Some Kind of Hero

'A warm-hearted, funny and affecting read'   *York Evening Press*

'Just when you think it's a comedy, the Kleenex moments sneak up on you'   *More*

Such a Perfect Sister

'This tale will make you love your own sister more than ever!'
Company

'[A] witty novel about tangled relationships'   *Hello*

'A fun and witty beach read'   *B magazine*

Kiss & Tell

'A very funny novel that soap fans will love'   *Woman's Own*

'Sparks fly and so do the pages in this irresistible book about love in the noughties'   *Now magazine*

'Do you love soaps and sordid kiss-and-tell stories? Then this is the novel for you . . . Hilarious, and with a ring of truth that keeps you reading'   *19 magazine*

Donna Hay's first novel, *Waiting in the Wings*, won her the RNA New Writers' Award, and since then she has attracted praise from critics for *Kiss & Tell* and *Such a Perfect Sister*. She writes regularly for *TV Times* and *What's On TV*, and has a weekly soaps page in *Chat* magazine. Her latest novel in Orion paperback is *Some Kind of Hero*, and her latest hardback novel, *Goodbye, Ruby Tuesday*, is also available from Orion. She lives in York with her husband and daughter.

By Donna Hay

Waiting in the Wings
Kiss & Tell
Such a Perfect Sister
Some Kind of Hero
Goodbye, Ruby Tuesday

Such a Perfect Sister

~

DONNA HAY

ORION

An Orion paperback

First published in Great Britain in 2002
by Orion
This paperback edition published in 2003
by Orion Books Ltd,
Orion House, 5 Upper St Martin's Lane,
London WC2H 9EA

Third impression
Reissued 2004

A CIP catalogue record for this book is available
from the British Library.

ISBN 0 75284 836 4

Typeset at The Spartan Press Ltd,
Lymington, Hants

Printed and bound in Great Britain by
Clays Ltd, St Ives plc

www.orionbooks.co.uk

To my goddaughter, Zoe Yenn,
in the hope that she may one day read it.

Acknowledgements

To Jane Quennell Ward, the best chef in the world, without whose culinary expertise this book might not have been written. And to Karl Ward, without whose expertise in downloading computer games it might have been written a great deal faster. To my husband Ken for not minding when I spent more time in my fictional kitchen than our real one, and to my daughter Harriet for learning to make coffee.

Chapter 1

It wasn't the most stylish entrance Phoebe Redmond had ever made, but it was the most memorable.

Her pink crinoline had been designed with a Daimler in mind. But due to a mix-up with the bookings, one of the wedding cars hadn't turned up. And since the bride's mother refused to travel in anything less than her promised Bentley, it was left to Phoebe to compromise. As usual.

Which was how she and several hundred metres of frosted tulle came to be jammed into the back seat of her Uncle Terry's Vauxhall Astra.

'All right, love?' He gave her a cheery wink in the rear view mirror. Phoebe gritted her teeth. The truth was, she felt hot, uncomfortable and just about ready to faint inside the rib-crushing satin bodice. Something had gone horribly wrong, she decided. Either the dressmaker had got her measurements confused with those of Naomi Campbell, or she'd been seriously overdoing the Hobnobs lately.

She looked out of the window at the gloomy April day. After two weeks of sunshine, the heavens were threatening to open. Clouds piled up like wet towels overhead. Her hair, sensing rain, had already begun to rebel. Despite a massive application of industrial-strength Frizz Ease, her dark curls were reasserting themselves. By the time they got to church she'd look like Jimi Hendrix in a rosebud tiara.

This was her fifth time of being a bridesmaid and it didn't get any better. The first time, she'd been six, and so excited, she'd wet herself in the vestry and had to slink back down the aisle minus her frilly pantaloons, much to her mother's mortification. Twenty-two years and several frocks later, the novelty had worn off.

Exiting gracefully from the back seat of the Vauxhall Astra was like trying to squeeze an elephant out of a telephone box. And it wasn't helped by Uncle Terry — a removal man by trade — standing on the pavement, waving his arms around and shouting, 'Left a bit. No, to you. Now to me. Blimey, love, you're worse than shifting a wardrobe!'

They'd drawn a small crowd by this time. Including the official photographer who, bored with waiting for the bride to turn up, was pointing his zoom lens down Phoebe's ample cleavage.

'Are you the bridesmaid?' he asked.

'No, I'm Little Bo Peep's evil twin. What does it look like?' With a final heave, Phoebe exploded out of the back seat and on to the pavement. A ripple of applause ran around the onlookers.

'I thought there were supposed to be two of you? Where's the other one?'

Good question. Phoebe looked around the churchyard. She could see her mother, dressed in a fetching navy two-piece and what looked like an eau-de-nil satellite dish on her head. And she could see her father trailing behind her, looking uncomfortable in his best suit. But there was no sign of her sister Alex.

This wasn't promising. The last time Phoebe saw her, she'd been buried under her duvet, sleeping off a late night. She'd mumbled something about meeting her at the church. At the time Phoebe had been in such a rush to get to the bride's house she didn't stop to argue. Now she wished she had.

She looked up at the clock tower. The wedding was due to start in five minutes. Alex was cutting it fine, even by her standards.

'Phoebe!' Auntie Brenda, the bride's mother, hurried towards her, heels slipping on the gravel. She was small and round, and her cream and black striped outfit made her look like a humbug. 'There you are. Can you keep an eye on the flower girl? She's already shredded two floral arrangements and thrown her shoes in the font. Her mother can't seem to control her, and the vicar's quite despairing. I told Bryony she was far too young to have in the wedding party but who listens to me?' She paused a nanosecond to take a breath, then said, 'Where's your sister?'

'Er – isn't she here yet?'

'Well, obviously she isn't, or I wouldn't have asked.' A look of panic crossed her face. 'Why isn't she with you?'

'She – um – er—' They were distracted by the bride's car drawing up. The ushers started to herd the stragglers towards the church.

'Oh dear, there's Bryony. I'm going to have to go in. But you can tell Alexandra from me that I'm not very happy with her.' With a last, severe look at Phoebe she followed the others into the church.

As if she ever listens to me, Phoebe thought. Alex might be two years older, but everyone always treated them as if Phoebe was the one in charge.

She crunched down to the gate to meet her cousin Bryony, who was standing with her father. She looked serene and beautiful, but her bouquet was shaking so hard the lilies were threatening to shed their petals over the path.

'You look stunning,' Phoebe said.

'I feel awful. We had to stop the car twice because I thought I was going to throw up.' She looked around. 'Where's Alex?'

'She's – um – on her way.'

'You mean she's not here? Oh my God, where is she?'

3

'I don't know. I'm sure she'll turn up,' Phoebe added lamely.

'I knew it! This whole day's turning out to be a disaster. How could she do this to me?'

Her face crumpled behind her veil. Phoebe exchanged worried looks with the bride's father, Uncle Maurice. 'She'll be here. Please don't get upset—'

'Upset? UPSET? One of my bridesmaids has gone AWOL and you tell me not to get upset? You just wait until she ruins *your* wedding and then you'll know what it feels like—'

She was drowned out by the wail of sirens. A brace of police cars screeched to a halt outside the church gates, blue lights flashing. Between them, Phoebe caught sight of a familiar metallic green Mazda.

She, Bryony and Uncle Maurice watched, speechless, as an officer jumped out of the front car and rushed to open the Mazda's door. Alex stepped out serenely. She wore the same frosted pink nightmare as Phoebe, but somehow on her supermodel figure it looked like a catwalk creation. She said something briefly to the policeman, then kissed him on the cheek and made her way over to them, smiling.

'Sorry I'm late. I got stopped for speeding.' She adjusted her headdress on top of her sleek blonde hair. 'But when I told them where I was going they offered to help me. Isn't that sweet?'

Phoebe shook her head. Only her sister could have charmed her way out of a speeding ticket and into a police escort. But Bryony didn't seem to find the situation remotely amusing. She grabbed her father's arm and stalked up the path towards the church.

'Did you see that look she gave me?' Alex made a face.

'I'm not surprised. First you nearly gave her a heart attack, then you upstage her at her own wedding.'

4

'She's lucky I turned up at all. I've got the world's worst hangover.'

Phoebe peered at her. She did look slightly green under the perfect make-up. 'Where did you get to last night?'

'You know where. I went to someone's leaving do at work.'

'Until three in the morning?'

'We ended up clubbing in Leeds.'

'You could have phoned and let me know. I tried to call you but you had your mobile switched off.'

'Yes, well, I wouldn't have heard it anyway, would I? God, Fee, you're worse than Mum! I am a grown-up, you know.'

Just then the organ struck up the opening bars of Wagner's Bridal March, the doors creaked open, and they all walked in.

Entering the church between willowy redhead Bryony and even more willowy blonde Alex, Phoebe felt like one of the ugly little dogs supermodels carried under their arms to make themselves look even more glamorous.

It didn't help that the first person she saw was Alex's boyfriend, Luke Rawlings. He was sitting on the end of the row beside her parents, his long legs stretched out into the aisle. Phoebe spotted him instantly among the crowded pews. Even the back of his head was handsome.

He turned round and looked at them. Phoebe flushed scarlet before she realised that of course he was looking at Alex and not her, but by then she was so flustered she'd dropped her bouquet. She looked around to see if anyone had noticed and realised the rest of the bridal party were already halfway down the aisle. Phoebe hastily gathered up what was left of her flowers and sprinted after them, her face a deeper pink than her dress.

As she rushed past, she caught her mother's tut of

disapproval and Luke's smile of sympathy. Why did she have to be such a klutz?

The service was excruciating. As she stood beside her sister, Phoebe felt certain the entire congregation was comparing the sizes of their backsides. Even her M&S hip-toning knickers were no match for a satin crinoline topped off with a huge and badly placed bow.

Finally it was over and they headed outside for photographs. The rain was still holding off, and a weak sliver of sunshine forced its way between the grubby clouds. As everyone gathered for the group photos, Phoebe noticed there was no sign of Alex. Typical. She'd probably sloped off for a sneaky fag. Better find her before the bride noticed she was gone and had another cardiac arrest.

She rounded the corner of the church and stopped beside a mossy, mouldering stone angel. Alex and Luke were standing under the yew tree at the far end of the churchyard, talking. Phoebe was just about to call out to them when she saw their faces and realised they were in the middle of a row. Alex had her arms folded, and was wearing the stubborn expression Phoebe knew so well. Luke was trying to reason with her. A pointless exercise, as Phoebe also knew.

She watched them for a while. Much as she adored her older sister, there were times when she felt that fate had been just a bit unfair. Alex had inherited a tall, slender figure, silky, pale-gold hair and incredible bone structure, while Phoebe had been left with her father's sturdy legs and wilful brown curls.

Even more unfairly, fate had given Alex Luke Rawlings, but made Phoebe fall in love with him.

She started to back away and leave them to it, but as she turned her shoulder collided with one of the angel's broken wings, knocking them both off balance. The angel rocked around in slow motion for a second or two. Then its moss-covered head fell off and thudded on the ground.

Alex and Luke were both watching her. Feebly, she raised her hand in greeting. 'They're, um, just about to start the photos.'

Luke stalked past her without a word. Phoebe waited for Alex. 'What was that all about?'

'Oh, nothing. You know what he's like.' Alex chewed her lower lip. 'Listen, I don't think I can face the reception.'

'But you've got to come. You're the bridesmaid.'

'So? I'm sure no one will notice if I'm not there. And I don't really feel like partying.'

'Has this got anything to do with Luke?'

'Of course not.' Alex didn't meet her eye. 'I want to go home and sleep off this hangover.'

'Well, don't expect me to cover for you.'

'Fee!' There was a wheedling note in Alex's voice.

'No, Alex, I mean it. You know I hate lying for you. If you don't want to show up for your own cousin's wedding, that's fine. But I'm not making excuses for you.'

'Go on Phoebe,' she pleaded. 'I'm not asking you to tell real lies. Just say I've got a headache or something. It's true, anyway.'

Phoebe sighed wearily. It wasn't as if she hadn't done it before. As a teenager she'd often persuaded her mother that Alex was studying at the library when she knew she was slapping on make-up at a friend's house, ready for an illicit date.

'Thanks, Fee, you're a star. I'll do the same for you one day.' Alex planted a kiss on her cheek.

'Hang on a minute, I haven't said I'd—'

But Alex was already sprinting towards the gate, her billowing skirt hitched up around her knees.

Chapter 2

Bryony's parents' home was a Tudorised mansion in a leafy suburb of Harrogate. It stood in its own grounds, a sprawling tribute to Uncle Maurice's success in the insurance business.

Auntie Brenda had gone all out to show it off to its full advantage for her eldest daughter's wedding. An enormous pink and white marquee dominated the lawn. A string quartet played a selection of well-known classics, while waiters in bow ties circulated on the grass with trays of champagne to welcome the guests. Phoebe helped herself to a glass and started to follow the others into the marquee. She was starving and longed to sit down and slip off her pinching shoes. She only hoped no one asked where Alex was.

Bloody Alex. It wouldn't have killed her to show her face for a couple of hours.

'It's Alexandra Redmond's sister, isn't it?' She turned round. Two women stood behind her, in toning Austin Reed pastels. 'I'm Vanessa Montgomery-Hughes. We were at Kingscote together, do you remember? Pippa and I were two years above you.'

Phoebe looked at them. Big teeth, braying voices, highlighted hair. No, she didn't remember them. Any more than she could put a name to any of the girls who'd made her life such a misery during that time. Her school years at Kingscote were just a blur now, thank God.

'We knew it had to be you when you dropped your flowers in church,' the woman continued. 'I said to

Pippa, "That's got to be Alex Redmond's sister." You were always so accident prone, weren't you?'

Her companion joined in. 'You used to make us howl, some of the things you did.'

'Really?' Phoebe gazed longingly at the marquee, wondering if she could make a run for it.

'Oh God, yes. Do you remember that time you left the gas tap on and blew up the science lab?'

Phoebe looked at Pippa's coral-painted lips stretched over her teeth. The last time she'd seen a set of dentures like those had been in the winner's enclosure at the Grand National.

'And then they put you in charge of mucking out the pets and you accidentally liberated the school rabbit?' Vanessa shook her head pityingly. 'So what are you doing with yourself now, er – ?'

'Phoebe.' She toyed with the idea of telling them she was a brain surgeon, then decided against it. 'I work in a restaurant.'

She couldn't have looked less impressed if Phoebe had said she ran a sewage-processing plant. 'You mean you're a cook?'

'A chef. Cook is what we do.'

'How alarming. Just think, you work with all those sharp knives and hot ovens. Wait until we tell the rest of the girls. They'll simply die, won't they Pippa?'

That would be too much to ask, Phoebe thought. She fixed a smile. 'I'd better be going. I'm supposed to be in the meeting and greeting line.'

'Yes, of course. Well, it was nice to meet you again, er – Fiona.'

'And you, *Victoria*.'

She walked away, still smarting. It didn't surprise her they hadn't remembered her name. In spite of what they'd said, she'd hardly made an impression at Kingscote. It wasn't easy to get noticed when her sister was around.

She'd joined the exclusive girls' boarding school two years after Alex, and from her first day she had been known as 'Alexandra Redmond's sister'. Phoebe wouldn't have minded if Alex hadn't been so impossible to live up to. She was good at everything, from Latin to lacrosse, without even having to try. In fact, Phoebe sometimes thought her sister might have been a genius if she'd actually applied herself, instead of hanging out in the local village and practising smoking like Lauren Bacall.

And she was popular. Everyone wanted to be Alex's friend. Somehow, Phoebe had got overlooked in the stampede.

It wasn't easy, being the sister of the coolest girl in the school. The only thing Phoebe excelled in was getting into trouble. It wasn't that she was any worse than the other girls, it was just she always seemed to be the one who got caught.

Alex was sympathetic at first but soon began to disassociate herself from her uncool sister, walking straight past her in the corridors and ignoring her if they ever found themselves sitting at the same table during prep.

While Alex fitted in at Kingscote, Phoebe always felt like the odd one out. She wrote unhappy letters to her parents, begging to be allowed home. Every holiday was a torture to her, as she ended up counting the days until she had to go back. She had the feeling her father might have let her stay at home, but her mother wouldn't allow it.

'Kingscote is one of the best girls' schools in the country,' she'd insisted. 'You'll settle in eventually. Alex hasn't had any trouble, has she?'

Then, one Sunday afternoon after a weekend at home, something inside her snapped. She didn't get off the train at Kingscote with all the other girls. Alex had spent the weekend down south with friends and no one else seemed to notice the girl who didn't join in with the push to be first off the train.

But even her running away was doomed to failure. After several hours wandering up and down the Scarborough seafront in the rain, she realised she hadn't really thought through her plan. She had no money, and she was cold, hungry and nervous as night closed in. She'd phoned home.

But her escapade did achieve something. She didn't have to go back to Kingscote. For once her father had put his foot down and insisted Phoebe should go to the local comprehensive school.

'You're just going to give in, are you?' her mother had protested. 'I suppose next time she wants something all she has to do is threaten to run away again and you'll let her have it!'

'Phoebe isn't like that,' her father said. 'It must have taken a lot to make her run away. Anyone can tell the poor lass is unhappy.'

The argument had raged on, with her mother shouting and her father quietly firm. In the end, much to Phoebe's relief, Shirley had said, 'Fine, if that's what you want, let her go and mix with the oiks. At least we'll save the school fees.'

So Phoebe had joined Sandshill Comprehensive, and it had changed her life. There no one had even heard of Alex Redmond. And with no one to compare her to her older sister, Phoebe had flourished. She'd come out of her shell and made friends. She'd scraped together a decent handful of GCSEs and won a place at college. Although, as her mother never tired of pointing out, her NVQ in catering hardly compared to Alex's psychology degree.

Inside, the marquee was a fantasy in pink and white.

Clusters of balloons floated from every table, with a matching arch of pink and white balloons dominating the top table at the far end of the marquee, where the now radiantly happy bride and groom sat flanked by their proud parents. Polished cutlery and glassware glittered, and the tent was alive with the hum of conversation, the clink of glasses and china, and the muted strains of the string quartet.

Phoebe joined the line of guests at the buffet table. Just looking at all the wonderful food made her stomach groan. She hadn't had any breakfast in a last-ditch attempt to starve herself into her dress. She piled up her plate with Coronation Chicken, quiche, vol au vents and potato salad, then made her way over to the table where her parents were sitting. She could tell from her father's patient but glazed expression that his wife was bending his ear about something. As Phoebe joined them, his expression changed to a warm smile.

'Hello, love.' Joe Redmond was in his early fifties but looked older. Her mother, on the other hand, looked much younger than her forty-eight years. She was slender and glamorous, her well-cut hair the same blonde as Alex's, but peppered with ash highlights to disguise the grey.

'Have you seen your sister?' she asked. 'I've been looking everywhere for her.'

'She's gone home. She didn't feel well.' She hoped her flushed face wouldn't give her away. She was useless at lying.

'Oh dear, poor love.' Her mother's brow creased with concern. 'Why didn't she tell me she felt ill?'

'You know Alex. She didn't want to make a fuss.' As she said this, Phoebe heard her father choke on his drink but didn't dare look at him.

'That's so typical of her, not wanting to spoil the

day for everyone. But really Phoebe, you should have told me.' She looked accusingly at her younger daughter.

'It's a lovely wedding, isn't it?' She tried to change the subject.

'Is it?' Shirley's mouth was pinched. 'I must say, this marquee's rather on the small side. And the garden's so unsuitable. It's clay soil, there's absolutely no drainage. If it had rained, we would have been wading through mud like the Somme.'

'Just as well it's been fine for the last two weeks then, isn't it?' Joe said mildly. His gentle Yorkshire accent clashed with his wife's strained vowels. Shirley's upwardly-mobile father had sent her and her younger sister Brenda to elocution lessons, and now she made the Queen sound down-market.

'It's all a bit showy, if you ask me,' Shirley went on, ignoring him. 'I don't know why they don't go the whole hog and wallpaper the downstairs toilet with five pound notes.'

Phoebe wasn't fooled. She could see the naked envy in Shirley's face. The Redmond family weren't exactly poor, thanks to her father's hard work in building up his electrical retail business. But they were nowhere near as rich as Auntie Brenda and Uncle Maurice.

All this must be killing her, Phoebe thought, looking around. And no doubt poor dad would pay for it when they got home. Shirley would be ringing up estate agents faster than you could say, 'mock tudor mansion with integral garage'.

Her father, as ever, was untroubled by it all. While Shirley fretted about what they had compared to other people, Joe Redmond took a more philosophical approach. As long as his family had enough to get by, he was happy. And, after years of hard work, he'd reached the age where he wanted to take things easier. But

Shirley had other ideas. It was a source of tension between her parents. One of many.

He smiled at Phoebe. 'You look lovely, lass. Doesn't she look lovely, Shirley?'

Shirley looked her up and down. 'Hmm. That shade can be very unkind with certain colourings. And I don't think you should be eating all that, either,' she added, with a disapproving nod towards Phoebe's plate. 'You know what they say, a moment on the lips, a lifetime on the hips.'

'Well, I think you look grand.' Joe smiled encouragingly at Phoebe as Shirley shifted her gaze around the marquee. Probably wondering how she could do it bigger and better when the time came, Phoebe thought.

Sure enough, a moment later she said, 'Of course, when Alex gets married there'll be no messing around with tents in the garden. I don't care if they are fashionable, it still reminds me of a beer tent at a boy scouts bring and buy. And as for that music—'

'Who says Alex will get married first?' Joe interrupted her. 'You never know, our Phoebe might beat her to it.'

Phoebe noted her mother's look of incredulity. 'Of course it will be Alex, she and Luke are practically engaged – ooh, talk of the devil. Hello, Luke darling. How are you? Come and join us.' Shirley patted the empty chair beside her. 'If you're looking for Alex, I'm afraid she's gone home. She's been taken ill. Isn't that right, Phoebe?'

'Hmm.' Phoebe stared at her plate, embarrassed to be caught with a whole mushroom vol au vent in her mouth.

'Really?' Luke frowned. 'She seemed OK earlier.'

'Yes, well, you know what these migraines are like,' Phoebe mumbled. 'They come on very suddenly.'

'Migraine! You didn't say she had a migraine.' Shirley looked dismayed. 'She shouldn't be driving back to York on her own, she could have an accident. Phoebe, why didn't you stop her? Joseph, we must go round there right away and check she's all right.'

'I'm sure she wouldn't want to ruin your day,' Luke said, to Phoebe's relief. 'And you wouldn't want to disturb her if she's resting, would you?'

'I suppose not,' Shirley agreed reluctantly.

They got through the rest of the meal without any mishap, but all the time, as her mother filled the silence around the table with a bitchy monologue about Auntie Brenda and Uncle Maurice's shortcomings, Phoebe could sense Luke watching her. Not, sadly, in a flattering, can't-take-my-eyes-off-you way, but as if he was waiting for the chance to talk to her.

And no prizes for guessing what he wanted to talk about. He wanted to bend her ear about Alex. After their row, Luke was obviously looking for a shoulder to cry on, but it was the last thing she felt like offering.

So it was a relief when the bride's teenage sister Becky sidled up and said, 'Mum wants to see you. She's in the house having a nervous breakdown.'

Outside the marquee, she eyed Phoebe's dress. 'Bryony tried to get me to wear one of those but I said I'd rather stick needles in my eyes.'

'I know the feeling,' Phoebe agreed.

Auntie Brenda was pacing around the kitchen, looking stressed. She pounced on Phoebe as soon as she walked in. 'Ah, Phoebe dear. Just the person. I wonder if you could help me? Apparently the caterers want this lot back tonight,' she waved her hand towards the worktops, which were all piled high with dishes, plates and bowls. 'I've loaded as much as I can into the dishwasher, but we're just going to have to do the rest by hand.'

Phoebe didn't like the sound of 'we'. 'Won't the caterers do it?'

'Well, that's the thing, you see. They might have

done, if we hadn't had a teeny disagreement.' Auntie Brenda toyed with her pearls. 'Just a silly misunderstanding, really, over the terms of the contract. I just thought the pavlovas weren't quite up to standard, so I tried to negotiate some kind of discount, and—'

Ah. So now it all became clear. Brenda might be rolling in money, but she also had Yorkshire blood flowing through her veins. She'd obviously tried some penny-pinching tactic on the caterers, and they'd had enough. 'They've gone, then?'

'Well, I wouldn't say – oh, all right, then. Yes, they've gone. And they've left us in this mess.'

There it was again. What was it with this 'we' and 'us'?

'I'm sure it won't take long between us,' She went on briskly. 'So if you could just make a start for me, I'll be back in five minutes to finish off.' Her fingers tightened around Phoebe's arm, preventing her escape. 'Becky will help.'

But Becky didn't help. Becky slouched in a kitchen chair, chewing gum and telling Phoebe what a mug she was. As if Phoebe, up to her puffy sleeves in hot soapy water, hadn't worked that out for herself. Finally she drifted off, leaving Phoebe to wonder where she went wrong.

There must have been a point where she could have said no, she thought. But somehow she always seemed to miss it. Which was why, when the rest of the world seemed to be out enjoying themselves, she was usually working unpaid overtime, or entertaining someone's fractious children, or doing the sodding washing-up.

The door opened behind her. Assuming it must be Becky, Phoebe said, 'If you've brought another load of plates you can forget it.'

'Actually, I've brought you a drink. You sound as if you could use one.'

She dropped the plate back into the bowl with a splash

and turned round. Luke was standing in the doorway, a glass in each hand.

He'd taken off his tie and undone the top buttons of his shirt. Phoebe looked up into his eyes and immediately felt her body go into meltdown.

'I wondered where you'd got to.'

'I got waylaid.'

He raised an eyebrow. 'Don't you mean lumbered?'

'It's not that bad. Auntie Brenda said she'd be back in five minutes.'

'Auntie Brenda is currently sipping champagne with her new in-laws.' Luke took the dishmop out of her hands and handed her a teatowel. 'Come on, Cinderella. It's time you went back to the ball.'

Back in the marquee, the tables had been pushed aside and a DJ had taken over from the string quartet. The dance floor was full of middle-aged men in shirtsleeves waving their arms to 'Hi Ho Silver Lining'. She briefly caught sight of her aunt quickstepping past in the arms of Uncle Maurice.

She and Luke looked at each other. Then he said, 'Let's get some air, shall we?'

The pale sun had finally given up and descended into purple dusk. Luke led the way down the garden to the terrace, which overlooked the fields beyond, and which Auntie Brenda had thoughtfully furnished with padded loungers and concealed lighting among the shrubs.

'No expense spared,' Luke grinned.

'Pity there's no central heating.' Phoebe shivered in her short sleeves.

'Here.' Luke took off his jacket and draped it round her shoulders. She snuggled into it, luxuriating in his body warmth which was wrapped around her. It was as close to the real thing as she was likely to get.

They talked for a while about nothing in particular — the wedding, the reception, her mother's jealousy of the

17

Johnson family. All the while, Phoebe watched him, drinking in every detail. How his hair, the colour of golden syrup, looked darker in the dusk. His perfectly chiselled profile, not a feature out of place. If a group of artists had got together and come up with The Perfect Man, it would have been Luke, she decided.

Phoebe sank back on the lounger, feeling so blissfully happy that she knew something would have to come along and spoil it.

And it did. They were both staring up at the bruised purple sky when Luke suddenly said, 'I rang Alex.'

'Hmm?' Phoebe closed her eyes. She might have known her sister's name would crop up sooner or later.

'There was no answer. Just the machine.'

'Yes well, maybe she left it switched on and took herself off to bed. You know what migraines are like.'

'Yes, I do. But Alex doesn't. She's never had one in her life.' There was a pause, then he said, 'She's avoiding me, isn't she?'

'How should I know?'

'I saw the two of you talking, before she left. I thought she might have said something – about us.'

'Like what?'

He searched her face. 'So she hasn't said anything?'

'Luke, I don't know what you're talking about. All Alex said was that she wanted to go home and would I cover for her. I don't know what's going on between you two.' And I don't want to know, she added silently. The last thing she wanted to do with Luke was discuss his love life.

He slumped back in his chair. 'I don't know either,' he admitted. 'One minute we're getting on really well, the next she's backing off. We've been seeing each other for six months now and I still don't know where I stand with her.'

Five months, two weeks, Phoebe corrected him silently. 'I'm sure you'll sort it out.'

'How can we, when she won't talk to me?' She knew what was coming next. 'Fee, I don't suppose you could – '

No, she wanted to shout. No, I couldn't talk to her. No, I don't want to sort out your love problems. I've got enough of my own, thank you very much.

'I'll see what I can do.'

Luke smiled. 'Thanks, Phoebe. You're a real friend. That's one of the things I love about you.' He reached out and squeezed her hand.

'And I thought it was my stunning looks and sparkling personality.'

'There is that too, of course.' Their eyes met in the darkness. If this was a romantic novel, Phoebe thought, this would be the point where he'd take me in his arms and then—

'I suppose we'd better be getting back to the party.' He was on his feet.

'I'll be with you in a minute.' She watched him head back across the lawn to the marquee.

It was just as well he didn't notice her, she reflected. Because no matter how much she adored him, there was no way she would ever do the dirty on her sister.

Chapter 3

It was nearly three in the morning when Alex slipped her key into the front door of her flat. She tottered carefully down the hall on her high heels out of habit, trying not to make a sound, even though she knew Phoebe was staying at the Johnsons' house after the reception.

She nearly fell over with shock as the light flicked on and Phoebe appeared in her bedroom doorway, wearing her old flannel pyjamas and a disapproving expression. Her dark curls stuck out all over her head.

'Christ, you nearly gave me a heart attack! What are you doing here? I thought you were staying at Auntie Brenda's?'

'I was, but Mum decided I should come home and take care of you, what with you being so *poorly* and everything. But I can see you're feeling a lot better.' Phoebe looked Alex up and down, her eyebrows rising at the clinging black slip dress, sheer stockings and high heels. 'I take it you haven't been down to the all-night chemists for a packet of paracetamol?'

Alex looked defensive. 'So I went out. There's no crime in that, is there?' She brushed past and headed down the hall. Phoebe followed.

'And what if Mum had come home with me? She nearly did, you know. She was worried about you.'

'So? I didn't say I was dying, did I? You said that, not me. I just asked you to cover for me.' Phoebe's eyes widened. 'Anyway, I'm off to bed.'

She headed for her bedroom and closed the door. She collapsed on to the bed and kicked off her shoes as the door opened. Phoebe stood there. Alex groaned. Didn't she ever give up?

'So where were you?'

'Out.'

'Who with?'

Alex stifled a yawn. 'Look, Fee, it's too late for the third degree. I'm shattered and all I want to do is sleep. We'll talk about it when I wake up, OK?' By then, hopefully, it would be lunchtime and Phoebe would be off to work.

It succeeded. After a moment's hesitation, Phoebe closed the door. Alex pulled off her dress, aimed it into the corner, then snuggled under her duvet, warm and happy, and drifted into a blissful sleep.

Five minutes later, she woke up again to the smell of hot coffee. Phoebe stood at her bedside, wafting a steaming mug under her nose.

'Coffee,' she announced. 'How are you feeling?'

'Bloody awful, thanks.' Alex squinted blearily at her sister. She was dressed as usual in jeans and a baggy sweater, her hair in a pony-tail. 'What time is it?'

'Nearly nine.'

'Is that all? I've only been asleep a couple of hours!' Alex pulled the pillow over her head, but Phoebe didn't go away. She put the mug down on the bedside table and sat down on the bed. Alex knew what that meant. The Spanish Inquisition was about to begin.

'So where were you last night?' she asked again.

'I told you, I went out.'

'I guessed that much. Who with?'

'Some friends.'

'Anyone I know?'

'I doubt it. Just a bunch of people from work, that's all.'

'Was this the same bunch you went out with the night before? The ones that almost made you miss Bryony's wedding?'

'As a matter of fact it was. Is that OK with you?'

'Not really. This was a family occasion, Alex. You should have been there. You're always saying you can't stand the people you work with.'

Alex pulled the pillow off her face and glared at her sister. 'And you're always telling me I should make more effort to get on with them. But when I do, you start accusing me of being up to something. I can't win, can I?'

'I'm not accusing you of anything.'

'It sounds like it to me.'

She turned over and tried to go back to sleep but she could feel Phoebe watching her. Finally she gave up.

'Bloody hell! Can't anyone sleep in this place?' She flung off the bedclothes. 'I'm going to have a shower. If that's all right with you, Mein Führer?'

She picked her way across the room through the trail of clothes and headed for the shower. She washed her hair, using the last of Phoebe's shampoo just to spite her, then cranked up the heat as far as she could bear and stood under the spray, enveloped in the scented, steamy fug.

The worst thing was, Phoebe was right. She had been up to something. Nothing truly terrible though. Well, not yet, anyway.

It had all started at the wine bar on Friday night. Claire, the Senior Account Manager, was leaving to have a baby, and the rest of the office had got together for a leaving do. Normally, nothing on earth would have persuaded Alex to join them – it was bad enough having to work with the witless morons – but she wanted Claire's job and she'd decided it might be a good chance to impress Frank Fleming, the MD, with her interpersonal skills.

But Frank was more interested in Rachel, the other

Account Executive and Alex's main rival for Claire's job. She'd been with Fleming Communications for longer, but as far as Alex could see, that was her only advantage. She was thirty, still wore a college scarf and duffel coat, and hadn't had her hair restyled since the Purdey cut was in. But despite having a round face and big teeth like a Disney cartoon critter, she'd still managed to capture Frank Fleming's attention.

Meanwhile, Alex was stuck at The Office Party From Hell, squashed on to a banquette between Gina from Finance, who was tipsy on Liebfraumilch and describing her episiotomy in great detail to a queasy-looking Claire, and Malcolm from Data Processing, who didn't get out much and kept asking Alex if anyone had ever told her she looked like Cameron Diaz. Alex was forced to flirt with Rachel's boyfriend James just to keep herself entertained.

She hadn't imagined Rachel having a social life, let alone a real boyfriend. And James wasn't bad. Not exactly George Clooney, but at least he didn't have gelled hair and the sparkling repartee of an amoeba like most of the men around the table.

He wasn't much of a flirt, either. Perhaps going out with squeaky clean Rachel didn't leave much room for talking dirty. It amused her to watch the fiery blush engulfing his face every time she spoke to him. And when he opened his mouth, he sounded as if he was being choked by his own anorak cord.

It had the added advantage of winding up Rachel. Alex watched her trying to talk to Frank while leaning in their direction to hear what was being said. Her smile grew more fixed when Alex reached up and brushed an imaginary speck off James' shoulder. And when she playfully rumpled his hair, Rachel finally muttered something about getting another round and stumbled off to the bar.

Strangely enough, no one else seemed to find Alex's antics remotely amusing. And when she went to the loo five minutes later, she overheard two of the office juniors discussing her.

'Well, I think she's a total bitch,' one of them whispered. 'She's not even interested in him, anyone can see that. She's only doing it to upset poor Rachel.'

'I don't even know why she bothered coming,' the other one joined in. 'Stuck-up cow—'

She broke off as Alex walked in. She smiled at them both. 'Oh please, carry on. Don't let me stop you.' She crossed to the mirror and coolly reapplied her lipstick, aware they were both blushing to their untouched roots.

Sod them, she thought. She despised the female office mafia, who cooed over each other's baby photos and went to the wine bar together on a Friday night. Frankly, she couldn't imagine anything more tedious than a girlie night out. Give her a man, any day. Men were more interesting, they liked fun and flirting, and they didn't bore everyone to death agonising about their feelings.

She left the juniors gaping at her and went back to the party. It was boring now she'd had her fun with James. She'd planned to go straight home but, as she was heading for the door, she walked straight into Tom Kavanagh, the Marketing Director, on his way in.

'Leaving already, Alex?' She was tall but he towered over her. He was in his forties, with silvery-fair hair and pale-blue eyes as penetrating as a laser beam. He wore the kind of understated suit that only he would know cost thousands.

Alex looked around at the party. If she had to sit with that lot any longer she would definitely slit her wrists. But an opportunity to schmooze the boss was too good to miss. Especially as she had a feeling Tom Kavanagh fancied her.

'Surely you don't have to rush off just yet? Why don't you join us for one more?' he coaxed.

She followed him to the bar, and tried not to look too impressed when he flicked a platinum credit card to the barman and instructed him to put everyone's drinks on it for the rest of the evening. He wasn't an especially attractive man, but he had a powerful aura that was quite compelling.

'I must say, I'm surprised to see you here. I didn't think you went in for this kind of thing?' She looked up from admiring his Patrick Cox shoes to see his strange, pale eyes staring at her.

'I could say the same about you.'

He smiled. 'You're right. But we all have to do our bit for staff relations, don't we?'

She hadn't done a lot for them so far, she thought, glancing over to where the others were still giving her daggers. But then again, they weren't the ones handing out promotion.

They went back to the table. Alex made sure she squeezed in next to Tom, ignoring James who, at her return, looked up from his pint like an eager spaniel.

'You're looking very tanned, Tom,' she said.

'A few weeks playing golf in the Algarve. I have a villa over there. Have you ever been there?'

'To your villa? I don't think so.'

He smiled. 'The Algarve. It's a fabulous place. You should go there sometime.'

'Is that an offer?'

'Would you like it to be?' Their eyes met. So he really did fancy her.

'I don't think your wife would appreciate it some-how.'

'So we won't tell her.'

He was smiling, but there was a look of deep intent in his eyes. Alex felt herself straying towards dangerous ground.

She loved this part of the game. The circling around each other, flirting, sizing each other up before slowly moving in for the kill.

It was only later that it got boring. Like a caveman who enjoyed chasing through the woods after the woolly mammoth, but didn't much fancy the idea of dragging it home to cook afterwards.

She looked down the table at Frank, who was still deep in conversation with Rachel.

'They seem to be getting on well.' Tom voiced her thoughts.

'Don't they? Looks like she'll be taking over from Claire if he has anything to do with it.'

'Just as well he doesn't then, isn't it?' She looked at him. 'Didn't anyone tell you? I've been given the job of appointing the new Senior Account Manager.'

Alex could hardly stop herself smirking as she glanced at Rachel again. She was wasting her time and she had no idea. 'And you don't think it will be her?'

'Possibly. She certainly has the qualifications for the job. But I'm looking for someone with a bit more style, an edge. Someone who isn't afraid to take risks.' He looked at her. 'Are you prepared to take risks, Alex?'

'I'd like the opportunity to show you what I can do.'

'Sounds promising.' He drained his glass. 'Why don't we go somewhere quieter and talk about it?'

They'd ended up at a private club Tom knew in Leeds, where they'd flirted and drank and talked about anything but her job prospects. The next thing Alex knew it was nearly four in the morning.

'Oh, shit, I've got to go. I'm due at my cousin's wedding at twelve!'

Tom had been very good about it. He'd arranged a taxi home, and paid the fare. He hadn't tried to kiss her, although he had made her promise to have dinner with him the following evening.

26

And so the game had begun.

When Alex crawled into the kitchen Phoebe was pottering around, making toast and humming tunelessly along to Shania Twain. She slumped at the breakfast bar that separated the living area from the tiny galley kitchen and cradled her head in her hands.

Phoebe put a fresh mug of coffee in front of her. 'Feeling better?'

'As if you care. If you had any sympathy you would have let me die in my sleep.'

'Sorry. Toast?' Phoebe pushed the plate towards her. Alex shuddered. 'Suit yourself.' She shrugged and crammed half a slice into her mouth. And Phoebe wondered why she couldn't zip up her jeans.

'I'd rather have a ciggie.' Alex looked around. Phoebe's Marlboro Lights lay on the worktop, just within reach. 'I don't suppose I could—'

'Get your own.' Phoebe snatched them up and stuffed them in her pocket. Alex could almost feel the waves of reproach coming off her, and knew what was coming next.

Finally Phoebe said, 'I talked to Luke yesterday.'

'What a surprise. I suppose he had a good whine to you about what a bitch I am?'

'No, but he had every right. Why are you being so vile to him?'

'Oh, that's nice. That's very loyal of you. Why do you always assume it's my fault? But then I suppose Luke can't do a thing wrong in your eyes, can he?'

'What's that supposed to mean?'

Alex saw her sister's face pale and felt a twinge of guilt. Phoebe's crush on Luke was supposed to be the secret of the century. But everyone could see she was besotted. Everyone except Luke, of course. Men could be very dense sometimes. 'Well, you're such a good friend of his, aren't you?'

'I feel sorry for him, if that's what you mean.' Her hands were trembling as she picked up the knife and buttered another slice of toast. If only Phoebe could hide her feelings the same way she hid her figure under those hideous, baggy clothes. 'I just don't think you're being very fair to him, shutting him out like this. The poor guy's totally confused.'

'*He's* confused?' Alex stared at her coffee.

'So what's it all about?'

'I don't want to talk about it. Anyway, it's none of your business.'

'After all the excuses I've made for you? I think that gives me a right to know what's going on. Come on, what did he do that was so awful?'

'If you must know, he asked me to marry him.'

She wasn't going to tell anyone, but it was almost worth it to see Phoebe's pole-axed reaction. She did her best to hide her shock, but it was there, written all over her face. 'He – did what?'

'He asked me to marry him. You know, proposed? Till death us do part and all that?'

'And what did you say?'

'No, of course. Well, actually, I laughed.' Alex rolled her eyes. 'Do you think I'd be avoiding him like this if I'd said yes? We'd probably be out there now, choosing the rings and going all gooey over wedding lists.'

'Why?'

Alex shrugged. 'Because that's what engaged couples do, I suppose.'

'No, I mean why did you turn him down?'

'God, Fee, can you seriously imagine me, married? A nice house in the suburbs, his and hers Volvos in the drive, a couple of kids and a bloody labrador? I'd go mad in a month. I'd turn into one of those women who sign up for courses in creative paint effects and enter Breakfast TV phone-ins.'

Alex looked up at her sister, who was cutting her toast into smaller and smaller pieces but not touching it, and realised that she may just have described Phoebe's ultimate fantasy. Phoebe would probably love being married. And it didn't take a genius to work out who she'd like to be married to, either.

Poor Phoebe. Alex hadn't gone out of her way to pinch her sister's man. But if she was honest, the idea that Phoebe already fancied him like mad hadn't exactly put her off, either . . .

She'd first met Luke at Phoebe's birthday party in November. Alex hadn't expected him to be so impossibly good-looking. From the way Phoebe talked about him – which she did constantly – she'd already built up a mental picture of some ghastly, over-achieving accountant who'd spend the whole evening trying to sell her a pension.

But when she spotted him in the corner, talking to her clearly besotted sister, she saw what all the fuss was about. He was tall, broad-shouldered and immaculately clean cut, but his eyes smouldered with sex. They sought her out across the room, and the instant attraction she felt was like an electric charge zinging right through her. Before she knew what she was doing, she was halfway across the room to join them.

'Alex!' Phoebe greeted her enthusiastically over the loud Craig David track. As usual, she'd covered up her curves with something long and shapeless in black velvet. Her hair escaped in wayward tendrils from its big silver clip, her cheeks were flushed and her dark chocolate drop eyes glowed with happiness. 'Luke, this is my big sister Alex. The one I'm always telling you about.'

'I feel as if I know you already.' His voice was irresistibly husky.

'Me too.'

And that was how it started. Alex had only meant to

chat him up because Phoebe didn't seem to be getting anywhere. But when Phoebe drifted off some time later, neither of them noticed.

As soon as she realised her sister was gone, Alex immediately felt guilty and tried to steer the conversation around to her. 'So, how long have you known Phoebe?'

'A year or so. She was one of the first people I met when I was transferred up to York from London. She's been really great.'

'That's Phoebe for you. Always looking after people, taking them under her wing. She's lovely, isn't she?'

'She certainly is.'

'And she has so many friends,' Alex went on, warming to her theme. 'People are always phoning or turning up on the doorstep, looking for a shoulder to cry on. Honestly, sometimes it's like sharing a flat with The Samaritans—'

'Look, I don't know why you're telling me this,' Luke cut her off. 'We're both agreed Phoebe is a wonderful person, but I'd really rather talk about you.'

That made her feel even more guilty, because that was what she wanted too. They ended up talking all evening. When Alex went to the bathroom, she passed Phoebe's bedroom and heard a muffled sound coming from inside.

'Fee?' She pushed open the door. 'Phoebe, are you OK?'

'I'm fine.' Phoebe sat up quickly and dabbed her face with her sleeve. 'Are you – um – enjoying the party?'

'It's great. How about you?'

'Oh yes, I'm – er – having a lovely time.' Her smile wobbled. 'You and Luke seem to be getting on very well?'

Guilt washed over her. 'Look, Fee, if you want me to stay away from him, you only have to say—'

'Don't be silly, why would I want you to do that?'

'I just thought you were quite keen on him—'

30

'Me? Keen on Luke? You must be kidding!' Phoebe managed a laugh. 'No, you've got the wrong idea. We're just friends, that's all.' She stood up. 'Well, I suppose I'd better get back to the party. Don't want everyone to think I've abandoned them, do I?'

After she'd gone, Alex noticed the small, battered-looking doll she'd been hugging on the bed. Helen had been Phoebe's pride and joy ever since they were young. And despite having a whole playroom of toys of her own, Alex had always coveted the tiny doll.

One day, when she was about six, she'd decided to play hospital with Helen as the patient. Phoebe had come in just as Alex was about to perform a complex appendectomy with a pair of nail scissors, and she'd gone into a rare frenzy, punching, kicking and screaming like a demon.

Their fight had brought Shirley running from the kitchen. She'd listened to both sides of the story, then calmly handed Helen over to Alex as 'punishment' for Phoebe's temper tantrum. At the time, even Alex could see how incredibly unfair it was, but Phoebe had said nothing. She'd just disappeared to her room and cried.

But the strange thing was, once Helen was hers, Alex didn't want her any more.

Now, nearly six months after she'd started seeing Luke, she was beginning to wonder if the same wasn't true of him.

Chapter 4

'So you see, she really did want to come but she's still not feeling too good.' Phoebe crossed her fingers behind her back and cursed her elder sister for forcing her to lie yet again.

Shirley Redmond didn't bother to hide her disappointment. It had been written all over her face the moment she flung open the front door of The Hollies and saw Phoebe standing there alone.

'Not that migraine from yesterday? Poor love, she really should see a doctor. I expect it's all that stress she's under at work. She does far too much, working all those hours.'

Phoebe nodded in agreement, although she knew Alex hardly put her heart and soul into her PR job, and that her well-worn claim to be 'working late' was usually an excuse not to visit her parents.

'I've brought you something.' Phoebe proffered her gift, a peace offering for arriving without Alex. 'It's a home-made sticky toffee pudding.'

'I wish you'd said you were bringing something. I've already got a lemon meringue pie from M&S.'

'You could always put the pie in the freezer?' Phoebe suggested. She was looking forward to the sticky toffee pudding. She never got the chance to eat desserts at home since Alex didn't touch them and even she, tempted though she sometimes was, drew the line at wolfing down a whole one by herself.

'No, I'll put this in the freezer instead. It's much too fattening anyway.'

Shirley looked disapprovingly at Phoebe's hips as she spoke. Her own were enviably slim in white tailored trousers, the result of a lifetime of self-denial and the Lorraine Kelly workout video. She wore a white sweater with a gold tiger motif on the front, and high-heeled gold mules.

She led the way into the house which was, as ever, immaculate. It had once been the show home on the executive style housing estate, and Shirley liked to keep it that way. In the sitting room, two peach sofas faced each other squarely on either side of the mock Adam fireplace. Cushions were placed at precise angles, their rose print matching the elaborately swagged curtains at the bay window. Between them was a polished repro-duction rosewood coffee table, bare except for a set of silver drinks coasters. The velvety, cream carpet was flawless, and the whole room was scented with lavender from the plug-in air fresheners Shirley insisted on having in every room.

Phoebe thought of their own less-than-ideal home. It was Alex who owned the flat, but Phoebe who kept it tidy. Or tried to. But with Alex's sluttish habit of leaving trails of washing through every room and stacking dirty cups under her bed, she was fighting a losing battle.

'Tea?' Shirley offered.

'Please.' Phoebe followed her into the kitchen. The spotless expanse of limed oak units looked as if they had never seen a cooking utensil in their life. 'Something smells nice.'

'It's roast chicken.'

Phoebe resisted the urge to ask if she could help. Even her culinarily challenged mother couldn't go far wrong with roast chicken. She only hoped Shirley had remem-bered to take the plastic bag of giblets out this time.

She leaned against the worktop, and watched her mother arrange the delicate china cups and saucers on a tray. Shirley Redmond would never entertain a mug. The silence between them stretched from awkward to downright embarrassing.

'So – er – where's Dad?'

'In the garden, as usual.' Shirley's mouth pursed as she poured boiling water into the pot. 'He might as well move his bed out to that potting shed, the amount of time he spends there.'

'I suppose there's a lot to do this time of year.'

'So he says.'

Phoebe gazed out of the swag-fringed window to the sunny garden beyond. She knew why her father stayed out in his garden, and it had nothing to do with pruning his shrubs.

She made a few more attempts at conversation, which were met by monosyllabic answers. Why was it so difficult to talk to her own mother? Alex never seemed to have any problem. When she was here, Shirley was a different person. She came alive, laughing and joking.

She picked up her cup and said, 'I'll just pop out and see Dad.'

'Good idea.'

If the house was Shirley's pride and joy, then the garden was her father's. What it lacked in size, it made up for in beauty and imagination. Around the immaculate lawn the gently curving borders were a profusion of white tulips. The apple tree dipped its blossom-laden boughs towards the ornamental pond. Her father had installed a new water feature since her last visit, and now the restful murmur of water bubbling over pebbles added to the general air of tranquillity.

Her father's potting shed was hidden around the side of the house, screened by shaggy ramparts of budding clematis montana.

'Dad?' she called out in greeting, but he didn't reply. She peered around the door, breathing in the smell of

34

damp earth and old wood that reminded her so much of her childhood.

Joe Redmond was hunched on a stool, a half-finished tray of seedlings at his feet. When he heard the creak of the door he looked up, a smile creasing his lined face. 'Phoebe, love!' He looked hopefully at the cup in her hand. 'Did your mum send that out for me?'

She hesitated, then handed it to him. 'I think she forgot to put sugar in. Sorry.'

'No matter, lass. As long as it's wet and warm.' He took it from her and set it on the ledge. Phoebe looked at him in concern. He looked older, his face drawn. His shabby old gardening cardigan seemed to hang off him.

'Are you OK, Dad?'

'Course I am, love. Why shouldn't I be?'

'No reason.'

'Come and sit down.' He hunched up on the bench to make room for her. The potting shed might have lacked the polished finesse of the rest of Shirley's des res, but it was warm and homely. Joe's old radio was set on the shelf so he could listen to the test match. There was a pile of gardening magazines, and a little fan heater for really cold days. She knew her father longed for a kettle, but Shirley wouldn't allow it. She said it was a fire hazard, but Phoebe suspected she just didn't want him to enjoy himself too much.

'What are you up to?'

'Just planting out a few tubs and hanging baskets. It's a bit early, but I'm risking it.'

'Been to the garden centre, have you?' Phoebe grinned at Joe's reproachful look. She knew her father took great pride in raising the bedding plants himself every year. He would never set foot in the garden megastores that sold everything from petunias to plastic patio furniture. If he had to shop for plants at all, he preferred small local nurseries where they knew their stuff.

As she watched him transplanting the young plants from their trays into the moss-lined basket, his calloused hands working tenderly in the soil, it was like going back in time. As a child, she would often end up out here with her father while Shirley took Alex out shopping or ferried her and her friends around. She didn't mind that she was so often left out. She hated trailing round the shops, Alex's friends made her nervous, and she was glad to escape occasionally from her mother's critical eye. She and Joe would spend hours in the garden, planting, pricking out seedlings, pruning, weeding and picking vegetables which Shirley would invariably cook to death.

It wasn't just gardening Joe taught her. He took her fishing, and explained the finer points of cricket and football. At the age of ten, she was the only girl in her class who could explain the offside rule.

'So where's your sister?' Joe asked, wiping the earth from his hands. 'Gossiping with your mum, I expect?'

'Um – she's not here.'

'Oh aye? And what's her excuse this time? Still in bed with that migraine, is she?' His eyes twinkled.

'Something like that.' Phoebe smiled back. 'Mum thinks she works too hard.'

'That'll be the day!' Joe shook his head. 'Your sister was never all that keen on hard work. If it doesn't come easily to her she doesn't want to know. And your mother hasn't helped, spoiling her all the time. She's grown up thinking she can have what she wants, so now she expects it.'

'And she usually gets it,' Phoebe said, thinking of Luke.

'Aye, more's the pity.' He threw down the cloth and stood up. 'Well, I suppose we'd better go in. Smells like dinner's almost ready.' Joe sniffed the air. Phoebe could smell it too. The unmistakable smell of burning coming from the house.

Shirley might have been a supreme home-maker, but her cooking skills were non-existent. She was the only woman in the world who used the smoke alarm as an oven timer.

Sure enough, as Phoebe opened the back door Shirley was waving a pristine pastel oven mitt in front of her face to dispel the smoke. 'It's ready,' she gasped. 'And you can take off those filthy boots. I'm not having you tramping mud all over my quarry tiles.'

Joe sat down on the step and pulled off his boots. It seemed to take all his effort, Phoebe noticed. Poor Dad.

They struggled manfully through the first course of dried out roast chicken, blackened potatoes and mushy vegetables. Phoebe and her father tried to make the right appreciative noises, knowing that the slightest criticism would send Shirley off at the deep end.

Phoebe was just thinking what a good thing it was that her mother considered her overweight, since it meant there was no possibility she'd be offered seconds, when the doorbell rang. The opening bars of 'Edelweiss' chimed merrily through the house.

'What a time to call.' Shirley threw down her napkin with a tut of annoyance. 'See who it is, would you, Phoebe? If it's Jehovah's Witnesses, tell them we're not interested. And if it's one of those down-and-outs selling teatowels, don't tell them anything. Just shut the door in their faces.'

But it wasn't Jehovah's Witnesses, or a teatowel sales-man. It was Alex with an armful of flowers. In her pale pink T-shirt and jeans, her blonde hair in loose, rippling waves over her slender shoulders, she looked a lot brighter than the last time Phoebe had seen her. Only her sunglasses concealed the unmistakable dark shadows of a night on the town.

'What are you doing here? I thought you weren't coming?'

'You're always nagging that I don't visit enough, so here I am. Aren't you pleased?'

Phoebe was sure there was more to it than that, but before she could say any more, Shirley appeared in the hall behind her.

'Who is it, Phoebe – Alex! I thought you were ill?'

'I was, but I knew how disappointed you'd be if I didn't come, so here I am.' Alex swept past Phoebe into the hall and handed the flowers to her mother. 'I bought you these, to make up for being so late.'

'Oh, how lovely! But you didn't have to. It's enough just to see you.' Shirley led the way back into the dining room, where Joe was starting to clear the table.

'Hi, Dad.' Alex kissed him on the cheek.

'Now, have you had anything to eat?' Shirley demanded. 'We've just finished, but I'm sure I could microwave something—'

'No! I mean, I don't want to put you to any trouble.' As Alex looked at the remains of Sunday lunch, Phoebe could see the relief on her face that she'd escaped that particular ordeal. 'I'm fine, honestly.'

Thanks to Alex's arrival, dessert seemed to have been forgotten. Shirley rushed off to put the kettle on, leaving Phoebe and Alex to finish clearing the table.

'So what's the story?' Phoebe whispered. 'Why are you here?'

'God, I can't do anything right, can I?' Alex rolled her eyes. 'I thought you wanted me to come?' She caught Phoebe's stern look and caved in. 'Oh, all right. If you must know, Luke came round for a heart-to-heart and I couldn't face it so I came here to escape. Satisfied?'

'Alex!' Phoebe shook her head. 'You've got to talk to him sometime.'

'I know, I know. I'll talk to him tomorrow, I promise.'

'What are you two whispering about?' Shirley appeared in the doorway.

Alex smiled at her. 'Oh, you know. Just bickering over whose turn it is to wash up, as usual.'

'No need for that. Just put it in the dishwasher, would you, Phoebe? Alex, love, come through to the conservatory and we can have a proper natter.'

She swept Alex away, leaving Phoebe to stack the dishwasher. Her father came in just as she'd finished wiping down the work surfaces. 'I'll make the coffee, love. You go and sit with your mum and sister.'

'It's OK, Dad. I might as well do it now I'm here.'

Joe nodded understandingly. He knew as well as she did that she wouldn't be welcome in her mother and sister's cosy little circle. She cleaned some congealed gravy spots off the hob while her father waited for the kettle to boil. Suddenly he said, 'She doesn't mean anything by it, you know.'

Phoebe stopped wiping. 'What do you mean?'

'Your mum.' Joe couldn't meet her eye. 'It's just she never sees your sister, so she's bound to get a bit excited—'

'I know, Dad. Don't worry about it.'

It might have bothered her father, but it didn't bother her any more. She had long since ceased to care that Alex was her mother's favourite. Alex had been born first, and she'd been coming first ever since, at least as far as Shirley was concerned. There was no point in getting upset about it. Alex couldn't help it, any more than she could help her blonde hair or long legs.

She took the tray into the conservatory. Alex and her mother were so deep in conversation they didn't notice her until Shirley looked down at the tray and said, 'No biscuits?'

'I'll get them.'

'No, I'll get them. You'll probably bring the wrong

39

ones, anyway.' She went into the kitchen, her high heels clicking on the polished parquet.

Alex collapsed back in her chair with a huge sigh. 'Oh, my God, why did I ever let you talk me into coming? Mum's been bending my ear about how fabulous Bryony's wedding was, and dropping hints about when I'm going to settle down.' She narrowed her eyes. 'You haven't been saying anything, have you?'

'Of course not.' Phoebe looked at the floor. 'Besides, there's nothing to say, is there?'

'That's right,' Alex said firmly. 'But all I need is for Mum to get hold of the idea and before I know what's happening I'll be Mrs Luke bloody Rawlings.'

Phoebe felt sick at the thought. 'I'll go and finish doing the pots,' she mumbled.

Halfway down the hall the sound of raised voices stopped her in her tracks.

'What are you saying? That I shouldn't be pleased to see my own daughter?' Shirley was shrill with indignation.

'No, I just think you forget sometimes you've got two daughters, that's all.'

'That's rich coming from you.'

'What's that supposed to mean?' Her father's voice lowered.

'Oh come on, it's always our Phoebe this, our Phoebe that—'

As Phoebe walked in, Shirley's open mouth snapped shut like a trap. She shot her husband a murderous look and flounced off.

Phoebe looked at her father. 'What was that all about?'

'Nothing, love. Why don't you come and help me pot up the last of those baskets?' He headed for the back door.

Chapter 5

Alex zipped in and out of the traffic on the M62, blithely ignoring the outraged horns blaring behind her as she rummaged in her make-up bag for her Touche Eclat. She was running late for work again. She'd forgotten to set her wretched alarm clock for Monday morning, relying on Phoebe to wake her. So really, she decided with a flash of moral outrage, it was all her sister's fault that, at twenty past nine, when she should have been at her desk for nearly half an hour, she was still on her way to Leeds, putting on her make-up and eating a chocolate croissant at the same time.

She turned up Minster FM, hoovered up the crumbs of her pain au chocolat with her finger and thought about the day ahead. Not much happening, as ever. An afternoon meeting with a new client, a brand of home cleaning products. And she was supposed to be organising the launch of a new DIY outlet somewhere on the outskirts of the city. She'd sent out the press releases and invitations to the opening do. Today, she would probably spend the whole morning – or what was left of it, by the time she finally got in – phoning the local papers and trying to persuade reluctant journalists to cover the event. It made her yawn just thinking about it.

The whole idea of PR and marketing had seemed quite glamorous when she stumbled into it after university. Long lunches, travelling the world, meeting people, organising parties. How was she to know that, nine years later, she'd be writing press releases for kettles?

But all that was set to change once she got her

promotion to Claire's job. And she would get it, she was certain. Once she set her mind to something, she was totally determined.

The job was as good as hers. She had Tom Kavanagh right where she wanted him, thanks to some judicious flirting and a veiled promise of more to come. By the time they'd drunk their way through three bottles of claret at dinner on Saturday night she was pretty convinced Tom would have made her Managing Director if he could. Missing Bryony's wedding reception had definitely been worthwhile.

Phoebe's lecture had given her a few conscience pangs about Luke. But it wasn't as if she was actually being unfaithful, she reasoned. She had no intention of it either, although obviously Tom Kavanagh didn't know that.

Besides, what Luke didn't know couldn't hurt him. And she'd buy him something fabulously expensive and frivolous to make up for it once she got her promotion.

Fifteen minutes later, as she pulled into the underground car park beneath the offices of Fleming Associates, a silver Mercedes glided like a shark out of the gloom ahead of her, and pulled into the space at the far end of the car park. A space clearly marked TCK. As in Thomas Charles Kavanagh.

'Good morning Alex.' As usual, he looked unruffled and totally in control, in a suit that she guessed was Ralph Lauren and a tie that probably cost as much as her month's mortgage. 'Late start today?'

'I – um – had a breakfast meeting,' she lied, brushing the croissant crumbs off her jacket.

'I see.' His eyes lingered on her bosom. 'You really should do something about your timekeeping, Alex. You're not Account Manager yet, you know.'

Maybe not, she thought. But from the way his eyes followed her legs up the stairs from the car park she had a feeling it wouldn't be long.

It was an experience, walking into the building with Tom Kavanagh. The doorman, who usually didn't bother to look up from the *Sun* when she arrived, suddenly leapt up to open the doors for them. People jumped out of his way, and held the lift doors when usually they'd take great delight in letting them close in her face.

So this is what power feels like, she thought. It was a heady, addictive sensation. No wonder so many people wanted it.

The office was silent when she walked in. Nigel, the third Account Executive, was flicking through the newspapers. 'Researching the market,' he called it, but he was really just looking up all his horoscopes. Debbie, the Secretary, was punching figures into her computer.

Rachel looked as if she'd been there the whole weekend. Her navy-blue suit did nothing for her mousy colouring. She might have got away with it if she'd worn a bit of make-up, but her face was bare and shiny and her short hair was pinned off her face with a whimsical pussy-cat hair slide. She looked about seventeen, and not at all like a potential head of department, Alex was pleased to note.

'Morning, everyone.' She greeted them cheerily as she made her way to her desk. It was an oasis of mess in the middle of zen-like tidiness, cluttered with piles of unfinished paperwork, sweet wrappers, a half empty bottle of Evian and a wilting pot plant. It looked as if someone had been holding a bring-and-buy in the middle of the office.

No one answered. 'The caterers called,' Rachel said, not looking up from her work, 'about the Home Sweet Home launch on Thursday. Apparently you haven't let them know final numbers.'

'Really? I'm sure I did.' Alex sat down and rifled through her in-tray, knowing perfectly well she hadn't.

'In fact, I definitely remember doing it on Friday morning. They must have lost the fax.'

'I gave them the rough figures anyway. That's all I could find in your file.'

'Thanks, Rach. You're a star.' Alex looked suspiciously at her.

'I bet she loved that,' she hissed to Nigel, as Rachel left the office with an armful of folders. 'I bet she couldn't wait to fire off an email to Tom Kavanagh telling him how crap I am.'

Nigel looked up from reading Jonathan Cainer's horoscopes. 'Not everyone's as big a bitch as you, you know.'

Alex stared at him in astonishment. Up until thirty seconds ago, Nigel had been her only ally in the department. He was twenty-five, gay, and they shared a passion for gossip and buying shoes. 'What's got into you?'

'I heard about your flirting antics at Claire's leaving do on Friday. It was a bit low, even for you.'

For a horrible second she thought he was talking about Tom Kavanagh. How did he know? If that got out, it could blow everything before it had even started. Then she realised he was talking about Rachel's ferrety boyfriend. 'Oh, that. It was only a bit of fun.'

'Rachel didn't see it like that. She was really hurt. She and James had a big row about it, and she hasn't seen him all weekend.'

'That's her problem, isn't it?' Alex switched on her computer, deeply annoyed. She'd been thinking of dropping a hint to Nigel about Tom, but now she was glad she hadn't. Sod him, she thought. Let him cosy up to his new best friend Rachel, if that's what he wanted.

It was a long, lonely morning with no one to gossip and bitch with. It looked as if the rest of Fleming Associates were ignoring her too. They kept coming in to deliver meaningless messages and pieces of paper just so they could look daggers at her. Rachel, meanwhile, was maintaining a dignified but martyred silence at the other end of the room.

Bloody hell, Alex thought. Anyone would have thought I'd dragged her boyfriend into the ladies' and bonked his brains out. Flirting with her was probably the most excitement he'd had in months.

She tried to lose herself in work but that was even more depressing. She was halfway down her list of press contacts and so far only three of them had definitely agreed to come to the DIY shop launch. At this rate they wouldn't even need caterers. She'd be able to do the job herself with a six-pack of Budweiser and a packet of Twiglets. She was just mulling over the impending disaster and its possible effect on her career when the phone rang.

It was Luke. 'Guess what I'm holding?' he said.

She smiled with relief at the sound of a friendly voice, even if it was the person she was supposed to be avoiding. 'Not in the middle of the office, I hope?'

Luke laughed. He had a very sexy laugh. 'It's actually two plane tickets. To Paris. Leaving on Friday.'

'Paris!' She suddenly felt wary. Had she forgotten his birthday, or something? 'Why?'

'Because I felt like it. Call it a peace offering.'

'Thanks. But you didn't have to.'

'I wanted to.' There was a silence. Alex gripped the phone, knowing what was coming next. 'Look, Alex, about what I said the other night—'

'Forget it.'

'That's just it. I think we should. Forget it, I mean. You were right, it was a stupid idea. Neither of us is ready for a big commitment like that.'

Relief flooded through her. 'I'm glad you see it that way.'

'That doesn't mean I don't want to marry you at some point. When you're ready. I don't mind waiting.'

You'll wait a long time, she thought. She couldn't imagine a time when she'd feel ready to get married.

She put the phone down, grinning at the thought of Paris and all those glorious shops.

'Something's put a smile on your face,' Nigel observed. So he was speaking to her again.

'That was Luke.'

'Hmm, that explains it. He could put a huge soppy grin on my face too.'

'He's taking me to Paris this weekend.'

'Lucky tart. I hear they've opened some fabulous new shops since the last time I went. Tell you what, why don't I fetch us a coffee? A real one from Starbucks, not that vending machine crap? Then we can plan.'

'Sounds good.' Alex smiled as she watched him go. Nigel couldn't stay mad at her for long. Not when there was an opportunity to talk retail.

She was looking forward to an in-depth discussion on the merits of Parisian shoe shops when the phone rang again.

She rarely had cause to speak to Angela, Tom Kavanagh's PA, so she didn't recognise the brisk voice that said, 'Is that Alex Redmond? Tom would like to see you in his office, if you have a moment?'

She'd only been into the Executive Suite once or twice, and never to Tom Kavanagh's inner sanctum. It was a vast expanse of blond wood and pale carpets. Alex immediately wanted to check her shoes for dog dirt.

He was waiting for her, relaxing in the sumptuous leather chair behind his desk. He'd taken off his jacket and his pale blue shirt matched his eyes.

'Thank you for coming, Alex. There was something I wanted to ask you.' He sounded cool. 'How do you fancy a working weekend? There's a marketing conference in Cheltenham starting on Friday, and I've been asked to make a presentation. I wondered if you'd like to come with me?'

She knew immediately what that meant. For working, read dirty. Tom must have noticed her hesitation, because he said, 'I know it's a bore working at the weekend, but it would be an excellent opportunity to make some useful contacts. It could be valuable to you if you get the Account Manager's job.'

He emphasised the word 'if'. Alex felt trapped. 'I'm not sure I'm free. I'll have to check my diary—'

'Fine. You do that.' Tom's smile dropped. 'And if you're not, perhaps I'll ask Rachel if she'd like to go instead. I'm sure she'd welcome the chance to further her career.'

'No! No, I'll come.'

Tom leaned back in his chair. 'Excellent. I knew you'd see the sense of it. I'll look forward to us working closely together.'

I bet you will, Alex thought as she stomped back to the lift. Bugger, what had she done? Overdone the signals, that was for sure. Now Tom Kavanagh was convinced he was on to a good thing.

Still, where was the harm in that, she thought. After all, it was only a weekend. Two measly days. She could keep him at arms' length for that long.

She skipped back into the office just as Nigel was unpacking the coffees from a brown paper bag. Alex grabbed him and planted a kiss on his cheek.

'Steady on, it's only a coffee. Bloody hell, I'm glad I didn't get you a muffin! What are you so happy about, anyway?'

Alex licked the cappuccino froth off the lid of her cup. 'Don't tell anyone, but you're looking at the new Account Manager.'

'What, you?'

'Don't look so shocked. You know I want that job.'

'And what makes you so sure you're going to get it?'

'Can you keep a secret?'

'Durr, no. But you're going to tell me anyway, aren't you?'

She told him about the conference, and about Tom Kavanagh. She waited for Nigel to whoop with joy, but he didn't. 'You mean you'd actually sleep with that wrinkly old creep just for some crummy promotion?'

'Not that crummy. Think of all the perks. Not to mention more money. And I could offload all my worst accounts on to you lot.' She couldn't wait to see Rachel's face when she told her she was handling Harley's Haemorrhoid Cream. 'Anyway, who says I'd have to sleep with him? There's a difference between having sex and just talking about it, you know.'

'Don't I just? It's the story of my life.' Nigel rolled his eyes. 'But I'd be careful if I were you. Kavanagh's such a slimeball, I wouldn't trust him an inch.'

'I know what I'm doing.'

'I hope so. When is this conference, anyway?'

'This weekend in Cheltenham. Do they have many decent shops there, do you know?'

'Not as many as in the Champs Elysées,' Nigel said. 'Sorry to burst your bubble, sweetheart, but aren't you supposed to be going to Paris this weekend?'

'Bugger!' Alex aimed the lid of her coffee cup at the bin and missed. 'It can't be helped, can it? We'll just have to make it some other time.'

Nigel stared at her in horror. 'You'd rather go to some poxy conference than Paris?'

'No, but I have to. This could make or break my career, Nige.'

'And what will Luke say about it?'

She hadn't really thought about that. 'He'll understand. He knows how important this is to me. Honestly, he'll be fine about it.'

'I still can't believe you're doing this.' Nigel looked more disgusted than impressed.

Alex stuck her tongue out at him. 'You're just jealous because you didn't think of it.'

'I wouldn't lower myself, love. And I certainly wouldn't risk losing someone like Luke.'

'I told you. He'll be fine about it.'

Chapter 6

'Ça marche, one calves' liver, one normandy pork, two pasta specials.'

Without pausing to think, Phoebe grabbed two pans from the overhead rack, set them on the burners in front of her and dolloped oil and butter into them with one hand. With the other she grabbed a slab of calves' liver from the reach-in and flung it into a pan of seasoned flour. Then she leaned over for a fistful of caramelised apples and threw them into yet another pan at the back. No need to worry about them now. But those chopped shallots sautéeing at the back would need deglazing before they turned too brown.

But first there was the pork to get started. Sweat ran down her face, stinging her eyes as she tossed an escalope into one of the sizzling pans. She could barely hear herself think over the clatter and hiss of the kitchen. The other chefs rushed around at their stations, shouting at each other, but Phoebe tuned out, focusing on what she had to do. On a busy Friday night she couldn't afford to let her concentration slip for a second.

Her eyes darted over the burners, working out what needed to be done next, constantly aware of the fluttering line of orders filling up the rack in front of her. On nights like this she felt like a circus clown spinning plates, trying to keep them all in the air, knowing she was always a moment away from disaster.

'Ready on seven? Let's go on seven.'

'What happened to that steak for table eight?'

'Got it here.'

Plates clattered up and down the line. Beside her Ronan, the other sous chef, was draining an industrial sized pan of pasta that could have fed the entire population of Tuscany. Further down the line, Ian manned the fryer, assisted by a new girl Phoebe hadn't seen before. A trainee from the catering college on work experience, judging by her pristine whites and terrified expression.

At the back of the kitchen, Dicky and Steve, the washers up, muttered together, their voices lost under the clatter of dishes. They were brothers from Newcastle, so Phoebe had heard, but she didn't know for sure because she'd never spoken to them. They never spoke to anyone except each other.

On her other side, Titus, the Head Chef, prowled the line, barking orders. He reminded Phoebe of one of the warriors from *Braveheart*, sandy-haired and awesome, his white jacket stretched over his massive shoulders, his eyes narrow slits of suppressed fury in his broad red face.

'Where the fuck is that pork for table four? Everything else is turning to shit waiting for it.'

'One minute, Chef.'

'One minute? Everyone else can get their act together, why can't you?'

'Dunno. Just incompetence, I suppose.' Phoebe added a splash of red wine vinegar to the shallots in the pan.

'You're bloody well right there. I don't know why I don't just sack you and hire a fucking monkey instead.'

'Good idea. At least you'd have someone to talk to.'

Titus moved away swiftly, but not before she glimpsed the twitch of a smile. She was the only chef in the kitchen who wasn't terrified of Titus McVey. He combined the coarseness of a Glaswegian docker with the temperament of an opera diva. His filthy temper frightened off kitchen staff on a regular basis, but despite being fired nearly every week somehow Phoebe had managed to stay in the job for two years. Over that time they'd developed a kind of mutual respect. She refused to let Titus' furious moods faze her, because she knew that, under all that bluster, he was a gifted chef who worked harder than the rest of them put together. In spite of what he said, she also knew Titus depended on her calm, unruffled presence as his second in command.

Not that she was feeling unruffled at that moment. Her white jacket clung with perspiration as she flipped the pork in the pan, put the seasoned liver in another and added a handful of fresh herbs to the shallots.

'What did you say?' Phoebe glanced down the line. Titus was bearing down on the new girl. Oh God. There was nothing he liked better than fresh blood.

'We – we've run out of chicken fillets, Ch-Chef.' The poor girl was trembling so much the fair curls poking out from under her white cap shook.

'I see. And it didn't occur to you to mention this small but dynamic fact before, did it?'

'I – um—' She was bug-eyed with terror. In spite of the hiss of the dishwasher, the clatter of pans and the muted roar of the extractor fan, the whole kitchen seemed to fall silent for a second.

'What's your name, love?' Titus' voice was deceptively soft.

'M-Molly, Chef.'

'Molly. Pretty name. Shall I tell you something, Molly? A friendly piece of advice?' She nodded dumbly. 'You don't tell people when you've run out of chicken fillets, Molly. You tell them *before* you run out. Otherwise there's fuck-all anyone can do about it, is there?' His voice was gathering to an angry crescendo. 'That's just common sense. Christ, what did they give you at that catering college, a fucking lobotomy?' Even Dicky and Steve stopped scraping plates and turned to listen. 'If this is the best you can do, I don't want you anywhere near my kitchen. In fact, I don't think you should be in any kitchen. I'm telling you now, you're never going to make it as a chef.'

As he ranted on, Phoebe could see Molly's eyes glistening with tears under the harsh fluorescent lights. She felt desperately sorry for her, but she knew there was nothing she could do. A public humiliation by Titus was a rite of passage all the chefs at Bar Barato had to go through. Especially the catering school trainees. Titus seemed to have a particular hatred for them, probably because he'd never been there himself. He'd come up the hard way through the ranks, first as a washer up in a hotel kitchen, then as a humble prep chef, and he felt that a catering qualification was no substitute for real, hands-on experience.

Finally the humiliation was over. With a curt order to find some more chicken fillets from the walk-in – 'And I don't care if you freeze your butt off, don't come back until you've got them' – Titus lumbered back up the line. 'Fucking useless college kids,' he muttered. 'Come out thinking they know everything. Two years learning about effing bacteria doesn't make them experts in the kitchen.'

'No, but it helps deal with the people who work in them,' Phoebe said calmly. She glanced back at the walk-in. Molly was still shaking, but at least she hadn't fled to the loo in tears. Titus would respect her for that. And if she could last the first couple of days, she'd probably learn more from him in a month than she would in a whole year at college.

'Chef, I've been thinking.' Ronan piped up beside her. He was in his twenties, a cocky little Irishman with dark hair and a thin, eager face.

'Did I give you permission to do that?'

Ronan laughed nervously. 'Well, no, but—'

'Then don't. When I want an opinion from you I'll give you one.'

'I—'

But Titus had already turned his back on him. Ronan shot him a sour look. Phoebe knew he couldn't wait to step into Titus' shoes – or hers, for that matter. He'd only worked at Bar Barato for six months and most of that had been spent sucking up to Guy Barrington, the owner. Phoebe knew Guy would never get rid of Titus. But she wasn't so sure about herself.

She was just putting the finishing touches to a chicken supreme when the double doors swung open and Karen, the manager, walked in, holding a plate.

'Customer on table three has sent the salmon terrine back. Says it tastes funny.'

Everyone froze and looked at Titus. He straightened up slowly. 'Funny?' he said. 'In what way funny?'

'I don't know. Just said he didn't like it. If it's any consolation he didn't like the position of the table, the state of the cutlery or the temperature of the wine either.'

But Titus wasn't listening. He'd moved over to the doors. 'Table three, you say? Which one is he?'

They all held their breath as Karen pointed him out. Titus was not known for his tolerance. None of them had forgotten the time he'd hurled a customer out of the restaurant because he'd asked for extra salt.

But to their relief he just nodded. 'I see. So what's he having next? The veal escalope? Perfect.' He turned to them all with a bright smile that was just the wrong side of manic. 'Let's see if we can't do better for him this time, shall we?'

As he went over to confer with Ian on the fryer, Karen turned to Phoebe with a heavy sigh. 'This is all I need. God, what a night. We're already packed out and turning people away. Oh, and your boyfriend's just walked in.'

'What?'

'The lovely Luke is having a drink at the bar.'

Phoebe dropped her hot pan with a clatter, and just managed to rescue the calves' liver before it skidded across the floor. 'Luke's here?' She hoisted the pan on to the work surface and rushed to the door, wiping her hands on a towel. Peering out into the dimly lit restaurant was a world she rarely saw from the kitchen, where she barely had time to look up from her burners. The customers were all tucking into their food, their chatter rising over the music. The servers in their black trousers and white shirts skimmed between the crowded tables. And there, over at the bar, was Luke.

He saw her peering out of the porthole at him and raised his hand in greeting. Phoebe waved feebly back and darted out of sight, embarrassed at being caught out, especially looking so terrible, with her face all sweaty and pink and her cap perched on top of her frizzing curls.

'What's he doing here?'

'I dunno, do I?' Karen shrugged. She was a couple of years older than Phoebe, tiny-boned with cropped dark hair and a fierce manner. But like Titus, she wasn't too bad once you got to know her. She was the only person Phoebe had confided in about her feelings for Luke. 'Go and ask him.'

'Don't you dare,' Titus roared across the kitchen. 'Your love life can wait. Table six can't. And I've got table three's veal here. Better take it to him before it gets cold.'

As Karen swung back out of the double doors, everyone started laughing. Phoebe frowned at them. 'What's going on? What are you lot sniggering about?'

They all looked at each other. Even Molly's shoulders were shaking as she arranged goose livers on a plate. Then finally Ian said, 'Titus has come up with a little surprise for table three.'

Phoebe turned to Titus, who shrugged. 'He deserved it,' he said. 'The guy's a professional moaner so I thought

I'd give him something to moan about, that's all. Something to get his teeth into, you might say.'

Everyone fell about. Phoebe folded her arms. 'Titus, what have you done?'

'I deep fried a beermat.'

'Titus!'

'What? I stuck it in breadcrumbs first.'

Phoebe darted a nervous glance at the doors. 'You could get the sack, you know that?'

'I'd like to see them try.'

Phoebe spent an anxious twenty minutes trying to concentrate on the orders coming through and watching the doors, expecting at any moment an irate customer to come charging in with a soggy lump of cardboard between his teeth. When Karen finally appeared with table three's tray, they all dived on her.

'Did he enjoy his meal?' Titus asked.

'Not really. Said the green beans were overcooked – what did I say?' Karen looked around, bewildered, at the hysterical chefs all doubled up over their stations. 'You're all mad,' she declared, pushing the tray over to join the others waiting for Dicky and Steve to scrape the plates and load them into the dishwasher. 'And talking of mad, you should see the bloke on table ten.'

Phoebe wiped her streaming eyes on a towel. 'Why, what's wrong with him?'

'See for yourself.'

They all abandoned their stations and crowded around the porthole to peer through.

He was sitting at a table in the middle of the restaurant. But it wasn't the fact that he was alone that made everyone look at him. It was the pale-grey morning suit he was wearing. His top hat was on the table, next to a half empty bottle of champagne.

'It looks like he's going to a wedding,' Phoebe said.

'Just come from one. He told me he was supposed to

be getting married today, but his fiancée dumped him at the last minute.'

'Lucky bastard,' muttered Ian, who had been married three times. 'I wish one of mine had done that, then maybe I wouldn't be paying all my wages to the CSA.'

'Why's he here?'

'Drowning his sorrows, I suppose, judging from the way he's getting through that bottle of champagne.'

'Good for him,' said Ian. 'He should be celebrating.'

But Phoebe could see that celebrating was the last thing on his mind. Behind that defiant expression his eyes looked forlorn and bewildered.

An hour later, Phoebe grabbed her break. She smoked a cigarette on the step in the back yard in the shadow of the rubbish skip. It was hardly glamorous, but she enjoyed the cool night air on her skin, and the chance to breathe in something other than the pungent aromas of garlic and olive oil.

'Phoebe?' She started guiltily. She'd been so rushed off her feet she'd forgotten all about Luke sitting in the bar. 'Karen told me you were taking your break. Mind if I join you?'

'Of course.' She shuffled sideways to make room for him on the step. She thought about whipping off her cap, then realised her hair probably looked even worse without it. 'Sorry I haven't spoken to you before but we've just been so busy.'

'I'm sorry for turning up out of the blue like this. But I had to talk to someone.'

'Really?' Phoebe offered him a cigarette. Here we go, she thought. Shoulder to cry on time again. She steeled herself to hear all about how much he was missing Alex now she'd been on this weekend conference in Chelten-ham for a whole five hours.

And sure enough . . . 'It's Alex,' he said. 'I think she's having an affair.'

Phoebe inhaled sharply and nearly choked. 'What makes you think that?'

'It's just the way she's been acting lately. Almost as if she doesn't want to know me.' He lit his cigarette and regarded her over the glowing tip. 'You know I asked her to marry me?'

'She – um – did mention it, yes.'

'Well, ever since then she's been really weird. I thought it was just the idea of commitment that put her off but now I'm wondering if she's got someone else. She just seems so preoccupied all the time.'

'She does have a lot on her mind at the moment,' Phoebe pointed out. 'I know she's been worried about this conference.'

'That's another thing. We were supposed to be going to Paris this weekend, but suddenly she blew me out because she had to work instead. Does that sound like Alex?'

Put like that, she had to agree it didn't. Alex would never in a million years give up the chance of a shopping trip to one of her favourite cities to go to a boring old conference. 'I suppose she does really want this promo-tion,' she ventured. 'And if her boss pressured her into going—'

Luke smiled at her. 'You're sweet, but we both know Alex doesn't do anything she doesn't want to. No, I'm pretty convinced there's someone else. I just wanted to ask you, as a friend. Has she mentioned anything to you?'

Phoebe found she couldn't meet his eye. Looking back, Alex *had* been behaving oddly the past few days. Like when they were kids and she had a smug little secret she was dying to pass on.

And then there was the stuff she'd packed for this weekend. Phoebe had joked about what all those sexy slip dresses and strappy tops might do to the middle-aged delegates' blood pressures. 'Everything else is in the wash,' Alex had replied. Now she wondered if there wasn't another reason for them.

'Look, you don't have to say anything.' Luke misinterpreted her silence. 'I shouldn't have put you on the spot like that. I'm sorry. It's just I don't have anyone else I can talk to about it.'

A roar from Titus was her cue. She stood up and dusted down her checked trousers. 'I'd better be getting back inside.'

'Perhaps I could wait until you finish and walk you home?'

'I've got my car.'

'Oh. Right. Some other time, then.'

She looked at his forlorn face. 'Look, why don't you come back to ours anyway? For a coffee?'

'Are you sure? That would be great.'

'Alex would want me to keep you company.' Except she wasn't convinced she was doing it for Alex. In fact, she wasn't sure why she was doing it.

Her good mood lasted precisely two seconds after she'd walked into the kitchen and found herself in the middle of World War Three. Titus and Ronan were squaring up to each other over the deep-fat fryer.

'But I only said—'

'I know what you said and I told you it's not going to happen.' Titus slammed a pan down on the burner. 'So you can just forget the whole thing right now.'

Phoebe looked blankly from one to the other. 'What's going on?'

Ronan shrugged. 'I just happened to mention there was a thing in the paper about Cameron Goode coming to York to film for his new TV series, and wouldn't it be great if he came here? But he said—'

'I said, if that wanker comes into my kitchen I'm walking out.'

'Why?' For once, Phoebe agreed with Ronan. Cameron Goode was the hottest new chef on television. He was young, good-looking and his breezy style made Jamie Oliver look like Delia Smith. As well as a successful TV series, he also ran his own wildly trendy restaurant in London. 'It'd be great publicity for the restaurant. And a real compliment to you.'

'I don't need any compliments from him!' Titus turned on her. 'This is a working kitchen, not some fucking game show. I'm not having some stupid bloody prat in a gimmicky hat poncing around taking the piss.' Flecks of spittle flew from his lips. 'I'm a professional chef, not a stooge for that moron. I take pride in what I do, even if you don't.'

At that moment Karen reappeared through the doors and called out, 'Titus, we've got another professional complainer on table eight. Do you think you could fry another beer mat?'

Titus looked around at them, his face growing even redder. Then he slammed down his pan, muttered, 'You take over, I need a fucking cigarette' and disappeared outside.

'Well, I still think it's a good idea,' Ronan said stubbornly. 'And I'm going to mention it to Guy at the next staff meeting.'

'I wouldn't if I were you,' Phoebe advised. 'You heard what Titus said. Don't upset him.'

Ronan looked disgruntled, but said nothing. Phoebe had the feeling he was going to do it anyway.

For the next couple of hours they were rushed off their feet by the post-theatre crowd. As Phoebe dashed around, Karen kept coming in with increasingly anxious bulletins about the jilted groom.

'He's very drunk.'

'I think he's crying.'

'He's on his second bottle of champagne and now he's trying to pick a fight with a hatstand.'

In the end Phoebe said, 'Why don't you just throw him out?'

'I can't. He hasn't actually upset anyone. Yet.' She looked at Phoebe. 'Talking of throwing people out, when is your boyfriend going to leave? He's been nursing one bottle of Becks for the past hour.'

Phoebe stared down at the lemon sole she was garnishing. 'He's waiting for me. He's – um – coming back to my place.'

'While your sister's away?' Karen gave a whoop. 'Phoebe Redmond, you fox!'

'It's not like that. He's just coming back for coffee and a chat.'

'Are you sure that's all he wants? It seems a bit keen to hang around all this time just for a cup of Gold Blend.' Karen looked knowing. 'If you ask me, he's after you. While the cat's away, and all that.'

'Don't be ridiculous!' Phoebe could feel her face flaming. 'He's in love with Alex. And even if he wasn't, do you really think I could cheat on my own sister?'

'Couldn't you?'

Their eyes met. Phoebe dumped a fistful of parsley on the sole and wiped her hands on a towel. 'Right, that's it. I'm going to cancel.'

'Don't you dare! Come on, I was only kidding. I know you wouldn't do something like that. Even though she did it to you,' she added.

'That was different. Luke wasn't my boyfriend and besides, Alex didn't even know I fancied him.'

'Yeah, and I'm having Brad Pitt's baby!'

For the next hour, Phoebe tried to convince herself Karen was wrong. It was all perfectly innocent. She and

Luke were old friends spending some time together. She'd known him first, after all.

But Alex wouldn't mind. Why should she? Luke was madly in love with her, anyone could see that.

When the restaurant finally closed she hurried around, cleaning up her station in record time. She dashed off to her locker, changed out of her whites and back into her jeans and baggy flannel shirt. She dragged a brush through her tangled curls and raced back to the restaurant.

Karen and Luke were standing over the jilted bride-groom, who was face down on the table.

'He's passed out,' Karen said. 'He's finished the second bottle. I knew I shouldn't have let him have it.' She looked down at him. 'What are we going to do?'

Phoebe didn't like the word 'we'. 'Just stick him in a taxi and send him home, I suppose.'

'In that state? Anything could happen to him. No, someone will have to take him home.'

Phoebe felt a chill creeping up her spine. She had a nasty feeling who that someone was going to be.

'He'll be fine.' She pulled him upright by the back of his collar. He didn't look fine, admittedly. Especially when she let go of his collar and he collapsed face down again with a nasty bump. 'If we chauffeured everyone who left here drunk, we'd be running a mini cab service.'

'This is different,' Karen said. 'He's obviously in a distressed emotional state. I feel sorry for him.'

'You take him home then.'

'My car's in for a service. And I'm not getting in a taxi with him. If he throws up it'll cost me fifty quid.' She looked at Phoebe. 'I don't suppose you could . . . ?'

'No, I couldn't. I've made other plans. Remember?'

'Karen's right,' Luke joined in. 'You'd better take him home, Fee. I don't like the look of him.'

Neither do I, Phoebe thought. In fact, she was liking him less and less every second. 'But – I don't even know where he lives.'

'Look in his wallet. It's bound to have his address in it,' Karen suggested.

'Brilliant idea.' Phoebe shot her an evil look, but Luke was already going through his pockets. He pulled out a wallet and handed it to her. It contained a couple of credit cards, a video club card, and a photo of an incredibly beautiful girl with dark hair, almond-shaped eyes and the kind of cheekbones you could hang a hat on. The runaway bride, Phoebe guessed. No wonder he was so devastated.

There was also his driving licence bearing the name William Jonathan Hutchinson, and an address off Bootham.

'You see, that wasn't too hard was it?' Karen smiled. Phoebe glared back.

Luke helped bundle him into the back seat of her Metro. He sprawled across the seat, snoring loudly, his mouth gaping open.

'I suppose this means we'll have to cancel?' Phoebe hoped he might offer to come with her, but he didn't.

'Maybe some other time,' he shrugged.

So that was it. She didn't know who she was more angry with, Mr Hutchinson for ruining her plans, or Luke for allowing her to drive a drunken stranger home alone. It struck her briefly that he and Alex made a good pair – they both had a selfish streak.

But since she couldn't take it out on Luke, she took it out on Mr Hutchinson. She was deliberately rough as she clicked him into his seat belt. He groaned, and she gave him an extra hard shove accidentally on purpose.

'He's going to wake up with one hell of a hangover,' Luke remarked.

If he wakes up at all, Phoebe thought. She was sorely tempted to dump him in the back alley among the dustbins and leave him there.

Chapter 7

She drove deliberately fast, not caring that he was being flung around in the back seat. All the way she kept up a bitter monologue about exactly why and how he'd managed to ruin her evening, and entertained herself by devising cruel and unusual deaths for him.

She passed through the ancient gate to the city down Bootham and past the crumbling walls of what had once been the Abbey, outlined in darkness. She scanned the darkened streets until she found the terrace of tall Victorian houses. She pulled up outside the right number and checked the address again. Top flat. Typical.

She got out of the car and banged the door. Her charge groaned, but didn't move. She yanked open the back door on his side, the one he'd been bundled up against. He slid slowly sideways until he was dangling out of the car, inches from the gutter. Deliberately she unclicked his seat belt, and watched with malicious pleasure as he fell head first on to the pavement.

'Ow! Bloody hell!'

'You're alive, then?'

'Not for much longer, if you have your way.' He crawled out of the gutter and staggered to his feet. 'Did you really mean what you said about stuffing my mouth with my socks and dumping me in the river?'

'I thought you were unconscious.'

'Wish I had been.' He held on to his head. 'I think you've fractured my skull.'

'Don't be a baby.' She started towards the house. As he

went to follow, his legs collapsed under him and he hit the pavement again.

He looked up at her. 'You could help me up,' he whined.

'I think I've done enough for you this evening, don't you?'

'Having trouble, Madam?' She swung round. A policeman stood behind her, his severe expression illuminated in the streetlight.

'Er – no, thank you, Officer. Everything's fine.'

'Are you sure about that?' His gaze moved down to the man scrabbling around at her feet. 'Are you all right, Sir?'

'He's fine.' Phoebe stepped in front of him. 'He's just, er, looking for his contact lens.'

The police officer began pacing around her car, eyeing up the Metro's chipped and rusting paintwork. 'Is this your vehicle, Madam?'

'Yes.' Thank God she'd finally replaced the Guinness label with an up-to-date tax disc. She only hoped he didn't notice the piece of string holding down the boot lid.

'What kind of a bloody stupid question is that?' She cringed as a voice rose indignantly from the gutter. 'I ask you. If we were going to pinch a motor we'd pick a classier one than this, wouldn't we? It hasn't even got air bags. And the brakes are very dodgy. I'd check them out if I were you.'

Phoebe saw the policeman reach into his pocket for his notebook, and cut in quickly. 'You'll have to forgive him, Officer, he's in an emotional state,' she babbled. She poised the heel of her boot over his hand, ready to crunch his fingers underfoot if he even drew breath. 'It was his wedding today.'

'I see. Congratulations.' The policeman looked at Phoebe.

'Oh no, I'm not the bride—' she started to say, then saw his raised eyebrows and shut up.

Fortunately, after warning her to get the man indoors before he caused a breach of the peace, the policeman wandered off. Phoebe hauled him to his feet, dragged him up the stone steps and dumped him on his doorstep. She went back to retrieve his top hat from the pavement and plonked it on his head.

'Aren't you going to see me inside?' he asked plaintively.

'No.'

'But I can't get up!'

'Tough.' She reached the bottom step and made the fatal mistake of turning round to look back at him. He looked so pathetic, slumped against the front door, his morning suit spattered with mud, his top hat sitting at a rakish angle over one eye. Cursing herself, she turned and stomped back up the steps. 'OK,' she said. 'Let's find your keys and I'll get you into your flat. But that's it. From then on, I never want to see you again.'

'Fine by me.'

It was hard going. First he couldn't find his keys. Phoebe watched as he fumbled in his trouser pockets, until she finally gave up and snapped, 'Oh for heaven's sake, let me.'

'I don't usually let strange women delve into my trousers.'

'Believe me, I'm not enjoying this any more than you are.'

'Oh, I didn't say I wasn't enjoying it. I just don't do it that often. My name's Will, by the way.'

'I know.' Phoebe found the key, and managed to get the door open. She hoisted him to his feet like a sack of potatoes and dragged him into the unlit hallway. She tripped over something in the darkness and fell headlong on to the cold tiled floor. Will fell on top of her and they both ended up in a tangle of arms, legs and spiky metal.

'Bugger! What kind of a moron leans a bicycle right where everyone can fall over it – no, don't tell me. Let me guess.'

'I'm not going to carry it up three flights of stairs, am I?'

Just then the light flicked on, blinding them. Squinting up the stairs, Phoebe could make out the dark outline of a figure on the first-floor landing. It was a small, fierce-looking woman, her head spiky with rollers.

'Evening, Mrs Warzovski.' Will waved a hand in greeting.

Her lip curled. 'Oh, it's you. I might have known.' She flipped off the light, plunging them back into darkness.

'Old bag!' Will shouted back. 'My fiancée's just left me, you know.' Somewhere upstairs a door slammed in response.

'Popular with the neighbours, are you?' Phoebe said drily.

'She's a cow.' Will made a half-hearted stab at disentangling himself from the bicycle and gave up. 'What's the sodding point?'

He sounded so defeated that Phoebe almost forgot what a pain he was. 'Come on,' she said, freeing herself from a bicycle wheel. 'Let's get you upstairs.'

'You know, we really shouldn't be doing this,' Will said, as she hauled him up the stairs. It was like wrestling a giant puppet.

'You're telling me. I think I've done my back in.'

'No, I mean, what if Nadine's there? What will she say?' She assumed he meant his fiancée.

Phoebe looked him in the eye – or tried to. It was difficult when his were pointing in different directions. His mouth was gaping and he stank like a distillery. 'I should think that's the least of your worries.'

She unlocked the door of his flat and threw him inside, then groped for the light switch. It was a surprisingly nice flat, an airy attic conversation, full of sloping ceilings and interesting angles. The huge living room had white walls, polished floorboards and two big squashy sofas. All very tasteful, considering its occupant. On the walls were some pieces of art – originals, from what she could tell – bright, bold still lifes and striking portraits. She was no expert, but they looked very good.

'Doesn't look like anyone's home,' she said.

'Didn't think so.' Will lay on the floor where he'd fallen. 'Oh God, what am I going to do?'

Phoebe looked down at him, sprawled out, his dark hair falling into his eyes. 'I think you should start with some strong black coffee.'

'I don't want coffee, I want Nadine!'

She stepped over him, found the kitchen and put the kettle on. Like the rest of the flat, it was modern and full of gleaming appliances, including several still in their boxes. Wedding presents, obviously.

She made the coffee, added some sugar, and brought it back into the sitting room. Will was still sprawled out, face down and snoring gently on the mat. She considered waking him, then thought better of it. Setting the coffee down beside him, she let herself out of the flat.

It only took about fifteen minutes to get home but it was still well after midnight when Phoebe parked her car behind the block of flats just off Fulford Road. The full moon cast an eerie, shadowy light over the rooftops. Every house was in darkness.

She was already thinking about a long, hot bath with the new Penny Vincenzi when she turned the corner and slammed straight into someone.

'Sorry, I didn't mean to startle you,' Luke said. 'I

thought I'd pop round and see if that drink was still on offer? I've brought a bottle of something stronger than coffee though.' He held it up in the darkness.

Typical. Let her struggle to get Will home, then just turn up when it was all over.

'I'm sorry I didn't come with you.' He seemed to read her thoughts. 'I realised as soon as you'd gone that I shouldn't have allowed you to go by yourself. Anything could have happened. That's partly why I came round, to check you were OK.'

Her annoyance melted. 'I'm fine,' she said. 'Just a bruised shin, that's all. It's a long story,' she added, seeing him frown. 'Let's crack open that bottle and I'll tell you all about it.'

It felt so strange to be alone with him. She kept expecting Alex to pop her head round the door and summon him to the bedroom. 'You get some glasses, I've just got to freshen up.'

Did she need it. Phoebe stared at her reflection in the bathroom mirror, appalled at herself. Her face was devoid of make-up, and her hair stuck up like an electrified Brillo pad. She looked like a warrior woman from Boadicea's tribe. She quickly washed her face and tried to brush her hair, but it was so tangled she gave up and pulled it back in a scrunchie instead.

Luke was sitting by the fire, his long legs stretched out, leaning back against the sofa, a glass of Chilean red in his hand. Candles flickered on the mantelpiece. If she didn't know better, she could have sworn the scene was set for seduction.

'There you are. I thought you'd gone to sleep on me.' He smiled up at her and patted the rug next to him. 'Come and sit here.'

'If I sit that close to the fire my hair will frizz.' Phoebe slipped off her shoes and curled up on the sofa a cautious distance away. Luke handed her a glass.

'I don't know why you make so much fuss about it. It always looks great to me.'

'Yeah, right!'

'Honestly. I think all those curls are really sexy.'

She took a gulp of wine and nearly choked. Did he really just say that?

'So,' she said. 'Alex.'

'What about her?'

Saying her name was like a talisman, breaking the spell that the wine and the candlelight were weaving around her. 'I wonder what she's doing now? In bed, probably.'

'Probably.' Luke stared into his glass. 'The question is, who with?'

Phoebe gazed at him sympathetically. 'Look, Luke, I really think you've got this all wrong. Alex wouldn't have an affair.'

'Wouldn't she?' He lifted his eyes to meet hers. 'We both know she's no angel, Fee. Even if she does look like one.'

'But she loves you!'

'That's just it. I don't think she does. In fact, I don't know if she ever did.' His expression was wretched. 'I reckon I've just been kidding myself all this time.'

'Don't say that.'

'You didn't see the way she looked at me when I asked her to marry me. She was horrified. That's the only way I can describe it.'

'It was the idea of marriage that horrified her, not you.'

'That's what I've been trying to tell myself, but I'm not so sure any more.' Luke shook his head. 'I really think we're coming to the end of the line. If we haven't got there already. This weekend proved that. Whatever she went to Cheltenham for, it wasn't just the confer-ence. She's trying to tell me something, and I reckon I've finally got the message.'

Phoebe looked at him. This was the moment she'd been longing for for the past six months. But now all she felt was overwhelming sadness for him. 'I'm sorry.'

'Maybe it's for the best? Maybe we should never have got together in the first place.' He refilled her glass. 'Anyway, let's not talk about it any more. What about you? How's your love life?'

'Even more depressing than yours, I'm afraid.' She stretched out her bare toes towards the fire. She hadn't eaten and she could feel the wine going straight to her head like a guided missile. 'I don't know if you'd noticed, but I don't exactly have a lot of gentleman callers.'

'Not even any offers?'

'I'm hardly inundated. It doesn't help that I work such weird hours. At least that's my excuse.'

Luke regarded her consideringly. 'You surprise me. I would have thought you'd be fighting them off. I'm serious,' he insisted, when Phoebe laughed. 'You've got so much going for you. You're warm, funny, you've got a great personality—'

'Oh, please! Why do people always say that when what they mean is that you look like the back of a bus.'

'You don't look like the back of a bus. Well, not all the time.' He grinned.

'Thanks a lot!'

'No, I mean it. You're lovely.'

'How much have you had to drink?' Phoebe wondered how he'd ended up on the sofa beside her without her even noticing.

'I'm serious. You're a very beautiful woman. You have a – what do you call it? An inner glow. It shines out of you.'

'You make me sound like a lava lamp!'

'Why do you always have to laugh at yourself?'

'To save everyone else the trouble?' She looked at

him. He was very close now, his eyes full of intent. No, she wasn't imagining it. He was coming on to her.

She ducked away. 'More wine?'

'Please.'

Actually, she thought he might have had too much already, the way he was carrying on. She refilled his glass, her hand shaking. She couldn't believe it.

'Anyway, about Alex—'

'Y'know, sometimes I wonder what would have happened if things had been different.'

'In what way?'

'What if I'd never met your sister?'

Phoebe took another gulp of wine. 'We wouldn't be sitting here for a start.'

'Wouldn't we?' He leaned forward. His hair was a deep, burnished gold in the candlelight. 'We had something going long before Alex came along, remember?'

Oh really? Is that why you had your tongue in her ear five seconds after meeting her? 'We were friends.'

'I think we could have been more than that, given time.'

Blimey, how much time did he need? She'd followed him around like a lovesick spaniel for nearly a year. 'I don't think so.'

'Why not? Didn't you ever fancy me?'

She stared into her wine glass. 'Maybe once.'

'But not any more?'

'You're my sister's boyfriend!'

'What if I wasn't?'

'But you are.'

He moved closer. 'Look, I told you, Alex and I are practically finished. To be honest, I don't really know why we got together in the first place.'

'Er, let me see. Could it be anything to do with the fact that she's stunningly gorgeous?'

'You're probably right,' he admitted gloomily. 'God, I'm so shallow, aren't I?'

'I wouldn't worry about it. Most men are.'

'I was so dazzled by her, I didn't care what she was really like as a person. And by then it was too late.' He turned to look at her. 'But I missed you, Fee. I could never talk to her like I could to you.'

She edged away. 'I don't think we should be having this conversation.'

'Then tell me to stop.' His gaze held hers. 'Look me in the eye and tell me you're not interested.'

She couldn't. She wanted to, but by then Luke had taken the glass out of her hand and was kissing her. Softly and tentatively at first, then deeper and more urgent. It was the sweetest, most dizzying sensation she could ever have imagined.

Her conscience reasserted itself and she broke away. 'Luke—'

'Shh.' He put a finger to her lips. 'Don't say it, Fee. Don't spoil this.'

He kissed her again and this time she didn't resist. It was hard to say anything when her body had gone into meltdown.

When they got to her bedroom she immediately rushed to switch off the bedside light but Luke stopped her. 'Don't,' he said. 'I want to look at you.'

Shyly she took off her clothes, sucking in her stomach, horribly conscious that Luke was staring at her. Comparing her to Alex, with her slender, toned body and endless legs. She half expected him to rush from the room screaming, but he didn't.

'You're beautiful,' he breathed. 'Come here.' She dived between the covers. Luke smiled and gently removed the duvet from her clenched fists. 'Relax. You're supposed to be enjoying this, remember?'

He started to kiss her, his lips and tongue moving

down her neck, and soon her desire for him overcame everything else.

It was the strangest feeling in the world, making love to Luke. It wasn't the best sex she'd ever had – she was far too nervous and self-conscious to enjoy it – but it was as if all her wildest fantasies had suddenly turned into hard, solid muscle. She savoured every sensation, running her hands through his thick soft hair, breathing in the clean smell of his skin, tasting his mouth on hers. But she couldn't look at him, didn't dare open her eyes in case, like all her other fantasies, he melted away.

It was only afterwards that the guilt set in. Just afterwards, in fact, barely before Luke had fallen asleep, his body still pinning hers, his dark-blond head heavy against her breasts.

Oh God, what had she done? Talk about stepping into dead women's shoes. Poor Alex wasn't even cold before she'd jammed in her size sixes.

It wasn't as if she and Luke had even split up properly. At least not as far as Alex was concerned. She was, at this moment, probably sweating over her conference notes, completely unaware that her bitch of a sister had just bedded her boyfriend.

Phoebe stared at the ceiling. The afterglow had worn off, leaving her feeling cold and utterly wretched.

But at the same time, she knew if she could turn back the clock she would probably do it all again. Just to know what it was like to feel his skin on hers, to know he wanted her, even if it was just for a moment.

She lay awake for hours, listening to the regular rhythm of Luke's breathing. How could he sleep like that, as if he didn't have a care in the world, when she felt so incredibly guilty?

Finally she couldn't stand it any more. She crawled out from under his body, careful not to disturb him, pulled on her dressing gown and padded into the kitchen.

It was nearly four in the morning. Phoebe made herself some tea and went back into the sitting room with it. Then she curled up on the sofa and waited for the dawn.

The ringing phone woke her up. Phoebe groped blindly for it, still half asleep.

'That was quick!' Alex's voice was like a bucket of icy water tipped over her. Phoebe jerked upright and nearly dropped the phone. 'Fee, are you there?'

'Yes. Yes, I'm here.' She put a hand over her racing heart. 'What time is it?'

'Just after eight. Sorry to ring so early but I just needed to hear a friendly voice.'

Friendly! If only she knew. 'So, um, you're not having a nice time, then?'

'No, I'm not. It's bloody awful, actually. I nearly came home last night, I was so fed-up.'

'Thank God you didn't,' Phoebe murmured.

'What?'

'I mean, thank God you didn't because you might have blown your chance of getting that promotion.'

'Sod the promotion. I don't think I even want it any more. You haven't seen Luke, have you?'

'No!' Phoebe squeaked in terror. 'No, of course not. Why should I?'

'No reason. I just tried to call him at his flat and he wasn't there.'

'Well, he's certainly not here!' Phoebe's voice reached an indignant falsetto.

'Calm down. I didn't think he was. I just wondered if you'd heard from him, that's all.'

'No, I haven't.' Phoebe darted an anxious glance at the sitting room doorway. 'What did you want him for, anyway?'

'Just to talk to him. And to tell him I'm sorry.'

'S-sorry? What for?'

'I've been a bit of a bitch to him lately. He fixed up a weekend in Paris and I turned him down to come on this rotten conference. I must have been mad.'

'Maybe he's gone to Paris on his own?'

'Possibly. I wouldn't blame him if he did. In fact, I wouldn't blame him if he ran off with a glamorous mademoiselle, the way I've been treating him.'

Phoebe looked down at her tatty dressing gown. Alex had got the glamorous bit wrong, at least.

'Anyway, if you see him, tell him I tried to call. And tell him I miss him.'

'You do?' Her throat constricted with guilt.

'Of course I do. Believe me, I'd much rather be with him than stuck here.'

Just at that moment Luke appeared in the doorway, barefoot and wearing just a pair of jeans. He started to speak but Phoebe frantically signalled to him to shut up.

'Phoebe, are you all right? Have you got someone there with you?'

'No.' She looked sharply at Luke, who backed out of the room.

'You have. I can hear someone moving around.'

'No, it's me. I'm, er, just getting the hoover out.'

'At eight o'clock in the morning? Come off it, Fee. You've got a man there, haven't you?'

'I told you, there's no one here.'

'Suit yourself. But you're a crap liar, Phoebe Redmond.'

If only you knew, Phoebe thought. Luke came back in as she put the phone down. In spite of everything, she felt her stomach curl with treacherous lust.

'That wasn't—' Phoebe nodded. 'Oh Christ.' He sank down on the arm of the sofa. He looked as sick and wretched as she felt. 'You didn't say anything to her, did you?'

'About us? Of course I did. I mean, we're sisters, aren't

we? We don't have any secrets from each other.' Phoebe rolled her eyes heavenwards. 'What did you think I was going to say, Luke? "Yes, I've taken your stuff to the dry cleaners. Yes, I remembered to water the house plants. Oh, and by the way, I bonked your boyfriend last night"?'

Luke ran his hand through his hair. 'I'm sorry, I'm just not thinking straight this morning.'

Not just this morning, Phoebe thought. She reached for her mug of cold tea. Suddenly she felt she needed something to hold on to, and Luke didn't look as if he was about to offer.

'So – are you going to tell her?' he asked slowly.

'Are you?' He couldn't look at her. 'I thought not. So I take it we're agreed last night was a big mistake?'

'Oh God, Fee, I'm so sorry. I'd had so much to drink last night, I didn't even know what I was doing—'

'That's a lame excuse, Luke Rawlings, and you know it!' Phoebe cut him off. 'You can't wriggle out if it by blaming it on alcohol. You knew exactly what you were doing last night, and so did I. So stop being so bloody feeble about it.'

'You're right.' Luke stared at the ground. 'I did know what I was doing last night. I just don't want to face up to what a heel I've been.' He looked up at her, his face wretched. 'The truth is, I was angry. I was lonely and pissed off at Alex for ditching me at the last minute. And for not wanting to marry me.'

'So you decided to get revenge by sleeping with me?'

'It wasn't like that,' Luke insisted. 'I wasn't just using you, Phoebe. Last night was really special.' He swallowed hard. 'I really do like you.'

'But you love Alex?'

'I wish I didn't. It would be a lot easier.'

You're telling me, Phoebe thought. She'd expected all this, agreed with it even, but it still hurt. Her chest ached with the effort of holding her emotions in. 'If it's any consolation, I feel exactly the same,' she said. 'I don't want to hurt Alex, either. So I think we should forget last night ever happened.'

'Really?' Luke looked like a condemned man who'd been handed a reprieve on his way to the gallows. 'You mean it? You won't say anything to Alex?'

'She's my sister, Luke. I don't want to see her hurt any more than you do.' She tried to smile but found she couldn't. 'It'll be our secret.'

Luke didn't hang around for too long after that. Phoebe didn't mind. It felt all wrong, having him there.

At the door he kissed her, an affectionate peck this time. 'Thanks,' he said.

'What for?'

'For being so good about everything. And for last night.' He looked down at her, and for a moment she saw a flicker of the way he'd gazed at her last night. It was more than she could bear.

'I thought we weren't going to mention that again?'

'You're right. Sorry.' He was just about to leave when Phoebe called him back.

'I forgot to tell you. Alex sends her love.'

'Did she?' His broad grin wrung her heart.

Phoebe closed the door on him and leant against it. Much as she loved Luke – and she really did love him – she knew she could never put a smile like that on his face. Not if she tried for a million years.

Chapter 8

Alex ducked under the hot, foaming water of the jacuzzi, thankful to be alone for the first time in twenty-four hours.

This weekend wasn't turning out how she wanted at all. The hotel was drab, with wall-to-wall beige hessian and piped musak. And the conference was even worse. All those tedious marketing people swapping business cards, flashing their laptops and texting messages on their mobiles as if the whole of western civilisation would die if they didn't stay online.

What was the point? she wondered. What did it really matter if people bought one brand of margarine and not another? But when she'd dared to voice her opinion they'd all stared at her as if she was a dangerous heretic who should be burned at the stake. She'd sat through one seminar on the Theory of Consumerism and then decided she'd had enough.

And she'd underestimated just how persistent Tom Kavanagh would turn out to be. She'd hoped he might be tied up with meetings most of the weekend, but he'd barely left her alone. Last night had been a close call. He'd made an oafish pass at her over dinner and she'd had to get him drunk so he passed out in his room and she could escape. She wasn't sure if she could manage it again tonight.

'There you are!' Speak of the devil. Alex fixed a smile on her face as Tom approached. In black Speedos, and without the clever tailoring of a thousand pound suit, his burgeoning paunch was clear to see. 'You naughty girl, sneaking off like that. Why didn't you tell me, then we could have played truant together?'

He slipped into the bubbling water beside her. Alex shifted along to make room for him, but he still sat too close.

'You've certainly charmed them all in there,' he remarked. 'They're all asking me where I found you. Seems you've made a real hit.' His breath was hot against her bare shoulder. 'There isn't a man in that conference room who wouldn't like to be where I am now.' She felt his leg brushing against hers under the water, and jerked away. 'Of course, when you're Senior Account Manager I expect there'll be lots more weekends like this.'

He made it sound like a threat. Alex suppressed a shudder. She didn't think she could stand it. 'I've been thinking. Maybe I'm not cut out for the job after all.'

He was closing in to kiss her neck as she said it. He drew back as if she'd suddenly announced she was in the early stages of leprosy. 'Why not? You'd be perfect for it.'

'I'm not sure it's what I really want.'

'You mean all that power and prestige? The big pay rise? The company Beamer?' She looked at him. No one had said anything about a Beamer.

Tom Kavanagh read the glint of interest in her eyes and smiled. 'You deserve it,' he coaxed. 'Or at least, I think you do. But if you don't think you're up to it—'

'Oh, I'm up to it.'

His leer was back in place. 'Good girl. Although I admit, it's going to be tough persuading old Frank Fleming.'

'But I thought you said it was up to you?'

'It is. But you know Frank has a soft spot for Rachel. She's been with the company longer, and frankly she's more qualified than you are. On paper, anyway. I'm going to have to persuade him that you have other –

qualities – you could bring to the job. But first you have to convince me.'

No prizes how she should do that. And it had nothing to do with psychometric testing. 'So what particular qualities were you looking for?'

'Drive. Ambition. The determination to do whatever it takes to succeed. Do you have those things, Alex?'

'I think so.' He was closing in on her again. She slid away. 'And I'd be glad for the chance to prove it to you.'

'What do you think we're doing now?' Suddenly his mouth was fastened on the bare, wet skin of her shoulder. Alex pushed him off.

'Hang on a minute! I bet you wouldn't do this to Rachel.'

'You're absolutely right. But then, I don't fancy Rachel otherwise I would have invited her this weekend and not you.' His surprise at being pushed away was hardening into anger. 'I do hope you're not going to start playing games, Alex? Because I have to tell you, I don't like games. I thought you of all people would know the score.'

'Oh, I know the score, all right. If I don't sleep with you I haven't a hope of getting the job, is that it?'

'Sweetheart, as things stand at the moment you don't have a hope of getting it anyway.'

'But I deserve that job. I'm bright, talented—'

'Your attitude's lousy and your timekeeping's even worse. And everyone in your department thinks you're an arrogant bitch.'

Alex gasped. 'That's not fair!'

'Isn't it? You think us lot on the top floor don't know what goes on? Come on, Alex, you've hardly bothered to hide your contempt for Fleming Associates and everyone who works there.'

'Only because I knew I could do better.'

'You haven't exactly shown a lot of promise so far,

have you? Whereas Rachel is hard working, well qualified and willing.'

'Rachel has about as much flair for PR as a tea cosy.'

'Maybe, but she's also got Frank Fleming in her
corner. Look, I'm not saying you wouldn't be perfect
for the job,' he said, as Alex smouldered. 'I wouldn't be
here if I didn't think you could do it. All I'm saying is
that in your position you need all the friends you can get.
And it helps to be nice to your friends, Alex. Because
you never know when you might need them to put a
good word in for you.'

He moved in again and Alex shouldered him off
coldly. 'You realise I could probably sue you for sexual
harassment?'

He looked unconcerned. 'You could try. But at best
you'd end up with a small compensation cheque and a
big reputation as a troublemaker. And you'd have to
convince the judge that you were so naïve you had no
idea what was going on when you came down here. And
frankly you don't strike anyone as the naïve type.' His
eyes dropped to her breasts and back up to her face. 'Plus
I doubt if any of your "friends" in the office would back
up your story. They all saw you flirting with me at
Claire's leaving party, and they saw us leave together.
And I don't suppose you could resist telling one or two
of them what you were up to this weekend? I thought
not,' he said, as Alex blushed. 'You'd have to ask them to
lie for you. And none of them really like you enough to
do that, do they?'

He was right, of course. They'd all close ranks against
her. Even Nigel would probably think she deserved
everything she got. They'd all love to see her fail.

Well, she wouldn't give them the satisfaction.

'It doesn't have to be that way, Alex.' Tom reached
out and tucked a damp strand of hair behind her ear. 'I
really don't want us to fall out over this. All you have to

do is be nice to me, and the job's yours. That's not too much to ask, is it? Just one night, and you'll have everything you want.'

She thought about it. He was right, of course. What was it, anyway? Just sex. It really was a small price to pay for what she wanted.

And what was the alternative? Saying no, then watching Rachel take the job. Her job. How could she work for a woman who thought Dorothy Perkins was the last word in tailoring?

Sensing her indecision, Tom moved in to kiss her again. This time she didn't push him away.

Chapter 9

Will Hutchinson opened his eyes, and immediately regretted it. The sunlight streaming through the open curtains drilled a laser beam of pain straight through to his brain.

He closed them again quickly. There was something wrong. Something very wrong indeed. He couldn't feel any of his limbs. The only thing he *could* feel was his head, which hurt like hell. His mouth was lined with what seemed to be the fur of a long-dead stoat. And there was something strange about his pillow. It was hard, rough and kind of hairy.

He risked opening his eyes again, more slowly this time. Everything lurched into focus around him, but in a strange way. He found himself eyeball to eyeball with what was under the sofa – pens, a few dustballs, an old copy of the *Evening Press*. Furniture reared up around him, towering over him. He'd never seen the world from this angle before.

And then, slowly and groggily, he realised he was on his sitting room floor, his face raw from the rough seagrass mat, his limbs dead from where he'd lain on them all night.

And Nadine was gone.

He gave up the effort of trying to open his eyes and collapsed back on the floor, not caring that the seagrass scraped the stubble from his face. What was the bloody point? Now Nadine was gone, there was no point in anything any more. There was no point in even living. He might as well stay here and wait to die. From the way he was feeling, it wouldn't be too long.

The phone rang, sending shockwaves through his brain. Will ignored it. It went on ringing, the sound worming its way into the pain centres, the only part of his body apparently left alive.

Then it suddenly occurred to him. What if it was Nadine? With his last ounce of strength Will threw himself on the phone, landing on the receiver just as it rang off.

He staggered into the kitchen, clutching his head in both hands. With every step he reckoned he could feel his brain sloshing around in his skull. He groped for the orange juice in the fridge and drank it straight from the carton, slaking his terrible thirst. Nadine would have gone mad if she could see him. But it was Nadine's fault he'd gone on such a bender in the first place.

He tried to piece together the events of the previous evening. He could remember the wedding, but after that things got distinctly hazy. Snatches kept coming back to him then receding again, like a tantalising glimpse out of the corner of his eye that disappeared when he turned his head to look at it. He couldn't remember how, but he had the feeling he'd behaved very badly.

Painkillers. That's what he needed. Still clutching his head, he crawled off to the bedroom to find them. There weren't any, just an empty foil packet. Increasingly desperate, the pain in his head growing worse every second, he pulled out the entire medicine drawer and emptied it on the bed. Scrabbling around among the athlete's foot powder and Rennies, he finally came up with an ancient sachet of Lemsip. Unable to summon the energy to boil a kettle, he tipped the packet's contents down his throat, followed it up with a quick slug of orange juice, coughed a lot, then staggered off to the bathroom.

He meant to have a shower but standing up was too painful, so he stripped off his clothes, climbed into the tub and ran the taps in around him. It was so blissful just lying there, lulled by the sound of rushing water, resting his aching head against Nadine's inflatable, lip-shaped bath pillow. His eyelids felt heavy, and before long he gave into the urge to close them.

Suddenly the bathroom seemed to be full of water and people, all shouting at him. Before he knew what was happening, someone had grabbed his arms and was hauling him over the side of the bathtub. He fell, spluttering and flapping like a landed cod, on the bathmat, a second before a pair of hot, wet and – judging from the taste of them – very male lips fastened against his.

'Christ!' He fought his way free. 'What the fuck are you doing?'

'I thought you were dead.'

'So you thought you'd cop a snog, is that it?' Will snatched a towel from the rail and clutched it against him as he struggled to his feet. 'What are you, desperate or something?'

'I was trying to save you,' complained his cousin Andrew. 'We thought you'd topped yourself, didn't we Tez?' He looked at the tall, gangly man beside him, who nodded vigorously.

'I was taking a bath!'

'With the taps still running? You were under the water when we got here. Another couple of minutes and you could have drowned. Come to think of it, we could have all drowned.' Andrew lifted his foot to show his dripping trainer.

Will looked around, registering for the first time that the bath had indeed overflowed and the carpet was soaking. Oh shit. He buried his face in his hands. This was all he needed. Any minute now the mad old trout from downstairs would be hammering on his door, complaining about the water coming through her ceiling.

'And there were all those drugs on the bed,' Tez said. 'We thought you'd taken an overdose or something. You gave us a fright.'

'I gave *you* a fright? How do you think I feel, waking up to find him trying to snog me?' He glared at Andrew.

'I was giving you the kiss of life.'

'Yeah? Well, here's a tip for you, mate. Next time don't use tongues. And you call yourself a bloody doctor.'

'No, I call myself a bloody research scientist.' Andrew pulled a couple of towels off the rail and started mopping the floor. He was three years older than Will, dark-haired and improbably handsome, even in those geeky glasses. In fact, he looked a lot like Clark Kent. 'I take it the lovely Nadine hasn't come back?'

'What do you think?'

Tez looked at Andrew. 'That's a tenner you owe me.'

'Oh great,' Will said bitterly. 'Very sympathetic. My life's in turmoil and you're taking bets. Why didn't you just go for an accumulator on whether I'd killed myself as well?'

They looked at each other sheepishly. 'Well, actually—' Tez began, but Andrew elbowed him.

'Thanks a lot. How did you get in here, anyway?'

'Mum gave me a key. She sent me round to see if you were all right. Apparently she tried ringing earlier but there was no answer.'

Will pulled his towel around him. 'Well, as you can see, I'm fine,' he said, with as much pride as he could muster.

'Well, you look bloody awful,' Andrew said. 'You go and get dressed while I make some coffee.'

Will was about to argue that Andrew had no right to order him about like they were kids, especially in his own flat. But he didn't have the strength and the idea of coffee was very appealing so he shuffled off to the bedroom.

87

The big, white bed gave him a pang but he ignored it and headed for his clothes, which as usual were heaped in a corner of the room where he'd slung them. He picked out a baggy old green sweater his Aunt Gina had bought him from M&S and teamed it with a pair of black Paul Smith jeans, knowing it would have driven Nadine mad. She was forever nagging him about his haphazard taste in clothes. It was a mystery to both of them how a woman who devoured the fashion pages of *Elle* and *Vogue* could have ended up with a man who was wearing grunge before and after it went out of fashion.

Was that why she'd gone? He had no idea. She hadn't said much when her father bundled her into the vintage Rolls.

He sat down on the bed and tried to piece it all together. Yesterday afternoon he had stood under the chandeliers in the flower-bedecked grand hall of the stately home with his friends and family, plus what felt like about a thousand of Nadine's relatives, feeling self-conscious in the morning suit she had made him hire for the occasion. His Aunt Gina was there, flanked by his other two matinée idol cousins. The third, Andrew, was beside him as his best man, while his best mates Baz and Tez were making a complete balls-up as ushers. Even his father had closed the surgery for a couple of hours to come along.

Then Nadine had appeared in the arched doorway on her father's arm, looking stunning in a slender, ivory dress, pearls woven into her black hair. She'd seemed nervous, of course, but then so was he. But as he reached for her hand to give it a reassuring squeeze, she'd suddenly stopped dead, whispered, 'I can't do this. I'm sorry.' Then she'd fled.

And that was it. By the time Will reached the steps of the stately pile she was already being helped into the car by her father. The last he saw of her was her tearful face looking back at him as the car sped off down the mile long drive.

After that came the embarrassment of going back inside and explaining to everyone what had happened. Luckily Andrew had taken charge of that one while Will had just stood there, too shocked to remember his own name. Baz and Tez had shuffled their feet and tried to crack a few limp jokes. Gina was all for forming a one-woman lynch mob and storming down to Nadine's parents' house in Leeds. His father, never one for big displays of emotion, had patted his shoulder in manly sympathy and headed off to open up the surgery.

Will looked around the room. It still bore traces of Nadine. Her perfume lingered on his sweater. Her make-up was scattered over the dressing table where she'd left it. It hurt to see it there, but at the same time it filled him with hope. She'd obviously decided to go on the spur of the moment so maybe she would decide to come back just as quickly? Besides, while her clothes were still here there was a chance he could see her again. She might walk out on him but she'd never abandon her shoes.

When he came back into the sitting room Andrew was pouring the coffee and Tez was zapping aliens on the Playstation. Guiltily he stuffed the console behind a cushion when Will walked in.

'How are you feeling, mate?'

'It's all right, you know, I'm not dying. You don't have to talk to me in that stupid voice.' He ignored the way Andrew and Tez looked at each other. 'Where's Baz, anyway? I can't believe he missed a chance to laugh at my expense.'

'He had to go in to work. Some big deal going down on a property and he stands to make a massive bonus. He said to let you know he's thinking about you.'

I bet he is, Will thought. Big Baz had all the sensitivity of a rhino.

He slumped down on the sofa between them and they all stared at the blank TV screen.

'So you're all right, then?' Andrew said.

'I wouldn't say that, no.'

'Oh. Right.' Silence. The room had the relaxed atmosphere of a vasectomy clinic waiting room.

If this was America, Will reflected, they'd all be throwing themselves into a group hug and having some kind of male bonding session by now. As it was, Tez and Andrew looked as if they'd rather have their colons irrigated by a Romanian shot putter than discuss their innermost feelings. He thought about bursting into tears, just to frighten them.

'So why do you think she did it?' Tez ventured. He was about eight feet tall, thin and gangly, with the pallid unhealthy complexion of someone who lived on pizzas and never ventured outdoors. Which, basically, was true. Tez worked in a computer shop. When he wasn't selling computers, or installing computers, or fixing computers, he was usually playing on them. He had an impressive knowledge of computer software. Frankly, it was the only impressive thing about him.

'God knows. Maybe she had a brainstorm. Maybe it was the wrong time of the month. Maybe she didn't like the way I looked in a top hat. Or maybe she's never really liked me, and this is all some kind of elaborate revenge fantasy she's been planning for months.' Will considered it. 'I think it's because I didn't take the wedding seriously enough.'

'What do you mean?'

'She's been planning this for ages. You know – string quartets, doves, six different types of bread roll, that kind of thing. But I never really took much interest. I think it got on her nerves.'

He remembered her horror when he'd presented her with his guest list, scribbled on the back of a Chinese takeaway menu.

'Baz, Tez, Smithy, Murgo, Dezza – this isn't a guest list, this is the cast of "Grange Hill". Don't you know anyone with a real name?' she'd demanded.

Come to think of it, he'd also shown a marked lack of enthusiasm when they trailed around House of Fraser compiling the wedding list. She wanted useless items like an electric wok; he'd wanted a GameCube. They'd ended up having a major tiff in the china and glassware department.

'That's it,' he said. 'It's because I didn't rave about ice sculptures and Welsh harpists. She's done it to teach me a lesson.'

Andrew sent him a sceptical look. 'Bit extreme, don't you think?'

Tez shook his head. 'I don't understand women.'

'I'm not bloody surprised,' Will said. 'You never get near enough to talk to one.'

'That's not true!'

'No? When was the last time you had a girlfriend? A real one, I mean, not one you downloaded off the Internet.'

A purple flush crept up Tez's neck. 'How did you know about them?'

'Excuse me, this isn't very constructive,' Andrew pointed out. Will gave him a dirty look. Typical Andrew, always so sane and reasonable. He'd been like that when they were growing up together, always coming up with good reasons why Will shouldn't skip school or set fire to things. And he was even worse now he'd grown up to be so sickeningly handsome with several degrees and a PhD. And his job involved researching cures for life-threatening diseases. Thank God he lived down in London. If Will had to see him every day he knew he'd end up killing him out of sheer envy.

'Well, if you ask me, you're better off without her,' Tez tried again. 'Actually, I reckon she did you a favour, dumping you.'

'How do you work that out?'

'Well, it's obvious isn't it? You're far too young to get married.'

'I'm thirty-two.'

'Marriage is a trap,' Tez went on, not listening. 'I mean, when was the last time you saw a happily married man? There's no such thing. Only those poor saps pushing their trolleys round Sainsbury's with that "somebody shoot me" look on their faces.'

'At least they've got a trolley.' Will had a sudden vision of a solitary wire basket filled with frozen ready meals for one, and all the checkout girls looking at him because they knew he had no one to share them with.

'When you're married, you have to spend your weekends buying flat pack furniture in Ikea instead of watching the footie,' Tez went on. 'And you can forget Saturday nights out with the lads. You have to have dinner parties. Which you probably have to help cook. And you don't get unlimited access to your computer games. Once you're married you can forget all about Level Twelve of *Total Armageddon* mate, because I'm telling you now that's never going to happen.'

They all sat in silence for a moment, letting Tez's utter stupidity sink in. Then Andrew said, 'So what are you going to do now?'

Will shrugged. 'God knows. Wait for her to get in touch, I suppose.'

'Why don't you try calling her?'

'I'm not that desperate!' Will saw their faces. 'OK, forget I said that. But I'm still not ringing her. I wouldn't know what to say, anyway.'

'How about, "Why did you ditch me in such a public and humiliating way, you inhuman, unfeeling bitch?"' Andrew suggested.

'Very nicely put. Yes, that should bring her running back.' Will sent him a scathing look. 'I suppose that's what happens when you spend your whole life locked in a laboratory full of diseased rats, is it?'

Actually, Andrew had a sickening amount of success with women. They adored the over-achieving swine, which was another reason for Will to hate him.

'Or you could come out with us and watch the footie?' Tez said.

Will stared at him. 'Do you seriously think that watching a bunch of hairy blokes running around a field chasing a ball is going to help?'

Tez looked affronted. 'Well, no, of course not.'

'Good.'

'Obviously we'd have to have a few pints as well.'

'Terence,' Will addressed him severely, 'I don't want to watch football, or drink pints. All I want is for that phone to ring right now and for Nadine to tell me she's coming home.'

The phone rang. They all looked at it, then at each other. Finally Will picked it up.

'Will?' She sounded different, her voice huskier. She'd probably been crying.

'Nadine? Where are you?' There were noises going on in the background he couldn't work out.

'Never mind about that. Look, we've got to sort things out.'

'Y-yes, of course. I know that.' He gestured for Andrew and Tez to leave the room. Neither of them moved an inch. 'Are you OK? You left so quickly yesterday, I didn't get a chance to—'

'Yes, yes, I'm fine.' More noises in the background. People talking. Phones ringing. It sounded familiar but he couldn't place it.

'I suppose you're wondering why I walked out on you like that?'

Will was taken aback. 'Well – er – yes, it had crossed my mind.'

'The truth is, you were crap in bed.'

'Wh–what?' Of all the things he'd been expecting to hear, this didn't even feature.

'I know it must be difficult for you to hear, but you just didn't satisfy me sexually. In fact, I've been faking it since I met you.'

'I– I—'

'Which is why I've been sleeping with Baz.'

'B–Baz? But—'

'He's a real man, Will. He's hung like a horse, and he knows what to do with it. Sorry.'

Will gulped for air like a drowning man, trying to make sense of what he'd just heard. Then there was an explosion of laughter on the other end of the line and suddenly everything fell into place.

'Baz!'

'Sorry, mate, I couldn't resist it.' Baz's voice boomed down the phone. 'Michelle was bloody good, wasn't she? Considering she doesn't even know what Nadine sounds like. She nearly had me fooled.' A few people giggled in the background. 'What do you think?'

'I think,' Will gripped the receiver to stop his hand trembling, 'I think you are a sad, sick fucker!'

He slammed the phone down. 'Ginger bastard,' he muttered.

'What was that about?' Andrew asked. Will was just about to explain when the phone rang again. He snatched it up. 'Yes?'

'Will?' This time he wasn't fooled. It didn't sound a bit like her.

'Ha ha, very bloody funny!' he snapped. 'You're about as amusing as a case of genital herpes. Why don't you and that fat git formerly known as my friend just piss off and screw up someone else's life?'

'Will? Is that you?' The voice sharpened, and suddenly he recognised it all too well.

'Nadine? Oh fuck.'

Chapter 10

'Nice greeting.'

'Where are you?' Will tried to stop his voice shaking.

'At my parents' house.'

Where else? The first hint of trouble, and Nadine would run home to Daddy.

Wonderful, wealthy Daddy with his big house, swimming pool and string of classic cars. Devoted Daddy, who still kept his little girl's favourite pony in the paddock behind the house, despite the fact that she'd outgrown it about twelve years ago. Possessive Daddy, who resented Will's presence in his daughter's life and made no secret of the fact.

There were so many things he wanted to say, questions he wanted to ask. But now he couldn't think of anything.

'How are you?' she asked.

'Oh well, you know. The woman I loved walked out on me at our wedding. My life's in tatters. I can't complain.'

'Will, I'm sorry. I don't know what else to say.'

'How about, "It was all a mistake and I'm coming home?"'

There was a pause. 'That's what I'm calling about, actually. I wondered if you'd be around today?'

His heart leapt. 'I'm in all day. Just say when and I'll be here.'

'That's just it. I was kind of hoping you wouldn't be.' Silence. 'I need to pick up a few bits and pieces. Clothes and things.'

Will's blood ran cold. So that was it. The shoes were going, and so was she. 'And you don't want me to be here?'

'It might be difficult. I don't really think we should see each other at the moment.'

'And what about me? What about what I think? Or doesn't that matter?'

'Don't lose your temper.'

'I AM NOT LOSING MY TEMPER!' He caught Andrew's warning look and forced himself to calm down. 'All right, so what if I am? Nadine, twenty-four hours ago we were about to get married. Now you don't even want to see me. Can you blame me for being a bit confused? I just want to know what's going on. Why did you walk out? Don't you love me?'

'I – I don't know. Yes, I think I do. But I don't know if that's enough.'

'Enough for what? It's enough for most people. It was enough for me.' He heard Nadine sigh.

'Will, I don't want to get into this now. I just want to come round and pick up my things. I've hardly got anything to wear except for this wedding dress.'

The mention of the dress stung him. 'Why don't you get Daddy to buy you a whole new wardrobe? I'm sure he wouldn't mind. Especially if it keeps you away from me.'

'Stop it, you're being childish.'

'So what if I am? He's behind it, isn't he?'

'No he isn't.'

'Bollocks. I bet he spent the whole journey to the wedding begging you not to go through with it. I've never been good enough for you, have I? After all, my dad's only a GP. That's no match for the man who invented self-cleaning cat litter!'

There was a clatter followed by a buzz as the phone crashed down. As Will stared at the receiver in his hand, Andrew clapped in mocking applause.

'My dad's better than your dad, eh? Very mature, well-considered argument, Will. You played a blinder there. If that doesn't bring her running back, I don't know what will.'

When Tez and Andrew had lost interest and drifted off to watch the football, Will attempted to settle down at his drawing board and work, hoping it might take his mind off Nadine.

He'd tried his hand at most things after leaving art school – graphic design, magazine illustration, he'd even managed to sell a few paintings, although most of his work still hung on his own walls rather than other people's. But for the past two years, most of his income had come from illustrating a series of children's books featuring a pair of lovable little scamps called Hunky and Dory. The books, written by a brisk, retired teacher called Roberta Forrest, were designed to introduce hard-hitting life topics to the under-eights in a gentle, non-threatening way. Poor old Hunky and Dory had already been through enough trauma in their short lives to keep Jerry Springer going for years, but thanks to Will they still managed to keep smiles on their chubby faces. So far they'd lived through bereavement (poor granddad and the family guinea pig popping their clogs in the same week), depression (Mummy lying down a lot) and homosexuality (why funny Uncle Leonard had such a wide collection of Shirley Bassey records). Now, by some horrible quirk of fate, they were coming to terms with divorce.

'Mummy and Daddy are splitting up,' went Roberta's relentlessly cheery prose. 'Daddy's found a new friend and now he's moving out. It's sad we won't all be living in the same house any more, but we'll see him at week-ends and we'll all have fun.'

Bugger that, Will thought. It was no good trying to

show splitting up positively because there wasn't a positive side. There was nothing smiley about seeing someone you loved walk out of your life. There was nothing cheery about the raw, gaping wound where your heart had been. For once he felt like defying Roberta and drawing his own, more accurate, illustrations. But it was impossible to draw the emptiness, or the terrible wondering where it all went wrong. Every line he put down on paper reminded him of what he'd lost.

But deep down, if he was honest with himself, he never believed they would get this far. When Nadine walked out on him at the wedding, she was only confirming something he'd suspected for a long time. He wasn't good enough for her.

He'd thought that ever since they first met at a men's magazine Christmas party in London. Will was invited along as a contributor because he'd done some illustrations for them a few months back. Nadine, a budding actress, was their Christmas cover girl, dressed in nothing but flashing reindeer antlers and some strategically placed tinsel. It was lust at first sight for him, and for most of the other men there. But with all of them hovering around her like wasps round a cornet, he never imagined he'd ever get the chance to do more than smile wistfully at her across the crowded room.

If it hadn't been for her lost bag it might have ended like that. She realised it was missing as they stood in the rain, both trying to catch a taxi. He'd helped her, lent her his mobile to call her flatmate, suggested she cancel her cards (she laughed that they were Daddy's account and he probably wouldn't mind because whoever nicked them would spend less than she did), and shared a taxi with her. He told her he was going to King's Cross to catch a train back to York. She told him her parents lived just outside Leeds. Half jokingly, he suggested she should look him up next time she was up there. She said she might. The taxi had made a lengthy detour to Finchley Road and Will had missed his train. She'd invited him to sleep on her floor.

And that was it. He'd gone through their long-distance relationship with a feeling of disbelief, as if it was a bubble that was going to burst at any moment. Every time he phoned he expected her number to have changed. When he went to London to visit, he imagined the police would be waiting to arrest him under the anti-stalking laws. Even when she agreed to move up to York and buy a flat with him he still expected her to call it off at any moment.

Then, on Valentine's Day, he'd got drunk and proposed and she — equally drunk — had accepted. It was at that point he'd breathed a sigh of relief and allowed himself to relax and believe that this was real, and it really was for ever.

Bloody ironic, come to think of it, that that was the point at which it had all started to unravel.

He fought the urge to have a beer, and lost. He knew drink wasn't the answer, but it helped dull the pain. Two dulled it even more. He was just wondering if he should go for three and total anaesthesia when he heard the key in the lock and Nadine walked in.

She wasn't wearing any make-up but she still looked gorgeous. She wore a T-shirt and faded Levis that showed off her incredible long legs. She stood there, her expression wary, ready to take flight at the first sign of trouble.

'Nadine!' Will stood up, nearly knocking over his drawing board. 'I didn't think you'd come.'

He made a move towards her. She backed away.

'I wasn't going to. But like I said, I needed some things.'

'I'm sorry. About losing my temper like that.'

'It's OK. You were upset, I understand that. And you were right, you do deserve an explanation.'

There was something so final about the way she said it, that suddenly Will didn't want one. He was too afraid of what he might hear.

'Would you like a drink?' It felt strange, treating her like a visitor when yesterday this had been her home.

Nadine eyed the empty beer cans beside his drawing board. 'No thanks. I can't stop.' There was an awkward pause. 'I'll make a start on the packing, shall I?'

'Help yourself. You know where everything is.'

He watched her go into the bedroom, mesmerised as ever by her slender, undulating body.

What the hell are you doing? a voice hissed in his ear. This could be the last time you see her. Are you really going to let her walk out without a fight?

He followed her into the bedroom. 'Do you, um, need any help?'

So much for putting up a fight.

'I can manage, thanks.' He watched as she hauled the suitcase from the top of the wardrobe on to the bed. As she unzipped it and threw it open, they both realised at the same time that it was packed with clothes for their honeymoon.

They glanced at each other, then without a word Nadine started taking the neatly ironed piles out and placing them on the bed.

'I guess this means I won't be going to the Seychelles,' Will quipped. He longed to make Nadine laugh, or even smile like he used to. But her face didn't crack.

'Sorry.' She went over to the wardrobe and started pulling out armfuls of clothes. 'I'm sure we can get at least some of the money back on the insurance.'

'I'm not sure the policy will cover it. Unless you think a broken heart counts as a medical emergency?' He stretched out on the bed. 'Maybe I'll go by myself?'

'Please yourself.' Her indifference appalled him. He could have announced he was taking the Dagenham Girl

Pipers with him and she wouldn't have batted an eyelid. 'We'll have to do something about the mortgage too, I suppose. Probably best if we sell this place.'

'No!'

'Why not?'

'I don't want to go through all that hassle. Besides, it's a bad time to sell. Baz told me.' The truth was, he didn't want to lose the last connection he had with her. 'I'll buy you out.'

'Are you sure?' On your pathetic income, her look said. 'The mortgage might be too much for one person. How will you manage?'

'I didn't know you cared.'

'I just don't want a bad credit rating against my name when you default, that's all.'

'I'll find a flatmate.'

'One of your friends?'

'Why not?'

'No reason. They practically live here anyway, it'll do them good to put their hands in their pockets for a change.'

Something acid in her voice made Will sit up. 'Is that why you left? Because you don't like my friends?'

'Don't be ridiculous. I don't give a damn about your friends.' She'd finished on the wardrobe and now began emptying the drawers of her dressing table. He felt as though his whole life was slipping like sand through his fingers. The tighter he tried to hold on to it, the faster it disappeared.

'So why did you leave, then? You still haven't told me.'

She didn't answer him. 'Have you seen my passport?'

'Is it me?' Will persisted. 'Do you hate me or something?'

Nadine straightened up and looked at him. 'No, I don't hate you.'

'But you don't love me?'

'I don't know how I feel.' She went back to emptying out the drawers.

Will sensed her weakening and jumped in with both feet. 'So why don't you stay until you do know?'

'Will—'

'I mean it. We could work it out. We could go to counselling or something.'

Nadine looked at him pityingly. Her green eyes were cool. 'It wouldn't work.'

'Why not? How do you know that until you've tried?'

'What the hell do you think I've been doing for the past year?' Nadine looked angry. 'I've tried to fit in with your life, Will. I gave up living in London to move up here with you, I even thought getting married might make me feel more settled. But it's all wrong. We're too different. We don't have the same goals.'

'I don't have any goals.'

'Exactly. You're just content to drift along, taking life as it comes. You're so laidback you're practically horizontal. It's one of the things I loved about you – at first. But now I realise it's driving us apart. I want to make something of my life, and you – well, you just don't care, do you?'

'I could care. I could have drive and ambition, if that's what you want.'

Nadine shook her head sadly. 'You can't change who you are, Will.'

'But I can! Just give me a chance. We could move to London. You'd like that, wouldn't you?'

She frowned. 'Why now? You've always hated the idea before.'

'I didn't stand to lose you before.'

She smiled at him sadly. For a moment he thought she was going to agree. Then she shook her head. 'It's too late,' she said.

'Why? I already said I could change. Who knows, I might even enjoy it if I—'

'Will, I've already made plans. I'm flying to LA tonight.'

He stared at her, stunned. 'Since when?'

'I booked a flight this morning. It's something I've been thinking about for a while.' She sat down on the end of the bed, as far away from him as she could get. 'You remember that film screening I went to in London a couple of weeks ago? The one you didn't want to go to because you thought it would be boring? Well, I met someone there.'

Will felt a cold trickle of dread down his spine. 'Go on.'

'Not the way you're thinking. Clint's a film producer, based in LA—'

'Clint?' Will interrupted. 'He told you his name was Clint and you didn't laugh in his face?'

'Like I said, he's based in LA.' Nadine ignored him. 'He was telling me how I could make a career over there. Maybe get into films.'

'Trying to chat you up, in other words.'

'That's what I thought. But I sent him my CV and some ten by eights and a few days later he phoned and said he'd talked to a couple of directors and fixed up some screen tests. He reckons British actresses are very hot out there now. He said I could be the new Kate Beckinsale. Isn't that incredible?'

'Unbelievable,' Will said. 'So you're going to drop everything – including me – and rush off to the other side of the world just because some dodgy bloke called Clint has told you he can get you into movies?'

Nadine looked offended. 'Trust you to be negative about it,' she sniffed. 'You've never had any faith in my career. Clint says I've got great potential.'

'And did you ask Clint what kind of movies he makes?'

'What's that supposed to mean?'

'I mean if you're not careful you could end up on one of those dodgy videos Baz is always getting from his mate in Amsterdam, co-starring with a ten-inch vibrator and a donkey.'

'That's right, bring it down to your level. God, and to think I agonised for so long about going. I haven't slept for the last week, thinking about it.'

'And you didn't think to mention it to me, so we could talk about it?'

'Why? I knew what you'd say. "Don't do it, Nadine. Stay here, Nadine." Or you'd just treat the whole thing as a big joke.'

'I wouldn't. I've always been very supportive of your career.'

'In which case you should be telling me to go.'

She had him there. Will was silent. 'I'm not saying it'll be for ever.' Nadine had put on that coaxing voice, the one she always used when she was about to persuade him to part with a lot of money for some useless household item. 'But I just need to go, to find out. Otherwise I might spend the rest of my life wondering about what might have been. And that wouldn't be any good for our relationship, would it?'

'You being thousands of miles away won't do much for it either.'

She ignored the comment as she reached out and took his hand. 'Who knows what will happen in the future? This whole thing could be a disaster, couldn't it? I could be home in six months pleading with you to take me back.'

'So I'm the fallback position, am I? Just in case your movie career doesn't work out?'

She drew her hand away. 'If you loved me you'd understand.'

'And if you loved me you wouldn't want to go.'

Silence. Stalemate. There was so much he wanted to say but he didn't dare. Every word he uttered just seemed to make things worse.

Finally Nadine stood up and hauled her suitcase off the bed. Will reached across and took it from her. 'Let me,' he said. Nadine looked as if she was about to argue, then thought better of it, and shrugged.

Out in the street, he helped load her bags into the boot of her sporty Nissan. He did it slowly, trying to drag out their last minutes together. Too slowly. Nadine was so impatient she nearly slammed the boot lid on his fingers.

'Well, this is it,' he said.

'It looks like it.' Was that a trace of regret in her voice? It was hard to tell. She'd put her sunglasses on so he couldn't see what was going on behind them. 'Bye, Will. I'll be in touch.'

She leaned forward and gave him a swift, awkward peck on the cheek. Stay cool, he told himself. Whatever you do, don't do anything stupid . . .

'Don't go, Nadine.' He was hanging on to the car door. 'Please don't go. I'll change. I'll do anything you want. Only please don't leave me.'

'Will, don't do this.' She sounded disappointed. If he hadn't blown it before, he certainly had now.

He let go of the door and she slammed it.

'Fine,' he said. 'Go, then. See if I care.' He raised his voice over the roar of the engine. 'But don't blame me if you end up in a porno movie called SIT ON MY FACE!'

As the car roared off, his last words rang around the eerily silent street. Will saw a curtain twitch on the first floor window. Mrs Warzovski's outraged face stared down at him, mouthed something, then disappeared. Will didn't even have the energy to mouth anything back. He sat down on the pavement, and started to cry.

Chapter 11

'Right, if you could just lean over the handlebars a bit, love. A bit further, that's it. Try to look as if you've had a good work out.'

Alex cranked her professional smile a fraction wider and tried not to glance at her watch. It was the official opening of a new city centre health club and Fleming Associates was handling the PR. Alex had allowed for a few nibbles and a quick run round the state-of-the-art equipment with the local press before dumping them in the capable hands of the fitness instructor.

But she'd reckoned without the club's owners putting on their own effort. Without her knowledge, they'd lined up a local celebrity, some musclebound soap actor called Brett Michaels, to perform the opening ceremony. For someone who wasn't gifted with two brain cells to rub together, Brett loved the sound of his own voice. In fact, he loved everything about himself. Their tour around the fitness suite had taken three times longer than it should have done because Brett kept stopping to flex his muscles and smooth his balding head in the full length mirrors.

As if that wasn't enough, the owner had then produced a sexy high-cut leotard and insisted Alex posed for press photos on an exercise bike. She would have told him where to stick his bike but with all the cameras pointing at her it seemed easier and quicker to go along with it.

'Come on, love, work up a sweat,' the photographer called out.

'I wouldn't mind working up a sweat with her,' Brett leered. He'd manoeuvred himself to the back of the shot to get the best view of her bottom.

Alex looked at her watch again. It was nearly lunch–time. She'd already missed most of the morning, thanks to this charade. And today, of all days, she really wanted to be in the office.

Because this was the morning Tom was finally going to announce she had Claire's job.

Two weeks had gone by since that weekend in Cheltenham. The following Monday she'd phoned Tom, who assured her he was taking care of it. But nothing happened. Over the next few days she'd tried ringing him a few more times, but his secretary always stalled her.

Finally, in desperation, she'd called his home number on Friday evening. He wasn't impressed.

'What the hell do you want? You realise my wife could have answered the phone?'

'Maybe you should have answered my calls in the office, then. Any news about the job?'

'For God's sake! I've had other things on my mind. I'll get round to it on Monday, OK?'

'I hope so,' Alex said sweetly. 'Otherwise I might have to call you at home again.'

'Bitch!' The phone slammed down. Alex smiled to herself. That had him worried. Now the tables had turned and she was the one in control.

She finally managed to escape from the press reception and change back into her suit. She'd chosen a sharp black trouser suit for the announcement. Authoritative, but with high heels and nothing underneath it, just the right hint of sexiness too.

She drove back to the office, Robbie Williams blasting out of the CD player, cheekily cutting in front of the other drivers. Soon she'd be behind the wheel of her brand new BMW. And all in exchange for a few minutes of clumsy, unsatisfying sex. Men were such simple creatures, so easily pleased.

Not everyone saw it that way. Nigel had been positively outraged when Alex told him what had happened.

'But you said you weren't going to sleep with him!'

'There was a change of plan.'

'What about Luke?'

'What about him?'

'Blimey, Alex, you slept with another man. How do you think he's going to feel?'

'He's not going to find out, is he? Anyway, it was only the once. It was just sex, Nigel, it meant nothing to me.'

'And that makes it all right, does it? You've got some twisted priorities, Alex.'

She turned away and pretended to tap some figures into her computer, not wanting him to see how his remark had hit home.

In spite of what she said, she did feel bad about what she'd done, especially as Luke had been so lovely to her since that weekend. They were getting on better than they had in ages.

She'd tried to shut out the memory of that night with Tom, but every time she thought of his hands pawing her she felt used and grubby. She'd never intended it to go that far. It was all Tom's fault. Which was why she was so determined to make sure he kept to his side of the bargain.

'You mean to tell me you wouldn't do the same thing if you had the chance?' she said.

'I hope I'd have more self-respect.'

Things had been cool between them ever since. Alex wasn't too worried. Once she was the boss, he'd want to get into her good books again, self-respect or no self-respect.

There was an odd atmosphere in the office when she

walked in. Nigel and Debbie were whispering about something, but they shut up when they saw Alex. She could feel their eyes following her to her desk. Had Tom Kavanagh made his announcement already, she wondered? He must have said something. You could cut the atmosphere with a blunt letter opener.

She glanced beyond the glass partition at Claire's empty office. She was tempted to go straight in there and claim her territory, but decided against it. Play it cool, she thought. She went to her own desk, sat down and had just picked up the morning's post when Rachel walked in.

'Alex!' She backed off a few steps when she saw her, and nearly dropped the armful of files she was carrying.

'Who did you expect, Lily Savage?' Alex smiled back.

Rachel shot a helpless look at Nigel and Debbie. 'I suppose you know – about Claire's job?'

'Oh that.' So he'd told them, had he? Pity he hadn't waited so she could be there to see their faces. At least it was all out in the open now. 'Of course I know.'

'Oh!' Rachel looked even more confused. 'I just didn't think you'd be in, that's all. Under the circumstances.'

Alex swung back in her chair, basking in satisfaction. 'Don't worry, I'm not going to start skiving off now—' Now I'm the boss, she was going to say, but stopped herself. 'As far as I'm concerned, nothing changes. We're a team, and we'll go on working as one.'

Rachel's face was flushed and beaming. 'You mean it? Oh, Alex, that's wonderful. You don't know how glad I am to hear you say that.' Crikey, steady on. Alex edged back in her seat. Any second now, Rachel would be snogging her with joy. 'When we first heard I was so worried. I mean, I know how I'd feel if it was me.'

Alex looked at her, bewildered. What was she on about? Did she think the power would go straight to her head?

Had she expected her to be carried in on a bier with a bevy of Nubian slaves?

'And you're right, of course we'll go on working as a team,' Rachel gushed on. 'As far as I'm concerned, there are no bosses in this department. We'll share all the work equally, and make all the decisions together—'

'Now hang on a second.' Alex sat up straight. This all for one, one for all business had already gone too far for her liking. 'I know I said we were a team, but the buck has to stop somewhere. Someone has to shoulder the responsibility for the smooth running of the department.'

'Well, yes, of course.' Rachel blushed to the same unflattering cerise as her blouse. 'I didn't mean it like that. Don't think for a second I'm going to be putting any more work on your shoulders, just because I'm in charge. I just thought—'

But Alex didn't hear any more. She sat bolt upright. 'What do you mean, *you're* in charge?'

'Did that sound a bit heavy-handed? Sorry.' Rachel blushed an even deeper shade of puce. 'I haven't really got used to this talking like the boss thing yet. I suppose it'll take a bit of time to get used to.' She giggled apologetically.

Alex stared at her. The truth began to dawn. 'You mean to tell me you got the job?'

A myriad emotions skipped across Rachel's broad face – confusion, disbelief, until her features finally settled on horror. 'I thought you said you knew about it?' She glanced across the office at Nigel. He was working away at his computer, head down, unable to meet her eye.

'And you thought you – oh God.' The full awfulness of it had finally sunk in with Rachel. She looked down at her, her large eyes full of sorrow. 'You thought you'd got it, didn't you? Oh Alex, I'm so sorry . . .'

The phone rang and Rachel hurried off to answer it.

Alex was relieved. Any more gushing sympathy and she might have slapped her.

Nigel glanced up. 'Looks like you backed the wrong horse, doesn't it?'

'We'll see about that.' Alex snatched up her phone and punched in Tom's number. 'Hello? Can I speak to him, please? It's Alex. Alex Redmond. What do you mean he's unavailable? I need to speak to him. OK, you can tell him if he doesn't want to talk to me on the phone I'm coming up there and he can talk to me face to face!'

She slammed the phone down.

'You haven't heard, then?' Nigel said.

'Heard what?'

'Tom Kavanagh was sacked this morning.'

She stared at him. 'I don't believe you.'

'Suit yourself. But it's all over the office. Financial irregularities, or something. Turns out they've been investigating him for months.' Nigel hit a few more buttons on his keyboard. 'Seems like he's been feathering his nest from the company profits. I always wondered how he managed to afford those expensive suits, not to mention the — where are you going?'

'Where do you think?' Alex grabbed her bag and stormed out of the office.

Angela, his secretary, wasn't at her desk. Tom's door was half open, and as Alex approached she could see him packing his files into boxes.

He looked up as she entered. 'I was wondering when you'd turn up. I take it you've heard?'

'Is it true?'

'Oh, it's true, all right. Frank Fleming called me into his office this morning. Had to make an example of me, he said. Self-righteous bastard. As if the rest of them weren't robbing the company blind behind his back. I'm not the only one with a villa in Portugal, you know—'

'I wasn't talking about you!' Alex slammed the door. 'What the hell's going on? You promised me that job.'

He looked at her uncomprehendingly. 'Alex, I've just been sacked. Doesn't that mean anything to you?'

'But we had an agreement.'

'Well, I'm not really in a position to honour that now, am I?' He sat down. Without his trappings of power she could see him for what he really was, a weak, sad, middle-aged man. 'I don't believe you. My life's in ruins and you're worrying about your bloody promotion. You really are a selfish bitch, aren't you?'

His words stung. 'It's better than being a loser like you!'

'You're the loser, Alex. Except you don't realise it.' His pale eyes narrowed. 'I really didn't expect you to sleep with me, you know. I didn't think anyone would give up their self-respect for a pay rise and a job title. But you did, Alex. I thought you had more class than that.'

'You bloody hypocrite! You used me.'

'Come on, Alex, we used each other. The only reason you're acting so outraged now is because you didn't get what you wanted. And as for being a hypocrite – well, it takes one to know one. I'd take a long, hard look at yourself before you start slinging mud around.'

There was no point in retaliating. Besides, she was so angry she probably would have ended up hitting him.

She turned to leave. As she reached the door he said, 'You know something? I wouldn't have given you that job anyway. You're not up to it. Your only talent is between the sheets and frankly you're not too great at that either!'

Back in the office, Nigel was perched on the corner of Rachel's desk. She was looking up at him, smiling at one of his stupid jokes, no doubt. Alex looked at the Starbucks cups in their hands. Once upon a time Nigel would have been sharing the coffee and gossip with her.

Now he looked at her as if she was something he'd just scraped off his loafers.

'Alex!' Rachel shot up, knocking over a pile of papers as Alex marched over to her desk and began emptying the drawers. 'Wh-what are you doing?'

'Getting out of this dump, what does it look like?' Alex went to stuff a half-dead spider plant into her carrier bag, then changed her mind and pitched it into the bin.

Rachel's hand flew to her mouth. 'Oh God, I hope this isn't because of me?'

'Don't flatter yourself.'

Rachel opened her mouth to say something, but Nigel put his hand on her arm. 'Leave her, Rach,' he whispered. So it was Rach now, was it? Well, he'd have trouble having a meaningful conversation with her about shoes, she thought bitchily. From the look of her feet, she was strictly a Marks and Spencer wider-fitting kind of girl.

She ignored them and concentrated on stuffing her belongings into a River Island carrier bag. There wasn't a lot to pack, mainly make-up and magazines. It shocked her to think that all she really did at Fleming Associates was fill in time between shopping trips.

Well, stuff them. She was better than this place, anyway. Rachel was welcome to the rotten job. She'd be floundering within a week.

It wasn't until she was out in the street with a carrier bag in each hand that reality started to sink in. It was just after three and she had nowhere to go. She couldn't even cheer herself up with a shopping spree because she was already overdrawn and she had no idea where her next pay cheque was coming from.

In desperation, she went to Harvey Nichols and bought herself a coffee. She felt as if everyone was looking at her as she nursed her cappuccino with her belongings at her feet. She'd been unemployed precisely ten minutes and she already felt like a dispossessed bag lady.

Inside she burned with anger. Fucking Tom Kavanagh. How dare he say those things about her. As if he was in any position to judge her performance in bed. He'd barely lasted long enough to find out!

Chapter 12

Phoebe fell through the front door, weighed down with Sainsbury's bags. She shouldered the door closed and hesitated for a moment. It was only five, Alex wouldn't be home for ages yet. Plenty of time to unpack the shopping, grab a quick coffee and think of some way of avoiding her all evening.

It was two weeks since that night with Luke, and Phoebe was still ridden with guilt. Every time she saw Alex she had to fight the urge to confess everything.

Instead she'd taken to avoiding her. She'd never worked so many double shifts in her life. She hadn't had a day off in a fortnight, and lived in a haze of exhaustion. It was only when she'd accidentally seasoned a lemon sole with a handful of demerara sugar that Titus had lost patience and refused to allow her to work that night.

She dragged the bags into the kitchen, put the kettle on, and started to unpack. She was reaching into the back of the fridge to retrieve a festering bowl of something that might once have been salad when she heard a voice.

'Is there any more vino in there?'

Phoebe rose sharply, cracking her head on the edge of the work surface. But she was so shocked she barely noticed the pain.

'Alex? Wh–what are you doing here?'

'I live here, remember?' Alex reached past her for the bottle and topped up her glass.

'But why aren't you at work?'

'If you must know, I quit.'

'But your promotion—'

'I didn't get it, did I?' Alex's eyes flashed with defiance. 'So I told them where to stuff their job.'

'Oh, Alex.' Phoebe didn't know whether to be appalled or admiring. 'So what are you going to do now?'

'God knows.' Alex drained her glass of wine. 'Get another job, I suppose.'

'Yes, but it's not that easy, is it? What are you going to do in the meantime?'

'I'll manage.'

'But what about your overdraft? And the mortgage on this place? And the—'

'I said I'll manage, didn't I? God, Phoebe, I thought you of all people would be on my side?'

'I am. I just think maybe you should have stayed in that job until you'd found another one, that's all.'

'And that's what you'd have done, is it? Good old Phoebe, never one to take risks. Well, for your information I couldn't stay there. Not after—' she broke off.

'Not after what?' Alarm bells rang in Phoebe's head. 'Alex, what is it? What's happened?'

'Nothing.' Alex refilled her glass. 'It's nothing.'

'There's something you're not telling me.' Phoebe's imagination ran riot. 'Alex, what have you been up to?'

'Thanks a lot. Why do you immediately assume it's something I've done? If you must know, I'm the victim this time.' She waved her glass. 'I've been sexually harassed.'

'*You*?'

'Yes, me.' Alex glared at her. 'And I don't see what's so funny about it.'

'Sorry.' Phoebe fought for control of her features. 'I just can't imagine it, that's all. So what exactly happened?'

Even while Alex was telling her, she still couldn't

believe it. Things like that just didn't happen to her sister. She was too confident, too sure of herself. No man would dare.

But Alex was almost in tears as she explained how Tom Kavanagh had promised her promotion if she slept with him, and how she'd refused and he'd given it to some upstart called Rachel instead.

But the whole time her sister was telling the story, something nagged away in the back of Phoebe's mind. An image of Alex packing all those sexy dresses for a work conference. 'So was Tom Kavanagh at this Cheltenham thing you went to a couple of weeks ago?' she asked.

'Yes.' Alex's chin lifted. 'Why do you ask?'

'No reason,' Phoebe said, but her face must have given her away.

'You think I did it, don't you? You actually think I slept with him.'

'No!'

'Yes you do, I can see it in your face. You really think I'd stoop that low. Well, if you're so clever answer me this. If I slept with him, how come I'm out of a job and not sitting in my new office?'

She was right, of course. Instantly Phoebe felt contrite. 'Alex, I'm sorry.' She reached out as her sister stumbled past her, wiping the tears from her eyes. 'Please don't go. I didn't mean it, honestly. I know you'd never do anything like that.'

Not like her. She was the guilty one, not poor Alex. She was just trying to pass off some of her own wretched feelings on to her innocent sister. How could she even *think* such a terrible thing of her?

'So what are you going to do now?' she asked.

'I don't know. Nothing, I suppose.' Alex sniffed back her tears.

'But you can't let him get away with it. What he did

was illegal. You can sue him for sexual harassment, can't you?'

'What's the point? He'll only deny everything, and it'll be my word against his.'

'So? I'm sure if you found yourself a good lawyer—'

'Look, Fee, I just want to forget it, OK? Can we just drop it, please?'

'If that's what you want.' Phoebe frowned. None of this made sense. She couldn't imagine Alex backing down over something like this. She would be in that office slapping down law suits before you could say 'Industrial Tribunal'.

'It's not that I don't want justice or anything,' Alex read Phoebe's mind. 'It's just Public Relations is such a small world. Tom Kavanagh has friends all over the place. If I make trouble for him I might not be able to find another job so easily.'

Phoebe nodded, hating herself for the small doubt that lingered in the back of her mind.

'Anyway, right now I just want to forget all about work, and bloody Tom Kavanagh,' Alex went on. 'Tell you what, why don't we have a girly night in? We haven't done that for ages, have we? Just you, me, a weepy video and a family-sized bar of Cadbury's Dairy Milk.'

Phoebe was about to refuse, then changed her mind. She couldn't really let Alex down, no matter how guilty she felt. 'Sounds good.'

'Great. You go and pick up the video and I'll chill some more wine, OK?'

Phoebe spent ages choosing a video, dithering between George Clooney and Hugh Grant until she realised there was really no contest. For an evening like this, it had to be George and a supersized bucket of popcorn. She bade Hugh a regretful goodbye and headed for home.

'I didn't know whether you wanted popcorn or tortillas, so I got both—' Phoebe walked into the sitting room with her arms full of confectionery and stopped dead. Luke was on the sofa, his arm around Alex.

From the stricken look on his face, he was still feeling as guilty about what had happened between them as she was.

'Look who's here,' Alex grinned, oblivious to the undercurrents surging around the room. 'Luke turned up, so I said he could spend the evening with us. That's OK, isn't it? He promises he'll keep quiet and not laugh when we start snivelling.'

Phoebe stared at Luke. She thought quickly. 'Actually, Titus just phoned and asked if I'd do an extra shift tonight.'

'Another one? But you haven't had a night off for ages.'

'I know, but they're a bit short-handed. Ronan's called in sick, and they've got a big party coming in. A birthday, or something.' Phoebe blathered on, convinced her burning face was giving her away.

'So when did he phone?' Alex asked.

'Sorry?'

'When did Titus call? You've only just walked in the door, and I haven't heard the phone ring.'

'No. You wouldn't. He – er – called on my mobile while I was out.'

'I see. So why did you bother bringing the video home, if you knew you weren't going to be here?'

'I thought you might like it anyway.' Phoebe thrust it at her. 'I'd better go and get changed. Have fun.' Her eyes met Luke's briefly, then she darted off to her room.

'So what was that all about?' Alex asked, when Phoebe had left for work.

Luke looked startled. 'What?'

'You and Phoebe. You didn't really think I believed

all that rubbish about her having to work, did you? How could Titus call her when her mobile's sitting over there on the table? It's pretty obvious she didn't want to hang around. I want to know why.'

'I don't know, do I? Maybe she thought we needed a quiet evening in together?'

'Or maybe she just didn't want to stay in the same room as you?' Alex looked at him shrewdly. 'There's something going on with you two, isn't there? Something happened while I was away.'

'I don't know what you're talking about,' Luke mumbled. But the mottled colour spreading up his neck gave him away.

'Come on, Luke, I know you both better than that. You've hardly been here the past two weeks, and neither has Phoebe. If you're not avoiding me, you must be avoiding each other. Did you have a row while I was away?'

'Course not. We hardly saw each other.'

'Well, there's definitely something wrong with her. You don't think it's man trouble?'

'How the hell should I know?' Luke snapped.

'OK, OK, no need to bite my head off. I just thought she might have mentioned it to you. As you're such good friends.'

'Who told you that?' He swung round to look at her. Alex stared back at him, perplexed.

'Luke, what's got into you?'

'Nothing. I just came round to spend time with you, not to discuss your sister's love life.'

'Fine. We'll change the subject.' Alex looked sidelong at his stony profile. She'd never seen him in such a foul mood. Just when she most needed some undemanding devotion, too.

She started to give him a carefully edited version of her leaving Fleming Associates, missing out any reference to

Tom Kavanagh's amorous advances. But halfway through her story she realised he wasn't listening.

'I can see I'm boring you,' she snapped. 'Shall we watch the video?'

'Whatever.' He went on staring into space, a million miles away. When Alex snatched up the remote control and switched it off he continued to watch the blank screen.

'For heaven's sake, Luke, what's wrong with you?' Alex hit him with a cushion. 'I might as well not be here for all the notice you've taken of me.'

'Sorry. I've just got a lot of things on my mind at the moment.'

'And I'm not one of them?'

Luke's smile was bleak. 'Actually, you're pretty near the top of the list.'

Looking at his face, this wasn't a very comforting thought. Alex remembered what Tom Kavanagh said about her taking people for granted, and felt wary. Was Luke having second thoughts about her? She wasn't sure she could face losing him and her job in one day. Especially now she'd realised she was quite keen on him after all.

Her worst fears were confirmed when he suddenly said, 'I think we need to talk.'

'Sounds ominous.' Alex covered her confusion with a nervous laugh.

'It could be.'

Oh God. She racked her brains for something she might have done to upset him. Quite a lot of things sprang to mind, from taking him for granted, to letting him down over Paris. And sleeping with someone else, of course. But he couldn't possibly know about that.

'Alex, do you believe in absolute fidelity?'

She nearly choked on her wine. 'In – in what way?'

'Do you believe a meaningless fling should be allowed to ruin a relationship?'

Who could have told him about Tom Kavanagh? Phoebe? No. But who else could possibly have known?

And then it came to her. Nigel. She wouldn't put it past him. He was outraged enough to blow everything.

She had to think fast. 'Luke, I don't know what you've heard—' she started to say, but he wasn't listening.

'Only I don't think I can go on like this,' he blurted out. 'I thought I could just forget about it, put it behind me – it didn't mean anything to me, you see. But I can't. I can't go on facing you, pretending nothing's happened. I can't go on lying to you.'

He buried his face in his hands. Alex watched him, relief giving way to misgiving. If it wasn't her, then it must be him. And if it was him . . .

She felt sick. In a calm voice she hardly recognised as her own, she said, 'Luke, what exactly is going on?'

Chapter 13

The following Friday was their parents' wedding anniversary, and Alex had come up with the bright idea of taking them to Bar Barato to celebrate.

'It'll save us cooking,' she'd explained. Phoebe didn't like to point out that she'd probably end up cooking it anyway. Despite telling her she looked exhausted five days ago, Titus had refused to let her have Friday night off.

'It's our busiest night. I need you here,' he'd insisted. 'Ronan spends more time poncing around than doing any work, and Ian's about as much use as a chocolate fireguard. You can take an extended break,' he added as an afterthought.

'I'm surprised you don't suggest we all eat out in the yard near the bins to save time,' Phoebe said. But she wasn't too upset. At least it would save her from watching her mother casting her over-critical eye around the place.

They'd barely got through the door before Shirley started. 'It's very crowded, isn't it? I would have preferred somewhere quieter.'

'It's Friday night,' Phoebe pointed out, knowing that if the place was empty her mother would have had something to say about it too.

She glanced at her father. He looked strained, and she guessed he must have been listening to her mother's complaints all day. She hoped Shirley wasn't going to be in one of her moods and spoil it for everyone.

Unfortunately, they walked in just in time to catch

Karen in the middle of an altercation with a group of middle-aged businessmen, one of whom was shouting into the mobile phone clamped to his ear and not listening to her. Knowing Karen's feelings about mobiles in the restaurant, Phoebe winced.

'Sir, would you mind not using your phone in here? You've been on it for half an hour and it's disturbing the other customers. Could I just ask you to go outside? Sir? If I could just . . . Oi, Dickhead, I'm talking to you!' She reached across the table, snatched the phone from his ear and dropped it with a splash into the water jug. 'Thank you,' she said, then stalked off to a ripple of grateful applause from the surrounding tables.

'Well, that's charming I must say,' Shirley said. 'If that's the way they treat their customers I'm amazed they have any left.'

'She did try to ask him nicely. And it can be very annoying for other people,' Phoebe started to explain. But Shirley's nose was already pointing northwards, a sure sign she wasn't listening.

'So where's our table?' She looked around. 'We've been standing here for ages and no one's bothered to look our way.'

Phoebe gritted her teeth. 'I think it's over here.'

'It's a bit close to the kitchens, isn't it?' Shirley wrinkled her nose.

'I asked for that one so I could keep sneaking out to join you.'

'Anyone would think you were ashamed of us.' Shirley cast a disparaging eye over the table, which Phoebe had made to look festive with a couple of foil balloons and a card with 'Happy Anniversary' on it. 'It looks like a kids' tea party. And, oh dear, are these paper napkins?' She picked up the offending article between cerise tipped fingers that matched her dress.

'Well, I think it looks lovely, lass.' Her father put his

arm round her. 'You did well to fit us in at such short notice. It's just a shame you have to work.'

'Oh well, you know. Someone's got to cook your dinner.' Phoebe frowned at her father. 'You do look tired, Dad.'

'I'm fine, love,' he smiled. 'Been overdoing it a bit in the garden, I think.'

Shirley thrust her coat at her. 'For heaven's sake, Phoebe, stop fussing. I don't think it will kill him to take me out one night. God knows we never socialise the rest of the year.' She sat down and flapped her napkin into her lap with a martyred sigh.

And whose fault is that, Phoebe felt like asking. When she lived at home she could remember her father pleading with her mother to go out dancing, or for dinner. But Shirley always refused, and as the years went by, Joe had given up asking.

She settled her parents at their table, made sure they had drinks and left them studying the menu while she slipped into the back and changed into her whites. After the tranquillity of the restaurant, walking into the kitchen was like catching a glimpse of Hell. The heat, the steam, the noise, and now and then the flash of whites as chefs ran around, narrowly missing each other with huge hot pans. She couldn't believe how frantic it all looked. Hard to believe that all those people dodging around yelling at each other were actually working together like well-organised ants.

'I wouldn't come in here if I were you,' Ian called out. 'Titus is in a right mood. The immigration people did a sweep this morning and took away half the casual staff.'

'It had to happen, didn't it? They've left us alone for too long.' Phoebe looked towards the back of the kitchen, where the kitchen porters and prepping staff usually worked. It looked deserted.

It was an occupational hazard in the catering business, where most kitchens relied on a shifting population of itinerants to cover the menial jobs. Some were homeless looking for casual work for a day or two. Some were on the run from the law or their families. Some were illegal immigrants who didn't have the necessary papers to get a proper job. Titus didn't mind if they had a criminal record or couldn't speak a word of English as long as they turned up on time, worked like dogs and didn't try to pilfer from the walk-in. But the immigration people were more fussy. Every so often they would descend for a purge on all the hotels and kitchens in the area and take them all away.

She looked at the empty sink area. 'What about Dicky and Steve?'

'Gone.' Ian shrugged gloomily. 'Immigration are re-patriating them.'

'Back to Newcastle?'

'Seems we were wrong about them. Apparently they were asylum seekers running away from the death squads in the People's Republic of Chiltonia.'

'Do you think it's true?'

'Dunno. I think Immigration are checking it out, but you can't be sure of anything with those two. Funny old world, isn't it?'

Phoebe was reflecting on this when Titus appeared from the office.

'And where the fuck have you been?'

'Entertaining my parents. It was supposed to be my night off, remember?'

'I don't recall agreeing to that.'

'No, well you wouldn't, would you? You've got the memory span of a goldfish when it suits you.'

He folded his arms across his chest. 'If you don't like it, you know what you can do, don't you?'

'You're right. After tonight I'm moving straight to the

Indian sub-continent to get a job as a child labourer. I hear the pay and conditions are much better.'

Titus opened his mouth to reply, but then Ronan emptied a whole pan of boeuf bourgignon all over the floor and he directed his stream of blistering invective at him instead. Phoebe straightened her cap and grabbed the next order as it rolled off the computer.

'Oh, and by the way – don't have the soup,' Titus broke off from roasting Ronan to say. 'There's just a chance that loopy Hungarian kitchen porter might have peed in it before they took him away.'

The next fifteen minutes were a blur of activity. Phoebe pan fried a couple of steaks, heated up some of the pepper sauce she'd made earlier that day, and passed them down the line for Ian to do the finishing touches with the vegetables. Then she slipped off her apron and went back into the restaurant to join her parents.

She reached the table just as Alex and Luke walked in. In spite of her embarrassment, Phoebe couldn't help staring at him, her eyes drawn to the tall, handsome figure in the well-cut suit.

He glanced at her, then looked away. He had guilt written all over his face. Phoebe was amazed Alex hadn't noticed it.

But apparently she hadn't, as she greeted them all. She looked slender and gorgeous in a pale-pink linen dress that made Phoebe feel fat and frumpy in her checked trousers and white chef's jacket spattered with the bourgignon Ronan had dropped earlier.

Alex looked around at the table. 'Gosh, this all looks wonderful, doesn't it? You've done a good job, Fee.'

'Yes, it's all very nice.' Shirley immediately forgot her carping. If Alex said black was white and England had the best cricket team in the world she would have agreed.

Phoebe glanced at Luke. He looked as thrilled to be there as a man on Death Row. 'Shall I get us all a drink?'

'Sit down, Phoebe. That girl can get them.' Alex snapped her fingers in Karen's direction. Karen ignored her. Alex snapped again. Karen banged down her order pad and was just advancing on them in a manner that suggested she was about to perform a complex surgical procedure involving her biro and Alex's nostril when she spotted Phoebe and switched on a sickly sweet smile.

'Yes? Can I be of some service?' Her voice dripped saccharine while her eyes spat venom.

They ordered more drinks and their food, and Phoebe slumped in her chair. This was even worse than she'd imagined. She hated the way Luke refused to meet her eye, as if what had happened between them was all her fault.

Alex, by contrast, was amazingly animated as she told Shirley all about her new job.

'I'm doing the marketing for a telecommunications company,' she explained. 'Quite a high pressure job, actually. I have to be on call all hours.'

'It sounds wonderful, darling.' Shirley looked impressed. 'You know, it's a pity you're not more ambitious like your sister, Phoebe, instead of working in a place like this.'

Phoebe gritted her teeth. She wondered if Shirley would be so impressed if she knew Alex's fabulous new career was actually a temporary job in a BT call centre. She'd taken it out of desperation when the bank manager called threatening to cut off her overdraft facility. 'But I like it here.'

'I know that, but it's hardly a career, is it? I mean, cooking.'

'Tell that to Jamie Oliver,' Phoebe retaliated. 'Or Cameron Goode. Or any of the others who've made a fortune doing it.'

'It's not quite the same, Fee. They work in famous restaurants, or they own their own. This place is hardly on the culinary map, is it?' Alex chimed in. Phoebe glared at her. Whose side was she on?

'We may not have any Michelin stars, or a place in Egon Ronay, but that doesn't mean you can sneer at it,' she said. 'I happen to be proud of what I do. And I enjoy it. And I consider myself lucky to work among some of the most brilliantly creative people I know.'

No sooner were the words out of her mouth than the kitchen doors flew open and Titus stood there, a blood-stained meat cleaver in his hand, looking like a mad Viking who'd just washed up after too many days on the long boat.

'RIGHT,' he roared, 'WHICH OF YOU BAS-TARDS IS LACTOSE INTOLERANT?'

A terrified silence fell. All eyes swivelled. Over in the far corner, a nervous-looking man put up his hand.

'You!' Titus stormed over. 'All right, explain yourself. Why are you here?'

'S-sorry?' The man shrank back in his seat and eyed the cleaver.

'Why are you here? Why do you bother coming? You clearly don't want to eat anything on the menu.' He thrust his face close to the man's. 'Why don't you just stay at home with your miserable little food fads, instead of coming here and ruining everyone's evening?'

'I- I can't help it. It's a medical condition.'

'Medical condition, my arse. Whining buggers like you make me sick. How dare you expect me to cater to your pathetic whims? Lactose intolerant! You're just a neurotic little shit who's trying to appear more in-teresting.'

The man put down his napkin. 'I don't have to stay here to be insulted.'

'No, you don't, do you? I expect there are lots of

places you could go.' Titus pulled himself up to his full six feet five. 'Go on, then, sod off. Go home and chew on a poxy rice cake. I don't want you in here.'

It was an unedifying sight. The customers pushing back their chairs, Titus waving his cleaver at them, herding them to the door while Karen tried to hold him off, her arms around his neck, hanging from his massive shoulders, her toes barely scraping the ground.

Finally the door closed and Titus rounded on them all, the blade of his cleaver catching the candlelight. 'What are you looking at?' he bellowed. 'Enjoy your meals!'

There followed the collective clatter of cutlery as everyone dived obediently into their food, terrified of being singled out. But Titus had already stormed off, the kitchen doors swinging in his wake. Karen followed him. In the awed hush that followed, her angry screeching could be heard from beyond the doors.

'Brilliantly creative, you say?' Shirley arched an eyebrow. 'He looks like a bit of a maniac to me.'

Everyone looked at Phoebe. 'He's under a lot of strain,' she shrugged.

The meal was fast turning into a travesty. Alex was the only one who looked happy. She was smiling away to herself as if she was enjoying some private joke. At least the food was good when it arrived, although Phoebe was too miserable to do anything but push it around her plate.

She waited tensely as the dishes were taken away, praying Titus wouldn't storm out and demand to know what was wrong with their meal, as he was inclined to do if a customer didn't clear their plate.

Mercifully, they all refused puddings. Just before Karen arrived with the coffee, Phoebe went back into the kitchen and collected the carefully wrapped gifts she'd bought for her parents' anniversary. There was a book on garden water features for her father, which she knew he'd love, and a crystal vase for her mother, which she was less certain about. She'd seen her admiring something similar in last month's *Homes and Gardens*, but Shirley's taste was capricious at the best of times.

'Happy Anniversary, Mum and Dad. From Alex and me,' she added, with a quick glance at her sister, knowing that, as usual, Alex was likely to have turned up empty-handed.

'Thanks, lass. It's just what I wanted.' Joe gave her a big hug. Shirley smiled tightly and put the vase down under her chair. As Karen poured the coffee, Alex suddenly said, 'Actually, those presents weren't from me. Luke and I have got a little surprise of our own. Haven't we, darling?' She smiled across the table at him. Phoebe noticed the cafetière wobble as Karen tried not to look as if she was eavesdropping.

'It's more of an announcement, really.' Phoebe's stomach lurched. She knew what Alex was going to say before the words came out. 'Luke and I are getting married.'

There was a whoosh of blood in her ears, followed a split second later by the sound of someone screaming.

'Jesus Christ! Jesus bloody Christ!' Luke leapt to his feet, clutching his groin. Everyone else jumped up too, apart from Phoebe, who was rooted to her chair, and Karen, who stood clutching the cafetière.

'Oops, sorry,' she said. 'My hand slipped. Here.' She grabbed the water jug and threw it over him. But somehow she missed his groin and soaked his shirt instead.

'You silly cow!' Alex yelled, as Luke fled to the gents.

'It was only a splash.'

'Only a splash? It was boiling coffee!'

'I'll take that, shall I?' The shock brought Phoebe back to life. She extracted the water jug from Karen, who looked as if she was about to let Alex have the rest. 'I think table four are waiting for their bill,' she said.

'Stupid woman,' Alex muttered, as Karen walked off. 'She could have scarred him for life. I want to see the manager.'

'She is the manager,' Phoebe said.

'Then I want to see the owner. I want her fired. And I want some kind of compensation.'

'It was an accident, love, anyone could see that.' Joe Redmond stepped in before Phoebe could reply. 'I'm sure Luke will be fine in a minute. I'll go and see how he is.' He got up, leaving Phoebe at the mercy of her mother and sister.

'Just think, my baby getting married!' Shirley was too overcome to care about what had just happened to her future son-in-law. 'So when did all this happen?'

'Earlier this week. Actually, Luke asked me ages ago, but I told him I needed time to think about it. Then, while I was away we both realised how much we meant to each other.' She looked directly at Phoebe when she said it. Almost as if she knew something . . .

But then she smiled and Phoebe's pounding heart slowed. 'We'll probably get married in the autumn. And of course you'll have to be my bridesmaid, Fee. You'd like that, wouldn't you?'

'Y-yes.' Phoebe stared at her. There was something malicious in her smile. Was it just the thought of making her wear peach taffeta, or was there something else?

'You're very quiet, Phoebe,' Shirley said. 'Aren't you going to congratulate your sister?'

Phoebe widened her smile just enough to stop her face cracking. 'Of course. Congratulations, Alex. I hope you and Luke will both be very happy.' She blundered to her feet. 'I'd better get back to work.'

Karen was already in the kitchen. By the silence that fell when Phoebe walked in, she guessed they must have heard the news.

'Before you say anything, it was an accident,' Karen

blurted out. 'But I would have done it anyway. That bastard deserved it. How are you feeling?'

'I don't know.' It was the truth. She was too numb to feel anything. But she was sure she would be making up for it once the shock had worn off.

'Smug bitch.'

'Why shouldn't she be smug? She's just got engaged.' Engaged. To be married. Phoebe felt a twinge. Maybe the numbness was wearing off already.

'But she doesn't deserve him. Bloody hell, she doesn't even love him, or she would have accepted his proposal first time.'

Phoebe said nothing, but the same thought had occurred to her. Four weeks ago Alex hadn't exactly been talking like a woman head over heels in love. She'd sounded more like a woman on the verge of doing a runner. 'Maybe she's had time to think about it. Or maybe it took some time apart to make her realise what Luke really meant to her. It certainly worked for him, didn't it?'

'That bastard.' Karen curled her lip. 'I hope I *have* scarred him for life. I hope he never gets another erection as long as he lives!' She shot an evil look at Ronan, who backed away. 'You should tell her, Fee. Tell her how he seduced you while she was away.'

'I don't think she'd be very sympathetic somehow. After all, he hardly had to nail me to the floor and have his evil way with me. I was as much to blame as he was.'

'Yes, but it might make her realise what a creep he is. And then she wouldn't want to marry him, would she?'

'And then what? He'd want to marry me instead? I doubt that somehow.' Phoebe mindlessly rearranged the seasonings in her *mise-en-place*. 'All that would do is spread the hurt around a bit more, and I wouldn't want that. No, I think it's best we forget that night ever happened.'

Luke certainly had. She remembered the expression in his eyes when he'd looked at her across the table. They were full of sorrow – and guilt. The sum total of his feelings for her. That was what hurt the most.

Another order whirred out of the computer. Phoebe grabbed it and stuck it up on the rack in front of her. Work. That's what she needed. Anything to take her mind off her troubles.

Except she couldn't quite make out the words. The more she looked at them, the more they blurred together . . .

'Phoebe.' She turned round. Titus was standing over her. Gently he reached up and took the order from the rack. 'I'll handle this. Why don't you give Ian a hand with starters and salads?'

There wasn't a lot to do. Like all the other chefs, Ian, the Garde-Manger, was very efficient. The salads were all ready and chilling in the reach-ins, and the starters were plated up ready for the finishing touches to be added at the last minute. But Phoebe realised it was Titus' way of being kind, and she appreciated the gesture.

She ended up prepping some vegetables for the following lunchtime. As kitchen jobs went, it was a fairly menial task, usually left to the lowly prep chefs. But Phoebe found chopping her way through a heap of onions was surprisingly therapeutic. Concentrating on the flying tip of her Wusthof, the noise from the kitchen blotting out her thoughts, she was able to forget the fact that her life was rushing towards a terrible abyss. Not only that, she had a good excuse to let the tears flow.

By the time she finished work two hours later, the rest of her family had gone. Only her father had stopped by the kitchens to say goodbye and thank her for organising everything. One thing was left behind – the crystal vase she'd given her mother. It was still tucked under the chair, forgotten in all the excitement.

Alex stared at the bedroom ceiling. It was well after midnight, but she couldn't sleep. She kept listening for the door, waiting for Phoebe to come home.

The first part of her plan had gone well. Seeing Phoebe's face when she announced she and Luke were engaged, watching her trying to smile. She would have gone on enjoying it if her sister hadn't scuttled off to the kitchen.

Well, she wouldn't escape so easily from what Alex had in store for her this time.

She hadn't believed it when Luke first told her. She'd even laughed, thinking it was some kind of sick joke. But then she'd looked into his eyes and realised that he was serious.

Part of her still couldn't believe it. She was Alex Redmond, and this kind of thing simply didn't happen to her. And certainly *Phoebe* couldn't do such a thing to her.

That was what hurt most. Not that Luke had slept with someone else. She could get over that. If anything, it made her feel better about her own less than spotless conscience. But that it had been Phoebe he'd slept with. Her own sister had suddenly become a rival. Alex didn't like that one bit.

Luke tried to defend her, of course. He insisted it was all his fault, that he'd made all the running. Alex had pretended to listen, to believe him, but she'd already made up her mind who was really to blame. Phoebe had always had a pathetic crush on Luke. It wasn't surprising she'd leapt at the chance of getting him into bed. She'd probably plotted and planned every single move.

The fact that Alex had been doing some plotting and planning of her own with Tom Kavanagh didn't trouble her. That was different. That was work, this was personal. Her own sister, for heaven's sake. Someone she'd always loved and trusted.

But not any more. Phoebe had let her down and shattered that trust. Now all Alex could think about was getting even.

She didn't know how she'd played it cool all week. It was so difficult to be nice to Phoebe, to pretend there was nothing wrong. The only thing that kept her going was the thought of getting her revenge.

And tonight she'd got it.

Poor Luke, he'd looked so dazed when she suggested they should go ahead and get married. 'But I didn't think you'd even want to see me any more?' he'd said.

Nor would she, if things had been different. But she felt vulnerable. Her self-esteem had already taken a battering when she failed to get her promotion. She'd lost her job, and she didn't think she could cope with losing her man as well. Especially not to Phoebe.

And she knew if she dumped Luke her sister would be only too delighted to pick up the pieces. She couldn't stand the thought of Phoebe being happy at her expense.

It seemed like ages before she heard her sister's key in the door. Alex hurried out of bed and headed her off in the hall.

'You're late,' she said.

'Alex! I thought you'd be in bed.' Phoebe's eyes were red-rimmed.

'I couldn't sleep. I needed to talk to you.'

'Can it wait until morning? I'm dead on my feet and I don't really feel like chatting.'

I bet you don't, Alex thought. 'Fine,' she shrugged.

She watched Phoebe go into her room and switch on the light. Then she waited. Sure enough, a moment later the door flew open and her sister's dark head appeared. 'What's going on? Why are my bags on the bed?'

'That's what I wanted to talk to you about. You see, now we're engaged it makes sense for Luke to move in here. I'm planning to sell this place and buy a house eventually, but Luke's only renting and anyway his place is much too small for the two of us. So I thought under the circumstances it might be better if you moved out. It's OK, you don't have to take all your stuff straight away,' she added. But Phoebe wasn't listening. She'd turned pale.

'Wh-what circumstances?'

'You and Luke, of course. Oh come on, Phoebe, did you really think I didn't know? He told me about your little fling while I was away.'

'He *told* you?' She didn't even try to deny it. Not that she could. She was always hopeless at lying, and her ashen face betrayed her straight away.

'Of course he told me. He also told me what a terrible mistake it had been, and how desperately sorry he was it had ever happened.' Alex saw Phoebe's huge, dark eyes fill with tears, but she didn't care. She wanted to hurt her, to make her suffer the way she'd suffered. 'So it looks like your little plan failed, didn't it?'

'Plan?' Phoebe looked confused, then realisation dawned. 'But it wasn't like that. I didn't plan anything, it just happened.'

'You really expect me to believe that? Come on, Phoebe, you've always had the hots for Luke. I bet you couldn't wait to get your hands on him.'

'But I didn't! I wouldn't do that to you.'

'I suppose you thought once you'd got him into bed, you'd somehow manage to split us up. Well, like I said, it hasn't worked. Luke hates himself for what he did, and we're going to put it all behind us and make a new start.' She watched Phoebe cowering in the doorway. It felt good to have the upper hand again. 'We're going to be married, Phoebe. And there's no way you're going to get your hands on him again.'

'And is that why you're marrying him?'

She spoke quietly but her words were like a barb,

hitting Alex where it hurt. 'What's that supposed to mean?'

'You didn't want to marry him a month ago. I just wondered what made you change your mind.' Phoebe was still pale, but there was a determined look in her eyes. 'I hope you're not just marrying him to get back at me, because that would be a terrible mistake for both—'

A ringing slap took the rest of the words out of her mouth. Alex looked at the red welt appearing on her sister's cheek. She didn't know who was more shocked, her or Phoebe.

'Get out,' she hissed. 'Get out and don't come back.' She turned back into her room and slammed the door.

She heard Phoebe's door close, and a moment later the sound of her sister's muffled sobbing came through the wall. Alex threw herself down on the bed and pulled a pillow over her head as her own eyes pricked with tears.

Chapter 14

Phoebe sat at the bar, nursing a cooling cappuccino and flipping through the Flats To Let column in the *Evening Press*. It was nearly five and her shift was over for the day but she was in no hurry to get home, mainly because she had no home to go to.

'Anything interesting?' Karen looked up from doing the bar orders.

'Nothing I can afford. There are a few places near the university, but I don't fancy sharing with a load of students. I'd feel too ancient.' She ran her finger down the column. 'Ooh, here's one. "Sexually ambiguous insurance broker seeks other to share house, bills and adventures." It doesn't say how much.'

'Who cares? You wouldn't want to live with someone like that.'

'What, sexually ambiguous?'

'No, an insurance broker.' Karen shuddered and helped herself to another cup of coffee. 'You know you can sleep on my sofa as long as you want.'

'Thanks.' It was kind of Karen to put her up, but after a weekend sharing a lumpy sofa with her three cats Phoebe was aching all over. The low point was when she'd woken up that morning to find one of them had left the gift of a dead mouse on her pillow.

'I can't believe your bitch of a sister just threw you out like that,' Karen said.

'She had good reason. I expect you'd do the same if you found out I'd slept with your boyfriend.'

'I'd give you a medal if you slept with any of the men I

go out with!' Karen grinned. 'But what I don't understand is, why blame just you? It takes two, doesn't it?
Why did he get away with it?'

'Search me. I suppose someone had to be the scape-
goat.'

'Jesus, Fee, why do you have to be so bloody reasonable all the time?' Karen looked exasperated. 'I bet if
you'd been around when Hitler marched into Poland
you'd say he'd got the map upside down and it was just a
misunderstanding!'

'This is my sister we're talking about, not Hitler.'

'Yeah, the same sister who's just got engaged to the
man you love, and thrown you out of your flat.'

'*Her* flat. And since I slept with her fiancé, I think that
makes us roughly even in the bitch stakes, don't you?'

Phoebe went back to flipping through the paper. It all
looked pretty depressing. Even bedsits in the less desirable parts of town were beyond her limited means.

'You're looking for a place to live? I know somewhere
that might suit you.' Guy Barrington, the owner of Bar
Barato, peered over her shoulder. He was in his forties
and a very wealthy man although no one would ever
think it to look at him. He favoured the Richard
Branson School of Millionaire Chic, in cargo trousers
and a dodgy pullover, his thinning hair growing peri-
lously close to his shoulders.

Karen smiled at him. 'That's sweet of you, Guy, but
somehow I don't think Phoebe could stretch to a penthouse on the money you pay her.'

'This isn't a penthouse. A bloke I know is looking for a
flatmate. His girlfriend's walked out and apparently he
needs someone to help make up the mortgage.'

'He's not a sexually ambiguous insurance broker, is
he?' Karen asked.

'I don't think so.' Guy frowned. 'Actually, he's an
artist.'

Phoebe looked doubtful. 'Well, that's very kind of you Guy, but—'

'He's a seriously nice bloke. I can give him a call for you, if you like?'

'Thanks, but no thanks.'

Guy shrugged. 'Suit yourself. Let me know if you change your mind.'

'Why did you turn an offer like that down?' Karen demanded, as soon as he'd gone. 'It sounded perfect.'

'It sounded like a nightmare.'

'Why? You don't even know the guy.'

'I know enough. He's a friend of Guy's, which means he's probably peculiar, and he's an artist, so he'll be broke the whole time. And his girlfriend's just left him. How desperate does he sound?'

'About as desperate as an impoverished Sous Chef who shagged her sister's fiancé and is out on the streets?' Karen suggested.

Phoebe glared at her. 'Point taken.'

She had to go back to the flat to collect the rest of her things. She'd been putting it off for two days, but she couldn't face rinsing her knickers out and leaving them to dry over the radiator for one more night. As she headed for the flat she just hoped Alex would still be at work.

There was a flashy Audi Coupé blocking the road outside the flat. Squeezed behind the wheel was a big man with cropped ginger hair. As Phoebe approached he levered himself out of the car and ambled towards her.

'Miss Redmond?' He gave her an oily, professional smile. His shiny grey suit was stretched over a bulky body. Obviously the only six-pack he was familiar with was the kind with Carlsberg Export in it. 'I'm Barry Orton, of Fraser and Duncan. The estate agents?' he prompted, as Phoebe looked blank. 'We had an appointment to value your property, if you remember?'

The penny dropped. So Alex really was serious about selling the flat. 'Oh, I see. You want—'

'I want to see inside your property, if that's all right with you?' Barry Orton looked at his watch. Like his suit, it was conspicuously flashy. 'We did say half-past five, and I'm running late.'

Probably the only running he ever did, Phoebe thought.

She looked up and down the street. Alex had obviously forgotten all about their appointment. And since Phoebe still had a key, she didn't want to be unhelpful and send him away.

'You'd better come in,' she said. As he stepped forward she almost gagged on the deadly cloud of aftershave that enveloped her. He stood close behind her on the step, and she could feel his impatience as she fumbled for her key. She just hoped for Alex's sake he was more efficient than he was charming.

'Would you like a cup of tea?' she offered, but he ignored her. Phoebe watched him swagger around the flat, muttering into his dictaphone and wielding his electronic measuring device from the hip like he was James Bond and it was his trusty Beretta. Talk about God's gift to women! She busied herself filling the kettle to stop herself laughing.

Then Alex arrived in a flurry of cursing. 'Bloody job! Bloody traffic!' She did a double take as Phoebe emerged from the kitchen. 'What are you doing here?'

'I've come to collect the rest of my things. You've got a visitor,' she said. 'This is Mr Orton, from—'

'Frasan and Dunker, I mean, Fraser and Duncan.' He stumbled over his loafers to get to Alex. 'Barry,' he said, holding out a pudgy hand. 'My friends call me Baz.'

Alex ignored his hand. 'The estate agent? Oh God, I'd completely forgotten you were coming.'

'Please don't apologise.' She hadn't, but he didn't

seem to notice. He'd turned into a ginger-haired blob of drooling lust. 'But if I could just take down your particulars—'

'Talk to Phoebe, would you?' Alex shouldered past him and headed down the hall. 'I'm off to have a shower. I take it you've finished in the bathroom?'

'What? Oh yeah. Fine. OK. You just carry on.'

Phoebe watched him sympathetically. She recognised all the signs. The dazed look. The loss of speech. The sudden urge to make a complete prat of oneself. Such was the effect her sister had on men.

'Would you like that tea now?' she asked.

He took a very long time noting down all the details. He showed a particular interest in the hall storage but Phoebe guessed he was hoping to catch a glimpse of Alex emerging naked from the shower.

Finally, after half an hour and two cups of tea, he gave up and slipped the sales details into his briefcase. Phoebe noticed it was monogrammed with his initials – B.O. How unfortunate, she thought. And yet, how appropriate.

No sooner had the front door closed than Alex came into the hall, wrapped in a towel. 'Oh dear, don't tell me the sex god's gone?' She bit her lip. 'Bugger. And I was so looking forward to dragging him off to my bedroom and shagging his brains out.'

'I think he was hoping for something similar.' Phoebe looked at her sister. Even with no make-up and her hair dripping around her face, Alex still managed to look utterly gorgeous and sexy.

'Did you smell his aftershave?' Alex rolled her eyes. 'I wonder if the Iraqis know about that stuff? It'd be great in chemical warfare.'

'That's probably where he gets it from. I expect he had it shipped over from Baghdad just before the last lot of UN arms inspectors turned up.'

'I bet the only way he gets a woman to go to bed with him is if he stuns her into unconsciousness.'

They laughed, then stopped abruptly, both remembering at the same time. 'So what did he say about the flat?' Alex looked away. 'Does he reckon he can sell it quickly?'

'Yes, he thinks he might have some potential buyers lined up. He reckons purpose-built flats this close to the city centre always go fast.'

'Great.' Alex flopped down on the sofa and reached for an orange out of the bowl. 'I can't wait to get rid of this place. Too many bad memories.' She looked up at Phoebe. 'What about you? Have you found anywhere yet?'

'Well, actually . . .' Phoebe was just about to tell her the truth, then found her pride wouldn't let her. 'Yes, I have found somewhere. A friend of Guy's is looking for a flatmate. It's a really nice place, apparently.'

'Sounds perfect.' Alex aimed a piece of orange peel at the bin, and missed. 'I just hope for their sake they don't have a boyfriend.'

The name and address seemed familiar. But it wasn't until Phoebe pulled up outside the terrace of tall Victorian houses that she finally realised she'd been there before.

She stared at the address Guy had scribbled down for her, then back up at the black front door with the row of stone steps leading up to it. It looked different in daylight, a bit shabby, its stonework chipped and kids careering up and down the street on bikes. But she'd know it anywhere.

She looked down at the piece of paper and groaned. Will Hutchinson. Whose girlfriend had just left him. She hadn't taken in the name before, but who else could it be?

Oh well, perhaps it wouldn't be that bad? After all, the flat was nice as she remembered. And the guy might be OK too, when he was sober . . . Plus she was desperate.

'Hello there.' She jumped as the big doughy face loomed in through the open car window at her. 'I know you, don't I? No, don't tell me. Yesterday, two-bedroom, purpose-built, Fulford Road area. Am I right?'

'Mr Orton.' Phoebe tried not to gag at the all-too-familiar smell.

'I knew it. I never forget a property. How's your sister?' Away from Alex's ego-shrivelling presence his confidence had reasserted itself.

'She's fine. A bit busy at the moment. You know – *planning her wedding*.'

His smile wavered. 'She's getting married?'

'Afraid so. She couldn't wait for ever for someone like you to come along.' Phoebe smiled up at him.

His eyes narrowed, as if he couldn't work out whether she was being serious or not. 'What are you doing here, anyway?'

'Flat hunting.'

'Not Will Hutchinson's place?'

'You know him?'

'We're old mates. As a matter of fact, I'm currently sleeping in the very room you're after.'

Phoebe's heart sank. Just as she'd talked herself into liking the place. 'So it's gone, then?'

'Well, yes and no. I'm sort of living there, except Will's being a bit funny about it. I think he's trying to get rid of me.'

'Really?' Will went up another few points in her estimation.

'I've told him I'll be moving on soon,' Barry went on. 'I just need a bit of time to get my act together. I mean, it'll all be easier once I've sold my parents' house.'

'Shouldn't be too difficult for you, being an estate agent.'

'Yeah, well, some places are harder to shift than others. Not everyone wants to buy a house where there's been a double suicide.'

Phoebe jerked back in her seat. 'What?'

'My mum and dad both killed themselves. I know it's been over a month and I should be starting to get over it by now, but it's tough, y'know? I can't face selling the place. I can't even bring myself to go there. Every time someone calls wanting to view it I chicken out. And of course, once they find out the history . . .' He shook his head.

'Oh my God, I'm so sorry. I had no idea.' Phoebe felt ashamed of all the awful things she'd thought about him.

'It's OK. Like I said, I'm slowly getting my act together. Once the house is sold I should have enough to clear all their debts. That'll be a weight off my mind, I can tell you.'

'Debts?'

'That's why they killed themselves. Dad's business went belly up and he turned to gambling. My mum couldn't cope and started drinking. They got themselves in such a mess that in the end they must have thought suicide was the only way out. I just wish I'd known how bad it was, then maybe I could have helped them. But I didn't know anything about it until it was too late.' He wiped his eyes. 'Anyway, that's why I'm staying with Will at the moment. Just until I get everything sorted out. I hate relying on charity, but I've really got no choice. I don't blame him for getting pissed off with me. He needs the money same as everyone else. I've told him it won't be long but what can I do?' He smiled bracingly. 'Anyway, that's my problem not yours. I don't want to stop you taking the room. It's a really nice flat. And Will's a great guy, if you don't mind—' He broke off.

147

'Don't mind what?'

'Nothing. He's just got a bit of a reputation when it comes to women, that's all.' Barry looked uncomfortable. 'I don't mean he's a pervert or anything. Well, nothing actually illegal,' he added. 'It's just one woman is seldom enough for him, if you know what I mean.'

'Really?'

Barry nodded. 'It's his fiancée I felt sorry for. I'm not surprised she walked out in the end. We were all just amazed she stood it for so long. All those other women and – things.'

'Things?'

'That's what finished it for her,' Barry said. 'She could cope with the other women, it was the kinkiness that got her down. Anyway, I shouldn't really be telling you any of this.' He changed the subject. 'Like I said, Will's a really nice guy deep down.'

'Even if he is trying to throw you out on the streets?'

'What? Oh, yes. Well OK, so he might be a bit of a bastard at times, but who isn't? Live and let live, that's what I say. And I'm sure he'll be fine with you. You seem like his type.' He looked her up and down. 'Just as long as you remember to keep your bedroom door locked. You wouldn't want to come home and find him going through your knicker drawer, would you? Ha ha.'

Phoebe stared at him. Was he for real, or just trying to wind her up? There was only one way to find out.

'It's up to you, anyway,' Barry went on. 'The last thing I want to do is put you off, although I can quite understand if you— where are you going?' He stepped back as she got out of the car.

'Where do you think?' As she headed up the stone steps, Barry's voice followed her.

'Fine. But don't say I didn't warn you.'

Chapter 15

The crash of the front door woke Will. He opened his eyes and blearily registered the fact that, yet again, he was head-crackingly hungover.

Wincing with pain, he searched his brain for clues. He remembered a mammoth clubbing session, and his mate Barry getting into an argument with the cab driver over the fare from Leeds. Or was that the night before? The last four weeks had merged together in a blur of alcohol, punctuated by horrific hangovers.

It all started in the Seychelles. Barry had insisted they use the tickets provided by Nadine's father, although they'd got some odd looks when they booked into the honeymoon suite together. As soon as they got there, Will realised it was a mistake, but by then it was too late. He had two weeks to get through, and getting drunk and cruising the bars and beaches looking for women with Baz was a lot better than sitting by himself in his hotel room crying because Nadine wasn't there to share it with him.

He'd meant to pull himself together and sober up when he got home, but somehow it just seemed easier to stay drunk. Except it wasn't fun any more. Somewhere along the line it had turned into desperation. Barry kept trying to talk him into picking up women but no matter how inebriated he was he'd always resisted. He knew if he went to bed with someone else it might block out the aching loneliness inside him for a few hours. But sooner or later the morning would come and he'd wake up hungover, hating himself and lonelier than ever.

Clutching his head, he climbed out of bed, in search of coffee and painkillers. The flat looked like closing time at the Next sale. It was mainly Baz's stuff. They'd been back from the Seychelles for nearly two weeks and he was still hanging around the flat like the remains of Will's holiday washing. He'd taken up residence in the spare room and kept coming up with reasons why he couldn't go home. The latest was that his flat was infested with cockroaches and the pest control men wouldn't let him back in until they'd cleared the place.

'I'm really squeamish about that kind of thing,' he said. 'I found a couple of the little bastards dead in their traps the other day and it turned my stomach.'

But Will suspected he'd got a taste for the bachelor lifestyle. He shared his riverside apartment with his long-suffering girlfriend Patti. According to Barry she'd moved back in with her parents due to the cockroach infestation, but once or twice Will caught him on the phone to her, explaining how he couldn't possibly come home yet 'because Will's still in the throes of grief and really needs my support'. His idea of support being to drag him off to nightclubs and dump him at the bar while he copped off with as many women as possible.

Will knew he had to get him to move out soon. Before his liver packed in or Patti discovered what Barry had really been up to.

He was chugging down a couple of aspirin and a glass of cold water when a girl walked in, wearing his old York City football shirt and little else.

'Morning.' She yawned and flipped the switch on the kettle. 'Coffee?'

She was small, pretty, and with her blonde hair in thick braids she looked frighteningly young. Will felt a rush of panic. 'Who are you?'

'I'm Shelley. We met at the club last night, remember?'

He couldn't even remember the club. He couldn't remember anything. The girl read his expression and smiled. 'You were a bit out of it at the time.'

'I must have been.' He looked her up and down. Surely he hadn't? Then it dawned on him and his shoulders sagged with relief. 'Baz,' he said.

Shelley beamed. 'He's lovely, your friend Barry.'

'That's a matter of opinion.' He was fed-up with Barry doing the dirty on poor Patti and treating his flat like a knocking shop. And he was even more fed-up with him leaving his cast-off women around like old socks for him to tidy up.

'No, he is. And he's had such an interesting life, hasn't he? I can hardly believe he was shot down flying Tornadoes in the Gulf War.'

'Neither can I.' Especially with his fear of heights. Barry got vertigo on the escalator at M&S.

'And fancy him fighting back from a bout of Mad Cow disease to start up his own chain of estate agents. He's really something, isn't he?'

'He certainly is.' Will watched her spooning coffee into two mugs. 'Look, um, Ellie—'

'Shelley.'

'Sorry. I don't want to be the bearer of bad news or anything, but I don't think you should get too hung up on Barry. He's – er – not quite what he seems.'

'Oh, I know that.' Shelley sloshed boiling water into the mugs.

Will stared at her. 'You do?'

'Of course. Barry told me all about his – you know.' She looked awkward.

Blimey, so Shelley knew about Patti, did she? 'And you don't mind?'

'I must admit I was a bit freaked at first, but then I just thought, what the hell? Besides, you can't actually tell, can you? I mean, I thought he'd have to unscrew it or something before we went to bed, but he didn't. And to see him dance you'd never know he even had one, would you?'

Will rubbed his forehead. He must still be drunk or something. 'What are you talking about?'

'His false leg. The one he got shot off the Gulf War?' Now it was Shelley's turn to look confused. 'Why, what did you think I meant?'

'I thought we were talking about his girlfriend.'

That was when she started crying. Ten minutes and half a roll of kitchen towel later she was still sobbing and Will was feeling like a total heel. He was about to ask her out himself just to make her feel better when the doorbell rang. Grateful for the distraction, he rushed to answer it.

A woman stood on the doorstep. She looked sort of familiar. Will wondered if she was the girl who'd just moved in on the ground floor, the one with all the cats. She looked like the kind who lived with cats, in that baggy jumper that didn't show the dirt, no make-up and her hair scraped back off her face.

'I've come about the room,' she said.

'The room?' Then he remembered Guy phoning yesterday to say someone would be coming over. What was her name? He screwed up his face, trying to think. Something weird. Phyllis? Fenella?

'Phoebe Redmond,' she said.

'Of course. Come in.' He led the way into the sitting room, on the way gathering up empty beer bottles and the greasy remains of a pizza. 'Sorry about the mess. I would have tidied up but Guy didn't say what time you'd be coming.'

'So you only tidy up when you're expecting someone, is that it?'

'Well, no.' Oops, wrong thing to say. 'It's my flat-mate's fault. He's a slob. Actually, he's not even my flatmate. He just thinks he is. I'm hoping he'll take the hint and bugger off soon.'

Phoebe looked disapproving. Maybe she didn't like swearing? Guy didn't say he'd sent a nun round. 'So you don't care if he's homeless and freezes to death in a cardboard box?'

Will stared at her. Guy hadn't mentioned she was mad, either. 'I shouldn't think he'd freeze to death at this time of year. Besides, he's a fat bastard. I expect his blubber will keep out the worst of the bitter May chill.'

He smiled. She didn't smile back. She muttered something that sounded a bit like 'insensitive wanker'. He decided he must be hearing things.

She was making him nervous now. He glanced sideways at her as she looked around the room, taking in the big brown eyes and the stray dark curls that escaped from her pony tail. She had a nice mouth, too. Or might have, if she smiled. As it was, she looked like the type who didn't shave her legs on principle.

He was just speculating on what kind of body she had under that shapeless sweater when she turned round and caught him. 'What are you staring at?'

'Nothing.' He backed off sharply. 'Would you like a coffee?'

'Yes please. White no sugar.'

'Why don't you come and take a look round the kitchen while I make it?'

Unfortunately he'd forgotten all about the near naked, weeping girl in there. She was still howling when he opened the door. Will tried to slam it shut again but Phoebe was already halfway through it.

The girl stopped crying and they both looked at Will. He felt sweat break out on his upper lip as he realised they were expecting him to introduce them. 'This is Phoebe. And this is – um – Kelly.'

'Shelley! Bloody hell, can't you even get my fucking

153

name right?' The girl started crying again. Will shoved Phoebe out of the kitchen and closed the door. 'Sorry about that,' he said.

Phoebe looked at the door. 'What's wrong with her?'

'Oh, you know. One night stand that went a bit wrong. I feel bad having to tell her it's over, but you've got to be cruel to be kind sometimes, haven't you?'

Phoebe's jaw dropped. 'You're not going to leave her in there?'

'Why not? She'll get over it in a minute. I don't suppose it's the first time it's happened to her— where are you going?' She was heading for the door. 'You're not leaving? But you haven't seen the rest of the flat.'

'I've seen all I need to, thanks.'

'But you can't leave now! At least have your coffee, first. Look, I'm making it now.' He dashed into the kitchen. Ignoring Shelley, who was still blubbing into the toaster, he grabbed two mugs off the draining board and heaped a couple of spoonfuls of instant into each.

Thankfully, Phoebe was still there when he got back thirty seconds later. 'There you are.' He thrust a mug into her hand. 'Now why don't we go back into the sitting room and have a chat?'

He tipped the newspapers off the sofa and found her a space to sit down.

'So, you – um – you're a cook, are you?'

'No, I'm a chef. Are you sure this is coffee?' Phoebe peered into her mug.

'Of course.'

'Then why is this old tea bag floating in it?' She pulled it out and held it at arm's length. Will snatched it away. Bloody Baz. He'd never quite got to grips with the true meaning of washing up.

'Here, have mine.' He handed her his mug, then remembered that it was the disgustingly chipped one

154

and snatched it back. 'In fact, let's not bother with the coffee. I'll just show you round.'

She followed him in silence. It was obvious she wasn't interested in the flat and he didn't care any more. He'd already made up his mind there was no way Phoebe Redmond was moving in. She was way too weird, not to mention unfriendly. He wouldn't have her as a flatmate if the bailiffs were at the door and she was clutching a lottery cheque.

She didn't speak until he'd finished showing her the bedrooms and they were back in the sitting room. Then she suddenly said, 'You don't remember me, do you?'

Will felt a flash of panic as he looked into her face. He thought she looked familiar. It suddenly occurred to him that she was probably one of Baz's conquests. He must have slept with her, forgotten to phone her and now she'd come round to exact her terrible revenge.

'Of course I do.' Better humour her. 'I wasn't sure you'd remember, that's all.'

'How could I forget a night like that?'

'Well, quite.' Trust Barry to cop off with a stalker.

He eyed her shoulder bag. It could be holding anything, from a lethal pair of nail scissors to a rusty hacksaw blade. In less than an hour he could be sitting in the A&E department of York District Hospital, clutching his own penis in a packet of frozen peas.

Phoebe's eyes narrowed. 'You really don't remember, do you?'

'I do, I do. It was McMillan's, wasn't it? Or Merlin's? No, don't tell me – it was definitely The Gallery—'

'Try Bar Barato. On your wedding night.'

Will felt sick. No, he hadn't. He couldn't have. Although he'd certainly been drunk enough . . .

And then it all came back to him. 'You brought me home. And you dumped me on the floor.' He might not be able to remember where he was last night, but the memory of those carpet burns would stay with him for ever. 'I meant to come round and thank you.'

'If I'd known what kind of a person you were I would have left you in the gutter where you belong.'

'Sorry?'

'Don't act the innocent with me. I know all about you. Your friend Barry told me.'

'How do you know Barry?'

'Never mind how I know him. Is it true you're throwing him out on the streets?'

'Hardly. He shouldn't even be here in the first place. I never said he could stay. Besides, he's got a perfectly good home of his own.'

'How can you say that?' Phoebe looked appalled. 'You can't expect him to live there. Not after what's happened.'

So he'd been bending her ear about the fictitious cockroach problem, had he? 'Oh, for heaven's sake, he's a big lad. He should be able to cope with finding a couple of bodies. It's not as if they were even alive or anything. They're not going to hurt him stone dead, are they?'

'A couple of—how can you be so heartless?'

She was obviously one of those girlie types who got all Buddhist about squashing bugs. Nadine used to be the same, but that didn't stop her napalming mosquitoes when they were on holiday.

Will sighed. 'Look, I know we're all God's creatures but frankly I don't think even the Almighty would be bothered with vermin like that. Besides, we don't know if Barry's telling the truth,' he went on, ignoring her gasp of outrage. 'I wouldn't be surprised if he'd stuck them in a box himself just so he'd have an excuse to stay here.'

'Stuck them in a box?' Phoebe looked as if she might faint. 'Are you saying he *murdered* them?'

'I don't know, do I? I wouldn't put anything past him.'

Will was beginning to lose track of the conversation. 'Anyway, we're missing the point. The sooner Barry goes, the sooner you can have his room.'

'If you think I'd take that room now you're even more insane than I thought.' Crikey, talk about the pot calling the kettle black. 'My God, I thought Barry was making it all up about you, but now I can see he was only telling me the half of it. You're evil. In fact, I'm not even sure you're human!'

Will started to feel seriously freaked. He eyed the door and wondered if he could make a run for it if she turned really nasty. 'Look, I don't mean to be rude or anything, but are you on some kind of medication?'

'Me? You're the one with the problem, not me.' She looked as if she was about to burst into tears. 'I come here and find some poor girl breaking her heart because you've just dumped her. Then you call your best friend's parents vermin and accuse him of murdering them!'

'What? When did I say that?'

'Don't try to wriggle out of it, I heard what you said. I wouldn't stay in this flat if you paid me. I wouldn't feel safe!'

'Believe me, the feeling's mutual.' As he stood up to ease her towards the door, Phoebe flinched away from him. 'Keep away from me! Barry told me exactly what you were like. Believe me, pal, you're not getting your hands on my knicker drawer!'

They looked at each other for a long time. Then, to her amazement, he laughed.

Phoebe drew herself up to her full height. 'I'm glad you find it so amusing.'

'You have no idea.' Will collapsed on the sofa.

'Perhaps you'd like to share the joke?'

'I wouldn't know where to start. Let's just say I reckon Baz has been taking both of us for a ride.' He looked up at her. 'So what exactly has he been telling you?'

She tried to tell him, but she had to keep stopping because he was laughing too much.

'So let me get this straight,' he said, when she'd finished. 'Barry told you his dad was a compulsive gambler who killed himself because he couldn't handle his debts?'

'More or less.' Phoebe faltered. 'Are you telling me it isn't true?'

'It's true Barry's selling their house. But only because they want to retire to Scarborough. As far as I know, the only debts his father has are the thousands Baz owes him.'

'And his mother isn't an alcoholic?'

'Not unless you count a sherry at Christmas.'

'And that girl – '

'One of Barry's conquests, I'm afraid. I was just breaking the bad news about his girlfriend when you arrived.'

Phoebe felt herself growing hot. 'The lying scumbag. I'm amazed you stay friends with him.'

'I'm used to him,' Will shrugged. 'He's been the same ever since we met at school. I was a first year and he threatened to stick my head down the toilet if I didn't give him my dinner money.'

'And what happened?'

'Nothing much. I went home with wet hair for a week until he got bored and decided to be friends with me instead.'

He smiled. He had a nice smile, Phoebe thought. In fact, he seemed like a really nice man. She wondered how she could ever have imagined he was a sexual pervert.

'I'm sorry I was so stupid earlier,' she said. 'God knows what you must have thought of me.'

'I must admit, I was beginning to wonder what kind of flatmate Guy had landed me with.'

The mention of the word flatmate brought a fresh

wave of embarrassment. As if he'd ever want to live under the same roof as her now. Which was a shame, because she'd started to like the flat. And Will.

She hitched her bag over her shoulder and stood up. 'Well, I won't take up any more of your time. Thanks for showing me around. And sorry again about the misunderstanding.'

He stood up too. 'So does this mean you don't want the room?'

He looked so crestfallen, Phoebe was puzzled. 'I didn't think you'd still want me to move in after what just happened!'

'Why not? Like you said, it was a misunderstanding. I'd like you to take the room, if you want it.'

'But you hardly know me.'

'I know you can't be worse than Barry! Tell you what, why don't I make us some more coffee and we can talk about it?'

It was real coffee this time, in stylish unchipped cups with no teabags floating in it. 'We got a cappuccino maker as a wedding present, so I thought I might as well make use of it,' Will explained. 'All the other stuff's waiting to go back. Unless you know anyone who can use an electric juice extractor?'

His smile didn't fool her for a moment. She could see the shadows of pain in his eyes. 'It must have been a terrible shock for you, your fiancée walking out on you like that.'

'You have no idea.' He looked lost for a moment. 'Still, it's not so bad now I know it's only a temporary thing. Nadine just wasn't ready for marriage, you see. I can quite understand how she feels. It's a big step after all, isn't it? And it's better she's honest about it now than a year's time, when it's too late.'

'Absolutely.' Phoebe nodded.

'And her career is far more important at this stage,'

Will went on. 'And when she got this chance to go off to America I just said go for it. I mean, you have to, don't you? Opportunities like that don't come along every day. You just have to grab them while you can.' He sounded as if he was reciting from a book. 'And it'll only be for a few months. Then she'll be back, and we'll take it from there.'

'So have you heard from her?'

'Not exactly.' His smile faded. 'But it's only been a few weeks, and I was away for the first two, so she might have tried then.'

'I suppose she's bound to be busy at first, with meetings and things?'

'That's what I thought.' He nodded eagerly.

'And she's probably written to you. The post takes ages.'

'Exactly.' She wondered if he really believed that, or if he was just playing along like her. 'Anyway, just as long as you know this flatshare thing may only be temporary. I mean, I want you to move in but I'm not sure how Nadine will feel about it when she gets back.'

If she gets back, Phoebe thought. 'We'll just take it as it comes, shall we?'

'Fine by me.' Will settled back in his seat. 'So, what else do you want to know, apart from the fact that I'm not a sexual pervert with designs on your knickers?'

Phoebe blushed. 'Nothing, I suppose. Except, will your friend Barry be dropping round very often?'

'I'm afraid so,' Will admitted. 'And a couple of others, too. Like my mate Tez. He's a computer nerd. Harmless, as long as you don't get him on to the subject of re-installing hard drives. Oh, and there are my cousins, but they're not around very often. One's a fabulously wealthy lawyer, one's an officer in the RAF and the other's a top research scientist. I'm the under-achiever of the family,' he grinned.

'I wouldn't say that.' Phoebe looked around. 'Those paintings look really good. I assume they're yours?'

'Not quite the same as finding a cure for cancer though, is it?'

They went on talking through another two cups of coffee. Phoebe found out that Will's mother had died when he was a baby, and he'd been taken in by his Aunt Gina when his father, a busy GP, found he couldn't cope.

But mostly he talked about Nadine. After twenty minutes, Phoebe knew every nauseating detail about her, from her favourite perfume (Calvin Klein's Eternity) to what she liked for breakfast (black coffee and a cigarette). She also knew that if she came face to face with the real thing she might have to kill her.

He listened, too, as she told him about her own family life, including a carefully edited version of why she had to leave Alex's flat in such a hurry. It was almost the truth – Luke was moving in, and the place would be too small for the three of them – she just forgot to mention the bit about her sleeping with him.

Somewhere in the middle of it all, Shelley appeared, dressed – if that was the word – in last night's clubbing outfit of micro skirt and boob tube, looking tearful. Phoebe was touched by the way Will looked after her, ringing a cab and offering her his last twenty quid for the fare home.

'You were very nice to her, considering it wasn't your problem,' she said, when Shelley was safely on her way back to Leeds.

'Someone had to be. I couldn't very well leave her stranded, could I?'

'You should have sent her round to your friend Barry's place.'

'Oh, yeah. I'm sure Patti would be delighted with that.'

'Maybe it's time she found out what her boyfriend's really like.'

'I expect she already knows. She just doesn't want to face up to the truth. Some people are like that. They can go on fooling themselves for ever, as long as no one comes along and rocks the boat.'

Like you and Nadine? Phoebe felt like asking, but didn't. If anyone was going to rock Will's boat, it wouldn't be her.

Chapter 16

'So who's this bird you've got moving in, then?' Tez asked. He was in his usual Wednesday night, straight from work position, slumped on Will's sofa with a can of Carlsberg.

'She's not a bird. Her name's Phoebe.' Will pushed his feet off the coffee table and swept an armful of last night's empties into a bin bag.

'Going to a lot of effort, aren't you? She must really be something. So what's she like? Blonde, leggy and a Page Three Stunna?'

'Try short, round and dead ordinary.' Barry aimed a can at the bin bag, and missed. He was still in a foul mood about being evicted, although that didn't stop him hanging around the flat making a nuisance of himself.

'You're kidding?' Tez looked as if someone had just told him the bad news about Santa Claus. 'Will, tell me this isn't happening.'

'No point in asking him.' Barry's lip curled. 'But I'm telling you mate, she's a wolf trap woman. You know, the kind where you'd rather chew off your own leg than wake up next to her?'

'Take no notice of him,' Will said. 'He's just pissed off because Patti's making him sleep on the sofa.'

'I won't be the only one in trouble when Nadine finds out about this,' Barry said. 'She's not going to be too pleased about you being shacked up with another woman.'

'Nadine's in LA.' Will threw a full can of Special Brew

into the bin bag. 'Anyway, she knows I'm getting a flatmate.'

'Yes, but does she know it's a woman?'

Will was silent. He didn't want to admit it to Barry, but the same thought troubled him. Phoebe might know it was only a temporary arrangement, but he wasn't quite sure what Nadine would make of it.

'I still don't understand,' Tez looked bewildered. 'I mean, what's the point of her moving in if she isn't a looker? Is she meant to be like a housekeeper or something?'

'She'll just be – a friend.' As soon as he said it he knew it sounded all wrong. The others stared at him.

'A friend? Are you mad?' Tez said.

'You can't have women as friends. It's a fact of life,' Baz declared.

'What the hell are you talking about?'

'It's true,' he insisted. 'I saw it on a documentary once. It all goes back to the cavemen, you see. Men have this biological imperative to procreate. When they see a woman, it's the first thing that occurs to them. Can I have sex with her? Do I want to have sex with her?'

'And if I do, will her caveman boyfriend hit me with his club?' Tez added.

'So that's all women are good for, is it?' Will asked.

'I'm not saying that. I'm just saying it's unnatural for a man to be with a women and not want sex. It's got to happen, they can't help themselves. That's also why, in theory, ugly women will eventually become extinct. No one will want to sleep with them, so their genes will die off. Sooner or later all women will look like Jennifer Lopez.'

'And when will this be, exactly?' Tez looked hopeful.

'In theory it should have happened several generations ago,' Baz said. 'But unfortunately evolution hasn't taken into account the powerful hallucinogenic effect of several pints of Stella Artois.'

Will shook his head. 'Have you two heard yourselves?'

'You can't argue with Darwin, mate.'

'You're talking bollocks. Of course you can be friends with a woman.'

'You can *think* you're friends with them. But sex is always going to get in the way. The best thing you can do is sleep with this flatmate of yours straightaway, satisfy your sexual curiosity.'

'But I don't want to sleep with her!'

'That's what you think,' Baz looked knowing.

'Can I?' asked Tez.

'Yeah well, some of us are a bit more evolved than others, aren't we?' Will shot Baz a hostile look.

'You mustn't feel bad about it,' he shrugged. 'Women can't be friends with men, either. They're always look-ing for commitment. They pretend they want to be mates, but secretly they're plotting to drag you off to their cave. You have to stick to your own species.'

'Aren't they all extinct, in your case?'

'Baz is right,' Tez agreed. 'You can't really go on the pull with a woman, can you? And they insist on having those stupid girly drinks. The ones that are bright pink and taste like bubble bath.'

'That's because they can't handle real alcohol. You give a woman a pint and she wouldn't know what to do with it.'

'And I suppose you think we have smaller feet so we can stand closer to the kitchen sink?'

They all turned. Phoebe stood in the doorway, a large cardboard box at her feet. She wore jeans and a big flannel shirt, her hair pinned untidily on top of her head. She was smiling, but the light of battle was in her eyes.

'Phoebe! How did you get in here?'

'I used the key you gave me.' She looked past Will at Baz. 'I may not be a hunter gatherer like you, but for your information, I never touch girly drinks. And I could drink you under the table any time.'

'How about tonight? Micklegate, nine o'clock?'

Will saw the malice in Baz's smile. 'Now hang on a second—'

'Make it eight.'

'You're on.'

'Fine.' They faced each other across the room like a pair of gunslingers at the OK Corral. 'And since you lot are such big strong men, maybe you can help me bring the rest of my stuff up from the car?'

Will waylaid Baz as they followed her out of the flat. 'What the hell are you playing at? We can't go out drinking with her!'

'Why not? Scared she might start looking attractive after a few pints?' Baz taunted him.

'It's not that. She's just – just—'

'A woman?'

Will fought the urge to punch him. 'You're only doing it to wind her up. You just want to see her get drunk and make a fool of herself.'

'It wasn't my idea. She was the one who wanted to prove herself. Although I admit, it would be a laugh.'

'I want you to cancel. Tell her she can't come.'

'No chance.' Barry shrugged. 'She's your *friend*. You tell her.'

Phoebe was unpacking her boxes when Will walked in. The place already looked as if a bomb had exploded, scattering the room with girly shrapnel, from the scruffy doll on the pillows to the clutch of photos on the bedside table. He tried not to think about what Nadine would make of it.

'Er – settling in OK?' He thrust his hands into his jeans pockets.

'Well, I've only been here twenty minutes, but so far so good.'

'Good. Great.' He picked up the nearest photo, just for something to do. It was a gang of people at a party, their heads crammed together as they all squeezed in for the camera. Phoebe was there, her face half hidden by a helium balloon, streamers round her neck, looking squiffy. She was propped up against some fair-haired, improbably handsome bloke with a square jaw like a Thunderbird puppet. 'Is this your boyfriend?'

'No, that's Luke. My sister's fiancé.'

She hadn't even asked which one he was looking at. And she was blushing like mad.

'So which one's your sister?'

'She's – um – not actually in the picture.' Phoebe's head was in the box so he couldn't see her expression.

Will put the photo back on the bedside table. Funny that she kept a photo of her sister's fiancé but not her sister. He would have asked her about it, but there was something else on his mind.

'So about tonight,' he began. 'You – er – don't really want to go out, do you?'

'Why not?'

'I just thought you might be tired, that's all. What with moving in and everything.'

'It's only a couple of boxes. Anyway, this might be just what I need. A chance to unwind and relax. Unless you don't want me to come?' she said. 'I don't want to gatecrash your night out or anything?'

'It's not that.' God, how could he put this? 'I'm just not sure if you'd enjoy yourself, that's all. You and Barry aren't exactly buddies, are you?'

'All the more reason to go.' Phoebe took a handful of books out of the box and put them up on the shelves. She had more books than clothes, Will noticed. 'If I'm going to be living here I ought to make an effort to get on with him. This evening could bring us closer.'

Will tried to smile, and failed. That's what I'm afraid of, he thought.

★

Phoebe swayed in her seat, beaming at nothing. She wasn't sure if the haze of coloured lights were coming from around her, or inside her head. She sensed she needed a pee but she wasn't sure her legs would carry her that far.

Strange she'd got so drunk so quickly. Usually she could hold her drink but for some reason the first half pint of lager had knocked her flat. Fortunately she'd hidden it well and no one else seemed to notice. There had been a nasty moment when she'd accidentally slipped on her way back from the ladies but she'd covered it with a kind of lunging dance movement and she didn't think anyone had seen her.

And to think she'd been nervous about going out with Will and his friends. They all seemed really nice. Especially Barry. Amazingly, he was the sweetest of all, the way he kept buying her drinks and laughing at all her jokes. And he and Tez had cheered all the way through her impromptu karaoke performance of Tina Turner's 'Simply The Best'. Barry said everyone in the pub had enjoyed it, and what the hell did it matter if the juke box was playing a Bon Jovi number? She'd done a hell of a job singing into an empty Becks bottle, and why didn't she think about going on 'Stars In Their Eyes'?

The only one who didn't seem to be enjoying himself was Will. He hadn't said a word all evening. He just kept glaring at everyone, especially her. And some time around the third drink he'd sprouted an extra head and about twenty pairs of eyebrows, it was a frightening sight.

Barry put another drink in front of her. Was it her fifth, or her sixth? She'd lost count since they'd moved on to tequilas. As she went to pick up her glass, Will leaned across and grabbed her wrist. 'Don't you think you've had enough?'

Phoebe glared back at him. 'You're a party pooper.'

'And you're making a fool of yourself.'

'You'd know all about that, wouldn't you? What about your wedding night?'

'Phoebe!'

Barry's eyes gleamed. 'What's this about his wedding night?'

'Nothing,' Will muttered.

'Didn't he tell you? That's where we met. I had to take him home because he was blind drunk and threatening to strip off in the middle of the bar.' She felt Will's grip tighten on her wrist, but it was too late. Her mouth had taken on a life of its own. 'He was all on his own, drinking champagne in a top hat. That is, he was wearing the top hat, not drinking out of it.'

'You're kidding?' Barry smirked at Will. 'Why didn't you tell us this?'

'It wasn't something I wanted to share.' He sent her a wintry look. It was probably meant to scare her but it just made her giggle. And once she started, she found she couldn't stop. She laughed and laughed, until suddenly—

'Oh God, I need the loo!'

She just made it. She sat there, the world spinning, feeling the walls of the cubicle closing in around her. She tried resting her head on her knees but it didn't help. Everything was going round and round. If only she could just close her eyes for a second . . .

'Phoebe! Are you in there? PHOEBE, OPEN THIS DOOR!'

The hammering shocked her back to life. She jolted her head back and stared at the door. 'W-Will? What are you doing in here? Go away.'

'Not until you come out.' She heard giggling on the other side of the door. Will's presence was obviously causing a stir.

She stood up, pulled herself together with effort, and

flushed the loo. As she staggered out of the cubicle, Will grabbed her arm. 'Come on, we're leaving.'

A gang of skimpily clad girls were watching him in the mirror while pretending to put on their lipsticks. 'But I haven't even washed my hands!'

'Later. Come on.'

'What's the rush? Are we going on somewhere?'

'The others might be. But I'm taking you home.'

'Why? I'm enjoying myself.'

'Well, the party's over.'

Phoebe couldn't argue. Her stomach was lurching and she was afraid to open her mouth.

The cool night air, scented with frying onions from the nearby kebab stall, hit her like a slap in the face and she felt her legs buckle. She would have crumpled to the ground if Will's arm hadn't been holding her up. He half-carried, half-dragged her through Micklegate Bar and down Queen Street. Phoebe had to break into a totter to keep up with him.

'Where are we going?'

'To the station.'

'Ooh, are we going on a train?'

'No, we're going home.' He dragged her to the station taxi rank and bundled her into a cab.

The driver glanced in the rear view mirror. 'She's not going to throw up, is she?'

'Not if I can help it.'

Phoebe tried to make a suitably cutting retort but her teeth had mysteriously been rearranged inside her mouth, so all that came out was an incoherent mumble. Her head lolled, watching the blur of lights flashing past the window. She could feel waves of anger vibrating off Will. Some kind of apology was called for.

'Shorry,' she mumbled. 'About the wedding night thing.'

'It doesn't matter.'

'I didn't mean to embarrassh you.'

'Believe me, the only person you embarrassed tonight is yourself.'

'I washn't that bad!'

'No?' He snapped a look at her, his eyes cold in the darkness. 'Dancing on the table? Falling over? Not to mention your entire repertoire of Cher's greatest hits!'

'Tina Turner, actually. And I wash not dancing on the table.'

'No, you weren't. You looked more like you were having an epileptic fit.'

He turned his face away. Phoebe slumped in her seat. 'Misherable bashtard,' she said. 'Jusht because your girlfriend's ditched you, you think no one else is allowed to have a good time.' Will ignored her. 'You don't have a mon- monop- you're not the only one who's ever been depressed, you know. I've been dumped too.'

'Now why doesn't that surprise me?' Will muttered under his breath.

'At least your girlfriend's on the other side of the world,' Phoebe could feel herself sliding into self-pity. 'At least she's not right under your nose. At least she hasn't moved in to your flat and married your bloody shishter!'

That got his attention. He turned round and gave her an odd look. So did the cab driver, which meant they whistled straight through a red light at the Bootham junction.

Three minutes later they were back at the house. Will paid the driver and hauled her out on to the pavement, but somehow the kerb moved at the last minute and she ended up on her knees.

'I'm sh-shorry,' Phoebe slurred, as Will dragged her to her feet. 'I really don't know what's the matter with me.'

'Could it be you're legless?'

'Legless! Very funny. It is funny, isn't it, because that's

what I am, isn't it? Got no legs, shee?' Just to prove it, she buckled again. This time Will caught her just before she hit the pavement.

'I don't see what's so bloody funny about it.' He slung her arm around his shoulders so she hung there, limp as a rag doll. 'For God's sake, why did you have to come tonight if you can't handle your drink?'

'I can!'

'Yeah, it looks like it. Half a lager and you were under the table.' He propped her against a wall and held her there with his shoulder while he struggled in his pocket for his key. With great difficulty he unlocked the door and manoeuvred his way inside, with Phoebe still draped around his neck.

As they struggled past his bicycle, still blocking the hall, there was a sound from upstairs. Phoebe flinched from the sudden burst of light as a figure appeared on the first floor landing, silhouetted against it. A short, dumpy figure, hands planted on hips.

'Yes, it's me again, Mrs Warzovski,' she heard Will say wearily. 'Yes, I know, it's typical, isn't it?'

The door slammed, plunging them into darkness again. Phoebe held on tightly around Will's neck. In spite of her drunkenness, she couldn't help noticing he had surprisingly broad shoulders. His arms were strong and muscled too. She rested her head against the rough cord of his shirt. 'Do you work out at all?'

'I don't need to. I get all the exercise I need hauling paralytic women around.'

That started her laughing again. Will's grip tightened around her. 'Will you shut up? This is hard enough as it is.'

'I know. I did it, remember? On your wedding night?' She tried to focus on his swimming face. 'I carried you over the threshold!'

'And dumped me on the floor.'

'Only because I thought you were dead.'

That made him smile. He really did have a nice smile, she thought. 'Well, you'll be pleased to hear I'm taking you to bed.'

'That's very kind of you, but I'm really not intereshted.'

He smiled again, although she could tell he was trying not to. He kicked open the door of her bedroom and hauled her inside.

As he laid her on her bed a sudden madness overcame her and she reached up, pulled his face down towards hers and kissed him. After a split second's surprise, he seemed to respond. Then he broke away.

'Bad idea,' he muttered. 'Really, really bad idea.'

She didn't know what time it was when she crawled into the bathroom and threw up. She didn't dare open her eyes in case the light fried her brain.

She rested her pounding head against the toilet seat and longed for death. It had to come soon. Surely she couldn't go on living like this? She was drenched in sweat but she couldn't stop shivering. She needed a drink but the thought made her stomach lurch.

What had happened to her last night? One minute she'd been fine, and the next – what?

And then she remembered. Groaning, she cradled her head in her hands and slid down the wall until she crouched on the floor. Dim images of the previous drunken evening kept swimming into her mind, each one more cringe-making than the last. What she'd said. What she'd done. More than anything, she could see Will's face, frowning in disapproval at her antics.

And then she'd kissed him. Phoebe curled, foetus-like, on the floor, remembering how he'd recoiled. 'A bad idea,' he'd said. More like catastrophic. Possibly her worst move since she'd tried to pierce her own ears when she was fifteen and nearly lost a lobe.

She staggered back to her room and pulled the duvet over her head. With any luck she would wake up and find it had all been a dream. Or not wake up at all.

She was woken up by the sound of someone moving around her room. She froze under the quilt. Maybe Will was packing her bags, ready to throw her out as soon as her eyes were open?

'Phoebe? I've brought you some tea.' She heard the rattle of a cup on her bedside table.

'Thanks.' She stayed under the duvet until she was sure he was gone. But as she fought her way bleary-eyed out of the covers, she suddenly realised he was standing at the end of the bed.

'How are you feeling?' he asked. He looked sickeningly fresh in jeans and a white T-shirt, his hair still damp from the shower. Phoebe, by contrast, felt she must look and smell like a dead poodle. She sniffed surreptitiously at her nightshirt.

'Terrible, actually.'

'I'm not surprised, after last night.'

She braced herself. 'I'm sorry,' she said. 'I can't understand it. I never usually get that drunk.'

'Yes, well, you probably never have people spiking your drinks.'

'What?'

'Barry rang this morning to see how you were. He seemed to think it was very funny, adding double vodkas to your lager.' Will looked grim. 'I told him he was bloody lucky he didn't kill you. I also told him not to show his face around here until I've stopped wanting to knock his teeth down his throat.' He looked at Phoebe. 'I owe you an apology. I was a bit rough on you last night, and I'm sorry. I thought you were trying to make an idiot of yourself on purpose.'

'Believe me, I never have to do it deliberately. It just sort of happens.'

Will sat down on the edge of the bed and handed her the cup. Him being so close reminded her of what else had happened last night. She knew she'd have to say something. 'I'm sorry about the way I behaved last night.'

'I told you, it wasn't your fault.'

'Maybe not, but I'm still sorry. About kissing you.'

'Oh that.' There was a long silence, then they both spoke at once. 'Look, Phoebe—'

'I just thought—'

They both stopped. 'You first,' he said.

'I just thought you ought to know I don't make a habit of that kind of thing. Kissing men I don't even know, that is.'

'I'm glad to hear it.' His dark eyes sparkled. 'And I don't want you to get the wrong idea, either. I mean, I really like you, but not in that way. You do understand that, don't you?'

'Of course.'

'Not that you're not a very attractive woman, or anything like that, but I love Nadine. As long as you know that. I don't need any more complications in my life.'

Talk about arrogant! 'Neither do I, as a matter of fact,' she said. 'You're not the only one with a complicated love life.'

'So I understand.' His eyes strayed to the photo of Luke beside her bed. What did he know about that, Phoebe wondered. She hadn't told him anything. Had she? Anyway, from now on there would be no more socialising. She would make sure their paths didn't cross unless they absolutely had to.

'I'm sure we can manage to keep our hands off each other as long as we're under the same roof.'

He looked amused. 'I'm sure we can.' He stood up. 'I'll leave you to it.'

As the door closed, Phoebe caught a glimpse of herself in the dressing table mirror. She was right. She did look like a dead poodle. No wonder he'd looked so amused. And no wonder he was worried she might fancy him.

Chapter 17

She was still feeling fragile when she crawled into the staff meeting three hours later. Guy's Thursday morning pep talks weren't exactly the highlight of anyone's working week. Except for Ronan, who never missed an opportunity to grease up to the boss.

Naturally, everyone else was already there, gathered around the restaurant tables facing Guy, who perched on a bar stool. All heads turned to look at Phoebe as she sidled to the back.

'Blimey, what happened to you?' Karen whispered.

'Don't ask.' Phoebe tried to light a cigarette with shaking hands. 'Have I missed anything?'

'Takings are down on last week, so Guy's on one of his economy drives. He's just been telling us how we've got to cut the cocktail cherries into quarters to make them go further.'

'Tight sod.' No doubt he'd be looking to slash the food budget too. That would put Titus in a good mood.

'And finally some good news,' Guy was saying. 'As you probably know, Cameron Goode will be visiting York some time in the next couple of months to film an episode of "The Goode Food Guide".' Phoebe had an awful feeling she knew what was coming next. She flashed a look at Titus' face. 'You'll be pleased to know I've been in touch with Talbot TV and they've kindly agreed to let Cameron do a segment of the show from here. Isn't that terrific? And I have to say it's all down to Ronan here for coming up with the idea in the first place. Great job, Ronan.'

But none of the kitchen staff was looking at Ronan. They were all staring at Titus.

At first he didn't move. Then, slowly, he rose to his feet. 'Since Ronan is the golden boy around here perhaps he'd better have my job.' He pulled off his toque and dropped it on the table.

He was halfway back to the kitchen before Guy galvanised himself to speak. 'Come on, Titus, don't be like that. Sorry to spring this on you, but I thought you'd be pleased.'

'Then you were wrong, weren't you?'

'But what's your problem? This is going to be amazing publicity for the restaurant. And for you. The TV people thought it would be great if you and Cameron Goode actually did some cooking together. What do you think of that? Fabulous, eh?'

His enthusiasm died in the face of the withering look Titus sent him. 'It's your choice,' he said. 'But I'm telling you, if that wanker sets foot in my kitchen, I'm walking out. Is that understood?'

He swung through the kitchen doors, leaving behind him a vacuum of silence.

'It's just another tantrum.' Guy tried to laugh it off. 'He'll get over it once he realises he's going to get his fat face on the telly.'

'I'm not so sure.' Phoebe looked towards the doors. 'He was too calm. I really think he's serious.'

'So what if he is?' Ronan desperately tried to build on his moment of glory. 'Let him walk out if he wants to. We don't need him. Phoebe and I could run the kitchen between us easily.'

No prizes for guessing who'd be in charge, Phoebe thought.

'Don't be an idiot.' Guy was dismissive. 'There's no way I'd want to lose Titus. The man might be a pain in the arse, but he's a genius.' He turned to Phoebe. 'You'll have to talk to him. Get him to see what a great idea this is.'

'Why me?'

'Because you're the only one he'll listen to.'

'The only one willing to get my head bitten off, you mean,' Phoebe muttered. But Guy was already pushing her towards the kitchen doors.

There was no sign of Titus. 'He must have gone home,' Phoebe said, unable to hide her relief.

'Then go after him. No, not now. Give him time to calm down. Tell him we're sorry. Tell him he can have a raise. Tell him anything, but just get him back here.'

'Can I tell him it's all off with Cameron Goode?' Phoebe asked. Guy sent her an incredulous look.

'And give up all that free publicity? Don't be soft.'

June had started with some dull wet weather that sent all the tourists scuttling for the museums. Consequently the maze of little streets around the restaurant were nearly empty as Phoebe left late that afternoon. Bar Barato was in the middle of Swinegate, an upmarket area of pedestrianised streets full of designer shops and fashionable bars. Usually it was buzzing with life, but as Phoebe hurried down Grape Lane, the pavement cafés were pulling down shutters and bringing their tables inside out of a sudden downpour. The smell of fresh coffee scented the air and she was sorely tempted to sneak in for a quick latte. Anything to stop her having to face Titus.

She really wasn't looking forward to this. Away from the kitchen, Titus guarded his privacy. He never talked about his family or his friends. No one had ever been invited to his home, or seen where he lived. Phoebe had a feeling she wouldn't get a warm welcome when she turned up on his doorstep.

She followed the directions she'd been given down Fossgate and over the bridge where the narrow ribbon of the River Foss snaked across the city, its banks so over-grown the bushes almost touched each other across its width. Icy drips ran down her collar as she plodded down Walmgate. Over a hundred years ago, the little back streets of narrow terraced cottages had been one of the poorest areas in the city, home to the families of Irish immigrants escaping the potato famine. It still felt like going back in time now, although the pubs had been smartened up and the flophouses had given way to newsagents, hairdressers and a tandoori takeaway. At the end of Walmgate she could see the imposing Bar, and beyond it Fulford Road, and what used to be her home.

But not any more. Would she ever stop thinking of Alex's flat as her home? It gave her a pang to think about her sister. She really missed Alex, but she couldn't blame her for shutting her out. Phoebe could only imagine how much it must have hurt her to find she'd been so badly betrayed. She just hoped she would have a chance to make it up to her some day. And another part of her never wanted to forget the memory of her night with Luke . . .

A gang of children were playing tig among the parked cars, ignoring the rain. When they spotted Phoebe they gave up and trailed after her instead.

She found Titus' door and knocked on it. There was no answer.

'Don't think he's in,' the tallest of the boys called out.

'Brilliant, Einstein.' Phoebe shivered from cold and hangover. She tried again.

'Told you he isn't in.'

'Shh.' Phoebe caught some movement behind the curtain. She went over to the window and shaded her eyes, peering inside. 'Titus? Are you in there? It's me, Phoebe.'

'Fuck off,' came the muffled voice.

'Come on Titus, let me in, please. I want to talk to

you.' She glanced over her shoulder. The children were crowding around, trying to catch a glimpse through the curtains too.

There were footsteps in the hall, and Titus' blurred outline appeared through the frosted glass of the front door.

'I suppose Guy fucking Barrington sent you?'

'Well, yes. But I would have come anyway. I wanted to see if you were all right.' Silence. 'Titus, do you think you could let me in for five minutes? It's pouring down out here.'

To her relief, the door opened. 'Five minutes,' Titus said. 'And you lot can piss off an' all,' he shouted at the children, who scattered like ninepins.

The hallway was dark, narrow, and smelt of damp. Titus led the way into the sitting room. This wasn't much better, with faded wallpaper, junk shop furniture and a cracked leather sofa that looked as if it had been left over from World War Two.

'Well, what do you want?' He confronted her, his arms folded across his chest. 'Say what you've come to say, and get going. I've things to do.'

Phoebe looked around the room. DIY wasn't one of them, obviously. 'Do you think I could sit down?'

His eyes narrowed. 'Aye, if you must. Only don't make yourself too comfortable.'

She perched on the sofa, feeling the springs groan under her. Being comfortable wasn't an option.

'I'm not doing it.' Titus cut her off before she could say a word. 'If he's sent you round to try to talk me into it, you're wasting your time. I've already told him where I stand. If that tosser sets foot in my kitchen then I'm gone. For good.'

'I know that, Titus. But what I don't understand is why you're so against the idea. As Guy says, it would be great publicity for the restaurant.'

'We don't need that kind of publicity!' Anger flared in his eyes. 'I've worked hard to give that place a decent reputation. I don't want the likes of Cameron Goode turning his nose up at it and making it into some pathetic sideshow.'

'But it won't be like that.'

'Won't it? You don't know Cameron. He'll take great delight in making us all look like a bunch of hicks from the sticks who wouldn't know a porcini from a Pot Noodle. Especially me. Oh yes, he'd love that.'

'You make it sound as if you know him?'

Titus stared at her for a moment. 'I should do. He's my brother.'

It was a while before she could react. 'You're kidding?'

'I wish I was. No, Cameron's my kid brother all right. Goode is our mother's maiden name. I suppose he thought it sounded fancier for the telly.' He looked bitter.

'But how come you've never told anyone?'

'Because I didn't want them to know. I'm only telling you now because I know you won't spread it around. And I want you to understand why I don't want that patronising little fuckwit anywhere near my kitchen.'

Phoebe nodded. 'Go on.'

'I don't care what anyone says, I know he's only agreed to this show so he can make a fool of me.' Titus sat down in the armchair opposite. 'He's been the same ever since we were kids. Everything I had, everything I did, Cameron had to go one better. If I got a cold, he got pneumonia. If I won a silver star at school, he had to get the gold. He's always done it. D'you know, he wanted to be a car mechanic until I got a job in a hotel kitchen? Next thing I know, he's chucked in his apprenticeship and enrolled in catering college.' His face was mottled with anger. 'For God's sake, he'd never even boiled an egg until he saw it was what I wanted to do. But of course, he had to be better at it then me. Had to try and make me look a fool.'

'But who says he's better than you? You're brilliant.'

'Yes, but I don't have a flashy restaurant in London, do I? Or my own TV series. All I've got is a job in a poxy little bar in the back end of nowhere. And now he's trying to take that away from me too.' His shoulders slumped. 'I've spent my whole life trying to get away from him. I thought I'd finally managed it, found somewhere I could be myself, earn a bit of respect. And then this happens.' He smiled sadly. 'You're right, I do like to throw my weight around, tell everyone I'm the greatest thing since Escoffier. But when Cameron turns up he'll show me up for what I really am. A crap chef who never made the grade.'

'But that's not true!'

'Maybe it is, maybe it isn't. But that's the way he makes me feel.' He looked up at her. 'I thought you of all people would understand, what with your sister.'

Phoebe was silent. The difference being, she really was inferior to Alex. Luke Rawlings had made her realise that.

'Anyway, now d'you see why I don't want him here?' His eyes searched her face for understanding. 'It's not that I'm jealous of him or anything. I don't care that he's famous, or rich, or that he's been round to Downing Street to cook for Tony Blair. I really don't. I just want him to leave me alone. That's not too much to ask, is it?'

'No. No, it isn't.' The problem was, how to convince Guy? 'Look, maybe if you told everyone about this—'

'No!' Titus roared. 'And I don't want you telling anyone either. I don't want anyone else to know, understand?'

'If that's the way you want it,' Phoebe agreed. 'But I don't see how we're going to change Guy's mind.'

She massaged her temples. The paracetamols she'd taken earlier were beginning to wear off. Titus frowned. 'Are you OK?'

'Not really. I woke up with a hangover and I haven't eaten all day.'

'I've got just the thing. Wait there.'

He disappeared off through a curtained doorway to the back room. Phoebe sank back into the sofa and closed her eyes. From beyond the curtain came the hissing of hot fat in a pan, and the unmistakable aroma of frying bacon. Intrigued, she followed her nose through the curtain into the kitchen.

It couldn't have been a bigger contrast to the shabby sitting room. No expense had been spared in here, from the gleaming expanse of stainless steel worktops inset with slabs of marble for pastry-making, to the industrial sized cooker with eight burners and a double oven. Row upon row of shining pans hung from a rack on the ceiling. Flourishing pots of fresh herbs lined the windowsill. On either side of the cooker were open shelves of spices and seasonings, everything easily to hand, just as it should be.

She should have known. This was where Titus was in his element, where he probably spent nearly all his time and money. No wonder the rest of the house had been so badly neglected.

He flipped the contents of a frying pan in between two slabs of white bread and handed her the plate. 'Here you go. Just what the doctor ordered.'

Presumably a doctor who didn't believe all that nonsense about cholesterol. Phoebe peered at the plate. 'What is it?'

'Fried egg, bacon and sausage sandwich, with extra ketchup. The best hangover cure in existence.'

Titus had garnished the plate with a fan-shaped sliver of cucumber and a radish rose. Old habits died hard, obviously.

'It – er – looks delicious,' she said faintly, 'but I don't think—'

'Eat it.' Titus' nostrils flared, and for a second Phoebe experienced the bone-melting fear of a customer who'd made the mistake of asking for his steak to be cooked a minute longer.

Titus stood over her as she took a bite. Each mouthful took about an hour to eat. She chewed and chewed it but her mouth was lined with sawdust and it didn't seem to want to go down. 'Could I have a cup of tea?' she pleaded.

'In a minute. Besides, I know you'll try to chuck it away while my back's turned. Go on, have another bite. It'll do you good.'

He was right. With every mouthful she could feel herself returning to normal. Her stomach settled, her hands didn't shake any more, even her head stopped pounding.

'It's a miracle,' she said.

Titus smiled. 'Told you. Now, if only I could get rid of my bloody brother that easily.'

Will wasn't home when she got back to the flat, but Barry and Tez were bouncing up and down on the sofa, hunched over a computer console. As Phoebe hung up her jacket she saw two cars flashing around the screen.

'Where's Will?'

'Gone out to get some more beers.' Tez glanced over his shoulder at her. 'Are you – um – feeling all right?'

'I'm not dead, if that's what you mean. No thanks to you.' She looked at Barry, who didn't respond. He went on jabbing the buttons on his console until Tez nudged him.

'What? Oh yeah, sorry about last night. It was only a joke, y'know?'

'Very amusing, I'm sure.'

'It was from where we were standing,' Barry sniggered. Phoebe smiled sweetly.

'I know. It's amazing what seems like a good idea when you're paralytic,' she said. 'But I expect a lot of your one night stands have told you that, haven't they?'

Will walked in before Barry could reply. 'Phoebe! Sorry, I should have warned you these two were coming round.'

'It's your flat,' Barry muttered.

'Why don't you join us? Fancy a beer?'

'Not for me, thanks.' Phoebe looked at the screen. 'What are you playing?'

'Formula One racing. The Monaco circuit.' Will wedged himself in beside the others on the sofa and cracked open a beer can.

'You wouldn't understand it,' Barry said.

'You mean a bunch of cars going round and round a track? I can see that would be mentally challenging.' Phoebe curled up in the armchair to watch, mainly because she knew how much it would annoy Barry.

After a few laps she couldn't understand what all the excitement was about. It was just like the old Scalextric her dad used to have in the loft, except you didn't have the hassle of putting the cars back on the track every time they flew off.

Finally Barry threw down his console and raised his arms. 'Ye-es! Still the undisputed champion! How does he do it?'

'Understeer,' Phoebe said. Three heads turned to look at her. 'You were braking too late on the corners,' she said to Tez. 'That meant you were having to overcorrect on the way out. It's a classic mistake.'

Barry's lip curled. 'So you're Michael Schumacher now, are you? Maybe you'd like to take me on?'

'Oh no, I couldn't.' Then she saw his smug face. 'Oh, go on, then.'

It took her half a lap to work out which buttons to press, by which time Barry's Ferrari was already blasting up the hill towards Casino Square. He made a bad mistake at Mirabeau and she managed to catch up with him. They entered the tunnel together and stayed side by side for the rest of the lap. It took all her concentration to keep going, so she hardly noticed when, during the tight right into Rascasse, Barry edged her off the track.

'Oi, play the game!' Tez protested.

'I was only taking the racing line. I can't help it if she can't stay on the road, can I? Bloody women drivers.'

He tried a couple more times to put her off. Once he nudged her nearside wing and, when that didn't work, he tried the psychological approach. 'Late into that corner,' he sneered. 'Stopped to put your make-up on, did you?'

But in spite of all his tactics, she was somehow winning. As they took the left-hander into Tabac for the final lap, she could hear Tez whooping with excitement. Barry had stopped making smart remarks and was hunched forward, jabbing buttons, a sheen of sweat on his upper lip.

'She's got you, mate!' Tez yelled, as the finishing line came into view. 'The unbeaten champion has finally eaten dust.'

Suddenly she was spinning through the air. The last thing she saw before landing nose first into the Armco was the flash of scarlet as Barry's Ferrari streaked past towards the chequered flag.

'Bloody hell, what happened?' Tez stared at the screen.

'I don't know. Must have pressed the wrong button.' She didn't look at Barry.

'I really thought she had you there, Baz. You were lucky.'

'It's only a stupid game, anyway.' Barry threw down the console and stood up. 'Are we going out, or what?'

'But it's not even seven yet.'

'So? We're wasting valuable drinking time.' As he grabbed his jacket and headed for the door, Will turned to Phoebe. 'What are your plans for the evening?'

She heard Barry's groan. As if she'd want to go out drinking with them again! 'I think I'll have a bath and settle down in front of the telly with Brad Pitt.'

'Are you coming?' Barry drummed his fingers on the doorframe. With one last look at Phoebe, Will followed him.

Chapter 18

It was blissful to have the flat to herself. Will was nice, but with Tez and Barry around it was like being with a bunch of overgrown schoolboys. How had Nadine put up with it for so long?

Time for some serious pampering, she decided. She put some smoochy soul music on the CD, slapped on a face pack and ran herself a bath, adding a splash of the Jo Malone bath oil Alex had given her for Christmas, which she saved for the most indulgent occasions.

The citrus scent made Phoebe think of her sister. What was Alex doing now, she wondered? Probably getting ready to go out for a romantic candlelit dinner with Luke. Or maybe they were having a cosy evening in, going over the guest list for their wedding.

Whatever it was, she certainly wasn't lying in the bath, staring up at the ceiling with tears rolling down her cheeks because she missed Phoebe.

She was just getting out of the tub when something made her stop. She listened at the door, straining to pick out the sound from under the soulful strains of Ben E. King. Someone was moving around the flat.

A thousand thoughts crammed into her mind, tumbling over each other. It must be Will, come back for his wallet or something. But he would have called out to her. And he wouldn't be creeping around like that either.

Adrenalin whooshed through her body. What to do? Staying locked in the bathroom seemed the best option. After all, unless the intruder was a clean freak on the hunt for soap, he wouldn't bother trying the door. He wouldn't even know she was in there.

But of course he'd know. Who left music playing in an empty flat? He was probably prowling around now, looking for her. He wasn't an ordinary burglar at all. He was a mad axeman.

And she knew what axes could do to doors. She'd seen *The Shining*.

And even if he was an ordinary burglar, how could she cower in the bathroom while he helped himself to the TV and video?

She suddenly remembered an old episode of *The Bill*, the one where there'd been a siege on the council estate and the Sun Hill brigade had sent for the macho cops with guns to sort it out. The one where that nice-looking one – what's his name – had ended up getting shot and no one quite knew whether it was one of the bad guys who'd done it, or . . . oh, well, it didn't matter. The point was, she remembered, that instead of just sneaking in and trying to catch the baddies unawares, they'd gone in literally all guns blazing, shouting and chucking smoke bombs around to try to confuse them.

She didn't have any smoke bombs, and she didn't have a gun either, unfortunately. But she pulled on her dressing gown and armed herself with the first things that came to hand. Then, with a banshee yell, she threw open the bathroom door and hurled herself through it.

She was so terrified she didn't dare open her eyes until she felt her loofah make contact with something solid and roughly human-sized. She heard a man's cry of surprise and let him have it with a blast from her aerosol, screaming and whacking at the same time. She didn't know what effect it was having on him, but she was scaring the hell out of herself.

'Phoebe!'

She stopped, hand raised, and looked around. Will was

standing on the other side of the room, watching her with disbelief and some dismay. 'What are you doing here?'

'Never mind me. What are *you* doing?'

She turned slowly to confront her assailant through a choking mist of lemon-scented body spray, only to find she'd been trying to kill the coatstand.

Will stared at her. 'Is it that time of the month?' he asked.

There was a twitch at the corners of his mouth she didn't like. She pulled the edges of her dressing gown together. 'I thought you were an intruder.'

'So you decided to perfume him to death? Or were you just acting on Impulse?' He eyed the can in her hand. His mouth was definitely twitching now. And there was the maddening hint of a twinkle in his eyes.

'I was acting to save your belongings.' She thrust the spray into her pocket. 'What are you doing here, anyway? I thought you'd gone out.'

'I decided I didn't feel much like drinking tonight. And I've got some work to finish. I did call out when I came in, but I guess you didn't hear me.' He looked her up and down. 'Thanks, by the way. For being a have-a-go hero. If I really was a burglar I'd have been shit scared.'

Mustering what was left of her dignity, she went off to get dressed. It wasn't until she was looking in the bathroom mirror that she realised why he'd been looking at her so strangely. In all the panic she'd forgotten to take off her face pack. Her face was chalky blue, riven with cracks like the Giants' Causeway. Christ, how awful.

She washed her face and pulled on jeans and a baggy green sweater. She felt like going to bed, pulling the duvet over her head and never emerging until Will had died or moved out, but it was only eight o'clock and besides, she was starving.

He was sitting at his drawing board. When Phoebe walked in he turned around and smiled with relief. 'That's better. I'm not being personal, but the Braveheart look really didn't suit you.'

'Very funny.'

She crossed the room to turn off the music, but he said, 'No, leave it on. I love Motown. I've got this CD myself, actually.'

Funny how two people's tastes could be so similar, and yet they themselves were so different, Phoebe reflected.

'Have you eaten?' she asked. 'Only I was going to cook something, and I wondered if you'd like to join me.'

He looked at her so strangely she wondered if she was still wearing the face pack. 'Cook? What, you mean – really cook? Proper food?'

'Don't look so surprised. That oven can be used for something other than drying your socks, you know.'

'Yes, but surely you don't want to go to all that trouble? I mean, you've been cooking all day.'

'It's no trouble. I'm only going to make an omelette, not whistle up a fifteen-course meal.'

She went into the kitchen. After a moment he followed her. She could feel him watching her with rapt fascination as she chopped onions, sliced peppers and whisked eggs, as if she was an alchemist performing the old base metal into gold trick.

'I can't remember the last time I ate something that didn't come out of a takeaway carton,' he admitted.

'I suppose you haven't felt much like cooking since Nadine left?' She saw the pained look that crossed Will's face.

'Nadine wasn't too keen on cooking either. We mostly ate out.'

How did I guess, Phoebe thought. The kitchen certainly looked a lot more lived-in since she'd put away all those ultra-smart but scarcely used gadgets and brought in her own trusty pots and pans.

'She wasn't that keen on eating either, come to think of it. She was obsessed about staying thin.'

Phoebe put down the hunk of French bread she'd been about to cram into her mouth and went back to softening the onions. 'It's a bit late for me to start worrying about that,' she said ruefully.

'You don't have to. You've got a great figure.'

She glanced at him. He was showing a sudden interest in her sauté pan, but she could see the blush spreading up his neck.

She'd dressed the salad and almost finished the omelettes when Will suddenly said, 'Why did you let Barry win the race?'

Her hand wobbled as she turned the omelettes out on to plates. 'I didn't.'

'Phoebe, you were driving that car like a pro. There was no way you would have smashed into the wall by accident. So why did you do it?'

She thought about it for a moment. 'I didn't want to humiliate him,' she admitted finally.

'He deserved it, after what he did to you last night.'

'But I've got to go on living here. And it would be a lot easier if he didn't hate me quite so much.'

'He doesn't hate you. OK, maybe he resents you a bit,' Will conceded. 'Barry thinks there's a time and a place for women. And it's not on a night out with the lads.'

'Did he resent Nadine?'

'A bit. But he tolerated her for my sake. And because she was so drop dead gorgeous it did his ego good to be seen with her.'

Unlike me. Phoebe almost wished she had thrashed him now. 'Let's eat, shall we?'

They talked as they ate, mainly about Nadine. Phoebe longed to talk about something else, but every time she tried to steer the conversation away, it seemed to come right back to her. Soon even the mention of her name was giving her indigestion.

The funny thing was, the more glowingly Will talked about Nadine, the less Phoebe liked the sound of her. Everything he said screamed 'self-obsessed'. But somehow Will couldn't see it.

And he wanted her back. When he should have been cracking open the champagne and toasting his narrow escape, he actually still wanted her. It was more than Phoebe could comprehend. Especially when it was obvious to anyone with half an eye and a basic grasp of human nature that she was about as likely to come back as Phoebe was of being hired as Kate Moss' body double.

'Anyway, we decided it would be best if she tried her luck in L.A., just to see if anything came of it,' Will explained for the millionth time. 'It's just for six months, to give her a chance to find out if there's anything out there for her.'

'And what if there is?'

Will blinked, not used to having his monologue interrupted. 'Sorry?'

'What if she makes a go of it out there and decides to stay? What will you do then?'

'She won't.'

'You mean she won't make a go of it? Or she won't decide to stay?'

'Of course she'll make a go of it. Nadine's very talented.'

It was a big claim for someone whose only acting role in the last six months had been a walk-on in a Mr Muscle commercial. 'I'm sure she is. In which case, won't she find it very difficult to walk away from all that success?'

His brows locked together. 'What are you saying?'

Oh Lord, why did she ever start this? Why not just let him enjoy his happy little fantasy? It wasn't really her

business anyway. 'I'm saying maybe you ought to pre-
pare yourself for the fact that she might not be ready to
come home after six months? Maybe she'll need a year,
or maybe—'

'Maybe she won't come home at all?' His tone
changed. 'You think she's dumped me, don't you?'

'Well, she did leave you standing at the altar. That
does suggest a lack of commitment.'

'She didn't dump me, she's pursuing her *career*. There's
a difference.'

Phoebe looked at him sympathetically. 'Are you sure
you're not kidding yourself?'

'Like you, you mean?'

The room suddenly went very still. 'What did you
say?'

'Forget it.' He dug at his food, his head bent.

'No, I won't. What did you mean?'

'OK.' He dropped his fork and looked up at her. 'It's
what you told me last night, when you were drunk.
About that Luke bloke.'

She felt the blood drain to her feet. 'What did I say?'

'Enough. And it seems to me someone who's obsessed
with her sister's fiancé isn't exactly qualified to hand out
relationship advice.'

Phew! Thank God she hadn't told him the whole
story. 'At least I'm not still waiting pathetically for him
to come back when the whole world knows that will
never happen!'

She saw his face darken and wished she hadn't said it.
'Will—'

'Forget it.' He picked up his plate and headed for the
kitchen.

Phoebe listened to him clattering around for a moment, then followed. He was standing at the sink but she
could feel the anger vibrating from the rigid lines of his
back.

'Will, I'm sorry. I should never have said anything. You're right, I'm hardly the one to be dishing out advice.'

He turned around to face her. 'No, it's me who should be apologising. You hurt me, so I lashed out. I'm really sorry.' He gave her a rueful smile. 'Friends?'

'Friends.' She smiled back.

They cracked open a couple of beers and slumped together on the sofa. This time it was Phoebe's turn to talk.

It felt strange, confiding in someone about Luke after keeping her feelings to herself for so long. But in a way it was easier to tell Will, just because she didn't know him so well.

She found herself telling him how they'd met when Luke moved up from London to run the Leeds office of an investment consultancy, how she had a huge crush on him for nearly a year. How they'd very nearly got together. And then Alex came along.

'Blimey, no wonder you had to move out,' Will said, when she'd finished. 'And you didn't even put up a fight for him?'

'What's the point? You've never met Alex.'

'It sounds as if you're in awe of her.'

'I suppose I am, in a way.' She'd never really stopped to think about it before. 'She's everything I'm not. She's confident, ambitious, she always gets what she wants. And she's stunning looking too.'

'You don't exactly look like the back of a bus yourself.'

There was an awkward moment. 'Anyway,' Phoebe brushed over it hurriedly, 'she and Luke are together now and there's nothing I can do about it.'

'And you've never been tempted to try and lure him away from her?'

He was joking, she could tell. And she wasn't about to

share the misery of Luke's rejection with him. 'There wouldn't be much point. Like I said, you don't know Alex.'

Will relaxed back on the sofa and propped his long legs up on the coffee table. 'We make a right pair, don't we? Both stuck indoors, breaking our hearts over other people. Maybe we should just forget about them and start enjoying ourselves instead.'

'What do you suggest?'

Their eyes met, and Phoebe felt the tiniest spark of electricity crackle between them. Will felt it too; she could tell from the flash of dismay in his eyes.

'I could always thrash you on the race track?' she said.

'You could try.'

The spark fizzled and died. She wasn't sure which of them was more relieved.

Chapter 19

The dress was exquisite. Ivory silk with a billowing skirt and strapless bodice traced with gold embroidery. It illuminated her skin and emphasised the curve of her bare shoulders. Alex stared at her reflection. It was like looking at someone else.

'Beautiful,' her mother sighed. 'Oh yes, that's definitely the one. What do you think, Alex?'

'It's – nice,' she murmured.

'Just think, my little girl a bride.' Shirley Redmond dabbed her eyes. 'You're going to look stunning, darling. Imagine what Luke will say when he sees you coming up the aisle in that.'

Alex stared back at her reflection and tried to picture it. She visualised herself entering the church; the swell of the organ music, the heavy scent of lilies, everyone turning to look at her as she swept down the aisle on her father's arm, to where Luke waited at the altar . . .

She felt the panic rising in her chest again, making it hard to breathe. She couldn't do it. Every time she reached the altar she blanked out.

'So, shall we get this one?' Shirley interrupted her thoughts.

Alex looked at the price tag, stalling for time. 'It's very expensive.'

'Oh, I wouldn't worry about the money,' Shirley dismissed. 'Your father and I only want you to have the best, you know that.'

Alex wondered if her father would feel the same when he saw the credit card bill. They'd already done it some serious damage buying her mother's outfit. 'I'm still not sure.' She looked back at her reflection and pretended to consider it. 'Maybe if it had sleeves. Or a different skirt. Or no embroidery.'

The sales assistant failed to suppress a sigh. No wonder. Over the past two hours they'd turned the shop upside down. Alex had tried on the whole range, from Scarlett O'Hara to medieval maiden, complete with tulle wimple.

'You're absolutely right,' Shirley agreed, clearly in no hurry to end the shopping trip of a lifetime.

'Perhaps you'd like to see something else?' Behind her fixed smile she could almost hear the assistant's teeth grinding. 'I'm sure we have something in the stock room you haven't tried on.'

'Maybe later,' Alex put in, as Shirley opened her mouth. 'Why don't we have some lunch first, and think about it?'

'Good idea. Let's go to Bettys. We used to go there all the time, remember?' Her mother's excitement made Alex feel even more guilty. She rarely went shopping with her these days, although she knew how much Shirley enjoyed it.

For once there wasn't a queue of tourists outside Bettys and they got a table immediately.

'I think you were right about that last dress. I must say I wasn't sure about the neckline,' Shirley chattered on as they looked at the menu. 'I think you'd have to have something to break it up. Some kind of chain, or maybe a choker? Perhaps you'd like some of my pearls? You know, something borrowed?'

'Hmm.' Alex hid her face behind her menu. The truth was, there was nothing wrong with the dress. She just wanted to put off buying one as long as possible. Somehow she felt if she actually bought a wedding dress she would be admitting to herself that it was all really happening. And she didn't want to do that.

'Anyway, I'm sure there are some shops we haven't tried yet,' Shirley said after they'd ordered. 'Maybe we could take a trip to Harrogate this afternoon?'

'Why don't we wait for Phoebe?'

Shirley stared at her in amazement. 'What on earth for?'

'I don't know. I just thought she might like to be involved.'

'If that's what you want, but I really don't know what she could contribute.' Her mother looked miffed. 'If that girl ever gets married it'll be in jeans and trainers.'

Alex smiled. 'You're probably right. She detests shopping.' It suddenly hit her how much she missed Phoebe. It was six weeks since she moved out, and in all that time Alex had hardly seen her. She couldn't remember when they'd gone so long without at least phoning each other.

She knew Phoebe was still ashamed about what had happened with Luke. But once her initial outrage had burned itself out, Alex had all but forgotten about it. What did that say about her feelings for him, she wondered.

Phoebe would understand. She would listen to her droning on about her problems. She might even offer her advice, although they both knew Alex wouldn't take it.

But there was no one else she could talk to. No one else she could tell how desperately worried she was about this whole wedding thing.

She gazed out of the window at the tourists in St Helen's Square enjoying the July sunshine. They sat on the benches, eating ice creams and watching the street entertainers. They looked as if they didn't have a care in the world. Not like her.

It was all happening way too fast. When she and Luke first got engaged the idea of actually getting married had seemed like a hazy prospect. Now the big day was hurtling towards her, becoming more real every minute, and Alex couldn't help feeling she was about to make the biggest mistake of her life.

Not that she could tell that to her mother. Shirley was in her element, pen poised over her Smythsons notebook, determined to go over every excruciating detail.

'We must talk about venues,' she said. 'We have to get something booked by the end of the week. We're cutting it fine as it is, all the best places will have been taken ages ago. You're not leaving yourself very long – there's only another three months until you get married.'

Alex felt her chest tightening again. 'Maybe we should put the wedding off?' she said. 'I mean, if we can't get anywhere decent—'

'Don't worry, I'm sure we can sort something out.' Shirley misunderstood her panicked expression. 'Now, I've got a few venues in mind.'

'Can't you sort it out?' Alex pleaded.

'But it's your wedding.'

'I know, but you're so good at that kind of thing. I'd really appreciate your help.'

The flattery worked. Shirley looked pleased and brushed an invisible speck off her Windsmoor two-piece. 'Well, if you're sure that's what you want?'

'It is.'

'But there are still things we have to discuss,' Shirley went on. 'The caterers, for instance. I'm going to need to know how many of the guests are vegetarian.'

'How should I know?' The waitress arrived just in time with the bottle of Chardonnay. Alex filled her glass while Shirley looked on, her lips pursed.

'You don't seem to be taking much interest in this wedding, I must say. Is there something you're not telling me?'

Alex looked at her over the rim of her glass. Now, she

thought. Now's the time to say something. She took a gulp of wine and the moment passed. 'I don't see why we have to have all this fuss, that's all,' she mumbled.

'But I want you to have a day to remember.'

'I'd remember it even more if we just ran away to Gretna Green.'

Her mother recoiled. 'You're not serious?'

'Maybe not,' Alex shrugged. 'But why can't we have a small wedding? Just friends and family?'

'We are having just friends and family.'

'I mean close family. You've invited aunts and uncles and cousins I've never even heard of, let alone met. Why do I need them at my wedding?'

'Darling, you have to have them.'

'No, *you* have to have them. Let's face it, this wedding isn't about what I want, is it? It's about putting on a show and impressing the relatives.'

She thought Shirley would argue back, but she didn't. She kept a dignified silence while the waitress brought their food, her trembling lips the only outward sign of her feelings. Then, when they were alone again, she said quietly, 'You're right, darling. This is your day, and you must have the wedding you want.'

Alex rocked back in her chair and stared at her. 'You mean it?'

'Of course.' She unfolded her napkin into her lap. 'The last thing I want is for you to have any regrets. Regrets are a terrible thing.'

Alex frowned. 'Surely you don't have any regrets about your wedding? It was huge, wasn't it?' She remembered seeing the photos once. It was like something out of a fairytale, complete with horse-drawn carriages, billowing frocks and a whole string of bridesmaids and pageboys. It had even made the front page of the local paper.

'Only because your grandfather wanted it that way.'

Shirley speared some salad with her fork. 'He wanted to show the world that we had nothing to be ashamed of.'

'Why should you be ashamed?'

'Oh, you know. With us coming from such humble beginnings. I suppose he wanted to show everyone how much he'd come up in the world.' She pushed her glass across the table. 'Do you think I could have some of that wine?'

Alex filled her glass and wondered why her mother wouldn't meet her eye. 'So why should you regret that?'

'Well, you know. I was nervous. Like you, I didn't really want any fuss.' Alex thought back to those wedding photos. In spite of the big glitzy occasion, she couldn't remember a single picture of her mother smiling from under those miles of spangled tulle. 'And the weather was far too hot. The hottest August on record, so they said—' she stopped dead.

'August?' Alex put down her fork. 'But you got married in May. We had a party a few weeks ago. Anyway, I know you got married then because I was born ten months later.' She saw her mother's trapped expression and the truth dawned. 'Oh my God! You were pregnant when you got married!'

'Shh!' Shirley darted a glance around the restaurant. 'Don't look at me like that, it – it was an accident. It happens to people all the time.'

Not to you, it doesn't. Alex stared at her mother, a woman so prim she even hid the loo rolls under frilly covers. She couldn't imagine her parents having sex after marriage, let alone before. It was such a ridiculous idea she couldn't help laughing.

'Bloody hell, no wonder Grandpa was desperate to get you up the aisle!'

'It isn't funny,' Shirley snapped. 'It may be trendy to be an unmarried mother these days but it certainly wasn't then. If Joseph hadn't offered to marry me . . .' her voice faltered, and she reached for her glass again. She was drinking so fast Alex could hardly keep up with her.

'He was hardly going to let you down, was he?' she said. 'Not Dad.'

'No. He would never let me down.' Shirley's neck was corrugated with tension. 'Joseph is a very decent man. He's hard-working, and a good provider. Your grandfather said I'd do well to marry him, and he was right.'

'Sounds like you didn't have much choice,' Alex remarked.

'No, you're right. I had no choice.'

The faraway look on Shirley's face worried her. 'Mummy, you did want to marry Dad, didn't you? I mean, you did love him?'

'What kind of question is that?' Shirley gave a little laugh and lifted her glass to her lips.

One she didn't want to answer, obviously.

She couldn't remember a time when her mother had shown her father any kind of affection. There was always an air of bitterness and regret around her. And now she knew why. Shirley had been railroaded into a marriage she didn't really want, through circumstances she couldn't control. And for the past thirty years she'd had to live with the consequences.

And what if she ended up like that, married to a man she didn't really love? What if their relationship disintegrated until she could hardly bear to be in the same room as Luke?

If she was having doubts now, what would she be like in thirty years' time?

Luke was away, spending a few days at the London office. Alex was dismayed to find what a relief it was to be without him.

More than ever, she missed Phoebe's presence in the

flat. She wanted her to be there, ready with a listening ear and a shoulder to cry on. She wanted her to put the kettle on, or crack open a bottle of wine, and for them to curl up on the sofa for a good giggle and a gossip. Most of all, she needed Phoebe to help her feel superior. No matter how awful her life seemed, compared to her hopeless kid sister she always felt better.

She called Phoebe's new number at the flat. No one answered, so she tried Bar Barato.

'She's not working tonight,' the snotty bitch who called herself the manager told her.

'Really? I've tried her flat and there's no answer.'

'So? Maybe she's out. She does have a life, you know.'

Alex ignored the jibe. 'If she comes in, could you get her to call me? I wondered if she fancied coming round tonight.'

'I'll mention it, but I happen to know she's busy tonight. She has a *date*.'

Alex put the phone down feeling annoyed, and not just because of the rude cow's attitude. This had never happened to her before. She needed Phoebe, and Phoebe wasn't there. She was out enjoying herself, while Alex was stuck at home feeling bored and resentful.

And she had a new man. Alex felt a stab of jealousy. Once she would have been the first person her sister told, and they would have dissected every detail of her love life together. Alex would have wanted to meet him. She would probably even have flirted with him, just for the hell of it. But now Phoebe was getting on with her life, and Alex obviously wasn't part of it any more.

The phone rang, and she snatched it up. 'Fee?'

'Hi, sweetheart.'

She felt guilty at the way her heart sank on hearing Luke's voice. Of course it was him. He rang this time every evening, like the loving, perfect fiancé he was. 'Hi yourself.'

'Missing me?'

'What do you think?' She tuned out while Luke chatted about his day, making interested noises, her mouth on auto pilot, her mind elsewhere.

Finally she hung up, switched on the answer machine, and made up her mind. If Phoebe could get a life, so could she.

Phoebe rushed from the kitchen and grabbed the phone just as it stopped ringing. Typical. She dialled 1471 and flinched when she heard Alex's number. Thank God she hadn't picked it up. It had been so long since she spoke to her sister she wasn't sure what to say any more.

She replaced the receiver, and flicked off the stray bits of rice that clung to it, then went back to put the finishing touches to Will's birthday supper.

She'd started earlier that day with good intentions, but now it was nearly eight and Will was due home any moment, she was beginning to feel a bit stupid. What if she'd gone over the top? What if Will was embarrassed? What if he thought she had ulterior motives?

She hadn't, of course. All she'd wanted to do was to try and cheer him up after the disappointment of not hearing from Nadine. He'd pretended he didn't care that she hadn't phoned or sent a birthday card, but Phoebe could tell he felt bad about it, and so did she. Hence her spending most of her day off preparing his favourite Thai curry and fragrant rice. It was just a gesture, that was all. She hoped Will wouldn't read anything more into it than that.

'What do you mean you're not going out? It's your birthday, for God's sake!'

'Exactly. It's *my* birthday. And I'd rather spend it at home than getting smashed out of my brain, thanks very much.'

Barry and Tez exchanged glances. 'I suppose Phoebe's got a cosy evening planned?'

Will stiffened. 'Meaning?'

'Meaning you two are spending a lot of time together lately. We hardly ever see you. We thought you two might be becoming a bit of an item, didn't we Tez?'

'I told you, we're just mates.'

'I dunno. Seems to me it's a bit more serious than that. You'll be off to B&Q next, choosing wallpaper.'

'Or arguing over the cereal in Sainsbury's,' Tez put in.

'Has she sent you down to Boots to buy her Tampax yet? They say that's when you know they've really got you pinned down.'

'Sod off.' Will sipped his pint. He was starting to wish he'd never agreed to meet them for an early evening drink. 'Look, just because I don't want to go out drinking every night and watching you two making fools of yourself over women it doesn't mean I've had a personality transplant.'

'If you say so, mate.' Barry looked sceptical. 'So, have you slept with her yet?'

'Oh, for God's sake!'

'I suppose that means no. Never mind, keep trying. I don't suppose she can be that hard to get. I mean, she's no Kylie Minogue, is she?'

'Why don't you just shut your fat face?'

'Ooh, touchy! I can see I've hit a nerve. Sorry to criticise your girlfriend, Will.'

'For the last time, Phoebe is *not* my girlfriend. We're just friends. Can you understand that? Just friends.'

'In that case, why can't you come out with us tonight? I mean, if there's nothing going on between you she's not going to mind, is she? And it is your birthday.'

Will rubbed his forehead. He was beginning to feel trapped. 'That's not the point. I've already promised

Phoebe I'd stay in. I don't want to let her down. What if she's waiting for me?'

'Bloody hell!' Baz wiped his mouth with the back of his hand. 'Look, if you're that worried about it we'll invite Phoebe as well. How about that?'

Will narrowed his eyes. 'I thought you didn't like her?'

'I don't. But if it'll stop you whingeing I reckon I can put up with her.'

'And you won't make nasty remarks to her?'

'I won't even speak to her.'

'Or spike her drinks so she makes a fool of herself?'

'As if!'

Will sent him a sidelong look. As usual, there was something in Barry's smile he didn't trust. 'OK, I'll ring her.'

'No, you get the drinks in. I'll ring her.' Baz pulled out his mobile.

They ended up at The Pitcher and Piano overlooking the Ouse. Barry must have been busy on his mobile because suddenly a whole load of Will's other friends were there, laughing and joking and plying him with drinks. Everyone except Phoebe.

'So what exactly did she say?' he asked.

'I've already told you a hundred times. She said she'd try to make it, but she was going out herself later.'

'But we were supposed to be staying in.'

'I suppose she got a better offer. Look, I told her where we'd be. You never know, she might pop in later. If she doesn't get lucky.' Barry pushed another bottle into his hand. 'So why not forget about her and get in the party mood?'

Will took the beer, his eyes still fixed on the door.

Forget about her, Barry had said. Hell, why not? She'd obviously forgotten about him.

Chapter 20

Alex ordered another glass of Sauvignon Blanc and tried to ignore the barman's speculative look.

This was a mistake, she decided. She'd never been to a bar on her own and she'd picked the wrong night to do it. Apart from the rowdy party going on in the corner, the place was packed with couples, and they all seemed to be looking at her. Either they thought she was on the prowl, or she'd been stood up by her boyfriend. She didn't know which was worse.

She'd picked the wrong thing to wear, too. She tugged her skirt over her thighs. The skimpy slip dress made her feel like a tart.

She wished she had some girlfriends to meet up with. It came as a shock to realise that, apart from Phoebe, she didn't have any close friends. She'd even thought about ringing Nigel from Fleming Associates, but her pride wouldn't let her admit she was that desperate.

'Excuse me, is this seat free?'

She sized up the man who'd approached her. Not bad-looking, medium height, medium build, medium every-thing. Normally she wouldn't have given him a second glance but tonight was his lucky night. 'Help yourself.'

'Thanks.' He picked up the stool and carried it to the other end of the bar, where his girlfriend was waiting. Alex saw the quick smile of malice on the other woman's face and a hot blush flooded her face.

She turned away, and found herself confronted by a fat ginger man. 'Miss Redmond?'

'I'm sorry, do I know you?'

'I'm Barry, remember? Barry Orton? Fraser and Duncan. The estate agents?'

She caught a whiff of his aftershave and it all came back to her. 'Oh God, yes of course. Have you found a buyer?'

'Not yet. But I'm giving it my personal attention. Your fiancé not around tonight?' He scanned the bar.

'He's away. I was supposed to be meeting some friends, but they're late,' she lied.

'Why don't you join us while you wait for them? It's my mate's birthday and we're having a few drinks.'

Alex looked over. 'Which one's the birthday boy?'

'Over there, in the corner.'

'He doesn't look too happy.'

'Woman trouble. In fact, you're not going to believe this, but—' he stopped. 'Forget it, it doesn't matter. Come on, I'll introduce you. Perhaps you can make him join in with the rest of us, instead of sulking by himself in the corner.'

I can't believe I'm doing this, she thought, as she followed Barry across the bar. How low had she sunk, that even a fat, ginger estate agent could rescue her from social embarrassment?

It was only for a minute, she promised herself. Just until she finished her drink. Then she'd be out of there. And if his friend turned out to be an estate agent as well, she wouldn't even bother to sit down.

As she got closer she saw that Barry's friend was rather a dish. He was tall, dark and angular. He was also more than slightly drunk. He sat at a corner table, shredding a beermat between his long, narrow fingers, ignoring the party going on around the next table.

'This is Will. Will, this is—'

'Alexandra.'

'Hi.' He didn't even look up.

'I said she could join the party. You don't mind, do you?'

'Suit yourself.'

'You'll have to excuse my friend. He has the social skills of a leper with agoraphobia.' Barry plonked himself down at the table and pulled out a chair for her.

Alex studied Will. He wasn't exactly good-looking but he was very sexy. He had the most incredible sleepy eyes, a full, turned-down mouth and his dark hair hung untidily in his eyes. He looked as if he'd fallen out of bed and thrown on his rumpled jeans and sweater in the dark. Alex, who usually liked her men perfectly coiffed and straight out of Armani, was utterly fascinated.

She slipped off her engagement ring and slid it into her bag.

'I hear it's your birthday. Many happy returns.'

'Thanks.'

She tried again. 'Are you an estate agent too?'

'Do I look like one?'

'No.'

'Good.'

'They wouldn't have him,' Barry said. Alex ignored him.

'So what do you do?' she asked.

'He draws pictures.' Barry pounced again. 'Pictures in kids' books. What kind of job is that for a grown man?'

'I could tell that, actually. You have an artist's hands.'

Will didn't react. Alex gazed at him, intrigued. She wondered who this woman was who'd stood him up. Whoever she was, she must be mad.

Barry made all the conversational running from then on. Alex answered him, but her attention was fixed on Will. She'd never met anyone like him before. Normally men fell over themselves to chat her up. Barry was certainly heading that way, edging his chair closer, thinking she hadn't noticed. To have a man ignoring her was a new and oddly exciting experience. She liked a challenge, and Will's indifference was totally compelling.

'Maybe this wasn't such a good idea?' Barry's breath was hot against her ear. 'Maybe we should just slope off to the bar and leave him to it?'

'No! I mean, we can't just leave him like this.'

'Why not? He's being a prat.'

'But it's his birthday. Why don't you get some more drinks in?' She batted her lashes at him, which was enough to send him scurrying to the bar.

'It's OK, you don't have to stay for my sake,' Will said, when he'd gone.

'I'm not.'

Silence. Alex tried again. 'Have we met before?'

'I don't think so. Why?'

'I just wondered. Only I seem to have upset you. I suppose it must have been in a past life or something.'

He almost smiled. 'Sorry. I've just got things on my mind.'

'Girlfriend trouble?'

He looked up sharply. 'What's Baz been saying?'

'Nothing. I just guessed.'

'I seem to spend my whole life waiting for women who want to be somewhere else.'

'I'm here. And I don't want to be anywhere else.'

Their eyes met and she felt a white hot jolt of lust go right through her. Then Barry came back.

'I see William's been keeping you amused.' He put the glasses down on the table. 'He's a laugh a minute, isn't he?'

Alex looked at Will. She felt sure he must have felt it too, but his eyes gave nothing away. 'He's very – enigmatic.'

Barry guffawed. 'That's one way of putting it!'

It was a long evening. Alex tried to flirt with him, with little response. Will seemed more interested in drinking himself into oblivion.

'Shouldn't we do something about him?' she whispered to Barry.

'No, leave him to it. If he wants to wallow in self-pity that's his business.' He leaned over and slid his hand on to her leg. 'But if you're fed up with him, we could always go somewhere by ourselves?'

Alex gritted her teeth. 'Why don't you get me another drink and I'll think about it?'

As soon as he'd shuffled off, she turned to Will and said, 'You wouldn't like to rescue me, would you?'

'Why? Don't you like Baz?'

'Are you kidding? Look, you're obviously not enjoying this party, and neither am I. So why don't we both go somewhere else?'

For a moment she thought he was going to refuse. Then, suddenly he pushed back his chair and stood up. 'Come on, then.'

They didn't stop running until they'd reached the far end of Coney Street. Alex collapsed, fighting for breath and clutching her ribs, against Waterstones' window. 'Where to now?'

'I don't know about you, but I'm going home.'

'You can't! I mean, why do you want to go home to an empty flat?'

His eyes narrowed. 'Who said it would be empty?'

'Just a guess. You don't act like a man who's got someone waiting for him at home.' She saw the defeated slump of his shoulders and knew she was right. 'Why don't you come back to my place? It's just round the corner.'

It felt strange, having another man in the flat. Alex showed him into the sitting room and then dashed off to the bedroom. She redid her make-up and spritzed herself with a generous dose of Obsession. Then, on impulse, she gathered up all the books, toiletries and clothes Luke had left lying around and threw them all into the wardrobe. Just in case.

Will was slumped on the sofa when she came back in

with a bottle of wine. He squinted up at her, then at the bottle. 'I think I need to sober up.'

'I don't.' He didn't argue. She poured him a glass and curled up beside him on the sofa.

'Do you live here on your own?' he asked. Alex glanced around, panicking that there might be something of Luke's lying around.

'I don't have a boyfriend, if that's what you mean.' It was practically true. Fiancés weren't the same thing, were they? 'What about you? Do you live with anyone?'

His brooding expression was back. 'I share a flat. We don't live together.'

'Was that the girl you were waiting for this evening?'

'I wasn't waiting for her. I didn't expect her to come. It's not like that with her.'

'But maybe you'd like it to be?'

'No! Bloody hell, why does everyone keep going on about it all the time?' He knocked his wine back and reached for the bottle.

Oops, she'd obviously touched a nerve there. But if this flatmate wasn't interested it was good news for her.

Alex did most of the talking, although Will relaxed slightly as they worked their way through the wine. He was funny and interesting, but she was more interested in his wonderful mouth and how she could get him to kiss her.

She could feel the moment wouldn't be far off, and she tingled with anticipation like a teenager. She'd never felt so turned on.

And then, just when she thought she was getting somewhere, he put down his glass and said, 'I'd better go.'

'You don't have to. You could stay the night?'

What was she doing? She'd never propositioned a man in her life. She'd never had to. But she knew Will wasn't going to make the first move. She also knew that if she didn't get him into bed she'd explode with frustration.

He stared at her for a minute. Then he shook his head. 'Not a good idea. My life's complicated enough.'

'Who said anything about it being complicated? It seems simple to me. I want you, and you want me. You do want me, don't you?'

He said nothing. Taking the initiative, Alex pressed herself against him and kissed him. Very gently, their lips barely touching, but it was enough. She pulled back and felt a surge of triumph at the spark of desire in his eyes.

'Call it a birthday present,' she said softly. 'Or you could just go back to that empty flat of yours?'

His hand closed around the back of her neck, pulling her back. His kiss, fierce and meltingly erotic at the same time, tasted of red wine. There was something else going on – revenge, spite, sheer lust – she didn't know what. But whatever it was, she meant to make the most of it.

She took his hand and, without a word, led him to the bedroom.

In the morning he was gone. Just like that. No note, no phone number, nothing. At first she couldn't believe it when she found the bed empty. She got up and wandered around the flat, convinced she was going to find him taking a shower, or making coffee. But all that remained were last night's wine glasses, side by side on the coffee table, mocking her.

'Bastard!' She picked one up and aimed it at the wall. How could he do this to her? OK, a one night stand might have been what she had in mind at first, but now? Now she wasn't at all sure that was what she wanted.

Chapter 21

Phoebe scraped the last of the leftovers into the bin. It went against her nature to waste food, but she was too embarrassed to let Will see the trouble she'd gone to.

That wasn't how she'd felt last night, when she'd left the dishes piled up in the sink. She'd half hoped Will might have seen them when he came home and been overcome with guilty remorse. But from the way he'd crashed about when he came in around dawn he probably hadn't even noticed.

She knew she had no right to feel angry, or disappointed. After all, she had no claim on Will. And he wasn't to know she'd spent the whole afternoon slaving over a hot stove. He hadn't asked her to. The only one she should be angry with was herself, for trying to make a casual arrangement more than it really was.

Her bitter disappointment worried her. Maybe it was a good thing Will hadn't shown up last night? The way she was feeling, she could have ended up making an even bigger fool of herself.

The doorbell rang. Phoebe glanced at her watch. Just after ten. A bit early for visitors, although with Will's friends you could never tell.

It rang again. She waited for Will to stir himself and answer it, but he was still comatose. In the end she went herself.

'Where the fuck is he?' Barry barged past her, looking furious.

'Baz! How lovely to see you.' Phoebe flinched as Will's bedroom door slammed.

She went back into the kitchen and tried not to listen, but it was impossible. Baz's voice carried round the flat like the mating cry of a frustrated elk.

'You bastard! Call yourself a fucking mate?' She couldn't hear Will's reply, but he must have said something because next thing Barry was yelling, 'Calm down? CALM DOWN? How do you expect me to be calm after you walked off with my bird? No, you leave Patti out of this, it's nothing to do with her. This is about you sleeping with that girl!'

Phoebe ran the taps full blast, trying to drown out his voice. But it was no use.

'What do you mean, she wasn't interested in me? Of course she was interested! Or she was until you stuck your oar in. I suppose you told her about Patti, did you? Or did you just give her the usual old sob story about poor broken-hearted Will, pining away for his fiancée and desperate to be loved? You just can't handle it, can you? Just because your love life's fucked up, you want to ruin it for the rest of us! You're such a loser, Will Hutchinson. No wonder Nadine left you. Well, from now on you're on your own! LOSER!'

Phoebe jumped as the bedroom door slammed again. She came out of the kitchen, and was nearly knocked off her feet by Barry the bulldozer.

When he saw her his face contorted with rage. 'And you can tell your sister I'm knocking two thousand off the asking price of her flat!' he shouted, then stormed out.

Phoebe stared at the door. What the hell was all that about?

She was up to her elbows in hot soapy water when Will staggered into the kitchen half an hour later. He was wearing jeans and no shirt, and judging from the deep shadows under his eyes, he hadn't had a lot of sleep.

'Morning.' She steeled herself to smile at him. 'The kettle's just boiled, if you want some tea?'

'Thanks.' He sat down at the table and buried his face in his hands. As Phoebe put the mug down in front of him she noticed a scratch down his shoulder. The kind that came from long fingernails.

She averted her eyes. Don't say anything, she warned herself. It's none of your business. Don't say a single word.

But her mouth was already open. 'Barry sounded upset.'

'You heard?' Will groaned. 'It was just a mis-understanding. I got drunk and did something stupid, that's all.'

Phoebe was alarmed at the quick stab of jealousy she felt.

'Anyway, what happened to you last night?' he asked.

'Sorry?'

'My party. What was so important that you couldn't make it?'

'I didn't even know you were having a party.'

'But Baz phoned you. And you told him you couldn't come because—' A look of sick realisation crossed his face. 'He didn't phone you, did he?'

'No one phoned. I was in all evening.' God, how sad did that make her sound?

'So you were here, waiting for me?' Not quite as sad as that, obviously. 'Phoebe, I'm really sorry. I had no idea, otherwise I would have come home.' He rubbed his hand through his hair, making it stick up. 'Jesus, what a mess. I hope you didn't go to any trouble? Make some-thing special, or anything like that?'

'No!' Phoebe's laugh came out as a squawk. 'Abso-lutely not. The thought never crossed my mind. If you had come home, it probably would have been cheese on toast. If I could even be bothered to put the grill on, ha ha.' She stopped, aware that he was staring at her.

'All right, steady on. You've made your point. Is there any tea left in that pot?'

As she poured another cup, Phoebe thought of the half ton of Thai curry festering in the bin. She had to get rid of it fast. 'I'll – um – just put the rubbish out.'

Will stood up. 'I'll do it.'

'No, you sit there. I'll do it.'

'It's the least I can do, after last night.'

'But it's my rubbish!'

There was a tussle over the bin bag, which then split, disgorging itself and the Thai curry all over the ceramic tiles.

For a second neither of them spoke. Then Will said, very quietly, 'What do you call this?'

'Leftovers?' Phoebe bit her lip.

'Was this meant for me? Shit, Phoebe, I thought you said you hadn't gone to any trouble? Now I feel really awful.'

'It's OK, honestly.' She turned away to search for a floorcloth in the cupboard under the sink. It gave her an excuse not to smile for a second. Her face muscles were aching.

'But you did all this, and I didn't turn up. What must you have thought of me?'

'It was a silly idea anyway.'

'No, it wasn't. It was a lovely idea.' She emerged from under the sink to find him crouching next to her. 'I've really blown it, haven't I? But I'll make it up to you, I promise.'

'You don't have to.'

'I want to.' Their eyes met and held. He reached out – and took the cloth out of her hands. 'I'll clear this mess up. It's the least I can do.'

She went to work at lunchtime and tried to put Will out of her mind. It wasn't too difficult. Titus was having a rare day off and they were so busy coping with the Sunday lunch crowd she didn't have time to think about anything but the next order.

She rushed backwards and forwards, plucking orders off the computer, calling out instructions and geeing up the kitchen staff who seemed to be taking advantage of Titus' absence to start a go-slow.

She was trying to sort out an order for two fresh tagliatelle with porcini and a veal escalope that had somehow been overlooked when Karen appeared and said, 'You've got to come and see this.'

Phoebe wiped away a trickle of perspiration from under her cap. 'If it's another bloke with a dodgy toupee, I don't have time.'

'Just come and have a look. Please!'

Sighing, Phoebe followed her. 'So what is it that's so urgent—' she stopped. There, in the doorway to the restaurant, were five bright helium balloons. Attached to the other end of them was a small boy, his chin out.

He looked straight at her. 'The man said I had to give these to Phoebe.'

'What man?'

'The one outside.' Phoebe looked up. There, with his nose pressed against the glass, was Will. 'He gave me 50p. He said I'd get a pound if I spelt the word right. I did, didn't I?'

Phoebe looked at the balloons. 'SRORY'. 'Close enough,' she said.

The boy handed over the balloons and went away, looking pleased with himself.

'Oh, my God.' There was a catch in Karen's voice. 'It's just like that bit in *An Officer and a Gentleman*, where Richard Gere turns up and sweeps Debra Winger off her feet in front of everyone. Do you think he'll do that to you?'

'Not unless he wants a hernia.' Phoebe watched Will as he made his way between the tables towards her. The whole restaurant had fallen silent.

'I told you I'd try and make it up to you.' He smiled sheepishly. 'You're not annoyed, are you?'

'Well . . .'

'Course she isn't. She thinks it's a wonderful gesture. Don't you, Fee?' Karen nudged her.

'I thought maybe I could take you to lunch. I booked a table at The Grange?'

'I—'

'She'd love to,' said Karen.

'I'm working.' Phoebe glared at her.

'We can manage.'

'But we're understaffed as it is.'

'I told you, we'll *manage*.' Karen was flashing neon messages with her eyes.

'But—'

'Excuse us a moment, would you?' Karen beamed at Will, then grabbed Phoebe's arm and pulled her aside. 'For God's sake, woman, what are you thinking? The guy's just made a wildly romantic gesture. More to the point, he's just asked you out. How many times do either of those things happen to you?'

They both looked around. Will was leaning against the bar, studying his shoes.

'You can't let this chance go,' Karen's grip tightened. 'You'll make him feel a complete idiot. Plus you'll regret it.'

As Phoebe looked at him again, he suddenly caught her eye and smiled. Karen was probably right, she thought. But then if she went, would she regret that, too?

She went over to him. 'Look, it was a lovely thought,

but I really can't. We're run off our feet in the kitchen. I can't leave the others in the lurch.'

'I understand.' Will's smile took on a fixed look. 'Um – some other time, maybe?'

'I'd love to.'

'OK. Fine. So I'll see you later, shall I?' He was backing away, reversing into tables and customers. 'Unless . . .'

Phoebe's heart, which had been sinking into her trainers, leapt again. 'What?'

'Maybe I could stay and help you?'

'What, you mean in the kitchen?'

'Why not? I could wash up, or peel potatoes or something.'

'Why would you want to do that? It's hard work. And it's not exactly fun.' She thought for a moment, then shook her head. 'No, I couldn't ask you to do that.'

'You're not asking, I'm offering. Call it a penance.'

Suddenly it seemed as if the whole restaurant was holding its breath, waiting for her answer. She could feel Karen's eyes burning a hole between her shoulder blades. It was a wonder her apron hadn't caught fire.

'Well, OK then. If you're sure?'

A sigh of satisfaction rippled around the room. Will grinned. 'Where do I start?'

He didn't seem remotely fazed by the huge piles of dishes needing to be scraped and rinsed before being loaded into the dishwashers. Thanks to his Spanish GCSE, he even managed to communicate with the Andalusian kitchen porter no one else had ever spoken to. By the end of the shift Luis, as he was apparently called, was inviting Will round to his house for tapas.

Phoebe was so busy she barely had a chance to speak to him, apart from a quick ten-minute ciggie break out by the bins. The first time they really talked was when he joined them for the usual staff lunch after the restaurant had closed, although he looked askance at the collection of food they were digging into.

'It's not exactly The Grange, is it?'

'It's whatever's left after the customers have gone home,' Phoebe explained. 'You're lucky. Once Titus over-ordered a whole load of monkfish, thinking it would be a good special. We were eating monkfish fricassee for nearly two weeks. Sorry,' she added. 'Today's been a bit of a disaster, hasn't it?'

'No way. I've always wanted to try – let's see – seafood angel hair pasta with a side order of lamb ragout.' There was a pause, and then he said, 'I went round to see Barry, by the way. To have it out with him about not phoning you.'

'And?'

'And he admitted he didn't. Another one of his stupid pranks, apparently.'

'I really don't know why you put up with him.'

'Neither do I. I suppose it's just because we've been friends for ever and he can be quite a decent guy when he wants to be.'

He put down his fork and laid his hand across her wrist. 'I'm really sorry, Phoebe. You're the last person I'd ever want to hurt.'

The scraping of cutlery against china stopped for a second, and suddenly it seemed as if everyone around the table was looking at them. Will was aware of it too. He took his hand away, picked up his fork and went on eating, his head down.

Later, as they were leaving, Karen pulled her to one side. 'I'd look after that one if I were you. Boyfriends like that don't grow on trees.'

'He's not my boyfriend. I've told you, he's just a friend.'

'Are you serious?' Karen rolled her eyes. 'Bloody hell. He spends three hours washing dishes and you tell me he's not in love with you. Either you're stupid or he is!'

It was a warm, sunny July afternoon, and the streets of the city were crammed with day trippers. Phoebe realised she was in no hurry for the day to end.

'Why don't we walk home along the river?' she suggested. 'It's not so crowded, and if you're good I'll even treat you to an ice cream in Museum Gardens.'

Will looked awkward. 'Actually, I promised I'd go and pick up my birthday present from my Aunt Gina. You can come if you like?'

Phoebe hesitated. She might not want the day to end, but she didn't want to hang around where she wasn't wanted either. 'No, it's OK. I'll go home.'

'Go on. Gina wouldn't mind. In fact, she'd love it. I've told her all about you.'

Me? Why? Phoebe wanted to ask, but Will had already taken her arm and was heading towards Skelder-gate Bridge.

Will's aunt lived in a Victorian terraced house just off Nunnery Lane. From what Will had told her about his idyllic childhood, Phoebe expected a plump mother-hen type with child-bearing hips and permanently floury hands from all the baking she did. So it was a shock when a tiny woman in black leggings and a Greenpeace T-shirt opened the door and said, 'Sorry, have you been standing there long? I've been out in the back, practising my tai chi.'

'We've just arrived. This is Phoebe, my flatmate.' Will nudged her forward.

'So you're Phoebe, are you?' Gina looked her up and down. She was in her mid-fifties with cropped grey hair and shrewdly assessing dark eyes. 'I was hoping Will would bring you round. Are you hungry?' She led the way down the narrow passageway to the kitchen. The house wasn't quite what Phoebe had expected either. Bold modern paintings, some of them Will's work, covered the walls, which were dotted with patches of different colours where someone had tried out a few matchpots and then got bored with the whole idea of decorating. Bright rugs covered the unpolished floorboards. 'I forgot to go to the supermarket again, I'm afraid. But I can make you a sandwich, if you like?'

'It's OK, we've already eaten. Sort of.' Will and Phoebe exchanged looks. 'I've been helping Phoebe out at the restaurant this afternoon.'

'You're kidding? You, make yourself useful in the kitchen? It must be serious.'

Gina lifted a pile of political science textbooks off one of the kitchen chairs for Phoebe to sit down.

'Been studying?' Will asked, ignoring her last remark.

'Trying to. But you know me, I keep getting distracted. There was a good arts programme on Radio 4.'

Phoebe looked around the kitchen. It was gloriously cluttered, warm and inviting. The mismatched assortment of china on the old Welsh dresser was almost hidden behind piles of letters, family photos and old copies of the *Guardian*. A fat ginger cat dozed by the Aga. The whole room was filled with the rich fragrance of cardamon and turmeric. Gina was obviously a dab hand with a Madras.

It was the kind of room Phoebe had always dreamed of having herself, a complete contrast to her own mother's joyless, interior designed kitchen, with everything ruthlessly in its place.

But then Gina was nothing like her mother, either. She could hardly imagine Shirley cracking open a bottle of Chianti, or drinking so much of it herself as Gina did later on in the garden, laughing and joking with her guests. It would be a sweet sherry in the lounge if they were lucky, a bone china thimble of tea and a resentful silence if they weren't.

As they soaked up the last of the sun's early evening rays, Phoebe listened to Gina and Will talking about her studies. At the age of fifty, Gina had decided to go back to college to catch up with her education. Five years later, she was in the middle of a political science degree. 'Something I should have done years ago, if I hadn't been such a silly beggar and got pregnant at seventeen,' she said.

She was vivid, full of life, and interested in everything around her. She made Phoebe laugh telling her how her husband had run off with the next door neighbour when Gina was pregnant with her third child.

'She borrowed my electric mixer and my husband and I never saw either of them again,' she declared.

'How awful!'

'I know. That mixer was brand new.' She cackled and poured herself another glass of wine.

While they were talking, Will drifted off to sleep on the lounger. 'Look at him, you've worn him out,' Gina said. 'He hasn't done a real day's work since he left art school.' She turned her sharp gaze round to Phoebe. 'So you're a chef, are you? That's odd. I thought all Will's girlfriends were actresses or models.'

Was she making fun of her? 'Well, I'm neither. And I'm not his girlfriend, either.'

'Really?'

'We share a flat, not a bed.' If Gina could be direct, so could she.

'I see. And does that mean you don't want to?'

Phoebe met her bold stare. 'I don't think that's any of your business.'

A glint of respect came into Gina's eyes. 'You're absolutely right, of course. It's because I don't have any love life of my own, I have to pry into other people's.' She glanced over at the lounger. 'But I do worry about Will. He's a nice lad, but an idiot when it comes to women. I suppose he's told you about Nadine?' Phoebe nodded. 'God knows how those two ever got together. I've never met anyone so totally up themselves. Everything had to be her way. And Will, bless him, was so besotted he just went along with everything she wanted.' She gazed fondly at Will. 'I mean, look at him, waiting for her to come back to him. I just hope she does him a favour and stays in America or wherever it is she's ended up. I could have told him she'd break his heart, but would he listen?'

'You can't control who people fall in love with.'

'Sounds as if you're speaking from experience?'

Phoebe thought about telling her to mind her own business again, then changed her mind. 'A bit. There was – is – someone. But he's in love with someone else.' She waited for the pang of misery. It took longer to come this time.

'I'm sorry.' Gina refilled her glass. 'But as you say, you can't control who other people fall in love with. You have to let them make their own mistakes, don't you? Which is probably why I've brought up four boys and none of them have managed to give me any grandchildren. They just keep falling for the wrong women, you see.' She smiled. 'Not that I'm in any hurry to be a grandma. I couldn't imagine myself knitting them their first bootees, could you?'

'You'd be more likely to take them down to the pub for their first pint.'

They both swung round. Will had opened one eye. 'Have you been listening to everything we've said?' Gina looked outraged.

'Enough.'

'Yes, well, you know what they say. Eavesdroppers hear no good of themselves.' She stood up and collected up the glasses. 'Now, who's for another bottle of wine?'

They were having such a good time they ended up staying far longer than they'd planned. Three hours and two bottles of wine later, they weaved their way un-steadily home down the river path. It was a warm, bright evening, and tourists lingered outside the cafés and bars all the way along the Ouse.

'So what did you think of Gina?' Will asked.

'She's quite a character.'

'I know what you mean. I should have warned you, she can be a bit intimidating. I hope she didn't give you too hard a time?'

'She was fine. I liked her.' She meant it. They'd had a couple of prickly moments, but Phoebe had proved she couldn't be bullied, and in the end they'd got on well.

'I'm glad. She liked you too, believe it or not.' He stopped to skim a stone across the dark water with great concentration, but Phoebe sensed he had something else on his mind.

Finally he said, 'She can be a nosey old bag, but she's right about one thing. It's time I forgot about Nadine and got on with my life.'

Phoebe looked at him sharply. 'How did you know she said that?'

'You didn't really think I was asleep, did you? With you two gabbling on?'

He sent another stone skittering across the still surface of the water. Phoebe wondered apprehensively what else he'd heard. She couldn't remember what she'd said to Gina. She just hoped it wasn't anything too embarrassing.

'I suppose I realised yesterday when she didn't call to wish me a happy birthday. She doesn't care. She probably didn't even remember.' His voice was bitter. 'I've just been fooling myself all this time, haven't I? Nadine won't be coming home. She's making a new life for herself over there, and I'm not part of it. The sooner I accept that, the sooner we can all get on with our lives.'

'And do you think you can do that?'

'I don't know. I wouldn't have said so, but something

happened last night that made me wonder.' He hesitated. Phoebe fixed her eyes on a red and white pleasure boat drifting past. She wished she was on it. She didn't want to hear what was coming next. 'Last night, after that party, I slept with someone. It didn't really mean anything – we were both a bit pissed at the time – but it proved something to me. It proved I could want someone else.' He looked across at her. 'I think I'm ready for another relationship.'

'So a one night stand changed your life?' She hated the bitterness in her voice. She couldn't understand why she didn't feel more pleased for him.

'And you.'

'Me?'

'You've been so great, listening to me droning on about Nadine all the time. I must have been a pain at times, but you've really helped me put everything in perspective. You're a good friend, Phoebe.'

He put his arms round her. It was the first close contact she'd had with a man since Luke, and it made her feel slightly dizzy.

She pulled away and started off down the path again. Will hurried after her. 'Are you OK? Was it something I said?'

'It's nothing.' She walked on, her head down. Will caught up with her and grabbed her arm, turning her to face him.

'I know what it is,' he said. 'It's Luke, isn't it?'

'What?'

'Oh God, Phoebe, I'm sorry. Here am I, rattling on about my miraculous return to the land of the living, and you're still not over him. But it'll happen, you know. Just give it time.'

They walked on in silence. Maybe he was right, Phoebe thought. Maybe that was why she felt the way she did. She was jealous because he was getting on with his life and she was stuck still in a rut, loving Luke. Misery loves company, and all that.

Or maybe there was something else? Something she'd felt when he took her in his arms just then.

Typical, she thought. Why did she have to discover feelings for Will Hutchinson just when he'd discovered other women?

Chapter 22

Alex stood outside the wedding dress shop and looked at her watch for the third time. Phoebe was nearly twenty minutes late. Alex, who'd deliberately set out to be ten minutes late herself, was deeply annoyed.

Maybe she wasn't going to turn up? The only time they'd clapped eyes on each other since the night of the big argument was when Phoebe had come round to collect the rest of her things. Alex's stomach was dancing with apprehension so heaven only knew what Phoebe must be feeling.

She'd put off phoning her for as long as she could, half hoping Phoebe would cave in and call her first. But with just six weeks to go before the wedding, she had to buy the bridesmaid's dress before her mother nagged her to insanity.

She was just about to give up and go home when she spotted her sister hurrying down the road towards her. When Phoebe caught Alex's eye she slowed down and for a moment she looked as if she might make a run for it. Then she straightened her shoulders and pushed herself forward.

'Sorry I'm late, I couldn't find anything to wear.'

Alex looked down at her sister's jeans, baggy T-shirt and trainers. It looked pretty much the same as she always wore. 'It's OK, I haven't been here long myself.'

They stood looking at each other. For once, Alex was at a loss. It was Phoebe who spoke first. 'So – shall we get this over with?'

'We don't have to go in straight away. Maybe we could have a coffee first and catch up with all our news?'

Phoebe looked reluctant. 'If that's what you want.'

Alex was looking forward to a giggly gossip, just like old times. But as they sat in Coffee Republic, nursing their cappuccinos and making small talk, she realised it was never going to be like that again.

There was so much Alex wanted to say, so much she wanted to explain, but she didn't know how to start. Time had opened up too much space between them, turned them into polite strangers.

And Phoebe wasn't helping. She stared out of the window, her chin cupped in her hand, as if she longed to be anywhere else. Alex felt irritated. She used to be able to claim all her sister's attention. Phoebe might be scolding her, or infuriated with her, or laughing at something outrageous she'd done, but at least she'd be listening to her.

Perhaps it was true what that bar manager had said on the phone? Maybe Phoebe did have a new life, and a new man? Maybe she didn't envy Alex for having Luke any more?

'So, how are you?' She put down her cup and made a brisk stab at conversation. 'How's work?'

'Oh, you know. Same as usual.'

Actually, she didn't know. She'd never taken that much interest in her sister's job. 'And what about your new flat? What's your flatmate like? Not as untidy as me, I bet.'

'He's OK.' Phoebe toyed with a spoon. Alex noticed the blush creeping up her throat.

'The flat seems really empty without you. I've missed you.' She waited for Phoebe to say she'd missed her too, but she didn't. 'Although I've been really busy lately, what with all the wedding plans and everything.'

She expected Phoebe to flinch. But all she said was, 'You must be very excited.'

Must I? Alex thought. She desperately wanted to tell

Phoebe how she really felt. She wanted to tell her about the sleepless nights, the sick feeling every time she thought about the wedding, the nagging worry that she was about to make the biggest mistake of her life.

The fact that she'd been so attracted to Will only confirmed her worst fears.

Over a month after they'd spent the night together, she still couldn't stop thinking about him. She kept telling herself that Will knew where she lived, if he wanted to find her.

But the fact that he hadn't, that he obviously didn't want to see her again, only fascinated her more. She didn't know if she was in love with him, or just piqued that she couldn't have him. But she knew she hadn't been so turned on by anyone in a long time.

'Actually . . .' She looked at Phoebe's blank face. 'Yes, I am. Very excited.'

'Great.'

'And I want you to know, I don't bear a grudge. About what you did.'

Phoebe looked embarrassed. 'Oh! Oh, right. Thanks.'

'It wasn't all your fault, I know that now. I was partly to blame. I neglected Luke, so he slept with you to punish me. That's more or less what he said, anyway.'

'Did he?'

Alex nodded. 'Anyway, I really should be thanking you. If you and he hadn't – you know – our relationship might have fizzled out. But now it's stronger than ever. Phoebe? Phoebe, are you listening to me?'

She looked up vaguely. 'Sorry? What?'

'I said Luke and I are closer than we've ever been.'

She studied Phoebe's face, watching for a reaction. A falter in her smile, a flicker in her eyes, anything to say the barb had hit home. But she just looked – bewildered. Almost as if she'd forgotten the whole incident.

'I'm glad,' she said, and even looked as if she meant it.

Was it really Phoebe sitting there? Or had she been abducted by aliens and replaced by a clone?

Surely it couldn't be that her sister was really over Luke?

She decided to make her try on some truly hideous bridesmaid's dresses. Put her in a few acres of pistachio satin and see if that didn't get a reaction. But Phoebe seemed to be in a trance. Even when Alex made her try on a turquoise taffeta creation with a huge shiny bow that made her bottom look like a battleship, she just nodded and smiled and agreed that yes, it was the loveliest thing she'd ever seen.

'Fine. We'll take that one, shall we?' Even the assistant looked dismayed when Alex pulled out her credit card.

'Are you sure you wouldn't like to see something else?' she pleaded. 'We do have others—'

'No, that's perfect.' Alex narrowed her eyes. And she'd make her wear a matching bow in her hair. That and a kitschy little basket of flowers.

'You mean, you actually want – that – at your wedding?'

Alex stopped short. She hadn't thought of that. In the back of her mind, it wasn't really her wedding she was planning. It was the only way she could get through all the endless arrangements, by telling herself someone else would be walking up that aisle on the big day.

They parted outside the shop. Alex was about to suggest they met up for a drink or a meal later in the week, but Phoebe was already rushing off, muttering some excuse about having a lot of prep to do in the kitchen before opening time.

She watched her sister disappear into the late afternoon crowds. She didn't look back and wave as she usually did. In fact, she didn't look back at all.

Phoebe wasn't due at work for another hour, so she called in at Karen's flat on the way to show her the dress.

The look on Karen's face confirmed her worst fears. She gazed at it for a long time, then at Phoebe. 'Bloody hell, she really does hate you, doesn't she?'

'Is it that bad?' Phoebe held it up against her. She'd hardly noticed, she'd been so preoccupied in the shop.

'Put it this way. No sane woman would be seen dead in it. I mean it, Fee. You can't wear it. You'll be a laughing stock.' A look of understanding crossed her face. 'I know what this is. It's a kind of penance, isn't it? For you and Luke? I don't know why you don't just go the whole hog and wear sackcloth and ashes. It's got to be more flattering than that thing.'

Phoebe looked at her reflection. God, it really was awful, she could see that now. But at the time she was so desperate to escape she would have agreed to a Mr Blobby suit just to get out of the shop.

'Oh, well, what does it matter? I'm going to feel like an idiot anyway, I might as well be dressed like one.'

Karen sighed. 'What's wrong with you? Apart from The Dress From Hell, that is?'

'Oh, I don't know. Everything, I suppose. Seeing Alex again today just made me feel so . . .'

'Jealous? Furious? Like punching her teeth down her throat?'

'Envious. Not because she's got Luke – I know he and I weren't meant to be – but just because she seems so happy. She's got everything she wants. I don't begrudge her any of it, I just wish I could be the same.'

'I think it's about time you stopped comparing yourself to her.'

'I can't help it, can I? And neither will anyone else when we walk down the aisle on her wedding day. They'll all be thinking there's Alex, looking radiant, about to marry the man she loves. And there's fat, frumpy Phoebe. What a loser!' She stared at her reflection in the mirror, then flung the dress aside. Even without it, she still felt ugly.

'Now, you listen to me, Phoebe Redmond.' Karen squared up to her, hands on hips. 'You're not fat or frumpy, and you're certainly not a loser. And tomorrow I'm going to prove it to you. We're going to Leeds to do some shopping.'

'But I hate shopping!'

'That's because you don't do it right. Trust me, I know. You're looking at the North of England shopping champion.' Karen grinned. 'You need a new image, something to boost your self-esteem. I'll help you find something sensational.'

Phoebe eyed her friend's lycra mini skirt and scarlet fishnets, finished off with a pair of hefty biker boots. It was the kind of thing she always wore when she wasn't in her sleek restaurant manager's uniform of white shirt and black trousers. 'That's what I'm afraid of,' she said.

Frankly she couldn't think of anything less likely to boost her esteem than seeing her faults in endless changing-room mirrors. But Karen seemed so excited she didn't like to dampen her enthusiasm.

'You know what I'd really like?' she said. 'I'd like to walk into that wedding with a man. Someone really special. Maybe I wouldn't feel so bad then.'

'Why don't you ask your cute flatmate?'

'No!' Phoebe stuffed the dress back into the bag. 'Anyway, he couldn't come. He's otherwise engaged, remember?'

'Well, I don't like to say I told you so. But I do recall advising you to hang on to him.'

'And I recall telling you there was nothing going on between us. And there isn't going to be, either. Not now he's got Minty.'

Minty, the feng shui consultant. Minty, who filled the house with essential oils and whale music, and who wouldn't even cross the road without consulting her tarot adviser. Minty, who made Nadine look like Lily Savage.

When Will said he was getting on with his life, she hadn't really expected him to start getting on with it so quickly. But he and Minty had been going out together for almost a month now. Four long weeks of healing crystals and wholefoods and not being able to see the TV for her practising her yoga.

'She's virtually moved in,' she grumbled. 'I don't think I can stand much more of it.'

'What does Will say?'

'Oh, he won't hear a word said against her. He thinks she's wonderful.' Phoebe looked bitter. She'd taken to sleeping with her Walkman on to drown out the sound of tantric sex.

'It sounds as if you might be a teeny bit jealous.'

'Jealous? Of her? Don't make me laugh! She just annoys me, that's all.' Since Minty arrived, everything had changed. And not just the arrangement of the furniture, although she'd made a huge fuss about moving the TV out of the wealth corner. Now Will spent all his time with her. It infuriated Phoebe to see how completely he'd been taken in by her. 'She's so obviously not his type, but after being rejected by Nadine he's vulnerable to anyone who shows him affection. It's a classic rebound thing.'

'He seems quite happy about it, from what you say.'

'That's because he's a man. He doesn't know his own mind.'

'And you do?'

'I just don't want him to get hurt again, that's all. Why are you looking at me like that? I've told you, I'm not interested in him in that way. I don't want him.'

Karen smiled shrewdly. 'But you don't want anyone else to have him, is that it?'

Chapter 23

The following morning was Saturday and her day off, so Phoebe got up late. She pulled on her dressing gown and headed straight for the kitchen, desperate for her caffeine fix.

She flicked the switch on the kettle just as Minty drifted in. She was wearing one of Will's shirts which showed off her endless, baby giraffe legs. Her short, dark hair framed an exquisite face. Even first thing in the morning without make-up she looked sensational. 'Morning. Would you like some carrot and beetroot juice?'

'No thanks.' Phoebe reached for the coffee jar. It was empty. 'Blimey, where's all this gone? It was full yesterday.'

'Er, that was me. I did it for your own good. That stuff's poison.' Minty saw Phoebe's expression and stepped out of her range. 'I've bought some camomile teabags instead. They're very calming.'

'I don't need calming.'

'Oh, but I think you do—'

'I TOLD YOU, I'M PERFECTLY CALM!' Phoebe reached for her bag and took out her packet of Marlboros. If she couldn't have a coffee, at least she could wake herself up with a quick jolt of nicotine . . .

As she took her first steadying drag, she noticed Minty's dismayed expression through the smoky haze. 'Yes? Is there a problem?'

'You're not – going to smoke that, are you?'

'Yes I already am, as a matter of fact. Since I

can't drink coffee, it's one of the few pleasures left to me.'

She took another drag. Minty put a hand to her chest. 'I'd really rather you didn't. It interferes with my chi flow.'

'Don't.' Phoebe waved the lighted tip at her. 'Just don't say another word OK? Because the mood I'm in, I might just interfere with your chi flow for you.'

Just then Will walked in. He was just wearing jeans, his hair damp and curling from the shower. 'Hi,' he said. 'Minty's just been practising her reiki on me.' He looked from one to the other as they stood at opposite ends of the kitchen. 'Is there a problem?'

'Your flatmate is smoking.' Minty pointed at Phoebe.

'And your girlfriend has hidden the coffee,' Phoebe retaliated.

'Oh. Right.' Will looked uneasy. 'I've been meaning to talk to you about that, actually, Fee. You see, Minty's very sensitive, and so I wondered if you wouldn't mind not smoking in here? You can do it all you like in your own room, of course.'

'Fine.' Phoebe ground out her cigarette and stuffed the butt back into the packet. 'So that's how it is, is it? Never mind that I actually pay rent for this place.' She glared at them. 'If anyone wants me I'll be in the shower. I take it I'm still allowed to do that?'

As she stormed out of the kitchen, she heard Minty whisper, 'She seems very tense. I wonder if there's a disturbance in her force?'

She makes me sound like flaming Darth Vadar! thought Phoebe. If she wasn't so utterly furious she would have laughed.

She stood under the shower, trying to calm down. It wasn't fair! How dare Will take Minty's side against her. And she thought they were friends. All those nights they'd talked into the early hours. All the hours she listened to him jawing on about Nadine, trying to be sympathetic, resisting the urge to tell him what she really thought. All the times they'd laughed till they cried. Didn't their friendship mean anything to him?

Obviously not. Now Minty had come along with her long legs and pert bottom and wretched chi flows, and suddenly Phoebe was about as wanted as last night's pizza leftovers.

Will was sitting on her bed waiting for her. Just to add insult to injury, he was smoking one of her cigarettes.

'Come in and make yourself at home, won't you?' Phoebe pulled her dressing gown tightly around her.

'I want to talk to you. About Minty.'

'Oh yes?' She sat down at the dressing table and dragged a brush through her damp curls. This is it, she thought. This is where he admits what a pain she is and says he's chucking her.

'I wondered if you had a problem? Only you seem very hostile towards her.'

'Me, hostile?' Phoebe twisted round to face him. 'She's the one who's thrown away the coffee and filled the house with cat's pee teabags. She's the one who won't let me play my CDs when she's meditating. And she's hidden the TV.'

Will regarded her with the same calm, slightly patronising look Minty did so well. 'I know she can be a bit over the top sometimes, but she's only trying to help. Why don't you give her a chance?'

'You would say that.' Phoebe turned away in disgust. 'And we all know why, don't we? She's introduced you to the joys of tantric sex.'

'Minty and I have a very special relationship.'

'Don't I know it. I can hear you through the wall.'

Will ignored her. 'She's kind, gentle, sensitive, and she's the first woman I've been able to feel anything for since Nadine left.'

That stung. 'Maybe that's why you're so keen on her?' Phoebe murmured.

'Meaning?'

'You could be on the rebound. Why else would you be interested in her? Let's face it, you don't have much in common.'

'Actually, Minty's a very interesting person. She's travelled all around the world, she's passionate about eastern cultures—'

'Exactly. The nearest you come to eastern culture is a takeaway curry in front of the TV.'

'Maybe she's raising my consciousness?'

She's raising something, and it isn't just your consciousness, Phoebe thought. 'And the fact that she also happens to be tall, leggy and shockingly similar to your ex doesn't come into it, I suppose?'

'What is this?' Will stubbed out his cigarette. 'Look, I'm just getting on with my life like everyone's been telling me to. It's a pity you don't do the same.'

Phoebe stopped brushing her hair. 'What do you mean?'

'All this business about Minty. If you ask me, you're just jealous because you've got no one to hang around feeling depressed with any more. You can't stand the idea of me being happy, because it makes you realise what a mess your life's in.'

'How dare you! My life's not a mess.'

'Really?'

'Really. I've got a job I love, loads of friends, a great social life—'

'What social life? You haven't had a date since you moved in here.'

'Oh, I get it. You don't think I can be happy or fulfilled without a man, is that it? God, you sound just like Baz.'

'I'm not saying that. I just think it's about time you

stopped being so hung up on your sister's fiancé and found someone of your own.'

'I am not hung up over Luke!'

'Then how come you still keep his photo by your bed?' Will held it up. 'And how do you explain the fact that you haven't even looked at another man for weeks?'

'Maybe I'm choosy. Unlike some.'

'What's that supposed to mean?'

'Think about it. Maybe I'm just waiting for some tall hunky Luke clone to come along so I can pretend I'm getting on with my life like you.'

'At least I've got a life!'

The hairbrush bounced off the door just as it closed. Phoebe sent hate vibes through the woodwork. Bloody Will. And bloody Minty, too.

But as her anger subsided, she began to wonder if he wasn't right. Maybe misery really did love company.

Or maybe it was just Will she missed?

'I really don't want to do this,' Phoebe insisted, as Karen dragged her down Briggate. 'I'm useless at shopping. Everything always looks awful. And the shop assistants all hate me.'

'Stop being paranoid.' Karen gripped her arm so she couldn't make a run for it. 'You're meant to be enjoying this, remember?'

How could anyone enjoy shopping? Phoebe wondered. Alex spent hours doing it, and loved every minute. But then Alex had cash to spare and looked absolutely gorgeous in everything. Phoebe was permanently broke, and her shopping trips tended to be the lightning strike variety, where she'd rush into Gap, buy the first pair of jeans or baggy shirt that came to hand, and rush out again.

So today was going to be absolute torture. Especially as Karen was heading for Victoria Quarter, where Leeds' most chic and expensive designer shops were. The vast minimalist spaces with their sparsely displayed beige and black merchandise terrified Phoebe, but Karen strutted around as if she owned the place, unfolding precisely arranged jumpers and discarding them again. The black-clad assistants, who had obviously realised Karen wasn't a woman to be messed with, quickly locked on to Phoebe. They prowled behind her, giving her trainers and jeans scathing looks from beneath their short black fringes, as if it was their mission in life to make her feel bad for being fat and poor.

'Can we go now?' she pleaded.

'Just a minute. How about this?'

'Not another pair of sequinned hipsters?' Phoebe was too despondent to bother looking.

'Hardly. Look.' Phoebe looked. It was gorgeous, she had to admit. A beautifully cut, very elegant shift dress in toffee coloured linen. It even looked good on the hanger.

'Very nice,' she agreed. 'But will you wear it?'

'Well, no. But I thought you might.'

'Me?'

'Why not? It'll look great with your colouring. Try it on.'

'I can't.' Phoebe looked at it again. It was beautiful, but far too sophisticated for her. 'Dresses always look awful on me. I haven't got the right legs. And I need sleeves, I can't have my arms showing. And I don't have the right shoes.'

'Oh, for goodness' sake!' Karen rolled her eyes. 'Just try the bloody thing on, will you?'

Phoebe stomped off to the changing room with a martyred sigh. Of course it would look hideous. That is, if she even managed to get into it.

But she did, and it didn't. She stared at her reflection, not quite able to believe what she was seeing. The fit was perfect, and so well-tailored it glided over her hips, making her look more curvy than fat. Her legs didn't look bad either. Perhaps if she had a pair of those kitten heels Alex always wore . . .

'Well? What's the verdict?' Karen flung aside the curtain. 'Blimey!'

'Is it that bad?'

'Phoebe, it's perfect. You look amazing.'

'I feel amazing.' She did a quick twirl in front of the mirror. She still wasn't exactly Kate Moss, but she didn't want to run out of the changing room screaming, either. 'You're sure it doesn't make me look too fat?'

'Fee, you've got a fabulous figure. It's just no one ever notices because you're always hiding it away under that old baggy stuff. That really shows it off. And the colour looks gorgeous.'

'It does, doesn't it?' Phoebe took a last wistful look at herself. 'I just wish I could afford it.'

'Who cares about that? You've got a credit card, haven't you?'

'Yes, but—'

'So why don't you use it? Come on, Phoebe, you can't be sensible all your life. Why not go mad and splash out for once? It would be criminal not to buy something that's so obviously made for you. And besides,' she lowered her voice, 'I've just knocked over the jumper display, and I don't think that assistant will let us out alive if you don't buy something.'

One dress, a beaded cardigan and a pair of kitten heeled mules later, Phoebe was still trying to work out how Karen had managed to get her to part with so much money she didn't have.

But it felt good. She hadn't recognised the glamorous woman in the changing room mirror. She'd never felt that good before. She'd spent her whole life compar-ing herself to Alex, bemoaning the fact that she didn't have her sister's long legs or blonde hair, never really taking in the fact that she might be attractive in her own way.

Maybe moving out had been a blessing in disguise? At least it had given her a chance to emerge from her sister's shadow. Now she looked back, she was amazed she'd stayed there for so long.

Her good mood lasted until she reached her front door. Then she remembered her row with Will and a gloom descended. She still felt annoyed at him for taking Minty's side against her, but she knew she should make the peace for the sake of domestic harmony. Minty was obviously there to stay, and she'd just have to learn to live with it. She might get to like the smell of patchouli oil one day.

'Anyone home?' She dumped her bags by the front door and eased off her trainers. 'Will? Put the kettle on, I'm shattered.'

'Sorry, he's out. Will I do?'

Phoebe looked up. There, standing in the kitchen doorway, was the most beautiful man she'd ever seen.

Chapter 24

'Will went out a couple of hours ago to some new age therapy session with that girlfriend of his. I think they've got to get their auras checked, or something.' His dark eyes smiled behind his glasses. 'You must be Phoebe. I'm Andrew, Will's cousin.'

'Pleased to meet you. Now let me see. Are you the high-flying lawyer, the fighter pilot, or the one who's single-handedly saving mankind?'

'The last one.' He grinned. 'Well, maybe not quite, but I do my best. I was just making a coffee. Do you want one?'

'I didn't think we had any?'

'Oh yeah. I heard the health police slapped a ban on it.' He smiled conspiratorially. 'Don't tell anyone, but I went down to Jacksons and smuggled a jar in. And an illicit packet of Hobnobs.'

'In that case, I'd love one.' She followed him into the kitchen and lingered in the doorway, watching him. He was too good-looking to be true, tall and dark, his faded jeans and black sweater showing off his lean hips, long legs and broad shoulders. Phoebe could just imagine him striding around the university research centre in his white coat, leaving a trail of drooling lab assistants in his wake.

He turned around and caught her staring. Phoebe feigned sudden interest in the ironing board. 'So – how long are you here for?'

'Just the weekend, unfortunately.' He handed her the mug. 'Shall we go into the other room and make ourselves comfortable?'

She sat in the armchair while he stretched out on the sofa. She didn't quite know what to say to him. 'Are you – um – a real doctor, then?'

He smiled. 'That depends.'

'On what?'

'On whether you've got anything wrong with you. For some reason once people find out I've got a medical degree they all want to talk to me about their backache or their housemaid's knee.'

'Damn. And I was going to get you to look at my ingrowing toenail.'

'I'll be glad to look at anything you want to show me.' Phoebe caught the look he gave her. If she didn't know better, she would think he was flirting with her. 'The fact is, although I'm a doctor in title, I haven't treated any patients in years. I'm more on the research side now.'

'Will says you're incredibly brainy.'

'Did he? That was nice of him.'

'He says you're finding cures for all kinds of diseases.'

'Actually, I spend most of my time trying to raise funds to keep my unit open. The university doesn't see saving lives as a priority, sadly.'

He had a lovely warm voice. Phoebe decided there and then that if she ever had a life-threatening disease he would be the one she'd want at her bedside, even if he was out of practice at treating patients.

'So how long have you known Will?' he asked.

'About four months. We met on his wedding night.'

'Really? I didn't realise he was such a quick worker.'

'It's not like that.' She explained briefly how they'd met, and how they'd ended up living together.

'So you know all about Nadine, then?'

'Enough to know I'd probably slap her if I ever saw her,' Phoebe checked herself. 'Sorry, I shouldn't have

247

said that. I don't even know her. She might be a really nice woman.'

'She isn't. And as for slapping her, I think you'd have to fight my mother for the privilege.' Andrew smiled. 'She wasn't exactly flavour of the month at home, even before she jilted Will.'

'What did you think of her?'

'I thought she was stunning. But a complete airhead. And this new one's not much better. I'd only been in the flat five minutes before she was accusing me of torturing innocent lab rats in the name of science.'

'And do you?'

'Of course not. I do it strictly for pleasure.' He laughed at her dismayed expression. 'Seriously, a lot of the work I do these days is on computer – you know, modelling molecular structures?'

She didn't know, but he could have recited the Yellow Pages in that gorgeous voice and she would have listened.

They chatted their way through two cups of coffee and half a packet of Hobnobs. Andrew was great company, really interesting and very easy to talk to. Once she'd got over her initial nerves, Phoebe found herself telling him all about Alex's wedding, and made him laugh about her hideous bridesmaid's dress.

'That's not it, is it?' He nodded towards the carrier bag she'd abandoned by the door.

'No, that's retail therapy. Although I'm not really sure I should have bought it.' Now the euphoria had worn off, she was beginning to wonder if the dress was an expensive mistake. 'It looked all right in the shop, but it'll probably look ghastly now.'

'There's only one way to find out, isn't there? Go and put it on.'

'Oh no, I couldn't.'

'Why not? I'll give you my unbiased male opinion.'

That's what I'm afraid of, Phoebe thought, as she went off to her room. If he laughed, or even smirked, she would have to kill herself.

She was pleasantly surprised to discover that the whole thing hadn't been an optical illusion in the shop, helped along by distorting mirrors and clever lighting. The dress still fitted her, and it still looked quite good, especially with the heels to give her a bit more height.

'Well, what do you think?' Andrew had his back to her, flicking through Will's CDs. He turned, and his smile froze. Phoebe froze in response. 'Oh God, is it that bad? I knew it, I look awful, don't I?'

'It's – it's—'

'Hi, we're back. I hope you haven't – fucking hell!' Will stopped in the doorway and stared at Phoebe.

'You took the words right out of my mouth.' Andrew said. 'You look amazing. What do you reckon, Will? Will?'

They both looked at Will. He went on staring at her. 'It's – um – different,' he said at last. Phoebe's happiness deflated like a balloon.

'Well, I think she's gorgeous.' Andrew looked past Will. 'Where's Minty? Don't tell me, she's got stuck in the full lotus and had to be carted off to hospital?'

'She's just locking up her bike.' He didn't take his eyes off Phoebe. 'So what's all this in aid of?'

'I just felt like a new image. Don't you like it?'

'I don't see what was wrong with the old one.'

Just then Minty walked in. 'You wouldn't believe what I've just seen in the – oh!' She caught sight of Phoebe. 'You look nice. Are you going for a job interview, or something?'

Phoebe felt even more deflated. How had she ever imagined she looked attractive, sexy even? Compared to Minty, in her tight jeans and cropped T-shirt showing off her flat brown stomach and pierced belly button, she looked like a middle-aged frump. No wonder Will was staring at her as if she'd gone mad.

'I'm desperate for a wheatgrass juice,' Minty said. 'Would anyone else like one? Will?'

'What?'

'Would you like a wheatgrass juice?'

'No thanks.' Why did he have to keep looking at her like that? She was beginning to feel very self-conscious.

'What about you, Andrew?' Minty said.

'I'd rather have another coffee. How about you, Phoebe?'

She caught the glint in his eyes. 'Yes, please. Extra strong.'

Minty's lips tightened into a thin line of annoyance. 'I thought we'd agreed coffee was a no-no? As a health professional, Andrew, you must surely be aware of its harmful diuretic properties, not to mention the effect all those stimulants have on the heart rate.'

'I know most doctors drink gallons of the stuff,' Andrew said. 'But if it offends your sensibilities that much, Phoebe and I will take ours into her room. If that's OK with you?' He looked at her.

Phoebe was just about to agree when Will interrupted. 'Don't do that. You can drink your coffee in here. In fact, I think I'll join you.'

Minty sucked in her breath. 'Will, can I have a word, please? In private.' She flounced off to the kitchen. Will followed her.

'Oops, looks like someone's in trouble,' Andrew remarked. 'How does he put up with her? She's a complete pain.'

'Try telling Will that. He's besotted.'

'Then he must be mad.' Andrew sent her a long look. 'D'you know, when Will first told me about you I thought there must be something going on between you two.'

'Me and Will?' Phoebe laughed, a bit too loudly. 'Oh no, we're just friends. Actually, we're not even that a lot of the time. Sometimes we barely speak.'

'More fool him, then.' Their eyes met and Phoebe felt a sudden jolt of attraction. 'So, do you have a boyfriend?'

'No.'

He opened his mouth to speak but Will came in with three coffees on a tray, and he shut up again, much to her frustration. She was so sure he'd been about to ask her out.

They drank their coffee in uncomfortable silence. Will had obviously had a set-to with Minty, because he was scowling and sullen. He sulked on the sofa between them, making conversation impossible.

Then, just as Andrew was telling her more about his work, he suddenly interrupted with, 'Shouldn't you be going?'

'There's no rush.'

'But Gina will be expecting you.' Will wrestled the mug out of his hands. 'You don't want to keep her waiting, do you? You know how much she looks forward to you coming.'

'All right, I know where I'm not wanted. Talk about making people feel welcome.' Andrew stood up. 'It's been nice meeting you, Phoebe. Even if it was only briefly.' He shot a look at Will. 'Tell you what, why don't we meet up again? Perhaps I could take you to dinner tonight?'

'I—'

'She's working,' Will cut in.

'Actually, I've swapped shifts with Ronan, so I'm free.' Phoebe frowned at him. What was he playing at? 'And I'd love to have dinner with you.'

'Great. I'll pick you up at eight, OK? Maybe you could book us a table somewhere?'

'I'll see you out.' Will shoved him towards the door. He came back in, looking boot-faced.

Phoebe jumped up and down. 'I don't believe it. I've got a date!'

'Don't get too excited, will you? He's only taking you to dinner, he hasn't asked you to marry him.'

Her smile faded. 'I thought you'd be pleased for me.'

'I am. I just don't want you building your hopes up, that's all.'

'What do you mean? He seems like a really nice guy.'

'He is. But he also lives two hundred miles away.'

'So what? Like you said, I'm not marrying him.' Phoebe glared at him. 'What's your problem, Will? Don't you like the idea of me going out with your cousin, or something?'

'I—' He was interrupted by Minty summoning him. 'I don't care who you go out with,' he said, and headed back to the kitchen, slamming the door behind him.

Phoebe clicked the top back on her lipstick and allowed herself a smile in the mirror. She hardly recognised the face that looked back at her, her eyes outlined in smoky pencil, her lips made fuller with rich berry gloss. It was amazing what a difference a touch of make-up made. She really should try it more often.

But it was the dress that really made the difference. It was like nothing she'd ever worn before. It definitely exposed more flesh than she was used to. She'd had to force herself not to change into her safe black trousers. At least she had the beaded cardigan to hide her suddenly goosepimpled shoulders.

Too nervous to do battle with the Frizz Ease, she'd given up with her hair and pinned it up, ignoring the wispy curls escaping around her face.

Five to eight. She jammed her feet into her kitten heels and went into the sitting room. Will was slouched in front of the TV. He'd been in a foul mood all day. Phoebe guessed he must have had a row with Minty.

The atmosphere had certainly been very frosty after Andrew left. Phoebe was doing her best to ignore him, but it was like living with a sulky teenager.

'How do I look?' She did a quick twirl in the sitting room doorway. Will looked at her, then back at the TV.

'OK, I suppose.'

'Thanks. Don't go overboard, will you?' Phoebe glared at him. 'You could try to sound a bit more enthusiastic, instead of going all moody on me.'

'I just hope he's worth it.'

Phoebe sat down and tugged her dress over her knees. At this rate Andrew would be able to see them knocking, as well as hear them.

'Are you going out with Minty tonight?'

'Probably.'

She checked her watch. Two minutes to eight. Will sent her a sideways look.

'Maybe he's not coming?'

'Why shouldn't he come?'

'No reason. I'm just saying, it wouldn't be the first time he's changed his mind.'

His words hung in the air. Phoebe took her mirror out of her bag and checked her lipstick again. Then Will suddenly said, 'You do realise he lives in London? The other end of the country.'

'So?'

'So it's hardly the basis for a relationship, is it?'

'You and Nadine did it.'

'Exactly. And look what happened to us.'

'Will, I'm only going out to dinner with him, we're not running off to Gretna Green.'

'That wouldn't happen. Andrew's commitment-phobic.'

Phoebe dropped her lipstick back into her bag. 'If I didn't know any better I'd say you were trying to put me off.'

'Why should I do that? I don't care who you go out with. I'm just a bit surprised, that's all. It wasn't that long ago you were breaking your heart over that Luke guy, and suddenly you're going out with someone else. You bounced back from that pretty quickly, wouldn't you say?'

Phoebe held on to her temper. 'A few hours ago you were telling me to find myself a new man. Anyway, what about you?'

'What about me?'

'You were getting married four months ago, remember?'

Will stared at the TV screen. 'That's different.'

'Why? Because you're a man?'

'Don't be ridiculous.'

'Why, then? Why shouldn't I go out with Andrew?'

He turned to her, an unfathomable look in his eyes. 'Because—'

The doorbell rang. Phoebe looked at her watch. 'Bang on time. Doesn't look like he's changed his mind, does it?' She picked up her bag. 'Have a nice evening, Will. Don't wait up for me, will you?'

She was still simmering with anger when she and Andrew reached the restaurant. She couldn't understand Will at all. One minute he was telling her to get over Luke, the next he was accusing her of being on the rebound. Which was rich, coming from him. It was pretty obvious why he'd started dating Minty, and it had nothing to do with a shared passion for alternative therapies.

She tried to forget him and concentrate on enjoying herself with Andrew. He really was gorgeous she thought, watching him across the table from behind her menu. He looked so good in that suit. Not like Will, who always looked as if he'd got dressed in the dark.

'Something wrong?' Andrew looked concerned. 'You were frowning. Don't you like the menu? We could go somewhere else.'

'No, no, it all looks lovely.'

'I suppose it's a bit of a busman's holiday for you?'

'I don't mind if someone else is doing the cooking.' Phoebe beamed over her menu at him, determined to enjoy herself. Why shouldn't she? Andrew was a wonderful man – good-looking, intelligent, considerate. Even more amazingly, he was actually interested in her. It wasn't every day she got the chance of a date with the perfect man.

They ordered their food, and she tried to concentrate. He was terrific company. Funny too, with outrageous stories about his time as a medical student. And he was fascinating about his work, too. She could have a proper, grown-up conversation with him, not like those bickering discussions she had with Will over whether David Beckham's hairstyle affected his playing ability.

She fixed her attention on Andrew's mouth and tried to listen carefully, while a different set of thoughts ran through the back of her mind.

Why was Will in such a foul mood? Had he really had a row with Minty? It was too much to hope they'd split up. That woman was harder to shift than a red wine stain.

'And I don't know if you're aware of this, but it's a medical fact that certain types of cancer risk can be reduced by regularly listening to Michael Ball CDs,' Andrew was saying.

'Really? I had no idea. How fascinating.' Phoebe caught the look in his eye. 'What? What's so funny?'

'You are. You haven't been listening to a word I've said, have you?'

'Of course I have.'

'Liar. You know, if I wasn't such a well-balanced, non-egotistical human being, I might take offence.'

'Sorry. It's not you, honestly. I've just got a lot on my mind.'

'Want to talk about it?'

Phoebe smiled. 'It's nothing, really. Just that cousin of yours winding me up.'

'Ah. So what's he done now?'

She hadn't meant to, but she ended up telling him the whole story of how she'd moved in with Will to escape her doomed romance with Luke, how they'd become friends, and how their friendship had been severely tested by the appearance of Minty. Somewhere in the middle of it, their food arrived, but Phoebe hardly noticed it, she was too busy talking about Will.

'And then he has the cheek to accuse *me* of being on the rebound!' she fumed. 'I don't know what's got into him. Sometimes he can be really sweet and other times he's completely maddening. I mean, what business is it of his who I go out with?'

'What indeed,' Andrew agreed.

'It's not as if he's exactly celibate. He's got Minty. Although God knows why he had to pick the most annoying woman on the planet. I know what you're going to say, it's none of my business either,' she went on, as Andrew opened his mouth to speak. 'And I know I should be glad for him because he's getting over Nadine. But he's making a huge mistake and he doesn't seem to realise it. I don't want to see him get hurt, that's all. Everyone can see Minty's not right for him. Everyone but him.'

'Maybe he can see it?' Andrew suggested. 'Maybe he's going out with Minty because he's too frightened to admit he's actually in love with someone else?'

'That's what I thought,' Phoebe nodded eagerly. 'I told him he was probably still in love with Nadine, but he didn't believe me.'

'I wasn't talking about Nadine.' He looked enigmatic.

What was it about the Hutchinson men and their unfathomable looks?

They finished their food, and Andrew called for the bill. Phoebe looked disappointed. 'Aren't we going to have another bottle?'

'I don't think there's much point, do you?'

She knew he was right. No matter how much she willed herself to feel it, the chemistry just wasn't there. What was the matter with her? The first time she'd met an attractive, available man, and she felt nothing.

She sighed. 'I've really messed this up, haven't I?'

'It's not your fault. Although I must admit it's not exactly flattering to listen to you talk about another man all evening. Even if he is my cousin.'

'I'm sorry.' So it was Will's fault. He'd screwed up her evening without even being there.

'Maybe he's the one you should be talking to, not me?' Andrew suggested.

'Yeah, right!' Phoebe snorted into her Chablis.

She decided to make one last, desperate effort to save the date. When Andrew took her home she invited him in for coffee. 'Please,' she begged. 'I want to make it up to you for spoiling your evening. And Will's gone out.'

But Will hadn't gone out. He was sprawled on the sofa, in much the same position as when Phoebe left him, idly flicking channels on the TV.

Phoebe felt her rage flooding back. 'Why are you here? I thought you were going out?'

'I said I'd probably go out. But I didn't. I decided to stay in and watch the match instead.'

'On a Saturday night? You never stay in on a Saturday night.'

'I felt like a change, didn't I?'

Phoebe stared at him in frustration. She felt like grabbing the remote control out of his hand and beating him to death with it. 'What about Minty?'

'What about her?'

'Why isn't she here?'

'I don't know. Possibly because I didn't ask her to come over.'

'Why didn't you ask her? She's supposed to be your girlfriend, isn't she?'

'We're not joined at the hip, you know.'

'Really? You could have fooled me.'

'Phoebe.' She heard Andrew's voice behind her, but she was too furious at Will to answer him.

'Well, you'll have to go to bed now,' she said.

'Who says?'

'I've brought Andrew back for coffee. We don't need you hanging around playing gooseberry.'

'I'm sure Andrew wouldn't mind. Would you, Andrew?'

'Well—'

'You see, he doesn't mind. Anyway, can I just remind you this is my flat? You can't just send me to my room like a little kid.'

'Why not? You act like one.' She stared at the TV, where semi-clad women were playing beach volleyball. 'I thought you said you were watching the match?'

'I was. It finished an hour ago.'

'So there's no reason for you to hang around, is there?' She grabbed the remote control and punched the off button.

'Hey! I was watching that!' Will made a lunge for it, but Phoebe jerked away. She overbalanced and fell backwards over the armchair. As she sprawled against the cushions, Will threw himself on top of her, pinning her down.

'Let go of me!'

'Not until you hand over that remote.'

She struggled, her screams turning to laughter and then silence as she felt Will's weight pinning her down, his face only inches from hers, so close she could feel his breath on her face.

The laughter died in Will's eyes too. For a moment they gazed at each other, caught in the moment, and Phoebe felt a jolt of electricity fizzing between them, far greater than anything she'd felt in a whole night's flirting with Andrew.

It took them both a moment to realise the remote control had fallen to the floor. It took her even longer to realise that Andrew had left, and she hadn't even noticed.

Chapter 25

Will was working on the new Hunky and Dory book when Andrew turned up the following morning.

'Working on a Sunday morning? You must be keen.' He looked sickeningly handsome as usual, in jeans, a white T-shirt and aviator sunglasses that made him look like a tall Tom Cruise.

'I had something to finish.' Will didn't look up from his drawing board. 'I suppose you've come to see Phoebe?'

'Actually, it's you I've come to see.'

Will pretended to concentrate on drawing Dory's hair. 'If it's about last night I'm sorry. I didn't mean to screw up your evening.'

'Yes, you did, but that isn't why I'm here. I came to tell you to stop playing silly buggers. Why didn't you tell me you fancied Phoebe?'

Ink splatted over Dory's face, but Will didn't notice. 'What?'

'Come on, it's obvious you're crazy about her. That's what last night was all about, wasn't it? You were jealous. That's why you didn't want to leave her alone with me.'

'I told you, I wanted to stay in and watch the match.'

'Suit yourself. But if it's any consolation nothing was going to happen. She spent the whole evening talking about you.'

'Did she?' Will reacted without thinking. Then he tried to hide it with a careless shrug. 'I can't help it if you're losing your touch, can I?'

'You'll lose her if you don't do something about it.'

Andrew gave him a big brother look over the top of his sunglasses. 'She's a great girl, Will. But she won't wait around for ever. Sooner or later she's going to get another offer. And the next bloke might not step aside like me.'

Will kept his head down, mopping up the spilt ink. 'Look, I don't know what you're talking about. I'm not interested in Phoebe. She's not even my type.'

'Of course she isn't. I mean, she's good-looking, she's fun, and she's not a self-obsessed airhead. Why the hell would you want anything to do with her?'

'So is that it?' Will said. 'Because if that's all you came for, I'm rather busy.'

'Don't worry, I'm going.' Andrew headed for the door. 'But a word of advice. If you haven't snapped her up by next time I come home, I'm definitely going to have another go myself. And I might try a bit harder this time!'

'And a word of advice to you. Only tossers wear sunglasses indoors!' Will aimed an ink-stained rag at the door and went back to work. Typical bloody Andrew, thinking he knew everything just because he had a string of medical degrees and had saved a few million lives.

But this time he was right. Only Will didn't want to admit it because he was still getting over the shock himself.

He couldn't ignore what had happened last night. For a moment there, as their eyes met over the remote control, he'd really wanted to kiss her. And he was sure Phoebe felt the same. Why else would she drop the remote and back off so quickly?

It couldn't be happening. Not Phoebe. She was a friend, someone to laugh with, to share a takeaway with, a shoulder to cry on. All those mornings he'd watched her flapping around the kitchen in her tatty dressing gown and no make-up and never thought of her as anything but his flatmate.

And then yesterday he'd walked in and seen her standing there in that dress, and suddenly he'd been floored by lust. It was as if he was seeing her for the first time, not as good old Phoebe, but as a sexy, desirable woman.

And he could tell Andrew thought the same. He'd watched them talking and laughing together, and felt like a prize gooseberry. Trust him to get in first. And of course, once Andrew asked her out, Will knew he'd missed his chance.

He couldn't stop thinking about the two of them together. That's what had triggered the big row with Minty. He didn't blame her for storming off like that. It couldn't have been much fun for her, watching him brood.

Now it turned out nothing had happened. He felt relieved, but confused and disturbed at the same time. Was he really ready for this? Deep down he wasn't sure if he was really over Nadine. He was terrified of getting involved with someone, of falling in love and being hurt again. Minty didn't count, he'd always known it could never be serious with her. Looking back, that had been part of the attraction. But now he felt as if he was on the verge of something huge, something that could snowball out of control, and he didn't know if he could cope with it.

And what if Andrew was wrong? What if Phoebe didn't feel the same about him? He knew that Luke character was still in her thoughts, no matter what she said. And she'd never really given much sign that she fancied him. Exactly the opposite, if anything. Like that time when Gina had asked if there was anything going on between them, and she'd practically bitten her head off. Her horrified reaction had stayed with him.

When Phoebe wandered in half an hour later, he was so keyed up he nearly knocked over his drawing board.

She was wearing that washed-out pink dressing gown, but he still fancied her. Her dark hair was a riot of curls – very sexy before she blow dried the life out of it – and last night's eye make-up was smudged under her eyes.

She yawned and flopped down on the sofa. 'Was that Andrew I heard earlier?'

'Yes, he just called round to say goodbye.' Will braced himself. 'Look, Phoebe, I want to talk to you—'

'Already? I thought he wasn't leaving until this afternoon?' Phoebe put her feet up on the coffee table. Will tried not to notice her shapely legs as he sat down opposite her.

'Yes, but I won't be seeing him. Phoebe—'

'Aren't you going round to your aunt's for lunch?'

'Phoebe, will you shut up and listen to me?' He saw her recoil. 'Sorry. I just wanted to talk to you about something.'

'Look, if it's about using your razor to shave my legs, I said I'm sorry—'

'It's nothing to do with that.'

'Leaving the top off the milk bottle? Hogging the phone?'

'Phoebe!'

'Sorry.' She looked contrite. 'What is it, then?'

'I just wanted to say . . .' He looked into her expectant face, and his throat dried up. 'Sorry if I messed things up for you last night. I behaved like a jerk.'

'Yes, you did a bit,' she agreed. 'But to be honest, there wasn't a lot to mess up. I don't think Andrew and I were meant to be.'

'Really? Why's that, then?'

'I don't know. Just chemistry, I suppose.' Phoebe shrugged. 'It's a shame, really. I would have liked someone to show off at Alex's wedding. Now it looks as if I'll be going on my own.'

'I'll go with you, if you like?'

At least she didn't shriek with laughter, which was something. 'You? Why?'

'Why not? You need a partner, and I've got nothing to do. And I do feel guilty for screwing things up with Andrew.' Thank God she couldn't hear his heart hammering.

'But what about Minty? Won't she mind?'

'Minty and I have split up.'

'Oh.' It was hard to tell what she was thinking, her face was a blank. 'When did that happen?'

'Yesterday. You were right, we weren't exactly suited.'

'I'm sorry.'

'Are you?'

'Well, no, maybe not. I can't say I liked her. But that doesn't mean I wanted you to finish with her.' She reached over and covered his hand with hers. 'Looks like we're both on our own again, doesn't it?'

He looked down at her fingers curled around his. Say something, Andrew's voice whispered in his ear. Say something before you miss your chance. He took a deep breath, 'That's what I wanted to talk to you about. You see—'

The phone rang. 'I'll get it.' Phoebe let go of his hand and reached over for it.

Will cursed silently. If that was Andrew, he'd have to kill him. There was nothing else for it.

But it wasn't. He watched Phoebe's expression change, her colour fading, and without knowing why, he started to panic.

She handed the phone to him. 'It's Nadine.'

'Who's that woman?' It was strange, hearing her again after so long.

'Just my flatmate.' He looked around but Phoebe had already beat a tactful retreat to the bathroom. He could hear the shower running.

'I had no idea.'

'I told you I was going to have to get someone to share the mortgage.'

'You didn't say it would be a woman.'

'I didn't think you cared.'

A sharp silence followed, prickly at the edges. Then she said, 'You're right, it's nothing to do with me.' She sounded – what? Subdued? Conciliatory? Surely not. 'How are you, anyway?'

'Oh, you know. Fine. How about you?'

'OK.'

There was a silence, then she said something else. Something he didn't quite catch. 'Sorry, what was that?'

'I said I've missed you.'

'Really?'

She laughed. 'Don't sound so surprised. It's not that unusual, is it?' Given the speed at which she'd left the flat, he thought maybe it was. 'Well, say something.'

'What do you want me to say?'

'You could tell me you've missed me too?' The silence lengthened. 'Well, have you?'

'You know I have.'

'I don't. How could I? For all I know you and your new flatmate could be sharing a bed by now.'

That was too close to the truth to be funny. He changed the subject. 'So what makes you call now? It must be the middle of the night where you are.'

'Actually, I'm back in Leeds. With my parents.'

His heartbeat quickened. 'How long for?'

'Not sure yet.' Another pause. 'Will, I think we should talk, don't you?'

'OK.' Stay cool, he told himself. 'When?'

'How about next Saturday?'

'But that's nearly a week away. Why not tomorrow? Or tonight?'

'Will!' She sounded exasperated but pleased.

'Sorry.' So much for staying cool. 'Saturday, then. Do you want to come round here?'

'I think we should meet on neutral ground, don't you?'

'You make it sound like we're going to do battle.'

'That depends, doesn't it?'

'On what?'

'On whether you put up a fight.' She laughed, a husky, seductive sound that stirred up all kinds of memories. 'You could take me to dinner?'

He tried again for some cool. 'Sure, if that's what you want. I'll book somewhere.'

'No, I'll book it. If I left it to you we'd probably end up having a kebab or something. How about The Blue Bicycle? Say, about eight?'

'I'll be there.'

'I'll look forward to it.'

He put the phone down, feeling dazed. I'll look forward to it, she said. Look forward to what? To seeing him again? To telling him she still loved him? To seeing his face when she finally told him it was all over for good?

He looked around the room. Everything was the same, but none of it looked familiar. The last few minutes had changed everything.

Then Phoebe walked in. Will jumped in his seat. He'd been so preoccupied he'd almost forgotten she was hiding in the bathroom.

'Everything OK?' She looked anxious.

'Fine – I think.' He looked at the phone. 'Nadine's in England. She wants us to meet.'

'What for?'

'I'm not sure.' He looked harder at the phone, as if he could somehow get a clue from it.

'Do you think she wants you back?'

'She didn't say.'

'Well, how did she sound?'

'I don't know. Sort of – normal, I suppose.' He couldn't remember a single thing she'd said.

Phoebe thought for a moment. 'Well, that's got to be good news, hasn't it?'

'Is it?'

'Of course.' Her smile was slightly strained. 'At least after Saturday you'll know where you stand.'

He looked at the phone again. That was the problem. He wasn't sure he wanted to know any more.

Chapter 26

The first wedding present had arrived, proudly displayed on the rosewood dining table. Alex took one look at the gold, horseshoe-print paper topped off with a huge bow, and felt her stomach knot up in panic.

'But the wedding's not for ages yet!'

'Only three weeks,' Shirley pointed out. 'Now, I thought you and Luke could open the presents as they arrive, then we could make a note of who sent what as we go along. Or would you rather leave them until after the wedding?'

What she really wanted to do was run screaming from the house and catch the first plane to anywhere. Her mind was blank with panic. Only three weeks to go. Three weeks before she made the biggest mistake of her life.

Much to Shirley's annoyance, she'd managed to avoid thinking or talking about the wedding. But it was still there. And it was getting closer.

And the closer it got, the more trapped she felt, and the more convinced she couldn't go through with it. It would be all wrong. Wrong for her, and wrong for Luke. He was a sweet bloke, he deserved better than this. Better than someone who didn't love him.

She knew she should have said something, put a stop to it before it went too far. But somehow she never found the right moment. She told herself she was biding her time, but deep down she knew she was just a coward. And everyone was putting so much work into it, she didn't want to let them down. Her mother, especially, was in her element, sending out invitations, ordering caterers around, confirming cars and finalising flowers. At first it seemed easier to let them just get on with it, but now she realised she'd let it go too far. She had to say something soon.

Only Phoebe seemed unhappier about it all than she was. She sat by the window, her tea untouched, staring into space. The wedding was obviously getting to her after all. Why else would she be looking so utterly miserable? Poor Phoebe, she longed to be in Alex's place. If only she knew how gladly Alex would have swapped.

Shirley was talking at her yet again. This time it was flowers. 'You still haven't decided what kind of arrangements you want for the reception,' she pointed out.

'Haven't I? Sorry.'

'The florists have got to get them ordered, especially if they're out of season and have to be flown in.'

'Flown in?' Her father, who'd been flicking through the *Evening Press*, looked up. 'And how much is that going to cost?'

'I don't know, do I?' Shirley looked irritable. 'Obviously they're not going to be cheap. Flowers don't grow on trees, you know.' Alex caught Phoebe's eye and they both smiled. Shirley turned pink. 'You know what I mean.'

'I don't see why we can't just get some flowers out of the garden,' Joe said.

'Oh yes, that will be very stylish, won't it? Tell you what, why don't we cancel the cars and you can drive her to the church in the Volvo? Or better still, we could get the milkman to drop her off in his float and save ourselves the petrol. How would that be?'

'Now you're getting hysterical.' Joe disappeared back behind his newspaper.

'I can't help it, can I? I seem to be the only person

taking this wedding seriously. So,' she turned back to Alex. 'Have you thought about flowers?'

'I'll get round to it,' Alex promised.

'Yes well, you should have got round to it ages ago.'

'I've been busy.'

'Busy doing what, exactly? Not organising this wedding, that's for sure. You still haven't sorted out an order of service to go to the printers, or even looked at those suggested table plans I did. The way you're going on anyone would think you didn't want to get married!'

'Maybe I don't,' Alex said quietly.

In the silence that followed she heard Phoebe's cup rattle in the saucer. Then Shirley said, 'Darling, you don't mean that.'

'I do.' Alex looked round at the three faces staring at her. She hadn't meant for it to come out like that, but now she knew there was no going back.

Shirley's smile wobbled, then reasserted itself. 'It's just pre-wedding nerves, all brides have them.'

'Not like this.' She looked directly at Phoebe, who'd gone pale. 'I don't want to marry Luke.'

'Why didn't you tell us before?' her mother asked.

'I didn't want to upset anyone.'

'Upset anyone? That's rich, coming from you!' They all looked round. Joe Redmond rarely raised his voice, which made it all the more shocking when he did. 'What do you think you're doing now, for heaven's sake? Do you know how much time and trouble your mother's gone to?'

'Leave it, Joseph.' Shirley stared down at her hands, her voice hushed.

'No, I won't leave it. It's about time she realised she can't go round upsetting everyone whenever it suits her.' Joe turned to her. 'It's just typical of you, isn't it? Letting everyone go to all this trouble, putting themselves out for you, spending a fortune, and then you pull a stunt like this.'

'It's not a stunt!' Tears sprang to her eyes. She hadn't expected her father to react like this. Her mother, yes. But she knew she could always talk her round. Not her father. 'Why do you think I didn't say anything before? I didn't want to cause trouble. I thought if I just went along with it, things would sort themselves out.'

'So what were you going to do, not show up on the day? Wait until we were all standing in the church and say, "Sorry, I've changed my mind"?' Alex had never seen him so angry. Even Phoebe looked stunned.

Alex looked down at her hands. The diamond solitaire on her left hand seemed to sparkle even more brightly through her tears. 'I – I don't know. I hadn't really thought about it.'

'No, you wouldn't. Never mind about anyone else, as long as you can do exactly what you want.' His face was mottled with fury, his breathing hard. 'And what about Luke? Have you mentioned any of this to him? He loves you, God help him. This is going to break his heart.'

'So you think she should go ahead and marry a man she doesn't love, just to please everyone else?' Shirley's voice rose over all of them. 'I wouldn't wish that on anyone.'

'Shirley.' Her father's anger disappeared, as he turned to face his wife. 'There's no need for this.'

'Why not? I've kept quiet all these years to please you and my father and everyone else, and look how I've ended up. I don't want my daughter to go through the same kind of misery I did. Not if I can help it.'

'Please don't say something you might regret.'

'Regret? The only regret I've ever had is letting myself get forced into marrying you!'

Alex glanced at Phoebe. There were tears forming in her big brown eyes, the way they always did when they were children and her parents argued.

'Mum, please,' she begged.

Shirley rounded on her. 'That's right. Stand up for your father. You always were a daddy's girl, weren't you? Your father's favourite, right from the moment you were born. And we all know why, don't we?' She turned glittering eyes to meet her husband's. The colour had ebbed from his face. He looked grey, drained and about fifty years older.

'Don't do this, Shirley,' he begged. 'Think about it. Once this is done, you can't go back.'

Alex felt prickles on the back of her neck. She wanted to run away, but she didn't know why. 'Stop it!' she cried, but no one heard her.

'You've never really cared about Alex, have you? Oh, you've played your part, just like you promised. But you've never really loved her.'

'That's not true. I love them both the same.'

'How could you? How could you possibly love her when she's not your daughter?'

A shattering silence followed her words. For a moment Joe Redmond sat frozen, just looking at her, reproach in his eyes. Then he got up and stumbled out of the room. Phoebe shot a look at her mother, the closest Alex had ever seen her come to hatred, and followed him.

Alex wanted to run too, but she couldn't. She stared at her mother. Shirley was unnervingly composed, her hands folded in her lap, staring down at her fingers.

'You had to know some time,' she said. 'I wanted to tell you before now but *he* wouldn't let me.' She nodded at the door. 'He thought you were better off not knowing. But you're my daughter, not his, and I think you have a right to know.'

Alex said nothing. Her whole world had tilted sideways on its axis. Nothing was the same any more, everything seemed strange, even the china ornaments on the mantelpiece. She looked around, trying to focus on something – anything – familiar, but it all looked totally different. 'I don't understand . . .'

'His name was Frank.' Shirley spoke as if she was reciting from a script. 'He was older than me – a friend of my father's.' She smiled wistfully. 'I fell in love with him the moment I saw him. He was the most handsome man I'd ever met. Tall, fair haired, such a wonderful smile. You remind me so much of him.'

Alex suppressed a shudder of revulsion. 'So why didn't you marry *him*?'

'He was already married.' The light went out of Shirley's eyes. 'Oh, as soon as he found out I was pregnant, he wanted to leave his wife but your grandfather wouldn't hear of it. He had his good name to think about. He didn't want any scandal. But he didn't want his daughter bringing an illegitimate child into the world, either. So he forced me to marry someone else. Someone respectable.' Her voice was bitter. 'Joseph worked for him. One of his rising stars, he always called him. My father promised to help set him up with his own business if he took me off his hands.'

'You mean he *bribed* him to marry you?'

'Not exactly. Joseph was always besotted with me, you see. My father spent months trying to push us together, but I never gave him a second glance. Not while I had Frank.' Her smile hardened. 'I suppose he saw this as his chance. Marry me and earn himself a reward at the same time. But I was fair to him. I told him from the start there was no way I would ever love him.'

Alex felt a flash of sympathy for her father. 'And what did he say?'

'He said he loved me, and he hoped that would be enough for both of us. But it wasn't.' Shirley fumbled in her pocket for a tissue. 'Oh, don't get me wrong. He did his best. But we both knew he could never be Frank.'

'What about Phoebe?'

Shirley's expression grew cold. 'I never wanted another baby, but I felt I owed it to Joseph to give him a child of his own.' She turned to Alex, a flash of defiance in her eyes. 'I did it for you, you see. That's why I married him, and that's why I've put up with it for all these years. I didn't want you to suffer for my mistake.'

She reached out and took her hand. Alex had to steel herself not to pull away from her bony, grasping fingers. Her mother's self-pity repulsed her. She couldn't feel any sympathy for her. If she felt sorry for anyone it was her father – or the man she'd always thought of as her father. He'd married Shirley knowing he was second best, and he'd never stopped loving her, even though she must have made him miserable for so many years.

And in spite of what Shirley claimed, he'd never, never made Alex feel she was anything but loved and cherished, although how it must have hurt him to look at her and see the man his wife really loved, she couldn't begin to imagine.

And then there was Phoebe. Poor, unwanted Phoebe, who'd been resented from the moment she was born, and who'd spent her whole life trying to earn her mother's love.

And now Shirley was weeping into her tissue, expecting Alex to feel sorry for her, to appreciate the sacrifice she'd made. Well, she couldn't. If Shirley felt she'd been through a lot in her marriage, it was nothing to what she'd put the rest of the family through.

'So where is he now – my father?' She could hardly bring herself to say the word.

'I don't know. He and his wife moved away shortly after I was married. She insisted on it. I think she knew it was the only way she would ever keep Frank away from me.' She dabbed her eyes. 'I wrote to him and sent a photo of you when you were born, but I don't know if it reached him. She probably found it and destroyed it before he even saw it. I don't know where he is or what he's doing now. He could be dead for all I know.'

Alex let go of her mother's hand and went over to the window to stare out at the garden. Her father's pride and joy. Except he wasn't really her father, was he? He was just a man who'd married a woman to save her from the shame of being an unmarried mother.

Her real father could be anywhere. He could, as her mother said, be dead. Or maybe he wasn't. Maybe he and his wife had children of their own. Maybe somewhere out there she had a whole set of half brothers and sisters. Had he told them about her, she wondered. Or had he forgotten all about the daughter he'd never known?

Did she look like him? She'd always thought Phoebe resembled their father while she'd inherited her tall, blonde good looks from her mother, but now she wasn't sure. She couldn't be sure of anything any more. Everything was so messed up and confused, she could barely think straight.

Suddenly there was a mass of questions crowding into her mind, demanding answers. But before she could say anything to her mother, the door flew open and Phoebe burst in.

'Quick, call an ambulance. Dad's collapsed!'

Chapter 27

Will stood at the ironing board, pondering over his shirt. He wasn't sure it was the right one. Nadine preferred the Versace she'd bought him, but that was still in the wash and he'd never felt comfortable in it. But should he drag it out and wear it anyway? Or should he go with his favourite grey one from Next, knowing she wouldn't like it?

The thought of her chilly disapproval had already made him change his socks three times and cut himself shaving. Was this what women went through every time they went out on a date, he wondered. If so, he was glad he was a man.

He knew he should be looking forward to seeing Nadine again, but he was so scared he felt like ringing up and cancelling the whole thing.

So what's the worst she can do, he reasoned. Walk out? She'd already done that. Or tell him she wasn't coming back? Come to think of it, the idea of her returning was what scared him most.

He couldn't have imagined it five months ago, but somehow he'd got used to life without her. Oh, he still missed her. But without him even noticing the pain had got less, until sometimes he barely noticed it.

And there were things he didn't miss, too. Like her always wanting her own way. The long, baffling silences when he had to play a tiring game of trying to guess what he'd done wrong. The way she organised his social life for him. The way she was always rude to his friends. The assumption that she always knew best, in any given situation.

And then there was Phoebe. He still wasn't quite sure what was going on between them. Nothing, judging by her reaction when he told her about Nadine. He'd sort of hoped she might try to talk him out of going, or at least express a smidgeon of jealousy. But she'd been upsettingly pleased for him.

'You've got to do this,' she insisted, when they sat down to talk long into the night about the fateful phone call. 'You need to see her, to find out if you're really over her. Otherwise you'll always be wondering about what might have been.'

But it was what might have been with Phoebe that really troubled him. He was fairly certain by now that Andrew must have got it wrong about her feelings for him. In which case, Nadine's phone call, coming when it did, had saved them both from a huge amount of embarrassment. He cringed to think about what might have happened if she'd called a nanosecond later.

He heard Phoebe's key in the lock. 'Thank God you're here,' he called out. 'Listen, do you think this shirt's all right? I know it's not exactly—' He stopped dead when he saw her leaning against the doorframe, her face the colour of sour milk. 'Christ, Phoebe, what's wrong?'

'Dad's had a heart attack.'

He dropped the iron on to his shirt and rushed over to her. She looked as if she was about to collapse herself. 'Sit down. Can I get you anything? A drink? How about a brandy?'

'No thanks. It's just a shock, that's all.'

She sank down on the sofa. Will poured her a brandy anyway and sat beside her, his arm around her shoulders. 'What happened? How is he?'

'We don't know yet. But it doesn't look good. He's in Intensive Care.' She swished her drink around the glass without touching it. 'I've got to collect some things, then I'm going back to the hospital.'

'Finish your drink first. You'll feel better.'

'I can't. I want to be with Dad.' She handed the glass back to him and stood up.

'I'll come with you.'

'What about Nadine?'

He'd forgotten all about her. 'I'll call her. She'll understand.'

'I don't think so.'

Neither did he. But it didn't matter any more. 'I can't let you go through this on your own.'

'No, Will. This is too important to you.'

'So are you.' The words were out before he'd had time to think about them. Luckily Phoebe didn't seem to notice.

'No, you go. I'll be fine. I'll probably be spending the night at the hospital, so you'll have the place to yourselves. If you want to be alone.'

It took him a moment to register what she meant. 'Thanks.'

They looked at each other. Neither of them seemed to know what to do next. Then Phoebe said, 'I'd better get those things,' and went off to her bedroom.

Will downed the brandy himself. Christ, he thought. What a bloody mess.

Nadine was late as usual. It was one of her favourite tricks, keeping everyone waiting so she could make a big entrance. Will never realised how annoying it was until he'd sat for half an hour, nursing a beer and ignoring the waiters' knowing looks.

He was just about to give up when she walked in. The blood sang in his ears when he saw her. He'd forgotten how incredibly beautiful she was. Her dark hair was drawn back in a plait, showing off her fabulous bone structure. Her simple black dress made her tanned limbs look even longer.

She saw him looking and responded with a cool smile. Will couldn't take his eyes off her as she slithered between the tables towards him.

'Hi.' She leaned over and brushed his cheek with hers. 'Sorry I'm late.'

'That's OK.' Everyone in the restaurant was looking at him. He felt like a spotty sixth-former who'd suddenly scored a date with Madonna. 'Would you like a drink?'

'Please.' She summoned the waiter and ordered a spritzer. Will tried not to stare at her. She was stunning. Those cool crème de menthe eyes, those cheekbones, the perfect, full lips. There wasn't a man in the restaurant who wouldn't have wanted to be sitting right where he was now.

So why was he thinking of Phoebe?

'Will?' He looked up. Nadine and the waiter were looking expectantly at him. 'Are you ready to order?'

'Oh, right. Yes. Sorry.' He scanned the menu and ordered the first thing he saw. Nadine, as ever, spent ages over her choice, questioning the waiter closely on the fat content and cooking method of every ingredient, before she finally ordered plain grilled chicken and steamed vegetables, something which wasn't on the menu. Will smiled to himself, remembering how much Phoebe hated it when customers did that.

'What are you grinning about?' Nadine looked half amused, half annoyed.

'Oh, nothing. Just something Phoebe said, that's all.'

'Phoebe?'

'My flatmate.'

'Oh yes. Your famous flatmate.' Nadine's smile was fixed. 'So what's she like?'

'She's . . .' He thought hard. How could he describe Phoebe? 'She's OK,' he said at last.

'Is that it?'

'What else do you want me to say?'

'What does she look like? Is she tall, thin, fat, or what?'

'She's . . .' Again he struggled over the words. Nadine was watching him closely. He suddenly felt as if the success of the evening depended on him getting the answer right. 'She's nothing like you.'

That seemed to satisfy her. Will ignored the smug gleam in her eye and made a determined effort to change the subject. 'So, how was L.A.?'

'Fabulous. I can't even begin to describe it. I went to some amazing parties, and made some really useful contacts. There was this one guy . . .'

As she went on and on, Will tuned out. A sudden vision of Phoebe, all alone in a hospital corridor nursing a cup of vending machine coffee, rose up in his mind. He shouldn't have let her go on her own, no matter how much she insisted. What kind of a friend was he?

'Are you listening?' He came back to earth to find Nadine looking annoyed. 'You haven't heard a word I've said, have you?'

'Sorry.' Poor Nadine, it wasn't her fault he felt so guilty. He really should concentrate. After all, this could be his big chance. He tried again. 'So – um – what made you come back to England?'

'Well, you know, like I said, L.A.'s great but it's not where I really wanna be right now.' She'd affected an annoying mid-Atlantic twang. Will tried not to notice. 'It's too false, too superficial—'

'In other words, you couldn't get a job?' The words were out before he could stop himself. Nadine looked offended.

'As a matter of fact I had several interesting offers, but nothing that fitted in with my long-term goals.' She toyed with the stem of her glass. 'Actually, I've just been offered the most amazing job over here. On TV.'

'Brilliant. What is it?'

'You know they have Animal Hospital and Children's

Hospital and all those real life medical series? Well, they're doing another one and they want me to front it. Imagine, me presenting my own TV series.'

'And where's this one set?'

Nadine's smile slipped just a fraction. 'In an old people's home. It's a fantastic opportunity, a definite stepping stone to—'

But Will wasn't listening. 'You? In an old people's home?'

'Don't look at me like that. I like old people. The producer says I have a natural warmth and empathy with them.'

'Nadine, you say they all smell of wee.'

'That's not true. Anyway, I won't have to do that much filming with actual old people. They'll have reporters to do that kind of thing. I'll just be the personality that holds it together.'

'So you're going to be the Rolf Harris of the geriatric ward, are you?'

'Thanks for being so supportive,' Nadine said sulkily.

'Sorry. I just can't picture it, that's all.'

'Look, if Gaby Roslin can mingle with a load of snotty kids and pretend to enjoy it, I'm bloody sure I can do it with a bunch of old gits. And it'll be great TV, all those sob stories, people dying all over the place . . .'

Dying. The word struck a chord deep inside him, and he remembered Phoebe's dad again. He wondered if there was any news? Perhaps he could slip away and phone the hospital. They probably wouldn't tell him anything, but maybe he could get a message to Phoebe, let her know he was thinking of her . . .

Their food arrived, and Nadine flirted with the waiter. Will knew she was doing it to wind him up, but he was too preoccupied to feel jealous. All through the meal, she went on talking about her future and her plans for a stratospheric career. Never once did she talk about how

Will fitted into them. Maybe he didn't? He was surprised how little he cared at that moment.

Finally, she snapped. 'Will, what's got into you? You've been on another planet ever since you got here.'

'Sorry. I'm just a bit distracted this evening, that's all.'

'You're telling me!'

'It's just Phoebe's dad is in Intensive Care, and she's really worried about him.'

'Oh. Sorry to hear that. Anyway, as I was saying—'

'Nadine, did you just hear what I said? He's had a heart attack.'

'So?'

'So he might die!'

'And I'm supposed to let that ruin my evening, am I?'

'Well, you could show a bit more concern.'

'Will, I've never even met the man. I'm not going to break my heart over someone I don't even know, am I?'

'I suppose not.' But Phoebe would have, he thought. Phoebe got tears in her eyes when the Andrex puppy got tangled up in the toilet paper.

'Anyway, I've got other things on my mind at the moment. Like our relationship.'

He looked up. 'I didn't know we had one.'

'That depends on you, doesn't it?' Her perfectly arched brows rose. 'I've been thinking, and I reckon we should try to make a go of it. We had something really special, Will. We shouldn't throw that away.'

'I wasn't the one who threw it away,' Will pointed out.

'Oh well, if you're going to start dishing out blame—'

'I wasn't.'

There was a silence. She looked as though she was waiting for him to apologise. He steeled himself not to.

Finally, she said, 'But if we are talking about blame, I think you should ask yourself why I felt I had to run away. I felt trapped, Will. Trapped in a life I didn't want, in a place I didn't want to be, just because that was the way you wanted it.'

'So what are you saying?'

'I'm saying if we're going to get back together, there have to be a few changes. I need to feel more fulfilled. I'm moving on with my life, Will, and I want you to move on with me.'

He suddenly felt wary. 'Go on.'

'Well, first of all I think we should move. I know you like it up here, but I hate it. I feel stifled, out of touch. And my new job is based in London, so I'm going to have to be down there most of the time anyway.'

'But what about my job? And my friends?'

'Will, you're freelance. You can work anywhere. If anything, I think your career will benefit from moving to London. And as for your friends—' Nadine gave a twisted smile. She didn't need to say any more. Will knew exactly how she felt about *them*.

'Anyway, who says we could afford to live down there?' He tried again. 'It costs about five million to buy a shoebox, doesn't it?'

Nadine smiled patronisingly. 'Don't exaggerate Will, you know nothing about it. It's not that bad. And anyway, Daddy says he'll put down the deposit on a place for us. Call it a sort of non-wedding present.'

Call it a bribe, Will thought. How did he know Nadine's father would be involved somewhere, pulling the strings to make sure his little girl got exactly what she wanted? 'Sounds like you and Daddy have got this all worked out.'

'It's not like that.' Nadine didn't meet his eye. 'Daddy can just see the sense in it, that's all. It's what we need. A new start for both of us. Together. It's what you want, isn't it?'

He looked at her. She'd never looked more beautiful. How could it not be what he wanted?

'What if he dies?' Shirley Redmond said for the hundredth time. She looked older, and not just because of the harsh, unflattering light in the hospital corridor. She'd cried all her make-up off in the first half an hour. It was the first time Phoebe had ever seen her in public without it.

'You mustn't talk like that. Dad's not going to die.' Phoebe felt like crying too, but she couldn't. Stupid really, she usually blubbed so easily. But her throat had closed up so much she couldn't even swallow her tepid coffee.

Meanwhile, Shirley was having enough hysterics for both of them. 'You don't know that!' she turned on her. 'You heard what the doctor said. The next couple of hours will be crucial.' She got to her feet and took a few steps up the corridor towards the Intensive Care unit. 'I should be with him.'

Don't you think you've done enough damage, Phoebe wanted to say, but she didn't. This was no time for recriminations, no matter how much she felt like it. 'He needs peace and rest. There's nothing you can do for him now.'

'I know, but I want to see him!' Shirley hiccuped into a sob. Was this really the same woman who had banished her husband to the shed for the past thirty years? 'Why won't someone tell us what's happening?'

'They will as soon as there's anything to tell.'

Shirley turned on her. 'How can you be so calm at a time like this? Your father could be dying!'

'Don't you think I don't know that?' Phoebe shouted back, her patience snapping. 'You might be making yourself feel better by shouting and screaming, but you're not doing anything for Dad, are you? So why don't you sit down and shut up for once?'

Amazingly, the fight seemed to go out of her and she

sank back into her seat. 'You're right. I'm sorry.' She looked so forlorn Phoebe almost felt sorry for her.

'It's OK. We're both a bit edgy.' The past few hours had been a blur. One minute Phoebe was talking to her father, trying to comfort him after the terrible things her mother had said, the next he was fighting for breath, his face contorted with pain.

And then the long wait at the hospital. Shirley had been allowed into the Intensive Care ward at first. But she'd caused such a disturbance with her wailing hysterics that the doctors had suggested she might be better off waiting outside.

They'd asked Phoebe if she wanted to sit with her father instead. But much as she'd longed to be with him, she felt her mother needed her more.

'Where's Alex? Why isn't she here?' Shirley was suddenly on her feet again, looking agitated.

'I think she went home after the ambulance arrived.'

'But she should be here. After all, he is—'

'Her father?'

Shirley's face crumpled. 'Oh God, what have I done? Joseph was right, I should never have said anything. I just thought she had a right to know, that's all. Now she hates me.'

'She's probably just in shock, that's all. Give her time, she'll come round.'

'You didn't see the way she looked at me. As if she despised me. I've ruined her life. I've ruined everyone's lives. This is all my fault!'

She started to cry again, fumbling in her bag for her handkerchief. Phoebe handed her a crumpled tissue. 'Mum, don't blame yourself. You heard what the doctor said. This heart condition would have been building up for a long time – maybe years.' She felt guilty too. She'd noticed how tired he seemed to be. If only she'd made him see a doctor.

'Yes, and that's my fault too.' Shirley dabbed at her eyes. 'I've led him a terrible life, I know that. I've been on at him for years, punishing him, blaming him, taking it out on him just because my life didn't turn out the way I'd planned. As if that was ever his fault.'

She sobbed. After a moment's hesitation, Phoebe put her arms around her mother's thin shoulders. She'd never hugged her before. It was always Alex who got the cuddles and the affection.

And now she knew why.

Poor Alex. No wonder she'd rushed off like that. Phoebe couldn't imagine how she'd feel if she'd just found out her father was some stranger she'd never met.

But strangely, even though everything was so awful, deep down Phoebe felt an odd sense of relief at knowing the truth. All these years, ever since she could remember, she'd blamed herself for the way her mother felt about her. If only she'd been prettier, or cleverer, or less clumsy, maybe she wouldn't be such a disappointment. It came as a relief to know that it wasn't really her fault. The way things were, Shirley would *never* have loved her the way she loved Alex.

'What time is it?' Shirley asked. Phoebe looked at her watch.

'Nearly ten.' Will would be with Nadine now. Maybe they'd be back at the flat, celebrating their reunion. She tried to push the thought from her mind. She had more to worry about than Will's love life.

At least Shirley had calmed down, although she seemed determined to talk. Phoebe stared at a health education poster extolling the virtues of a low-salt lifestyle, while Shirley rambled on about her teenage love affair, and how she'd ended up pregnant.

'I've been deceiving myself for years,' she said. 'All this time I let myself believe that my father kept us apart and forced me to marry Joseph. But that's not the way it happened. Alex's father never wanted to marry me. He couldn't get away fast enough once he found out I was pregnant.' Her mouth curled in self-disgust. 'I couldn't bear to think of how he'd let me down, so I pretended to myself that we were being kept apart. And as the years went by I started believing my own silly lies. Pathetic really, isn't it?' She smiled shakily. 'The truth is, I would have been lost without your father. Poor man, I thought he wasn't good enough for me, just because I was the boss' daughter. But it was me who wasn't good enough. What other man would take someone like me, knowing I was pregnant with another man's child? And what man would let me live with my stupid romantic delusions for nearly thirty years, just because he didn't want to hurt me?'

She started crying again, and Phoebe realised there were tears running down her face too. 'I kept telling myself Alex's father was the love of my life. But Joe's shown me more love and devotion than I ever deserved. And what have I given him? Nothing but heartache. And now it's too late to tell him I'm sorry.'

Phobe cuddled her closer. 'Dad will pull through, you'll see.'

After much persuasion, she finally talked her mother into going to the canteen for something to eat. 'But I'm not hungry,' Shirley protested.

'All the same, you've got to eat,' Phoebe insisted. 'And maybe you should put some more make-up on? You don't want Dad to see you looking a state, do you?'

'That's true. He'll probably have another heart attack.' Shirley gave a thin smile. 'You're a good girl, Phoebe,' she said. Phoebe felt more hot tears pricking her eyes. It was the nicest thing her mother had ever said to her.

And then she was alone. All the effort of being strong for her mother had left her feeling exhausted, and now she had nothing left for herself. She'd spent all her time being a shoulder for everyone else to cry on, but she had no one to lean on herself.

'Phoebe?'

Will was coming down the corridor towards her. She stood up, her legs trembling. He started to run, and the next second she was in his arms, sobbing with relief and gratitude. She'd never been so pleased to see anyone in her life.

Chapter 28

Phoebe woke up, stiff and disorientated, to find she'd fallen asleep on Will's shoulder.

'Sorry.' She jerked upright, then realised why she'd woken up. The doctor was standing over them. 'What is it? What's happened?'

'It's good news, Miss Redmond. We've taken your father off the ventilator. He's out of danger.'

'Oh, thank God.' She looked around. 'Where's Mum? Does she know?'

'She's just gone in to be with him. You can go in too, if you like?'

Phoebe looked at the door to the IC Unit. 'In a minute. I'll let Mum have some time with him first.' They had a lot to say to each other. She just hoped her mother wouldn't forget herself and upset him all over again.

It wasn't until the doctor left that Phoebe realised she'd been gripping Will's hand so tightly she'd scored deep grooves with her nails.

'Sorry.' She let go of him, deeply embarrassed.

'S'OK.'

'What time is it?'

'Just after seven.'

'In the morning? You mean you've been here all night? Why didn't you go home?'

'I wanted to stay here.'

'You didn't have to.'

'I told you, I wanted to.' Their eyes met. Phoebe looked away first.

'How did it go with Nadine last night?'

'It didn't.'

'Don't tell me she didn't turn up?'

'She turned up all right. Full of plans, she was.'

'And did they include you?'

'Let's just say I'm not what she wants any more. And she's definitely not what I want.'

So what do you want? Phoebe longed to ask, but Will changed the subject. 'You look shattered,' he said. 'Why don't we grab a celebratory coffee? I think the canteen's open.'

'You go. I'd like to stay here.'

'Are you sure? I'll stay too if you want.'

She felt a warm glow, seeing the concern in his eyes. 'No, you go. I'll be fine. Bring me a coffee.'

She waited until the doors had swung closed on him, then tiptoed into the IC Unit. It was dimly lit, silent except for the beeping of machines. At the far end of the tiny ward she could make out her father in the bed, wired up to a monitor. Her mother was sitting beside his bed, holding his hand. Phoebe felt tears pricking the back of her eyes. She'd never seen them do that before. She watched them for a moment, then crept away, closing the door behind her.

Alex stood at the end of the corridor, looking pale and tragic, her face bare of make-up. Luke was with her, his arm around her shoulders. Obviously she hadn't told him the wedding was off yet. Or maybe it was back on?

Phoebe felt a surge of anger. 'You've finally turned up, then?'

Alex said nothing, but her eyes swam with tears. It was Luke who asked, 'How is he?'

'Out of danger, thank God.' Phoebe rounded on Alex. 'Why weren't you here?'

'I – I didn't know if I should. After what happened.'

'For God's sake, Alex, he's still your father!' Exhaustion and pent-up worry made her snap. 'Whatever Mum said doesn't wipe out thirty years of caring for you. You owed it to him to be here. And you owed it to Mum, too. She needed you.'

'I know – I'm sorry.' Alex burst into tears. Luke pulled her into his arms.

'It's OK sweetheart, don't get upset.' He frowned at Phoebe over her head. 'You shouldn't take it out on her. She's been worried too, you know. She hardly slept a wink last night.'

'She should have tried sleeping on one of these chairs,' Phoebe muttered. Then she looked at Alex and some of her anger ebbed away. 'I'm sorry, I shouldn't have snapped. I'm just tired, that's all.'

Alex pulled away from Luke and rushed into Phoebe's arms. 'Oh Fee, this is so awful. I feel so terrible.'

'I know, I know,' Phoebe stroked her hair. 'But it's going to be OK now.'

'She's ruined my life. Why did she have to do it? Why did she have to tell me?'

Never mind you, what about Dad? Phoebe wanted to retort, but she stopped herself. Alex had had a terrible shock. She wasn't really being selfish.

She was still hugging Alex when Will came down the corridor, a cup in his hand. He hesitated for a moment when he saw them all standing there, then headed towards them.

'Sorry, I didn't realise you were—' he began to say. Then Alex turned round to face him.

His reaction was almost comical. His jaw dropped and the cup rattled in his hand, slopping hot coffee into the saucer.

'Bugger!' He patted his pockets, searching for a tissue.

'Here.' Alex took one out of her bag and handed it to him with a smile. Phoebe recognised that smile, and instantly felt wary.

Luke must have noticed it too, because he stepped in quickly. 'You must be Phoebe's flatmate. I'm Luke, and this is Alex. My fiancée.'

'Your – fiancée? So that makes you—'

'My sister,' Phoebe said. What was the matter with him? She was used to men reacting to Alex, but Will had turned to jelly.

Alex was gazing intently at him. 'Have we met somewhere before? Only you look very familiar.'

'No! I mean, no, we haven't. We can't have. It's impossible.' Will looked flustered.

'You're probably right. I'm sure I wouldn't have forgotten you.'

She was flirting with him, her heartbreak apparently forgotten. Phoebe instantly wanted to rush over and throw herself between them. Luke was obviously thinking the same thing, because he said, 'Now we're here, Phoebe, why don't you go home and get some rest? You look as if you need it.'

Thanks for pointing that out, Phoebe thought. As if she didn't feel a big enough frump in last night's crumpled clothes. Especially next to Alex doing her Anna Karenina bit.

'He's right,' Will said. 'We can come back and see your dad later. And you'll feel better when you've had a few hours' sleep.'

Phoebe nodded. There wasn't much she could do anyway. And anything was better than watching Alex making eyes at Will.

She slipped into the IC ward to say goodbye to her father and was pleased to find that, in spite of the tubes and drips, he seemed much better. When she came out, Will and Alex were alone in the corridor, whispering. They jumped apart when they saw her.

'Ready?' Will's smile didn't reach his eyes.

'Where's Luke?'

'I sent him to the canteen to get me some breakfast.' Alex turned to Will. 'Well, goodbye Will. I hope we meet again soon.' Phoebe felt the cold grip of dread around her heart.

Oh please, not him too, she thought.

She knew she'd have to say something. As they walked home, she mulled over her words until she finally said, 'What were you and Alex talking about?'

'We weren't talking.'

'Yes, you were. When I came out of the ward you were whispering about something.'

'Oh, that. We were just – um – talking about your dad.'

'So why were you whispering?'

'People always whisper in hospitals. Look, what is this?'

'Nothing. I just wondered, that's all.' They crossed the footbridge over the railway line, then headed down Bootham Crescent towards the main road. 'So what did you think of Alex?'

'She seemed – very nice.'

'Oh, come on, Will, your jaw practically scraped the floor when you saw her!'

'OK, so she's beautiful. That good enough for you?'

He thrust his hands in his pockets and marched up the road. Phoebe hurried to catch up with him. 'She seemed to like you. She was flirting like mad.'

'Was she? I didn't notice.'

'Funny, everyone else did. Even a couple of people in a coma in the next ward noticed.'

Will stopped dead, and she cannoned into the back of him. 'So she was flirting with me. So what? You may find this hard to believe, Phoebe, but I'm not remotely interested in your sister. She could perform Riverdance naked down Coney Street and I still wouldn't be interested. Satisfied?'

He strode off, head down. Phoebe watched him go. You're right, she thought. I do find that hard to believe.

They walked home in silence. Once they were through the front door, Phoebe collapsed on to the sofa and pulled off her boots.

'Thank God that's over. All I want now is a hot bath, a decent cup of tea and about a hundred hours' sleep.'

'That can be arranged. You start your bath, I'll put the kettle on.'

'You're an angel.'

She ran the taps, then went into her bedroom to put on her dressing gown. She was so tired she lay on the bed, listening to the sound of running water from the bathroom. Her aching limbs seemed to melt into the welcoming softness of the mattress after all those hours on a hard hospital chair. It wouldn't hurt to close her eyes, just for two minutes . . .

Next thing she knew, Will was standing over her, a mug in his hand. He'd swapped his suit for a T-shirt and jeans. His expression was tender in the dim light of the bedroom.

'I wasn't sure if I should wake you or not.'

Phoebe blinked up at him for a moment. Then she remembered. 'Oh hell, my bath.'

'Don't worry, I turned off the taps a couple of hours ago.'

'What?' She struggled to sit up. 'How long have I been asleep?'

'Quite a while. You looked so peaceful I thought I ought to let you rest.' He sat down on the end of the bed. 'I'm sorry I got in a mood earlier. About your sister.'

'Oh, that.'

'I don't know if she was flirting with me or not. But even if she was, I wouldn't be interested.'

That's what they all say, Phoebe thought. 'It doesn't matter. It's nothing to do with me anyway.'

'That's just it. It's everything to do with you.' He traced the pattern on the duvet with his finger. 'Phoebe, there's something you should know. We've been friends for a while now, and since you moved in – well, not since you moved in, exactly, but certainly over the past few weeks – I've kind of grown to think of you as more than a friend.'

'Yes?'

'You've been there for me when I needed someone. And I want you to know that I really appreciate that.' She could almost feel the heat coming off his face. 'But I also want you to know—'

'What?' She leaned forward so they were practically nose to nose.

'I just thought I should tell you—'

The phone rang. 'Don't answer it,' Will said.

'I've got to. It might be the hospital.'

But it wasn't. It was someone called Sammy offering her a free estimate on her double-glazing. It was all Phoebe could do not to throw the phone out of the window.

She raced back to the bedroom, but Will was gone. She found him in the bathroom, running another bath.

'So what was it you were going to say?' she asked.

'What? Oh, it doesn't matter. It probably wasn't the time or the place anyway.' He smiled at her. 'I'll leave you to it, shall I?'

She lay in the bath, trying to soak away her frustration. She'd been so sure he was about to tell her he loved her.

And she was all ready to tell him she loved him, too.

She hadn't really been ready to admit it until now. Even when Minty came on the scene, she told herself it wasn't really jealousy she was feeling, just a natural dislike for someone who wore an excessive amount of patchouli. But then when Nadine phoned, she finally realised how she really felt.

It had nearly killed her to smile and act positive when inside she'd been tearing herself apart at the thought of Will getting back with his fiancée. All those lonely hours in the hospital, when she wasn't worrying about her father, she was tormenting herself by picturing the two of them together, laughing over old times, realising what they'd missed while they were apart.

And when Will turned up at the hospital it wasn't just the fact that he was a friendly face that made her rush up and throw her arms around him. It was sheer relief that he wasn't on a plane back to L.A.

She was fairly sure he felt the same way. If that wretched double-glazing woman hadn't phoned, she might even have found out. Now all she could do was wait. And hope.

'Good to see your dad's feeling better, isn't it?' Luke said, as they came out of the Intensive Care Unit.

'What? Oh, yes.' Alex was so preoccupied she didn't even bother to point out that he wasn't really her dad.

Seeing Will again had been a shock. Seeing him with Phoebe was an even bigger one.

Was there anything going on between them? It was hard to tell. She'd certainly kept it a secret if there was.

But it couldn't be serious. After all, it wasn't that long ago that she and Will had spent the night together. And to think all this time Phoebe had been sharing a flat with him. In a small place like York she shouldn't have been too surprised, but it was still a weird coincidence.

Luke was rabbiting on, even though she'd stopped listening to him. 'You know, you mustn't blame yourself,' he said.

'What?'

'This heart attack. I suppose you're thinking the strain of the wedding must have had something to do with it. But it could have happened at any time.'

'I know that,' she snapped. If anyone had caused it, it was her mother. Seeing her weeping at the bedside had filled Alex with rage. She was nothing but a bloody hypocrite. 'Can we get out of here? Hospitals give me the creeps.'

'Don't you think we should hang around and offer your mum a lift?'

'Let her take the bus. It'll be good for her.'

'Alex—'

'Look, if you want to give her a lift, that's up to you. I'm going home.'

She strode off. He followed, as she knew he would. Alex almost wished he'd argue sometimes.

She hadn't told him she'd changed her mind about the wedding, but she knew she would have to soon. His compliance bored and frustrated her.

Not like Will. She was silent in the car, thinking about him. His reaction when he'd seen her had been so comical. He looked like a little boy who'd been caught with his hand in the biscuit tin.

When Phoebe had gone in to see her father, Alex had immediately sent Luke off to the canteen so she could be alone with him.

'Long time, no see,' she'd said. 'Small world, isn't it?'

'Very.' He didn't smile back. His eyes were fixed on the door of the IC Unit.

'I didn't expect to see you again. Not after you disappeared with the dawn like that. Not a very gentlemanly thing to do, by the way.'

'I know. I'm sorry.'

'You seem very edgy?' Alex glanced in the direction he was looking. 'I take it Phoebe doesn't know anything about us?'

'What do you think?'

Of course Phoebe had to choose that moment to appear, just as things were getting interesting. The look on her face when she saw them together was enough to tell Alex how she felt about Will.

But did he feel the same way about her? Maybe it was time to find out.

'You look happy,' Joe Redmond said as he watched his daughter unpacking her Sainsbury's carrier bag on to his bedside table.

Phoebe looked up, a bag of Golden Delicious in her hand. 'Any reason why I shouldn't be? You're on the mend.'

'No, it's more than that. Something's put a smile on your face. It's not that young man who was here last night, is it?'

'Dad!' Phoebe ducked her head to avoid his shrewd gaze. God, was it that obvious? 'I couldn't get you lemon barley so I got you orange instead. Is that OK?'

'I'd rather have a pint.' He smiled at her. 'That young man of yours has promised to take me out for a drink when I get out of here.'

Phoebe rearranged bananas in the fruit bowl. 'He's not my young man. And I'm sure Luke would go out for a drink with you, if you're that desperate.'

'Aye, and I'd need to be, to go supping with him.'

'Dad! I thought you liked Luke?'

'Oh, I do. Don't get me wrong, I think he's a grand lad. But all he ever talks about is work and Alex. Your Will seemed much more my kind of man. Yours too, I reckon.'

'Has the consultant been round yet? What did he say?' She changed the subject before her face caught fire.

'Not much. You know the kind of thing these doctors come out with. Never look you in the eye, never give you a straight answer.' He grasped her wrist. 'Phoebe, love, I want to ask you. Has the doctor said anything to you?'

'Only that you've had a major scare, and you've got to learn to take it easier,' Phoebe said. 'A healthier diet, gentle exercise, no more stress.'

'And that's it?'

'As far as I know. Dad, what is it? What's this about?'

'That's what I'm wondering.' His face creased with anxiety. 'I was just worried, you see, because your mother—'

'I'm back. Sorry I had to rush off earlier, I wanted to catch the library.' They both turned around. Shirley stood in the doorway, her arms full of flowers. Phoebe nearly fell over with shock at the sight of her. She looked as if she'd thrown on the first old sweater and pair of slacks that came to hand. Her hair was less than immaculate and her lack of make-up showed the lines of strain around her eyes. But she looked softer and more attractive than Phoebe could ever remember her.

Even more shocking, she was actually smiling. A real smile, not just her usual twitch of mouth muscles. It was so unexpected Phoebe had to look round to check no one else had sneaked into the room behind her.

She watched with astonishment as Shirley moved over to the bed and planted a kiss on the top of her husband's head. It was a bit awkward, but by Shirley's standards it was roughly the equivalent of a full-on snog. 'How are you feeling now?' she asked.

'No different to how I was the last time you asked.' Joe glanced at Phoebe. See, his expression said. No wonder he thought he wasn't long for this world. 'You don't have to come in three times a day, you know. You must have other things to do.'

'Nothing as important as seeing you.' Shirley put down her bags and plumped up his pillows. 'Now, have you had your medication yet? They were late yesterday, as I remember. I know the NHS is supposed to be overstretched, but—'

'I had it an hour ago. Stop fussing, woman.' Joe pretended to be cross but Phoebe could see he was as pleased as he was confused by all the attention.

'That's all right, then.' Shirley sat down and rifled through her bag. 'Now, I've changed your library books. I got you the new Ruth Rendell, I know you like her. Oh, and a couple of gardening magazines. Not that you'll be doing much of that for a while,' she added severely.

'Who says? I'm supposed to exercise, remember?'

'Yes, but not to overdo it. I know you, once you get out in that garden you'll be pulling up weeds and hauling that lawnmower all over the place.'

'So who's going to do it if I don't?'

'I suppose I'll have to.'

'You?' Phoebe and her father both stared at her. She looked defensive.

'Why not? I'm not completely useless, you know.'

Phoebe was fairly sure Shirley didn't know a rose from a radish. As far as she was concerned, the garden was a place to sit and sip gin and tonics.

'Anyway, you can show me, can't you? For heaven's sake, it can't be that difficult. We could do it together.'

Now she really was entering the twilight zone, Phoebe decided. The last time her parents had done anything together was conceiving her. And that was such a disaster they'd never tried it again.

She decided to leave before things got really strange. Gathering up her bags, she kissed her father goodbye.

'Can I have a word?' Shirley said. They went outside. 'How did he look to you? I wonder if the doctors did the right thing, moving him to a general ward so soon.'

'He'll be fine,' Phoebe reassured her.

'What if he isn't? What if they did it just because they needed the bed? I knew we should have gone private—'

'Mum, they know what they're doing. And Dad likes

having other people around him. He enjoys the company.'

'I hope you're right.' Shirley bit her lip. Phoebe couldn't remember the last time she'd seen her worried about anything but the state of her hair. 'I know I can't make up for the past thirty years, but I really feel as if I've been given a second chance. And I mean to make the most of it this time.'

Phoebe smiled. 'Perhaps you should tell Dad that? With you being so nice, he's terrified the doctors are keeping something terrible from him.'

'Is he really? Oh God.' Shirley rolled her eyes. 'I really do have a lot of making up to do, haven't I?' She paused. 'Have you seen Alex recently?'

'Not since she turned up at the hospital three days ago. Hasn't she been in since then?'

'Your father hasn't seen her. He keeps asking.' She sighed. 'I suppose it's all my fault. I've driven her away.'

'She'll come round eventually.' Phoebe made a mental note to call her sister. Even if she was upset, that was no excuse to neglect her father.

She gave her mother a quick, embarrassed peck on the cheek. But as she turned away Shirley suddenly grabbed her and enveloped her in a big hug. 'You really are a good girl, Phoebe,' she said. Then, before she had time to faint away with shock, Shirley added, 'It's just a pity you can't do something nicer with your hair.'

Phoebe grinned. It was good to see some things hadn't changed.

It was Wednesday afternoon, and the streets were quite empty. As she walked across the hospital car park, the air was filled with the delicious smell of chocolate from the Nestlé factory further up the road.

Her father was right, she was in a good mood, although she didn't really know why. Nothing had happened between her and Will since Sunday, but she had a feeling that might all change soon. He'd been so sweet to her, going in to visit her father when Phoebe had to work. Surely he wouldn't go to that trouble if he didn't feel anything for her?

Then, as she turned the corner from Bootham into Will's street, a glint of metallic green caught her eye. Alex's car was parked in her space outside the house.

She abandoned her Metro further down the street and ran back to the house, feeling sick with exertion and panic.

Let me be wrong, she prayed. Please let me be wrong.

But she wasn't.

Chapter 29

They were at opposite ends of the sofa, but Phoebe could feel the tension the moment she walked in.

'Phoebe!' Will shot to his feet. 'I was just telling Alex I didn't know what time you'd be back. How's your dad?'

'Getting better.' Phoebe looked at Alex. 'It's a pity *you* don't take a bit more interest in his welfare.'

'I've been phoning the hospital every day.' Alex's chin lifted. She was still looking pale and tragic, but she'd done her hair and put on some make-up.

'You could have gone in to see him.'

'I wasn't sure he'd want me to.'

'I'll – um – just nip downstairs and see if the evening paper's arrived.' Will beat a tactful retreat, leaving Phoebe alone with Alex.

'Of course he wants to see you. You're his daughter.'

'Not according to our mother.'

'It was Dad who brought you up and loved you for thirty years. What the hell does it matter who was there at the conception?'

'Quite a lot, actually. But then you wouldn't understand that. You haven't just had your world turned upside down, have you?' Tears started to brim. 'You know, I've always thought there was something about the way he treated me. He never loved me like he loved you.'

'That's rubbish.'

'You were always his favourite.'

'Only because Mum wouldn't let him near you!' Phoebe was exasperated. 'Look, as far as he's concerned we're both his daughters. Nothing can change that. And it's really hurting him that you haven't been to see him.'

'I don't know. I just don't think I'm ready to face either of them.'

'For God's sake!' Phoebe's temper cracked. 'The way you're going on anyone would think it was you in hospital! Dad nearly died. Can't you stop worrying about yourself for five minutes and think how someone else might be feeling for once?'

Alex burst into tears just as Will walked back into the room. He sent Phoebe a reproachful look, then disappeared off to the kitchen.

Phoebe sat in the armchair and waited for her sister's weeping to subside. Which it did, about three seconds after Will had left the room. 'So what are you doing here, anyway?'

'I had nowhere else to go. I had to talk to someone.' She wiped her face on her sleeve. 'I've split up with Luke.'

Phoebe sat upright. 'What? Why?'

'I told him I didn't want to marry him, like I told you. Then I realised I didn't want to be with him either. We just weren't making each other happy. I suppose you think I'm a complete bitch,' Alex guessed her thoughts. 'But I'm not doing this just for myself. Luke deserves to be with someone who can truly make him happy.' She smiled shakily. 'He'd have been better off with you.'

'He didn't love me.'

'He slept with you.'

Phoebe glanced at the door, expecting Will to appear. 'That was a mistake.'

'It may be for you, but actually I think that's part of the reason Luke and I finished. I couldn't really forget what you and he did. I found it impossible to trust him any more.'

'Of course you could trust him!'

'You're a fine one to tell me about trust! Does Will know you slept with my fiancé?'

'No, he doesn't.'

'And you don't want him to? I don't suppose he'd be too impressed.'

'Too impressed with what?' Will came back into the room with the evening paper.

'Oh, nothing. Just girl talk. Anyway, the bottom line is we're finished. I'm free and single again.' She waggled her diamond-free left hand at Phoebe and Will. Especially at Will, although he pretended not to notice.

'So where's Luke now?' Phoebe asked.

'Trust you to be more worried about him! He's still at the flat. I said he could stay there for a while, since he's got nowhere else to go.'

'Won't that be awkward for you?' Phoebe caught Alex's look and suddenly knew what was coming next.

'Actually, I was wondering if I could stay here for a few days? You're right, it would be awkward at the flat. I wouldn't be any trouble, honestly. You wouldn't even know I was here.'

Having shared a flat with her for three years, Phoebe doubted that very much. 'Why can't you just tell Luke to move out? It is your place, after all.'

'I know, but I feel really guilty about throwing him out. Especially as it was my idea for him to give up his flat and move in with me. And he doesn't have anyone else he can stay with. All his family are in London, remember? Although I suppose you could always let him move in here. I expect you'd like that, wouldn't you?'

Phoebe ignored the look Will shot her over the top of the *Evening Press*.

'Anyway, I don't really feel like being on my own right now.' Alex looked appealingly at her.

'What about Mum? I'm sure she'd appreciate the company while Dad's in hospital.'

'I don't think Mum and I have much to say to each other at the moment.' Alex's smile disappeared. 'Besides, he'll be out in a few days. Please, Fee?'

'It's not my flat. Will's the one you should be talking to, not me.'

Alex swivelled around on the sofa to face him. 'So what do you think, Will? Can I stay here for a few days? I can sleep on the floor in Phoebe's room.'

They both looked at Will. Suddenly it felt as if everything depended on his answer. If he said no, it would mean she still had a chance with him. But if he said yes . . .

'I don't see why not,' he shrugged.

'That's settled, then. I'll get my stuff from the car, shall I? I brought it with me, just in case you said yes,' she explained, seeing Phoebe's look of surprise.

'And what if I'd said no?'

'I knew you wouldn't.' Alex planted a kiss on Phoebe's head. 'You wouldn't let me down, Fee. You're too nice.' She turned to Will. 'I don't suppose you could give me a hand? Only it's a long way up and down those stairs.'

'I'll do it.' Phoebe was on her feet, but Alex practically pushed her back down.

'Oh no, you sit there. This is a job for a big strong man.' She grinned at Will. 'Tell you what, Fee, why don't you nip down to the off-licence and buy a couple of bottles of wine? Then we can have a nice evening in. Just the three of us. Won't that be cosy?'

Will gazed at the boot of the car, crammed to bursting with boxes, suitcases and carrier bags. 'I thought you said you were only staying a few days?'

'I don't believe in travelling light. Besides, you never know, you might get to like having me around.' Her eyes flashed with meaning.

'I doubt it.' He reached into the boot for the first box.

'You don't seem very cheery. Have I done something to upset you?'

'Yes, since you ask.' He turned to face her. 'You told me you'd come round to see Phoebe. You didn't say anything about moving in.'

'You could have said no.'

'Then I would have had to tell her why I didn't want you around.'

'And why is that?' She leaned closer. He caught a whiff of her perfume, sharp and sexy. 'Why exactly don't you want me around, Will?'

'You know why.' He held the box in front of him, like a shield.

'Is it because you're afraid you won't be able to resist me?'

Their eyes locked. 'What are you playing at?' he said. 'Why are you here?'

'I told you, I had nowhere else to go.'

'Are you sure that's the only reason?' He hauled the box up the stairs. Alex followed him, empty-handed.

'Of course. Why?' She laughed. 'You're not worried I'm going to do a *Fatal Attraction* number and start stalking you?' Will said nothing. 'You are! You think you're going to come home from work and find me boiling your bunny?'

'Don't be ridiculous.' He shouldered open Phoebe's door and put the box down on the bed.

'Sorry to disappoint you, Will, but Phoebe's the cook in the family. My talents lie in other directions.'

When he turned around, she was blocking the doorway. Her eyes roved up and down his body. 'And so did yours, if I remember correctly.'

Will edged past her and went downstairs to fetch another box.

When he got back to the bedroom Alex was waiting

for him. She stretched out on her stomach on the bed, watching him with lazy amusement.

'Are you playing hard to get, or are you just shy?' she teased.

'Neither. I just don't think this is a good idea, that's all. Phoebe will be back any minute.'

'So? We're not actually doing anything, are we? Or are you thinking about it?'

He dropped the box on the floor. 'Are you going to start unpacking this stuff, or what?'

'In a minute. Why are you so worried about her finding out, anyway? It's not as if she's your girlfriend, is she?'

'No, but—'

'If you ask me, I don't suppose she'd even care. There's only one man she's interested in, and that's my ex-fiancé.'

'She's over Luke. She told me.'

'And you believed her? Did you not see the look on her face when I told her we'd split up? If I know Phoebe, she'll be round there by tomorrow, offering him a shoulder to cry on.'

She slid off the bed and stood up in a sinuous movement. 'Looks like they won't need either of us much longer, does it? Still, we could always keep each other company. I seem to remember we did quite a good job of consoling each other last time around.'

'That's not an experience I really want to repeat.'

'Isn't it?' He could feel himself growing mesmerised as she gazed deeply into his eyes. 'I think you do, Will. That's why you're so afraid of having me around.'

'For God's sake, Phoebe, why don't you just tell her to pack her bags and piss off?' Karen's advice was, as usual, short and to the point.

'How can I? She's my sister.' Phoebe flinched as the

crash of what sounded like an avalanche of pans came from beyond the kitchen doors, followed by great deal of swearing.

It felt strange to be sitting in an empty restaurant at lunchtime. Bar Barato was closed for two days while they filmed 'The Goode Food Guide'. The set builders were hard at work transforming the kitchen, while researchers and production assistants buzzed around with clipboards and stopwatches.

The rest of the kitchen staff had been given the day off, but since Titus was still stubbornly insisting he'd resigned, Phoebe had been dragged in to help. Which was how she came to be propping up the bar with a glass of Pinot Grigio watching Karen fill in her weekly drinks order.

'And you reckon she's definitely making a move on Will?'

'She's about as subtle as a love-starved rhino. I caught her coming out of his bedroom this morning. She said she'd been taking him a cup of tea but they both looked very shifty about it.'

Phoebe pushed her glass away. Alex had been in the flat for nearly a week. Six days of utter misery, watching her move in on Will like a heat-seeking missile. She kept talking about her 'pain' and how she was 'still grieving' but her grief certainly hadn't affected her ability to flirt.

'And what does he say about it?'

'Not a lot. He pretends he's ignoring it, but it's pretty hard to see how anyone could ignore Alex flitting around in a push-up bra and thong.'

The most hurtful thing was, he seemed to be ignoring her too. As if it was somehow her fault Alex was there. As if he wasn't secretly enjoying it.

Any hope she'd had for the two of them had faded the moment Alex turned up. They never seemed to have a moment alone together any more. And if they did, Will always seemed preoccupied and distant.

Phoebe's response had been to try to preserve what there was left of her dignity. She deliberately kept him at arms' length, pretended she didn't care. It hurt, but at least it saved him the effort of avoiding her. Unfortunately, it also left a yawning gap between them just waiting for Alex to come along and fill.

'What I don't understand is why she has to do it,' she said. 'She could have any man she wanted. Why does she always want mine?'

'Maybe that's part of the fun?' Karen refilled her glass. 'Anyway, you don't have to let it happen, do you?'

'What do you suggest I do? Put a twenty-four-hour guard on his bedroom door?'

'You could tell him how you feel about him.'

Phoebe laughed. 'And make an even bigger fool of myself? It's pretty clear he's not interested.'

'So you're not going to put up a fight for him?'

'What's the point? Alex will only get him in the end. Besides, it's not as if I'm actually his girlfriend, is it? Will's a free agent, he can do as he likes.'

She knew her friend's advice made sense. If it had been Karen, she would have been in there, claws out, ready to fight for her man. But she also knew that it would do no good. Sooner or later Alex would get her way.

Chapter 30

But Alex wasn't getting her way. She lay in the bath and adjusted the tap with her toe, maliciously taking the last of the hot water, knowing Phoebe would want a shower when she got home.

She was deeply frustrated. She'd been in the flat for a week now, and the only time she'd lured Will into the bedroom was to retrieve her ancient coffee cups lined up under the bed. She must be losing her touch.

And the less interest he showed, the more she wanted him. It had got to the point where she couldn't stop thinking about him. She'd never failed to get any man she wanted. Having Will had become a matter of pride, as much as anything else.

Even more unthinkably, he actually seemed more interested in Phoebe. Phoebe, who slopped around the flat without make-up and dressed like a bag lady. Yet Will looked at her as if she was Claudia Schiffer in head-to-toe Vivienne Westwood.

Bloody Phoebe! Alex felt the old anger building up. Why did she have to have everything? Why did everyone seem to love her? Even their mother, who'd always been Alex's most devoted ally, seemed to be singing Phoebe's praises these days.

And she had Will. Even if she was too stupid to realise it, and spent most of her time running away from him.

In the meantime Alex had nothing. She didn't even have a boyfriend, for heaven's sake! And her temp job had come to an abrupt end after the boss found out she was using valuable customer call time to order from the Next Directory.

Still, being unemployed had its advantages. For one thing, it gave her a lot of time alone with Will.

He was working at his drawing board. He didn't even look up as Alex came into the room.

'Doing anything interesting?' she asked.

'Just finishing the last illustration for the book.'

She came up close behind him to peer over his shoulder. 'And you actually get paid for that? They look like little stick men to me.'

'That's because you're not six years old.'

She stared in frustration at his back. 'Will, I think we ought to talk, don't you?'

'What about?' He carried on working but his pen hesitated a fraction, she noticed.

'Do you want me to move out?'

That made him look up. She noticed his expression change when he saw she was wearing nothing but a big fluffy towel, her wet hair snaking over her bare shoulders. He wasn't as immune as he liked to think, obviously.

'Why?' he asked.

'Oh, come on. You obviously don't like having me around.'

'It's not that—'

'Will, you run a mile every time I come near you. You're making me feel as welcome as a leper at an orgy.'

'I'm sorry.'

'So do you want me to go?'

'Phoebe wants you to stay.'

'I'm not talking about Phoebe, I'm talking about you. Do you want me to stay, Will?'

He turned back to his drawing board. 'It's nothing to do with me.'

'I think it is. Why do you think I split up with Luke? It was because of you and that night we spent together.'

'Now hang on a minute—'

'Don't panic, Phoebe's not going to walk in the door. We've got hours. And I think it's about time we both put our cards on the table, don't you?' She went around to the other side of his drawing board to face him. 'I meant what I just said. That night changed everything, Will. As soon as we made love I knew I couldn't go back to Luke.' She reached out and touched his shoulder. His muscles were hard under his shirt. 'Look at me. Look at me and tell me you haven't thought about that night too.'

He lifted his head. His eyes moved slowly up her body to rest on her face. 'That night was a mistake,' he said.

'How can you say that? We were great together.'

'So you keep telling me. But the fact is I was so drunk I don't remember a thing about it. I didn't even remember what you looked like until I saw you in that hospital corridor.'

'That's not true!'

'I'm sorry, but it is.' His voice was more gentle. 'Look, maybe you're right. Maybe it would be better if you moved out. You're obviously expecting something from me that I can't give you.'

'Because you're in love with Phoebe, you mean? I told you, you're wasting your time there.'

'So you keep saying.' He picked up his pen and went back to work. Alex stared at him, infuriated. She wanted to lash out, to hurt him like he'd just hurt her.

'I wonder how she'd feel if I told her what happened that night?'

'You wouldn't.'

'I might have to. She is my sister after all. We always tell each other everything.' She examined her nails. 'I expect she'd be quite interested to know what you were doing on your birthday, while she was waiting here for you all alone.'

He looked up at her, contempt in his dark eyes. 'Why?' he said. 'I can understand why you'd want to hurt me, but why her? What's she done to you?'

'Because . . .' Because she's got everything, she wanted to blurt out. 'Because I think she deserves to know the truth.'

The stairs up to the flat felt like the north face of the Matterhorn. Phoebe trudged up them, barely noticing when Mrs Warzovski appeared on the first-floor landing for her customary tutting session.

She hadn't touched a pan or sliced so much as an onion, yet she felt as tired as if she'd single-handedly covered an entire Saturday night session.

She'd imagined that filming in the kitchen would be a simple matter of moving in a couple of cameras. But she reckoned without the director, Malcolm, the Laurence Llewelyn Bowen of cookery programmes. He'd moved in with a crew of burly set builders and virtually dismantled and rebuilt the kitchen to his own specifications. They'd taken down shelves and refitted cupboards, put on new doors and changed the lighting. Phoebe had tried to stop them, but it was like standing in front of a 500-ton juggernaut.

'But we've got to work in here!' she'd protested as they began to empty the walk-in.

'So have we, dear.' Malcolm flicked back his hair. 'And at the moment it's just not right. There are too many – things.'

'It's a kitchen,' Phoebe pointed out through gritted teeth, 'there are meant to be things.'

'Yes, but these are the *wrong* things.'

In desperation she'd sought out Guy, who was busy bragging to his friends on his mobile.

'It's a disaster,' she complained. 'God knows what Titus is going to say.'

'There's nothing he can say, is there? I asked him to come in and supervise, but he's decided to stay at home and play silly buggers instead.' He smiled at Phoebe. 'Still, I'm sure you can sort it out, Fee. I have every confidence in you.'

In other words, don't bother me about it, Phoebe thought. She looked around the barren wasteland that had once been a working kitchen. Titus would definitely go ape. If he turned up. But with Cameron Goode due the following day, he and Guy were still in a stand-off situation.

By three o'clock there was nothing left to supervise and the crew had gone home for the day, leaving Phoebe with a thumping headache and a dull feeling of dread about what lay ahead. With any luck, the headache would turn into a migraine and she wouldn't have to go in at all.

The voices were so loud she heard them halfway up the stairs. Will and Alex were in the middle of an argument. She was just about to rush in and break them up when something made her stop and listen instead.

'You're right,' she heard Will say. 'But I should be the one to tell her, not you.'

'You wouldn't dare.'

'Why not? I don't want to go on deceiving her.'

Phoebe froze as she heard Alex's voice, clear and mocking. 'You mean to say you're actually going to tell her we slept together?'

'Like you said, she deserves to know the truth.'

'But she'll be devastated. And she'll hate you.'

'That's a chance I'll have to take, isn't it?'

Alex said something else after that, but Phoebe didn't wait to hear it. She turned and fled back down the stairs, nearly knocking over Mrs Warzovski who'd come out to complain about the noise.

★

'You're bluffing,' Alex said.

Will shrugged. 'Maybe, maybe not. But I know I can explain better than you will. If I tell her, maybe there's a chance she'll understand.'

'You're asking a lot.'

'I know. But I can't let something like this hang over us. I can't go on for ever, wondering if you're going to say anything. If Phoebe and I are to have any chance, we've got to get this in the open.'

Anger boiled through her veins. 'If you're so worried about getting things out in the open, perhaps you'd better ask Phoebe if she's got anything to hide too.'

That got him. 'What are you talking about?'

'Ask Phoebe. Ask her what she and Luke got up to while I was away at a conference a few months ago.' She turned to walk away but Will grabbed her arm. 'Ow, you're hurting me!'

'Tell me!'

'All right, then. While I was away working, your precious Phoebe was sleeping with my boyfriend in my flat. Probably in my bed for all I know.'

He let go of her. 'I don't believe you.' But she could see the doubt in his eyes.

'Fine. I don't care anyway. But ask Phoebe. Ask her what she did while I was in Cheltenham.' She rubbed at her wrist where he'd gripped it. 'You see, she's not such an angel after all, is she? I don't think you've got anything to worry about, telling her about us. After all, how does a quick one night stand compare to sleeping with your sister's boyfriend?'

Chapter 31

Luckily Karen was still at the restaurant, locking up. Phoebe caught her at the front door.

'Oh hi, I thought you'd gone home.' She took one look at Phoebe's stricken face, unlocked the door and pushed her inside.

She sat her down at the bar, poured two large brandies and handed one to her. 'Tell me,' she said.

Phoebe told her, in between crying fits and bolstering sips of brandy. Now the shock had worn off, she felt more stupid than angry. Why hadn't she known? The clues must have all been there, staring her in the face. Why hadn't she guessed? It felt as if there was some huge joke and she was the only one who wasn't in on it.

'So how long has this been going on?' Karen asked, when she'd finished.

'I don't know. Since she moved in, probably. It wouldn't take her long. Look how quickly she moved in on Luke.' She blew her nose on a paper napkin. 'Why couldn't they tell me? Why did they have to make a fool of me?'

'I don't know, love.' Karen refilled her glass. For once she seemed too stunned to be angry. 'All I know is that if Will can let himself be taken in by someone as shallow as your sister, he really isn't the man I thought he was.'

Phoebe buried her head in her hands. 'Oh God, Karen, what am I going to do? I can't go back to the flat, not with them together. I don't think I could bear it. Not again.'

'You don't have to,' Karen said briskly. 'You can stay

317

at my place tonight. We'll get drunk and have a takeaway and bitch about men.'

'But what about tomorrow? I've got to go back sooner or later, if only to pick up my stuff.'

'We'll worry about that when the time comes.' Karen topped up her drink. 'In the meantime—Oh Hell, that's all we need. What's he doing here?'

She looked past Phoebe's shoulder towards the door. Phoebe turned round. Luke was peering in at the door, shading his eyes with his hand. Phoebe felt plunging disappointment. For one insane moment she'd hoped it might be Will.

'I'll get rid of him.' Karen started to move from behind the bar but Phoebe stopped her.

'I'd better see what he wants.'

Karen sent her a look that spoke volumes, but said nothing.

She unlocked the door. Luke looked uncertain as he stepped inside. 'I wasn't sure whether to come.'

'Just because you and Alex have split up, it doesn't mean we can't still be friends.' Phoebe forced herself to smile. 'Would you like a drink?'

'Please.'

Karen glowered at him from behind the bar as she poured another brandy. Then she went down to the other end of the bar to fold napkins, leaving them alone.

For a long time they sat in silence. Then Luke said, 'I suppose she's staying with you?' Phoebe nodded. 'I thought she might be. I've tried ringing there a couple of times, but I always get the answer machine. I just need to know, because some post has come for her and I don't know where to send it. Do you think she's going to be staying there long?'

Karen snorted and did some extra fast folding.

'I get the impression she's not in any hurry to move on,' Phoebe said carefully.

He sipped his drink. Then, just as Phoebe was getting used to the silence, he put his glass down and said, 'I don't know what went wrong. One minute we were fine, and the next she's telling me she never really loved me. I don't suppose you know what happened?' Phoebe shook her head. 'But she must have said something to you? You're her sister, she tells you everything – Phoebe, what is it? Why are you crying?'

'I'll tell you why, you selfish bloody oaf!' Karen stormed down to their end of the bar, elbows out, looking furious. 'At this very moment your oh-so-precious ex-fiancée is having sex with Phoebe's flatmate. Who, incidentally, Phoebe happens to like very much.'

She could feel Luke looking at her. 'Is this true?' She nodded, not trusting herself to speak. 'I can't believe it. She swore to me there wasn't anyone else.'

'Well, there is now.' Karen, never one for sparing anyone's feelings, chimed in again. 'And I'll tell you something else. She's been doing it to Phoebe for years.'

'Karen—'

'He ought to know the truth.' Karen turned to Luke. 'Why do you think she was so interested in you? Don't flatter yourself she went for your winning personality. The only reason she wanted you was because she knew Phoebe was in love with you!'

A black hole of silence followed. Phoebe wanted to throw herself into it and disappear for ever. As it was, she could only stare at the pale ash wood surface of the bar and wish herself a million miles away.

Karen must have realised she'd said too much because she collected up her neat pile of folded napkins and disappeared into the back room.

'Phoebe, I had no idea.' There was a catch in Luke's voice.

'It doesn't matter.'

'It does matter. Christ, I knew you had a crush on me,

but I never realised—' He ran his hand through his hair. 'So that night we spent together – it really meant something to you?' She looked down at her hands, too embarrassed to answer. 'But you seemed so OK about it the next morning. I thought you didn't care.'

'I didn't have much choice, did I? I knew how you felt about Alex.' She forced herself to look at him. 'Take no notice of what Karen said. Alex did love you. Why else would she want to marry you?'

'I'm beginning to wonder.' There was a faraway look in his eyes. 'I thought it was strange at the time. One minute she hated the idea and then suddenly—' he stopped, a thought occurring to him. 'She didn't want to know until I told her about us. Maybe your friend's right? Maybe she really did only want me because you did?'

He looked so forlorn Phoebe said, 'I don't know if anyone really understands what goes on in Alex's head. Sometimes I wonder if she knows herself.' Even now, in spite of everything she'd done, she couldn't help defending her.

'I don't hate her. Although I have to say it makes it a lot easier to leave. I've asked for a transfer back to London,' he explained, seeing Phoebe's face. 'I'm leaving on Friday.'

'So soon?'

'There's not really anything to keep me here, is there?'

'You're probably right. I just wish I could escape that easily.'

They were both silent for a moment, lost in their own thoughts. Then Luke said, 'So what are you going to do now?'

'I don't know. Karen says I can sleep at her place tonight. But I've got to pick up my stuff from the flat sometime.'

'Do you want to do it now? I could come with you.'

'I don't really think that's a good idea, do you? Alex might be there.'

'So? It'll give me a chance to say goodbye.' He smiled. 'Don't worry, I won't make a scene or try to lay one on your boyfriend.'

'Why not? He deserves it.' Karen appeared from the back room at such speed Phoebe wondered if she'd had her ear glued to the door the whole time. 'I think it's a great idea. You don't really want to face those two on your own, do you?'

Phoebe looked from one to the other. She didn't really want to face them at all.

She was trembling so much she could hardly get her key in the door.

'Are you sure you want to do this?' Luke asked.

'No, but I'm here now, aren't I?'

'That's my girl.' He put his arm around her and gave her a reassuring squeeze, just as the door flew open and Will stood there.

'I thought I heard—' His face fell when he saw Luke. 'What do you want? Alex isn't here.'

'I haven't come to see Alex.' Luke moved towards the door but Will blocked his way.

'Then what do you want?'

'He's here with me.' Phoebe walked past him into the flat. 'You wait here while I get my things, Luke. I won't be a minute.'

She left them squaring up to each other like a pair of cats in an alleyway. They'd probably be fighting over Alex in a minute, she thought bitterly.

She'd only been gone a few hours, but already it didn't feel like her bedroom. Alex's clothes were strewn all over the room, despite the fact that Phoebe had taken half her own stuff out of the wardrobe to make space for them. How long before she moved into Will's room, she wondered. The thought made her feel sick. At least she wouldn't be around to see it.

She pulled out the few clothes she had and laid them on the bed. Then she spotted the dress Karen had talked her into buying. She remembered Will's startled reaction when he'd walked in and seen her wearing it.

Looking back, perhaps that had been her chance? But she'd been looking the wrong way and had missed it.

Will came in just as she was emptying her dressing table drawers. 'He says you're moving out. Is that right?'

'Looks like it, doesn't it?'

'Am I allowed to ask why?'

'I would have thought that was obvious, don't you?'

'Not to me.'

Talk about spelling it out! 'Look, Will, I know about you and Alex.'

She still clung to the tiniest glimmer of hope that she'd got it wrong. But one look at his face told her she hadn't.

'She told you?'

'No, you did. I overheard you arguing about it earlier. So did the rest of the street, actually.' She turned away, pretending to sort through her tangle of underwear, hoping he wouldn't hear the emotion clogging her voice.

'So you've decided to leave, just like that? You don't even want to hear how it happened?'

'To be honest I don't really care.' The last thing she wanted to hear was a blow-by-blow account of how they'd both been overcome by lust. 'I've heard it all before, remember?'

'No, I don't suppose you do care. This all fits in very nicely with your plans, doesn't it?'

'What plans?'

'Alex told me what you and Luke got up to while she was away.' Will's voice was rough with anger. 'So don't try to make me feel guilty about Alex, because as far as I'm concerned you've done a lot worse!'

322

She didn't realise what she'd done until she saw him recoil, his hand on his cheek, and felt her stinging palm. 'Get out!'

But he'd already slammed out of the room.

She finished her packing quickly. Luke was waiting for her in the sitting room, but there was no sign of Will.

'All ready? I'll start loading up the car then, shall I?'

He picked up an armful of boxes and started off downstairs. Phoebe stood for a moment, looking around. She'd had some of her happiest times in the flat, as well as some of her worst. But it was all behind her now.

She waited a moment longer, hoping Will might appear, but he didn't. Finally she gave up. She dropped her keys on the coffee table, picked up her cases and left the flat.

She didn't allow herself to cry until they were safely in the car. Then, once she'd started, she found she couldn't stop. She worked her way through Luke's clean hanky, all the scrappy tissues in her bag and had resorted to the sleeve of her sweater by the time they got to Karen's flat.

Luke helped her unload her bags and boxes. 'Now, are you sure you'll be all right?' he asked, as she followed him back to his car.

Phoebe nodded. 'I'll get this lot moved down to Mum and Dad's in the morning. I'm sure they won't mind storing it for a few days.'

They hesitated for a moment, like strangers, both lost for words. Then Phoebe said, 'Well, have a great time in London, won't you? Don't forget to send me a postcard.'

'Why don't you come with me?'

'What?'

'You said you wanted to escape. So why don't you come to London with me? We could get a place to-gether, and you'd get a cheffing job dead easy. It would be a new start for both of us.'

They looked at each other, and she suddenly realised he was offering her what she'd always longed for.

She also realised it was far too late.

He seemed to know it too, even before she spoke. 'I really did blow it, didn't I?' he said softly. 'Come here.' He pulled her into his arms, holding her close. 'Be happy, Fee,' he whispered into her hair. 'If anyone deserves it, it's you.'

They hugged each other for a long while, both thinking about what might have been. For the first time ever, it was Phoebe who let go first.

Will was sitting on the sofa in the dark, nursing a glass of bourbon when Alex came home. He flinched as she switched on the light.

'Bloody hell, you frightened the life out of me!' She clutched her chest. 'What are you doing in the dark?'

He looked up at her. She was still dressed in her gym clothes – cycling shorts, baggy sweatshirt, her hair tucked up inside a baseball cap. Even after several Jack Daniels she still looked amazingly sexy. 'Phoebe's gone,' he said.

'What? You're joking. When did this happen?'

'About an hour ago. She turned up with her new boyfriend and packed her stuff. She's taken everything.' He still couldn't quite believe it. Just like he hadn't been able to believe the keys on the coffee table, or her empty room. All that lingered was her light, flowery perfume. He'd always meant to ask her what it was. Now he'd never know.

Alex frowned at him. 'What new boyfriend?'

'Your ex. It looks like you were right about them.'

'Luke? Luke was here?'

'I just said so, didn't I?'

'Did he ask about me?'

'No. I told you, he was with Phoebe.' He looked up at

her. 'Why are you so surprised? It was you who said they had a thing going on, remember?'

'I know, but I didn't think they'd be so quick off the mark, that's all.' She gnawed her thumbnail. 'Are you sure he didn't say anything about me?'

'Not a word. He just stood there, smirking.' Will still felt the urge to punch him. 'Like I said, you were right about him and Phoebe.'

Alex flopped down on the sofa next to him. 'And now you're drinking to forget?' She eyed the bottle.

'Can you think of a better way?'

'Actually, I can.' She took the glass out of his hand. 'I made you forget her once before, remember? I'm sure I can do it again.'

She leaned over and kissed him, her mouth engulfing his protests. Her perfume was sharp and sexy and nothing like Phoebe's. Which, at that moment, was a good thing.

It would be so easy, he thought. So easy to just give in and blot out the all-consuming misery just for a while.

To forget Phoebe, just like she'd forgotten him.

Chapter 32

Chaos greeted Phoebe in the restaurant the following morning. The tables had been pushed aside to make way for TV cameras, hot lights blazed overhead, cables snaked across the floor, and the place seemed to be crammed with more people than on a busy Saturday night.

Guy was in the corner talking to Malcolm, the director, while Karen applied more lipgloss in the mirror behind the bar. Phoebe crept past them, feeling tired and washed out, and headed straight to the office.

At least that was what Titus laughingly called it. It was little more than a cupboard off the kitchen where he did his ordering. There was room for a desk, and a phone, and not much else.

Someone was already in there. A pleasant-faced man with cropped sandy hair and lively green eyes sat with his feet up on the desk, smoking a cigarette. Phoebe recognised him immediately as Cameron Goode, the star of the show. He was wearing his trademark towering toque and zebra-print chef's trousers.

'Oops, sorry.' He sat up. 'I didn't realise anyone else would be using this room. I can get lost, if you like?'

'It's OK.'

She was just about to leave when he said, 'I like to get away and have a quiet smoke before a show. It calms my nerves.' He offered her the packet. 'Want one?'

Phoebe hesitated, torn between her loyalty to Titus and her need for a nicotine fix. Her craving won. 'Thanks. Would you like a coffee?' she offered. 'It's only my secret store of instant, I'm afraid. I'd make you the real thing, only the kitchen's a bit upside down at the moment.'

'Instant's fine. It's all I drink at home. But don't tell anyone, you'd ruin my cred. The rest of the world likes to think I spend my whole life making my own pasta and sun drying tomatoes.'

'And don't you?'

'In East Acton? You can't even dry your washing, let alone a tomato.'

Phoebe smiled back. It was difficult to dislike him. She could see what Titus meant about him being charming.

Then, as if he was reading her thoughts, he suddenly said, 'I don't suppose my brother's shown up yet, has he?'

Phoebe shook her head. 'He was threatening not to come.'

'That sounds like Titus.' Cameron looked grim. 'Pig-headed bugger, always cutting off his nose to spite his face. Doesn't he realise this could be fantastic publicity for him?'

'I don't think he sees it that way,' Phoebe said carefully. 'I think he's more worried about you making a fool of him. That's why he still hasn't told anyone you're his brother.'

Cameron looked genuinely surprised. 'Me? Why?'

'Look at you,' said Phoebe. 'You're a huge celebrity with a whole constellation of Michelin stars and he's just a chef in a restaurant no one's ever heard of. He's going to look a bit sick in comparison, isn't he?'

'I never thought of it like that. I just thought I was doing him a favour.' Cameron looked hurt. 'Why has he got such a massive chip on his shoulder?'

Phoebe shrugged. 'I don't suppose it's easy being overshadowed by your brother all the time.' God knows she knew how that felt.

'But I never overshadowed him. If anything I always envied him.'

'You, envy Titus?' Now it was Phoebe's turn to look astonished.

'Of course. The guy's a culinary genius, you must know that. Why do you think I decided to go to catering college? I wanted to be just like him, ever since I was a kid. Although I always knew he was the one with the talent.'

'But you're a star! You've got your own TV show and everything.'

'So? I've just been lucky. OK, I'm not a bad cook but my real talent is in charming people into believing I'm better than I really am.' He grinned wryly. 'But Titus could have been the real star, if he hadn't been such a grumpy bastard. He puts too many people's backs up, that's his trouble.'

Don't I know it, Phoebe thought. 'I really wish you'd tell Titus that.'

Cameron looked at his watch. 'Doesn't look as if I'm going to get the chance, does it?'

Just then a researcher appeared. 'We're ready for you now, Cam.'

'Has my brother turned up?' Cameron looked hopeful.

''Fraid not. Malcolm says we'll just do a quick interview with the owner, then go to a demo in the kitchen. We can't waste any more time waiting for him to show up. Is that OK?'

'Looks like it'll have to be, doesn't it? The show must go on, and all that.' Cameron shrugged apologetically at Phoebe then followed the researcher out of the office.

Ten minutes later, Phoebe went to sneak a look at what was going on in the kitchen. It wasn't easy to see at first. Everyone was crowded in there, from the waiting staff to the army of TV people. Guy and Karen lurked behind the cameras, watching the monitors. The kitchen staff had been huddled into a corner, all dressed in their best pristine whites, just in case they managed to get into the shot. Cameron stood at the work surface, an array of chopped vegetables around him, facing the camera, very professional. The director lined up the camera, checked the lighting levels, gave him his cue and then—

'What the fuck is going on in here?' Titus burst in like an angry bull. 'What have you done to my kitchen? It looks like a fucking tart's boudoir!'

Everyone went white and held their breath, apart from Cameron, who turned calmly to his brother and said, 'Titus! Glad you could make it. We all thought you'd chickened out.'

'The day I run away from a snivelling little bastard like you will be the day I feed my own bollocks into a blender.' He slammed a meat cleaver down, missing Cameron's hand by just inches.

His smile didn't waver. 'So what kept you? Bad case of food poisoning, was it?'

'As a matter of fact it was. I tried one of your recipes last night and didn't get off the toilet for six hours.'

Everyone looked terrified but Phoebe could see the beads of nervous sweat on Titus' upper lip. He was more scared than any of them.

The cameraman glanced nervously at the director, who gestured for him to keep the camera rolling. He stared at the monitor, transfixed.

'So what are you ruining today, then?' Titus sneered.

'I was about to demonstrate pan fried salmon with lemon and dill.'

'Jesus Christ, how boring is that? You can buy it ready-made from Sainsbury's.'

'And I suppose you can come up with something better?' Cameron looked unoffended. 'Perhaps you'd care to give us all the benefit of your wide culinary experience? How many Michelin stars did you say you had?'

This time Phoebe held her breath. How could he be so cruel, after everything he'd said? But Titus' eyes glinted with the light of battle. 'I don't need a poxy star to know what to do with a bit of salmon,' he growled. He snatched the offending fillet from his brother's hand. 'Find me some shiitake mushrooms and I'll show you how it should be done, sonny.'

A few minutes later, Phoebe realised what Cameron was up to. He needled his brother gently, until Titus was so fired up with fury he rose to the challenge. Phoebe had never seen him work so well. Or use such strong language. But Cameron gave as good as he got. They made a great team, she decided, Cameron so dry and unflappable, Titus just plain mad.

And she wasn't the only one who thought so. 'We've got to get this pair signed up,' Malcolm the director whispered. 'They make great telly. They could be the Two Fat Ladies for the new Millennium.'

'You couldn't put them on before the watershed though, with all that effing and blinding,' the production assistant hissed back.

Then, suddenly, it was all over. As Titus tipped his sizzling pan-fried salmon out on to a bed of lightly wilted Chinese greens, drizzled with a warm Oriental dressing, the crew broke into a spontaneous round of applause. He looked up, blinking at the bright lights, as if coming out of a trance and seeing them for the first time.

'Get the fuck out of my kitchen!' he roared, then stormed off, slamming the door so hard the pans rattled.

Cameron smiled unwaveringly at the camera. 'I see my brother's forgotten to take his medication again,' he said mildly. Everyone laughed, the tension was broken, and the director called a wrap.

'That was brilliant,' he said. 'Utter genius. Ainsley Harriott meets The Terminator. I love it.'

Cameron beamed at Phoebe. 'I told you he was a genius,' he said.

As the TV cameras began to pack up and the crew dispersed back into their vans, Phoebe went outside to look for Titus. She found him round the corner in one of the pavement cafés. He was smoking ferociously, an espresso going cold in front of him.

Phoebe sat down next to him. 'Titus, you did it. You were a star.'

'I don't care.' As he raised his cigarette to his mouth she could see his fingers were trembling.

'But they were all raving about you in there. They're talking about giving you and Cameron your own TV show. You could be a celebrity.'

'I'm not interested in any TV show, and I don't want to be a celebrity. *He* can do that if he wants.' He blew a smoke ring into the air. 'I did what I set out to do today, and that's all that matters.'

'And what was that?'

'I faced my demons.' He turned to face her, and she saw the glitter of tears in his eyes. 'My whole life I've been convinced he was better than me, that I could never measure up. But the truth was, I was always too scared to compete. I didn't want to find out I was right, I suppose.' He ground out his cigarette. 'Well, today I did find out. I faced him. And do you know what? I'm as good as he is after all.'

'Of course you are.' Phoebe reached for his hand.

'And so are you.'

She frowned in confusion. 'Sorry?'

'I faced my demons, Phoebe. Now it's time for you to face yours.' He nodded over her shoulder. Phoebe looked round. There, standing behind her, was Alex.

She looked different somehow. Some of her old

331

confidence seemed to have deserted her as she stood a few yards away, the early autumn breeze lifting her hair across her face.

'The weather's changing,' she said, as Phoebe approached. 'I don't think it would have stayed fine for my wedding day, do you?'

'What do you want?'

'We need to talk. Shall we have a drink?' She pointed to the table Titus had tactfully vacated. 'I don't know about you but I could do with one.'

They sat down. Alex ordered a glass of wine but Phoebe refused. The way she was feeling, she didn't think she'd be able to swallow a single mouthful.

'If it's about you and Will you're wasting your time. I already know.'

'This isn't about me and Will. I just want to know if it's true what he told me. Are you and Luke really together?'

'What if we are?' Phoebe's chin lifted. 'Don't tell me, you've decided you want him back again, is that it?'

Alex ignored her. 'You're making a big mistake, Fee. Luke isn't the right man for you. It's just a rebound thing.'

'Because he must still be in love with you, you mean? That's just typical of you, isn't it? You think the whole world revolves around you, you can't imagine anyone being happy without—'

'I'm not talking about Luke, you silly bitch. I'm talking about you.' Phoebe stopped dead, her mouth hanging open. 'Anyone can see you're mad about Will. And I reckon he feels the same about you.'

'Which is why he's sleeping with you?'

'Not sleeping. Slept. Past tense. It was just the once and a long time ago. I had no idea he was your flatmate and he certainly didn't know I was your sister. Otherwise he probably wouldn't have come anywhere near me,' she added under her breath.

But Phoebe was in no mood to listen. 'You mean you had a one night stand with him while you were still engaged to Luke?'

'Keep your hair on, these things happen, you know. We're not all born-again romantics like you.' Alex sipped her wine. 'Anyway, I haven't come here to talk about my love life. I'm just telling you not to do anything stupid, just because your pride's been hurt. It was just one night, Fee. It meant nothing, honestly.'

'So why have you been throwing yourself at him since you moved in?'

Alex gnawed her lip. 'OK, so it might have meant something to me,' she admitted. 'But not to him, apparently. He made that very clear last night.'

'Why? What happened?'

'I don't want to talk about it.' Alex blushed. 'Let's just say I overplayed my hand. That's when he told me it couldn't happen again, because he was in love with you.'

Hope leapt inside her. 'He said that?'

'Well, not exactly.' Hope sank again. 'But only because he's as proud and stupid and bloody idiotic as you are. He thinks you don't care about him, Phoebe. He thinks you want to be with Luke.'

'But why should he think that when—' she saw her sister's expression and guessed the truth. 'You told him, didn't you? About me and Luke?'

'I was angry and it just slipped out, OK?' Alex looked defensive. 'Anyway, I don't know what you're getting so steamed up about. You shouldn't have done it in the first place, should you?'

Maybe not, but she was certainly paying for it. No wonder Will had been so angry when she turned up at the flat with Luke. It all made sense now.

'He seems to think you two are moving in together. Is that true?'

'Of course it isn't true. Luke's going back to London on Friday.'

'Is he? Now there's a coincidence.' She smiled at Phoebe over the rim of her glass. 'So there's nothing to stop you and Will getting together, is there?'

'No – except that thanks to you he now thinks I'm a man-stealing slut.'

'Yes, well, I've said I'm sorry, haven't I?'

Another hostile silence fell. Alex gazed into the distance while Phoebe brooded on what she'd just said.

It was over between her and Will, whatever Alex seemed to think. There were just too many bridges to mend.

And even if they did, how was she ever supposed to forget that he'd slept with her sister? To Phoebe, that was just about the worst betrayal he could ever inflict on her.

'Looks like you've both got a lot to forgive each other for, doesn't it?' Alex seemed to guess her thoughts.

'Maybe it's too late for forgiveness.'

'And does that go for me, too?' They looked at each other. Phoebe tried to say no, but the word just wouldn't come. Alex had hurt her too deeply, and for too long.

Once again, her sister seemed to guess her thoughts. 'Don't worry, I won't be around for much longer. Luke's not the only one who's moving down to London.'

'You're going to London? Why?'

'An old contact of mine rang and offered me a job. She's setting up her own PR firm. And there's not really anything to keep me up here, so I thought I'd give it a go.'

'I'll miss you,' Phoebe murmured.

'No, you won't. You'll be glad to see the back of me. I would, if I were you. Don't look at me like that, you

334

know I've always been a pain,' she went on. 'But I never meant to hurt you, you know. The truth is, I was jealous of you.'

'Jealous? Of me?' Phoebe looked shocked. 'But you had everything.'

'I never had what you had,' Alex said. 'Everyone loves you, Phoebe. Even really awful people, like that fat chef and that horrible spiky Karen. You've just got a way with everyone. I never had that.'

'You've always had loads of boyfriends.'

'Only because of the way I look. Men are easy.' She shrugged dismissively. 'Anyway, they may have fancied me but deep down they all loved you. You were the one who made them cups of tea and gave them a shoulder to cry on when I dumped them.'

'Luke loved you,' Phoebe said.

'Luke liked the idea of loving me. But we were never really suited. Not like the two of you. I think you might well have ended up together if I hadn't come along.' She smiled bracingly. 'Anyway, you'll have an easier time of it when I'm gone. No more "poor old Phoebe", always the bridesmaid, never the bride.' She reached in her pocket and handed Phoebe a key. 'Here's my key to Will's flat. You might want to use it later.'

Phoebe looked down at it, freshly cut and shining in her hand. She doubted she would ever use it again, but somehow it made her feel better, as if there was still something connecting her to Will. 'So where will you stay?'

'Never mind about me, I'll be OK. I might book into a hotel for a few days. Just until I leave.'

'You could always go to Mum and Dad's? I know they'd love to see you.'

Alex smiled sadly. 'I don't think so. I might phone them in a day or two, just to let them know what's happening.'

'They're still your parents, Alex. Whatever you might think.'

'I know.' She hoisted her bag over her shoulder. 'Anyway, just in case I don't see you again before I go, I just wanted to say take care of yourself, little sis.' She ruffled Phoebe's hair.

'Oh Alex!' Half an hour ago Phoebe could never have imagined herself crying over her sister, but now she was sobbing and clinging to her as if she never wanted to be parted. 'You don't have to go, you really don't.'

'I think I do. I need some space to get on with my life and so do you.' Alex hugged her fiercely. 'Phoebe,' she whispered. 'Don't lose him. You'll both regret it for ever.'

Will wasn't at the flat. His drawing board was still set up with the Hunky and Dory illustration he'd been working on. A cold mug of coffee sat beside it, and a soulful Motown CD autoplayed over and over again. 'What Becomes of the Broken Hearted?' Very appropriate, Phoebe thought. But what had become of Will?

While she was wondering, the phone rang. It was Gina.

'I don't suppose you've seen Will, have you? Only he was supposed to be coming round for supper and he hasn't turned up. You don't think anything's happened to him, do you?'

'I expect he just forgot. You know how absent-minded he can be.' Phoebe promised to get him to call as soon as he came home, but she was even more worried as she put the phone down. It really wasn't like Will. What if he'd done something to himself?

The anxiety was enough to make her do the unthinkable. She went round to see Barry.

His eyes narrowed when he saw her on the doorstep. 'What do you want?'

'Have you seen Will?'

'Yeah, I've seen him.'

'Is he here? I need to talk to him.'

'You've got a nerve showing your face after what you did to him.'

'I didn't do anything.'

'No? Then why is he so upset? I knew you'd be trouble the minute I saw you. I didn't like you then and I don't like you now.'

'The feeling's mutual. Now where's Will?' She tried to peer past him, but Barry blocked her way.

'I don't know where he is, and even if I did I wouldn't tell you. So why don't you just go back to your boyfriend and leave him alone?'

But Phoebe wasn't listening. She'd spotted Will's battered leather jacket hanging in the hallway. So he was there.

'OK, I'll go,' she said. 'But I want you to give him a message. Tell him I'm not moving in with Luke, whatever he might think. I never was. It was all just a misunderstanding. Tell him if he wants to find me I'll be at my parents. He's got the address.' She took a deep breath. 'And tell him – tell him I love—'

But Barry had already slammed the door in her face. She knew he wouldn't pass the message on. She could only hope Will had caught something of what she said.

Chapter 33

It felt strange to be back in her old room. All her books and things had been cleared away, but other than that nothing had changed since she was a child. There was the same pink carpet, the same pine furniture, and the same faded kitten-print curtains.

She'd always hated those curtains. As a teenager, she'd longed for pretty Laura Ashley ones like her friends, but her mother had insisted she keep them. 'There's still a lot of wear in them, it would be a crime to throw them away,' she said. They'd come from Alex's room after it was redecorated. Alex, needless to say, had got the Laura Ashley.

Those curtains summed up everything that was wrong in her life. They were secondhand and second best.

And Will. She wasn't sure how she felt about him any more. Part of her would always love him, but she wasn't sure she could cope with knowing that her sister had got there first.

Anyway, it didn't really matter now. She'd been at her parents' house for two days and he hadn't bothered to contact her. She'd stopped waiting for the phone to ring, or listening for the doorbell. And she'd stopped trying to tell herself that perhaps her message hadn't got through to him. Whatever Alex or anyone else said, she had to face the fact that it was over – not that it had ever really begun.

'There you are. What are you doing, moping about in here like a teenager?' Her mother breezed in and pulled back the hated curtains, flooding the room with light.

'It's a beautiful afternoon. Why don't you go outside and get some fresh air? Your father's in the garden. I'm sure he'd appreciate some company, and I've got shopping to do.'

Joe Redmond sat in a lounger, looking out over the lawn, a cup of weak tea in his hand. 'Grass could do with a cut,' he remarked. 'I wonder if your mother would notice if I got the mower out?'

'Yes, she would. And she'd probably have a fit. I'll do it.'

'Are you sure?' Her father looked sceptical. 'Have you ever handled a mower before?'

'You make it sound like the family Porsche. I'm sure I can manage. Anyway, I expect you'll tell me if I'm doing it wrong, won't you?'

And he did. The garden was on a slope, gently undulating to the naked eye, but like the foothills of K2 when you were pushing a heavy petrol-driven lawn-mower. Phoebe could feel perspiration trickling down the inside of her shirt as she dragged it from one end of the lawn to the other.

Meanwhile, her father called out orders from the terrace like a commander mustering his troops. 'Try to keep a straight line . . . no, you're going off to the left again . . . keep it moving, you don't want to damage the grass.'

'Never mind the grass, I think I've damaged myself.' Phoebe turned off the engine and flopped over the handlebars, fighting for breath. She wiped off the grass clippings that stuck to her sweating face. 'Why can't we get a Flymo like normal people?'

There was no answer. Phoebe looked up. 'Dad?' Oh God, her massacre of his precious lawn had probably brought on another coronary.

But he was talking to Will.

Phoebe was so shocked to see him she leaned on the

switch and started the motor. There was a roar, a flurry of turf and clippings, and by the time she got the wretched thing switched off again she'd churned up a bald patch bigger than Prince Edward's.

'I hope you haven't done any damage?' Her father called out from the terrace.

She turned around, and jumped when she saw Will behind her.

'That's quite a bald patch,' he remarked. He looked leaner than she'd remembered, and there were shadows under his dark eyes.

'Maybe I could cover it up?'

'You'd need more than a turf toupee for that. You've practically dug a pond there. Maybe that's the answer? Maybe you should turn it into a water feature?'

'And you have a lot of horticultural experience, do you?'

'Of course. I never miss an episode of "Ground Force".'

He grinned, and her heart flipped over. 'I – um – didn't expect to see you.'

His smile faded. 'I would have come sooner but I had a lot of thinking to do.' He looked around. 'Is there anywhere we could go to talk?'

Her father graciously gave her a break from her mowing duties. 'Perhaps Will could lend you a hand later on?' he suggested, his eyes twinkling. Phoebe smiled back. She didn't like to disappoint him, but she had the feeling Will wouldn't be staying that long.

They went into the conservatory. Phoebe chose the seat furthest away from Will, half concealed by a towering parlour palm. She hadn't had time to look in a mirror, but she knew she must look a mess. She was pretty sure she smelled iffy, too.

'I wasn't sure if you'd still be here,' he said.

'Why? Where else would I be? Alex's flat is under

offer so I couldn't go back there. I thought Baz might have told you that.'

'Baz and I aren't on speaking terms at the moment. Not since I had to wring it out of him that you'd been to see him. He wouldn't have told me, but Patti happened to overhear the two of you.'

So that was why he hadn't been round sooner.

'I thought you might have gone to London,' Will said.

'With Alex, you mean?' Phoebe shook her head. 'I've had enough of living in my sister's shadow, thank you very much. I'm tired of being second best all the time.'

'I meant with Luke.' Will scuffed at the tiled floor with his boot. 'Is that why you didn't go off with him? Because you thought you'd be second best?'

'I never intended to go off with Luke.'

He looked up sharply. 'But Alex said—'

'Alex said a lot of things, but that doesn't make them true.' She chose her words carefully, knowing how important they might be. 'That night I slept with Luke, I didn't do it to try and split them up. I thought they'd already separated. I was pretty sure Alex had someone else on her mind that weekend.' She still didn't know for sure, and probably never would. 'But as soon as it was over I knew it wasn't going to work with Luke and me. Whatever he said, I knew he was always going to want Alex more than he wanted me. And like I said, I'm sick of being everyone's second best.'

'You're not *my* second best.'

It took a moment for the words to sink in. Even when they did, she still couldn't believe them. 'How can you say that? I've seen the kind of women you go out with, Will. They're all so beautiful—'

'So are you. You just don't seem to realise it.' He smiled at her. 'That's what I like about you. You're more interested in other people than you are in yourself. You'd never spend hours preening yourself in front of a mirror.' Is it that obvious? Phoebe pushed back a stray curl and some grass clippings fell out of her hair. 'You don't know the effect you have on people,' Will went on. 'I didn't even know it myself, until I'd fallen in love with you.'

She felt light-headed, but she forced herself to keep calm. 'And was that before or after you slept with my sister?'

He looked pained. 'I didn't know she was your sister, did I? She was just some woman I met in a bar. I know it doesn't excuse what I did, but I was lonely, I was drunk, and I was pissed off because it was my birthday and I thought you'd stood me up.'

So that's when it had happened. 'You stood *me* up, remember? I was waiting for you at home.'

'I didn't know that, did I? Barry said he'd phoned you, and you told him you were going out. I assumed you must have got a better offer.' He stared moodily at the ground. 'Then this woman started coming on to me, and I just thought – why not? If you could find someone else, why shouldn't I? It was only the next morning I realised how stupid I'd been. There couldn't be anyone else.'

'But you still went out with Minty.'

'That was another mistake,' he agreed. 'I tried to tell myself I was getting on with my life. It wasn't until I saw you with Andrew that I realised you were the one I really wanted to share it with. And then Nadine turned up, and that just complicated things even more.' He looked at Phoebe. 'But seeing her again made me realise that it really was you I wanted, not her. If she hadn't come back, that doubt might have lingered on for years. For both of us.'

Phoebe silently agreed. But now there was another doubt lingering in her mind. 'What about Alex?' she had to ask.

Will's face grew cold. 'What about her?'

'Will, you slept with my sister. You of all people should know how that makes me feel.'

'I know, and if I could turn the clock back believe me I would. I had no idea she was your sister, or that she was going to turn up on our doorstep.'

'You seemed very keen for her to stay when she did.'

'Only because I thought it was what you wanted. Do you really think I enjoyed sharing a flat with her, being constantly reminded of what an idiot I'd been? Not to mention her throwing herself at me the whole time.'

Phoebe shredded a palm leaf between her fingers. 'How do I know you resisted?'

'What do you mean?'

'All that time you were alone in the flat. You'd done it once. How do I know you didn't do it again?'

There was a long silence. For one terrible moment she thought he was going to confess he had. Then, finally, he said, 'I have to admit I was tempted. That night, after you turned up with Luke. But nothing happened. I promise you that.'

Phoebe plucked another leaf off the parlour palm and pleated it between her fingers. She was desperate to believe him, she really was. But there was still the nagging doubt in her mind. How could he have resisted Alex? No man could.

'Look, I realise you think your sister is the most desirable creature on the planet, but I have to tell you she isn't. Not as far as I'm concerned, anyway.' There was an edge to his voice. 'I love you, Phoebe. And I'd never knowingly do anything to hurt you. But I can't live my whole life feeling guilty. And I can't spend it trying to make you trust me if you feel you can't.' He stood up. 'It's up to you. Either you learn to trust me or we finish this right now.'

She watched him go, fighting the urge to call him back. She still couldn't convince herself that anyone would want her more than Alex. But she knew she had to try, or lose Will for ever.

She caught up with him halfway down the drive. 'Will!' He turned around and she flung herself into his arms. Suddenly she didn't care about her shiny face, or the grass clippings in her hair, or her three-day-old shirt. And from the way he kissed her, neither did Will.

'You do realise,' she said, when they finally came up for air, 'that if you ever so much as look at my sister again I'll kill you?'

'As if I would, when I've got you,' he said, and kissed her again.

And, for the first time in her life, Phoebe believed it.

All Orion/Phoenix titles are available at your local bookshop or from the following address:

Mail Order Department
Littlehampton Book Services
FREEPOST BR535
Worthing, West Sussex, BN13 3BR
telephone 01903 828503, *facsimile* 01903 828802
e-mail MailOrders@lbsltd.co.uk
(Please ensure that you include full postal address details)

Payment can be made either by credit/debit card (Visa, Mastercard, Access and Switch accepted) or by sending a £ Sterling cheque or postal order made payable to *Littlehampton Book Services*.
DO NOT SEND CASH OR CURRENCY.

Please add the following to cover postage and packing

UK and BFPO:
£1.50 for the first book, and 50p for each additional book to a maximum of £3.50

Overseas and Eire:
£2.50 for the first book plus £1.00 for the second book and 50p for each additional book ordered

---

BLOCK CAPITALS PLEASE

name of cardholder ....

address of cardholder ....

....

....

postcode ....

delivery address
(if different from cardholder)

....

....

....

postcode ....

☐ I enclose my remittance for £.............................

☐ please debit my Mastercard/Visa/Access/Switch (delete as appropriate)

card number ☐☐☐☐☐☐☐☐☐☐☐☐☐☐☐☐☐☐

expiry date ☐☐☐☐   Switch issue no. ☐☐

signature ....

prices and availability are subject to change without notice